AUG 1 9 2009   PR

O9-BSA-198

RAPUNZEL'S REVENGE

Shannon Hale
and
Dean Hale

illustrated by Nathan Hale

BLOOMSBURY

NEW YORK BERLIN LONDON

Also by Shannon Hale

THE BOOKS OF BAYERN
THE GOOSE GIRL
ENNA BURNING
RIVER SECRETS

PRINCESS ACADEMY

BOOK OF A THOUSAND DAYS

For adults
AUSTENLAND

Also by Nathan Hale

THE DEVIL YOU KNOW

YELLOWBELLY AND PLUM GO TO SCHOOL

BALLOON ON THE MOON (illustrations)

Published by Bloomsbury U.S.A. Children's Books
175 Fifth Avenue, New York, New York 10010
Distributed to the trade by Macmillan

Library of Congress Cataloging-in-Publication Data
Hale, Shannon.
Rapunzel's revenge / by Shannon and Dean Hale; illustrated by Nathan Hale.—1st U.S. ed.
p. cm.
ISBN-13: 978-1-59990-070-4 · ISBN-10: 1-59990-070-X (hardcover)
ISBN-13: 978-1-59990-288-3 · ISBN-10: 1-59990-288-5 (paperback)
1. Graphic novels. I. Hale, Dean. II. Hale, Nathan. III. Title.
PN6727.H246R36 2008 741.5'973—dc22 2007037670

Book design by Nathan Hale
Balloons and lettering by Melinda Hale
HushHush and Storyline fonts by Comicraft

First U.S. Edition 2008
Printed by South China Printing Company Ltd. China
4 6 8 10 9 7 5 (hardcover)
2 4 6 8 10 9 7 5 3 (paperback)

All papers used by Bloomsbury U.S.A. are natural, recyclable products
made from wood grown in well-managed forests. The manufacturing processes
conform to the environmental regulations of the country of origin.

For Christine Hale, aka Mom,
who, but for a lack of mile-long hair
and spiteful imprisonment by a witch,
could have been the hero of this story
—S. H. AND D. H.

To Lindsay, Leigh, and Layna:
three cowgirls, my sisters
—N. H.

Part 1: Once Upon a Tower

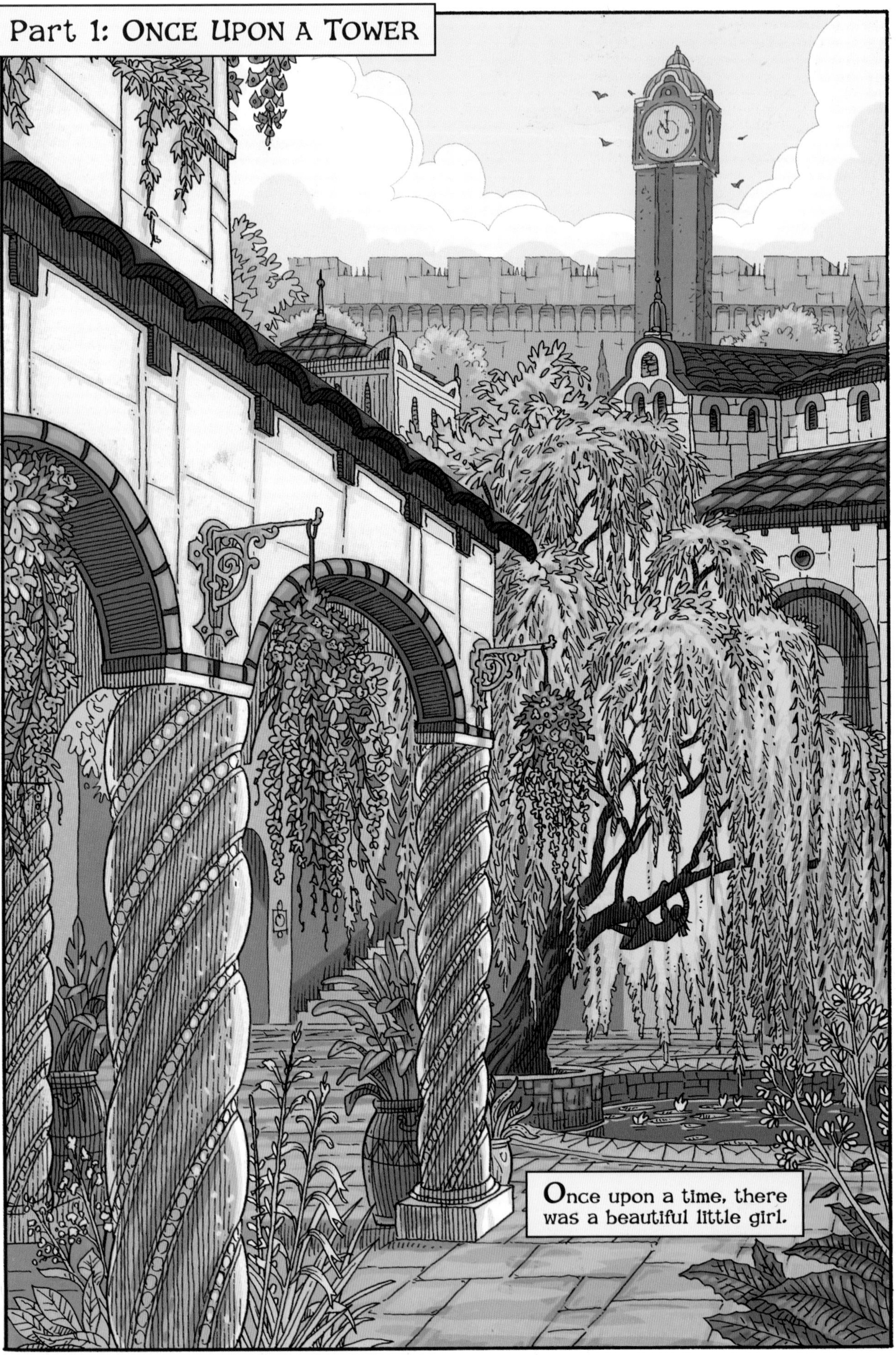
Once upon a time, there was a beautiful little girl.

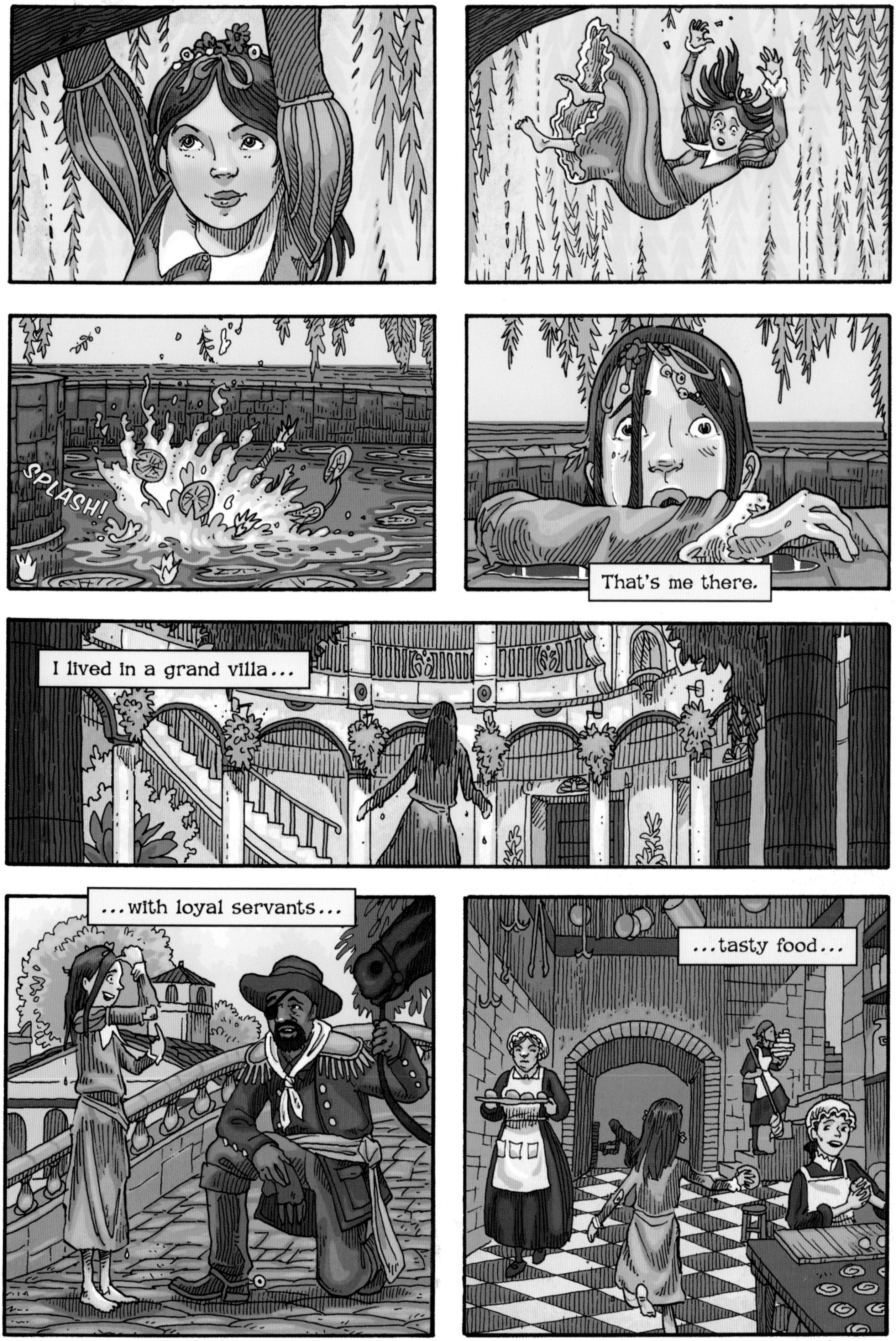
SPLASH!
That's me there.
I lived in a grand villa...
...with loyal servants...
...tasty food...

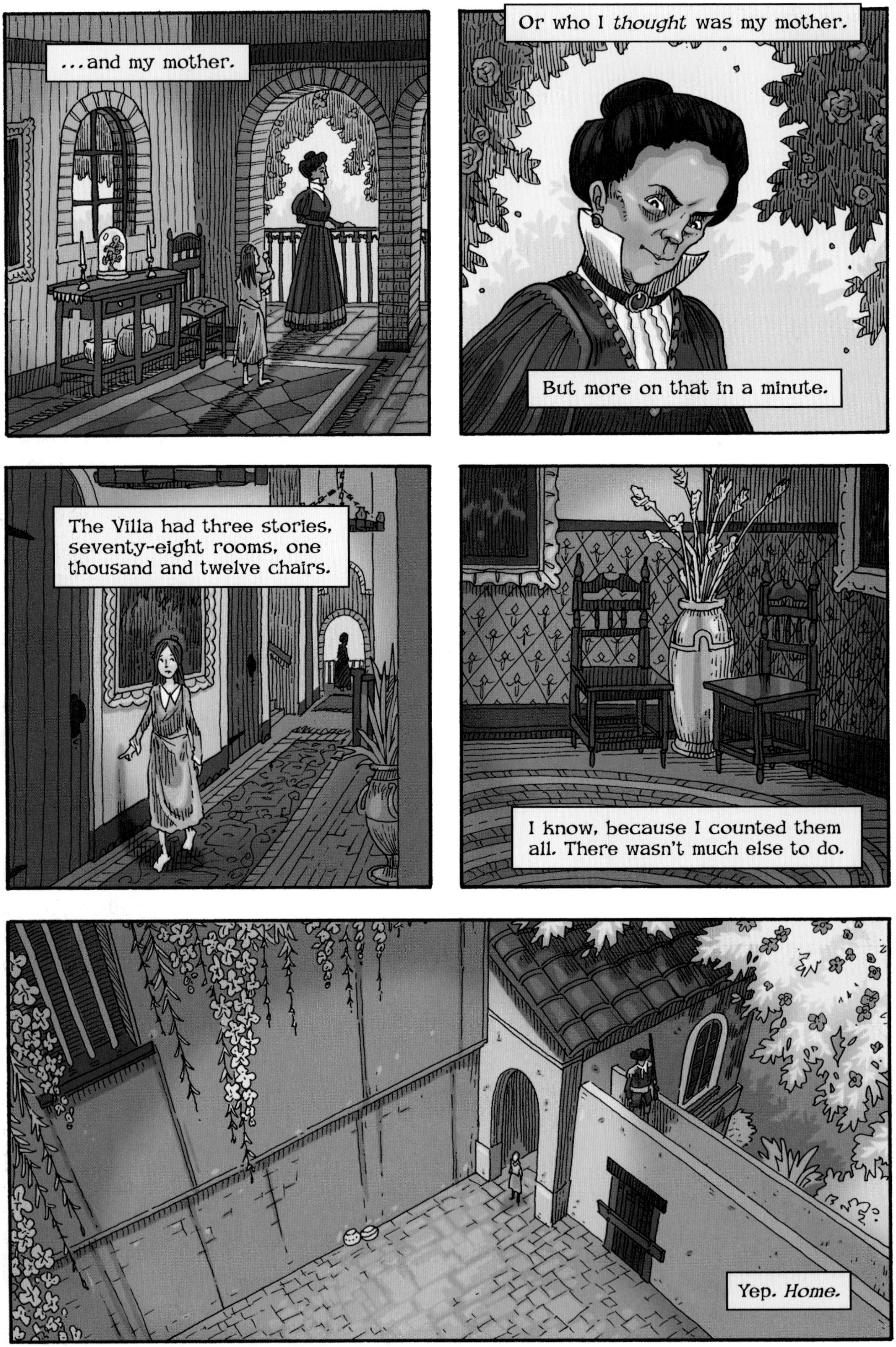
...and my mother.
Or who I *thought* was my mother.
But more on that in a minute.
The Villa had three stories, seventy-eight rooms, one thousand and twelve chairs.
I know, because I counted them all. There wasn't much else to do.
Yep. *Home.*

No one was horribly mean to me or anything.

In fact, one of the guards—Mason—he was right kind.

He taught me tricks when he thought Mother wasn't looking.

Now it seems so strange that I lived all those years in the Villa...

...and never realized what was going on.

Never saw who Mother really was.

...MY FARM CAN'T GET BY WITHOUT YOUR GROWTH MAGIC... I SWEAR WE'LL PAY DOUBLE NEXT YEAR...

And the kinds of things she was capable of doing.

I didn't understand then why I felt the way I did—

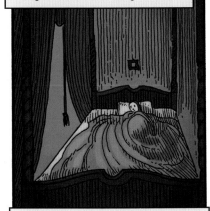

—like something lost, like a toy left out in the rain.

And I didn't know why I had that dream again and again.

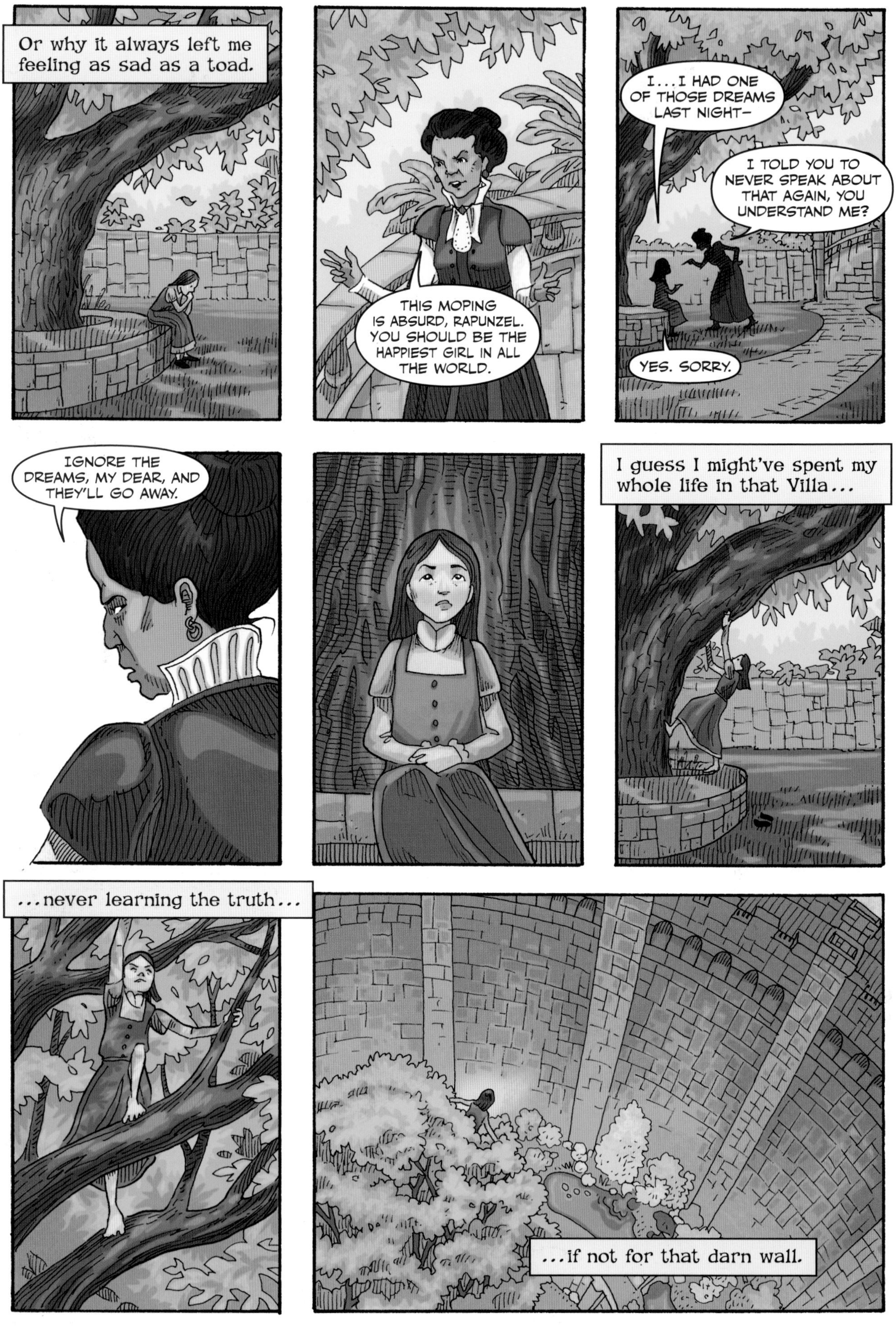

Or why it always left me feeling as sad as a toad.
THIS MOPING IS ABSURD, RAPUNZEL. YOU SHOULD BE THE HAPPIEST GIRL IN ALL THE WORLD.
I...I HAD ONE OF THOSE DREAMS LAST NIGHT—
I TOLD YOU TO NEVER SPEAK ABOUT THAT AGAIN, YOU UNDERSTAND ME?
YES. SORRY.
IGNORE THE DREAMS, MY DEAR, AND THEY'LL GO AWAY.
I guess I might've spent my whole life in that Villa...
...never learning the truth...
...if not for that darn wall.

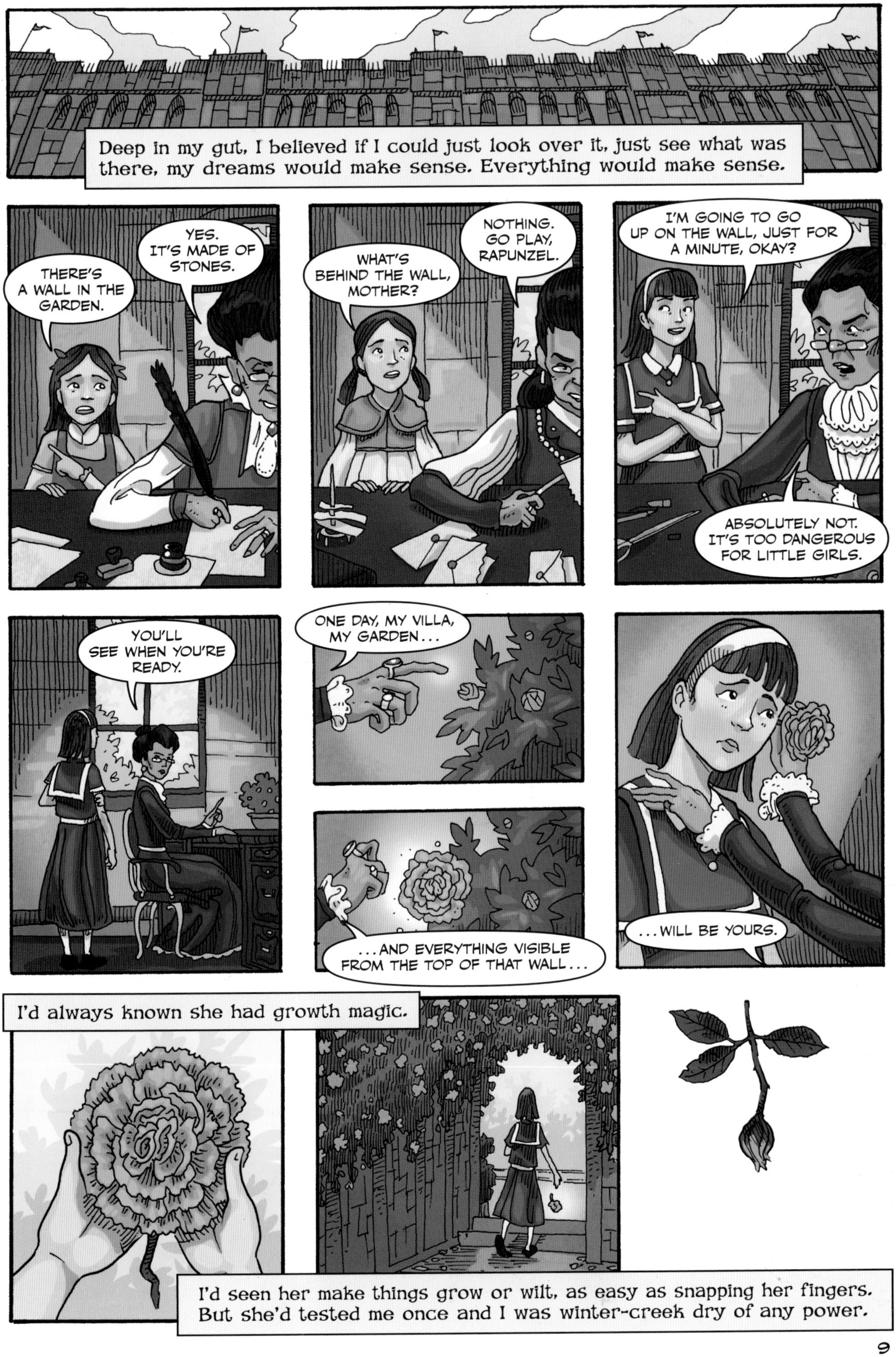
Deep in my gut, I believed if I could just look over it, just see what was there, my dreams would make sense. Everything would make sense.
THERE'S A WALL IN THE GARDEN.
YES. IT'S MADE OF STONES.
WHAT'S BEHIND THE WALL, MOTHER?
NOTHING. GO PLAY, RAPUNZEL.
I'M GOING TO GO UP ON THE WALL, JUST FOR A MINUTE, OKAY?
ABSOLUTELY NOT. IT'S TOO DANGEROUS FOR LITTLE GIRLS.
YOU'LL SEE WHEN YOU'RE READY.
ONE DAY, MY VILLA, MY GARDEN...
...AND EVERYTHING VISIBLE FROM THE TOP OF THAT WALL...
...WILL BE YOURS.
I'd always known she had growth magic.
I'd seen her make things grow or wilt, as easy as snapping her fingers. But she'd tested me once and I was winter-creek dry of any power.

I'd never dared disobey Mother before, but on my twelfth birthday, I couldn't stand it anymore. I needed to see what was over that wall...

HAPPY BIRTHDAY RAPU

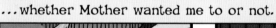

...whether Mother wanted me to or not.

After all, what was the worst she could do to me?

SNIP

The stairs had too many guards.

So I found another way up.

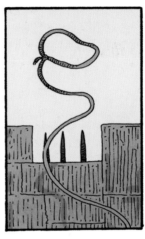

BOING!

AAAAA...

WHUMP

Call me a numbskull if you like...

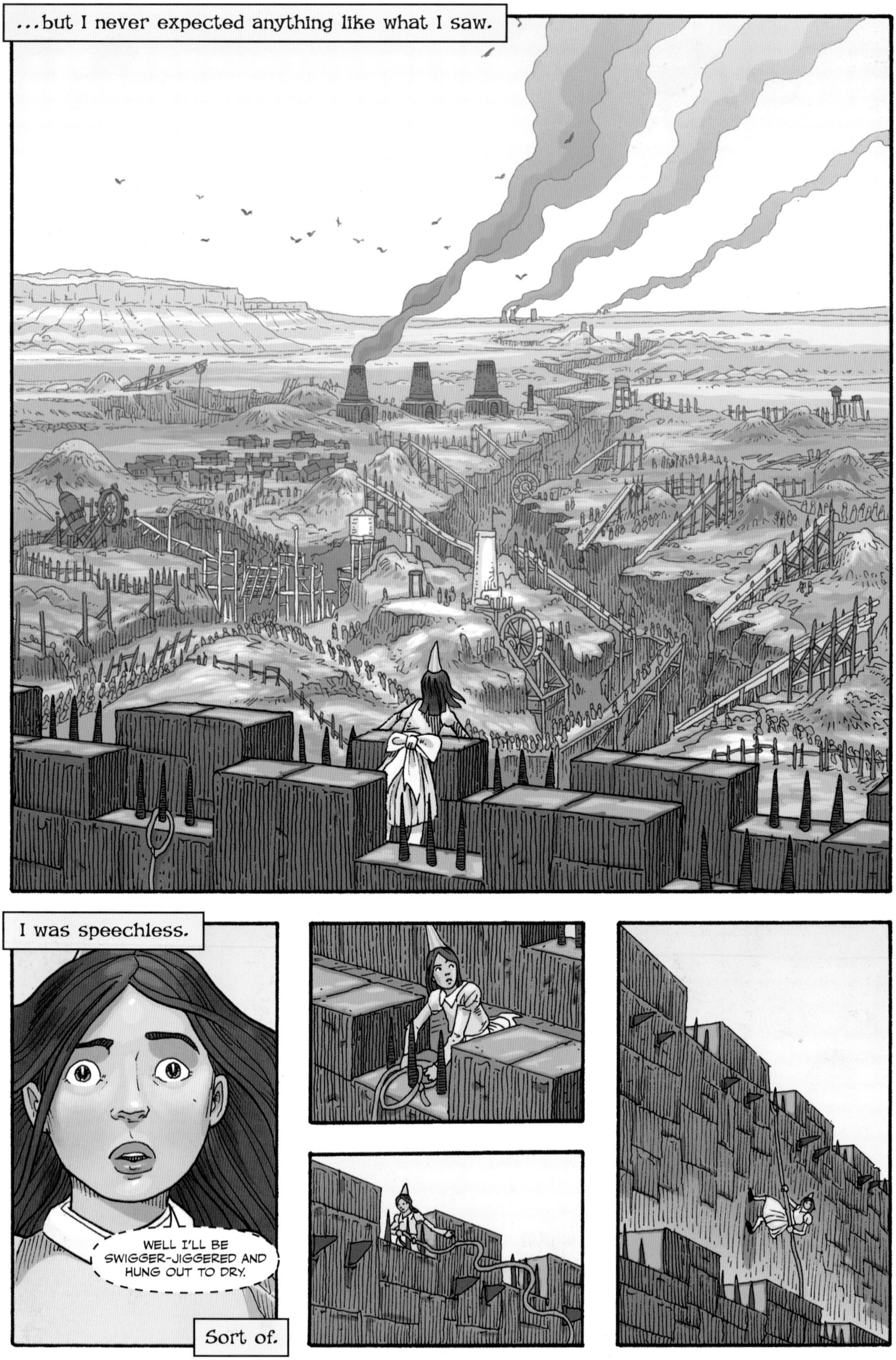
...but I never expected anything like what I saw.
I was speechless.
WELL I'LL BE SWIGGER-JIGGERED AND HUNG OUT TO DRY.
Sort of.

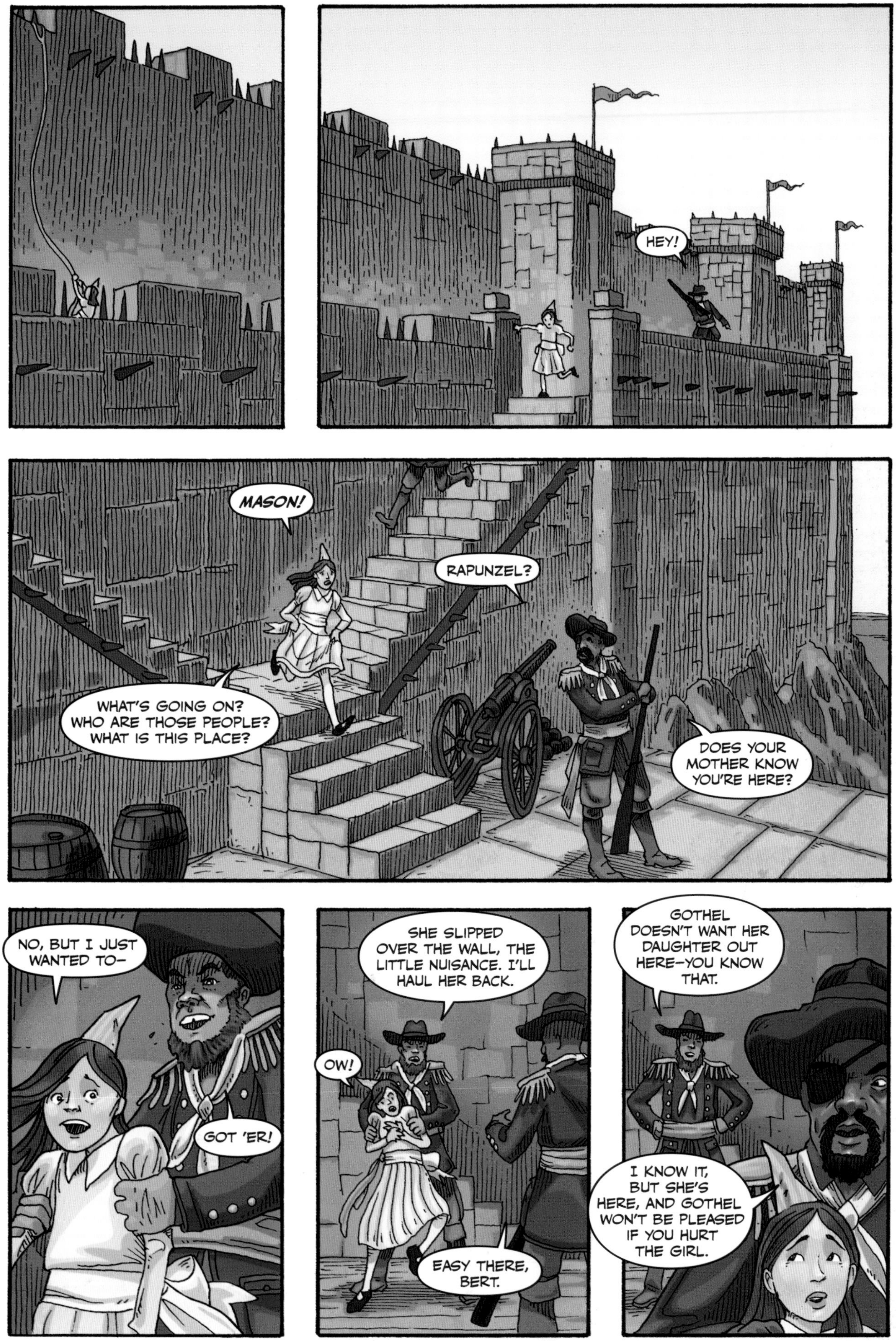
HEY!
MASON!
RAPUNZEL?
WHAT'S GOING ON? WHO ARE THOSE PEOPLE? WHAT IS THIS PLACE?
DOES YOUR MOTHER KNOW YOU'RE HERE?
NO, BUT I JUST WANTED TO–
GOT 'ER!
SHE SLIPPED OVER THE WALL, THE LITTLE NUISANCE. I'LL HAUL HER BACK.
OW!
EASY THERE, BERT.
GOTHEL DOESN'T WANT HER DAUGHTER OUT HERE–YOU KNOW THAT.
I KNOW IT, BUT SHE'S HERE, AND GOTHEL WON'T BE PLEASED IF YOU HURT THE GIRL.

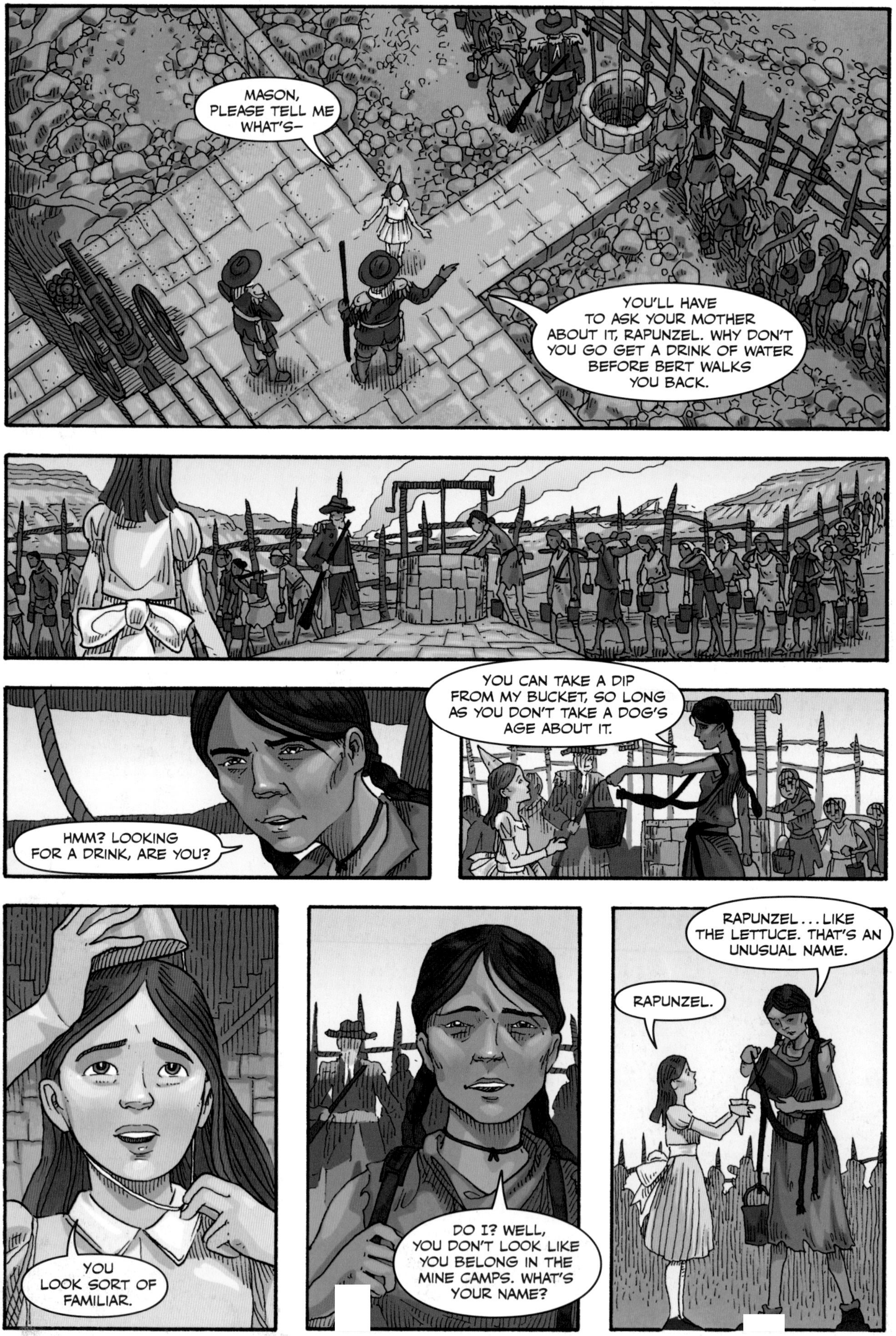
MASON, PLEASE TELL ME WHAT'S–
YOU'LL HAVE TO ASK YOUR MOTHER ABOUT IT, RAPUNZEL. WHY DON'T YOU GO GET A DRINK OF WATER BEFORE BERT WALKS YOU BACK.
HMM? LOOKING FOR A DRINK, ARE YOU?
YOU CAN TAKE A DIP FROM MY BUCKET, SO LONG AS YOU DON'T TAKE A DOG'S AGE ABOUT IT.
YOU LOOK SORT OF FAMILIAR.
DO I? WELL, YOU DON'T LOOK LIKE YOU BELONG IN THE MINE CAMPS. WHAT'S YOUR NAME?
RAPUNZEL.
RAPUNZEL... LIKE THE LETTUCE. THAT'S AN UNUSUAL NAME.

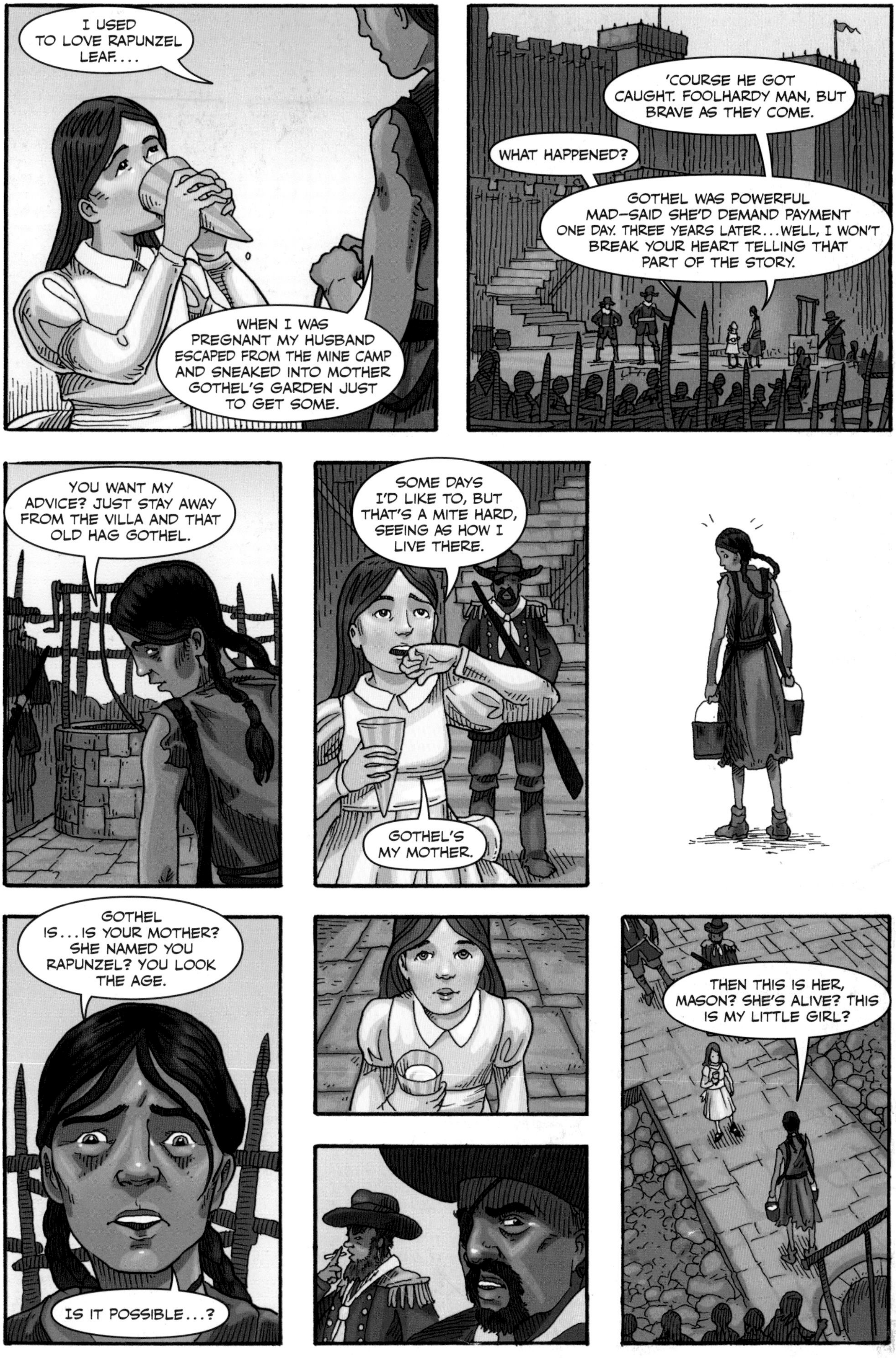
I USED TO LOVE RAPUNZEL LEAF....
WHEN I WAS PREGNANT MY HUSBAND ESCAPED FROM THE MINE CAMP AND SNEAKED INTO MOTHER GOTHEL'S GARDEN JUST TO GET SOME.
'COURSE HE GOT CAUGHT. FOOLHARDY MAN, BUT BRAVE AS THEY COME.
WHAT HAPPENED?
GOTHEL WAS POWERFUL MAD—SAID SHE'D DEMAND PAYMENT ONE DAY. THREE YEARS LATER...WELL, I WON'T BREAK YOUR HEART TELLING THAT PART OF THE STORY.
YOU WANT MY ADVICE? JUST STAY AWAY FROM THE VILLA AND THAT OLD HAG GOTHEL.
SOME DAYS I'D LIKE TO, BUT THAT'S A MITE HARD, SEEING AS HOW I LIVE THERE.
GOTHEL'S MY MOTHER.
GOTHEL IS...IS YOUR MOTHER? SHE NAMED YOU RAPUNZEL? YOU LOOK THE AGE.
IS IT POSSIBLE...?
THEN THIS IS HER, MASON? SHE'S ALIVE? THIS IS MY LITTLE GIRL?

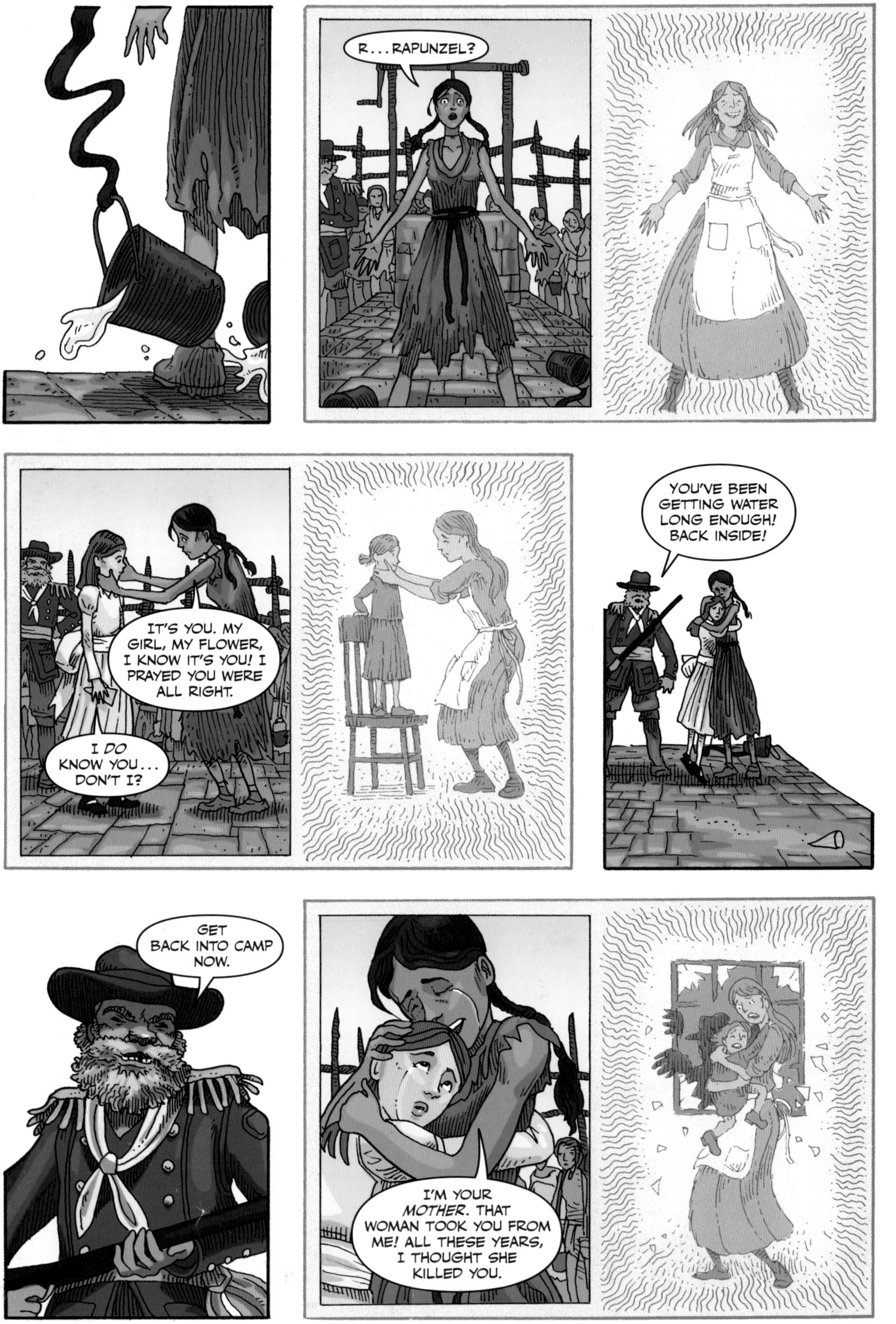
R . . . RAPUNZEL?
IT'S YOU. MY GIRL, MY FLOWER, I KNOW IT'S YOU! I PRAYED YOU WERE ALL RIGHT.
I *DO* KNOW YOU . . . DON'T I?
YOU'VE BEEN GETTING WATER LONG ENOUGH! BACK INSIDE!
GET BACK INTO CAMP NOW.
I'M YOUR *MOTHER*. THAT WOMAN TOOK YOU FROM ME! ALL THESE YEARS, I THOUGHT SHE KILLED YOU.

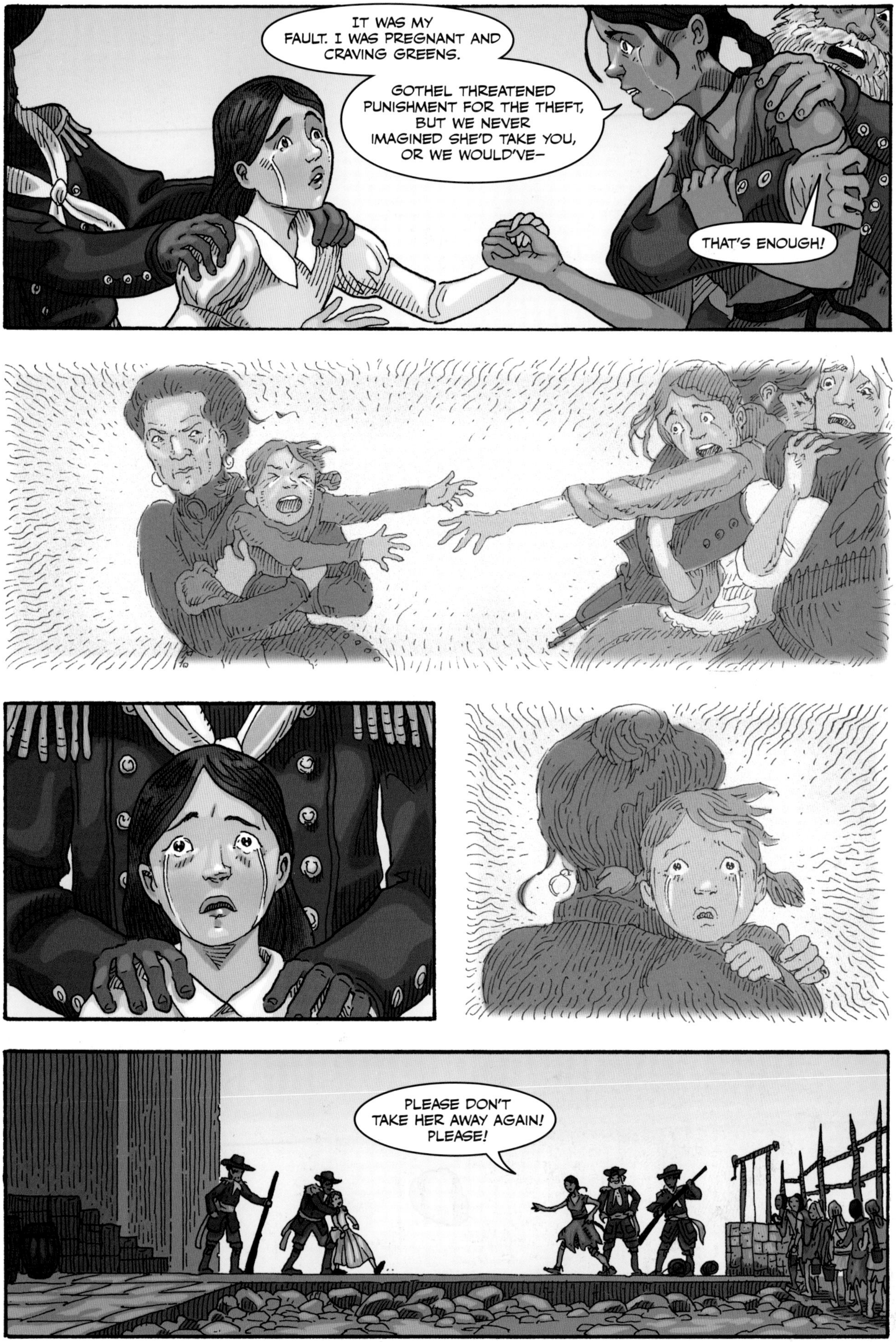
IT WAS MY FAULT. I WAS PREGNANT AND CRAVING GREENS.
GOTHEL THREATENED PUNISHMENT FOR THE THEFT, BUT WE NEVER IMAGINED SHE'D TAKE YOU, OR WE WOULD'VE–
THAT'S ENOUGH!
PLEASE DON'T TAKE HER AWAY AGAIN! PLEASE!

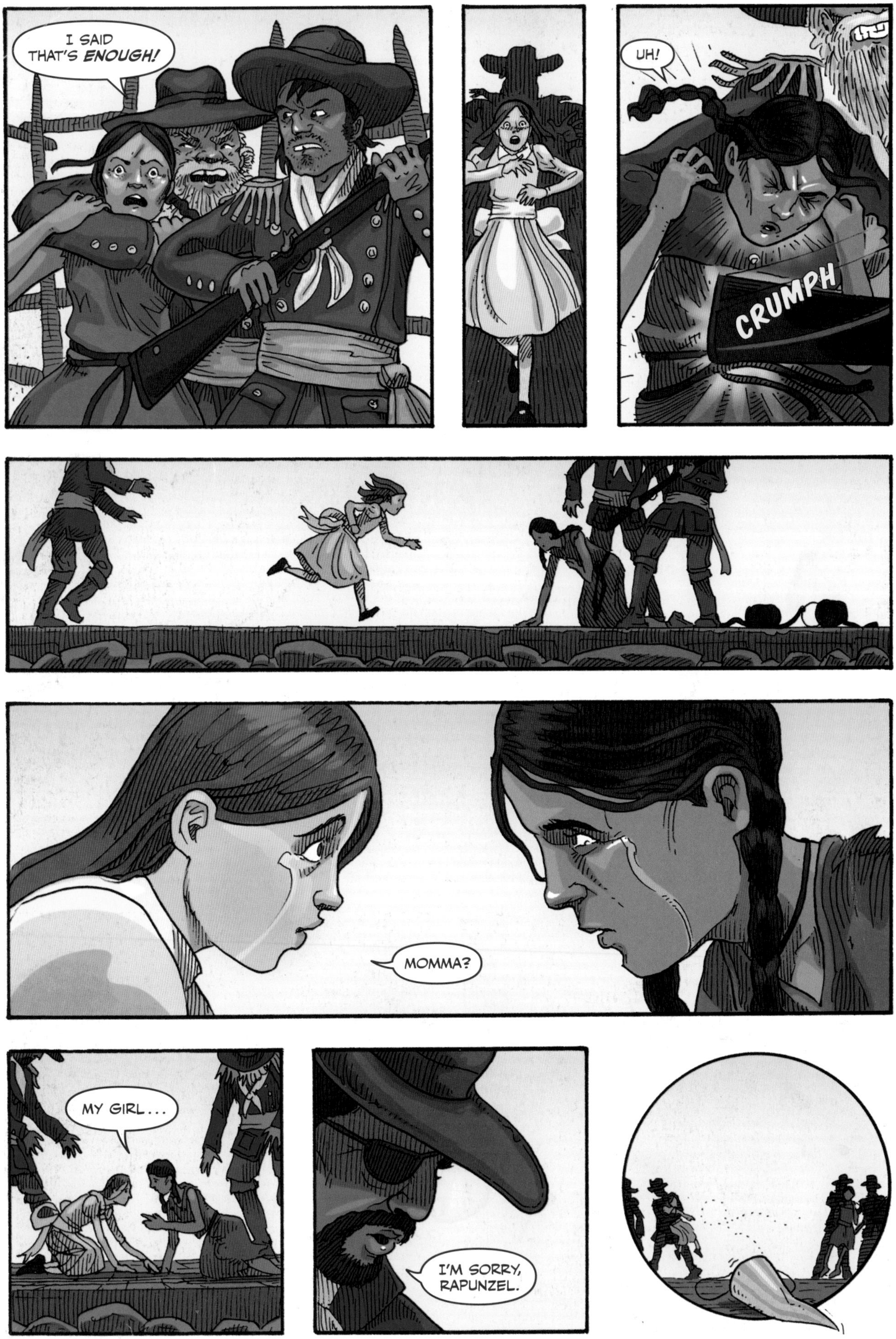
I SAID THAT'S ENOUGH!
UH!
CRUMPH
MOMMA?
MY GIRL...
I'M SORRY, RAPUNZEL.

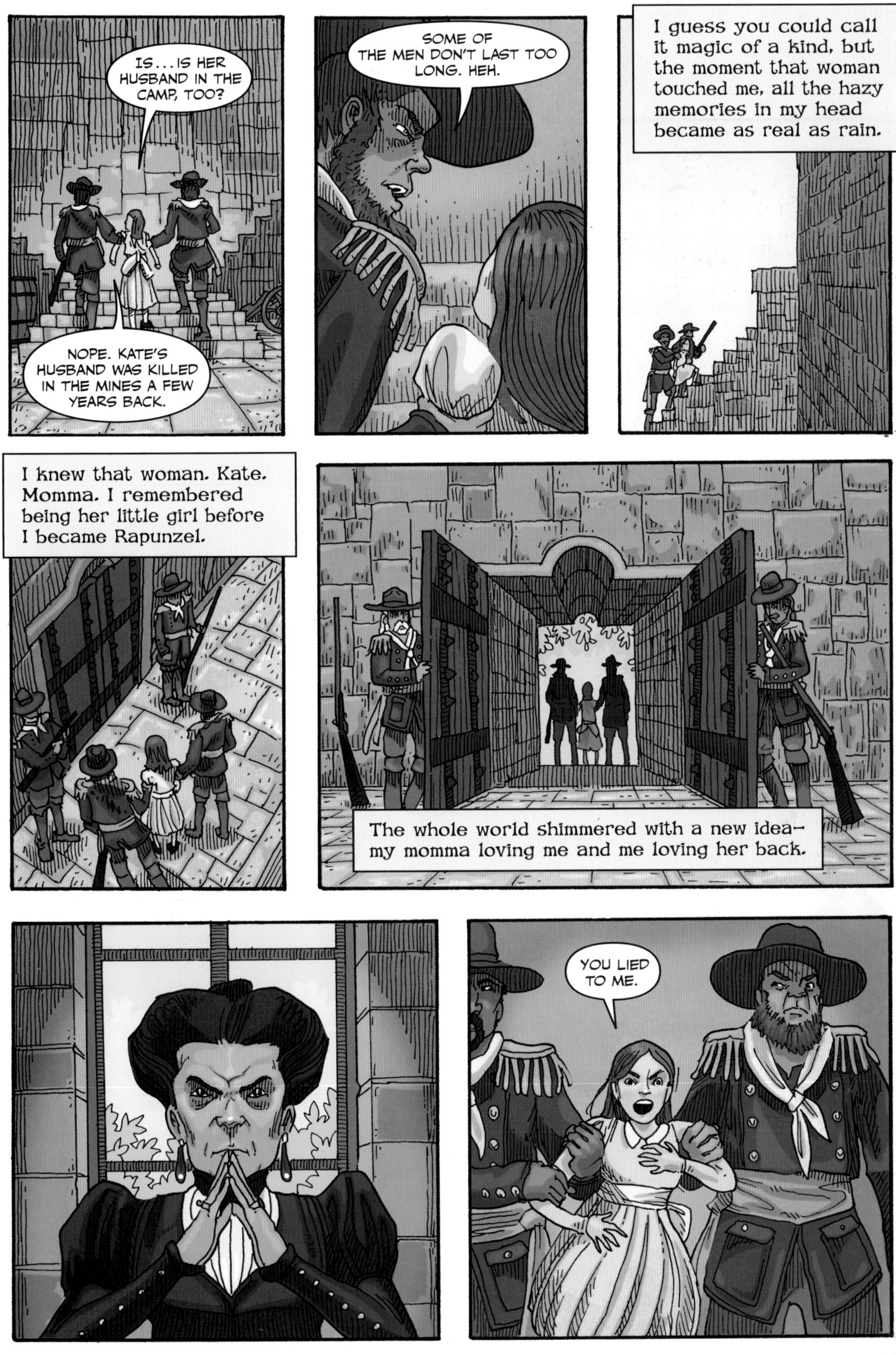
IS... IS HER HUSBAND IN THE CAMP, TOO?
NOPE. KATE'S HUSBAND WAS KILLED IN THE MINES A FEW YEARS BACK.
SOME OF THE MEN DON'T LAST TOO LONG. HEH.
I guess you could call it magic of a kind, but the moment that woman touched me, all the hazy memories in my head became as real as rain.
I knew that woman. Kate. Momma. I remembered being her little girl before I became Rapunzel.
The whole world shimmered with a new idea– my momma loving me and me loving her back.
YOU LIED TO ME.

BACK THEN I DIDN'T HAVE SUCH A GOOD WALL. NO ONE WILL STEAL FROM ME AGAIN.

SO IT'S ALL TRUE?

YOU SAW HOW THAT WOMAN LIVES. THINK WHAT I SAVED YOU FROM.

SHE'S ONLY IN THE MINES BECAUSE YOU—

UNGRATEFUL CHILD, SLAVES ARE NECESSARY TO BUILD UP MY EMPIRE. OUR EMPIRE.

OUR? IF I'D KNOWN WHAT WAS GOING ON, I WOULD'VE RUN AWAY LONG AGO!

When she quit arguing, I actually thought I'd won. For one amazing moment, I really believed it was going to be happily-ever-after right then and there.

I didn't anticipate the whole sticking-a-sack-over-my-head thing.

Her henchman, Brute, used to give me piggyback rides. This time, being thrown over his shoulder wasn't so fun.

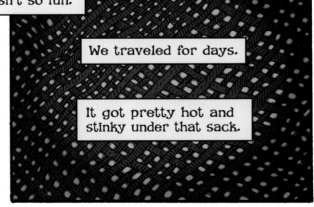

We traveled for days.

It got pretty hot and stinky under that sack.

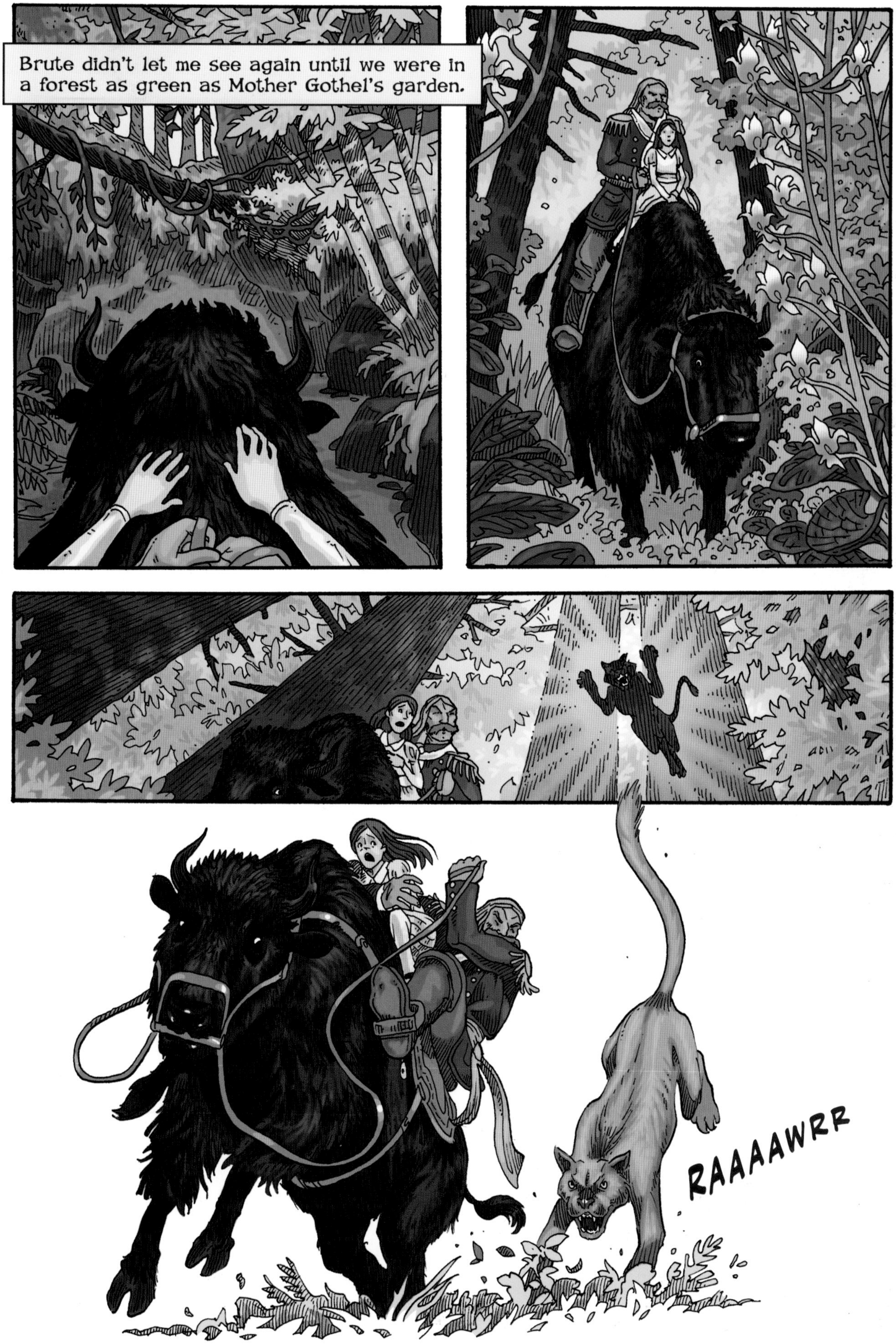
Brute didn't let me see again until we were in a forest as green as Mother Gothel's garden.
RAAAAWRR

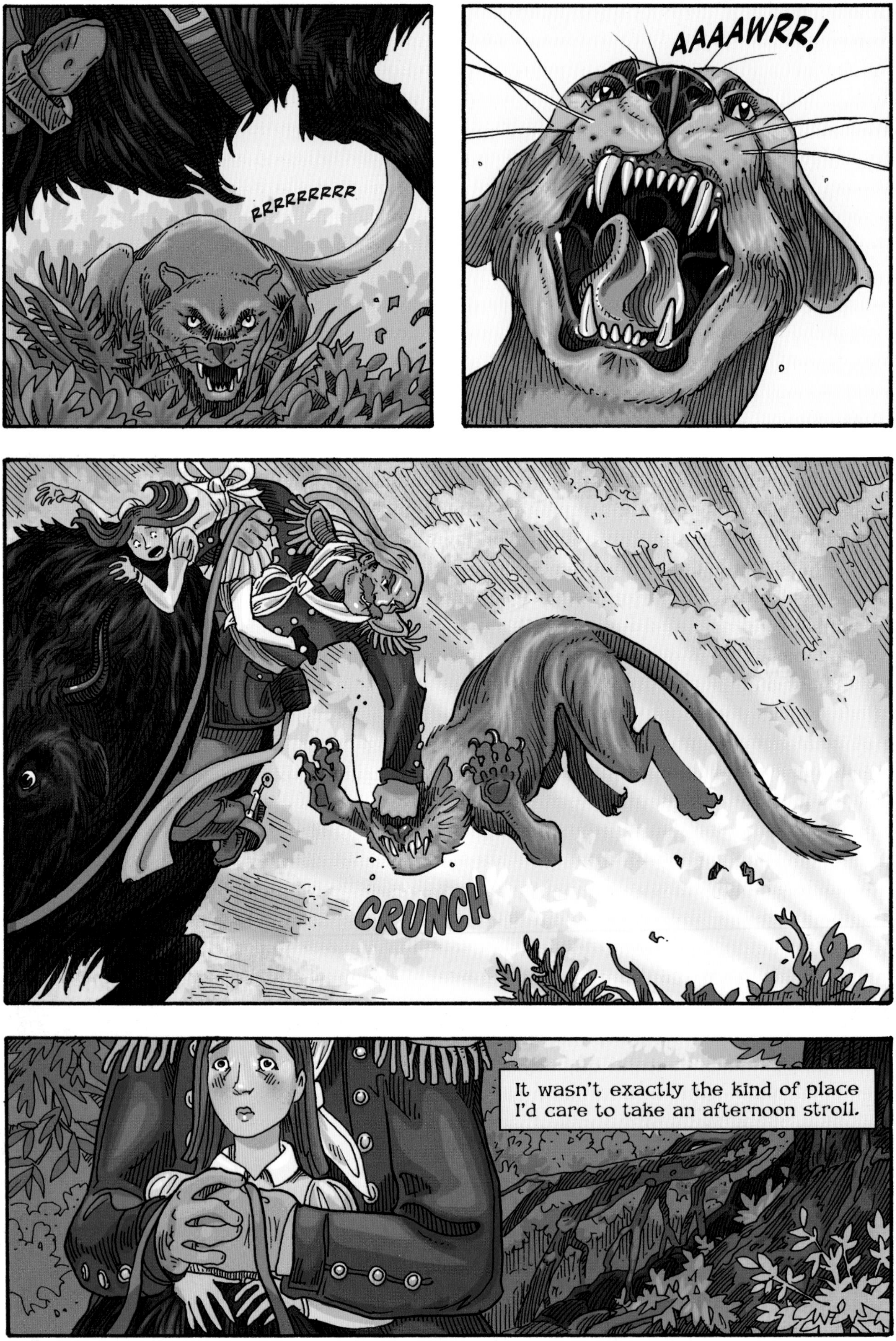
RRRRRRRR
AAAAWRR!
CRUNCH
It wasn't exactly the kind of place I'd care to take an afternoon stroll.

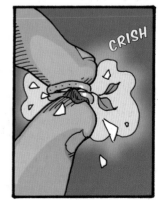

CRISH

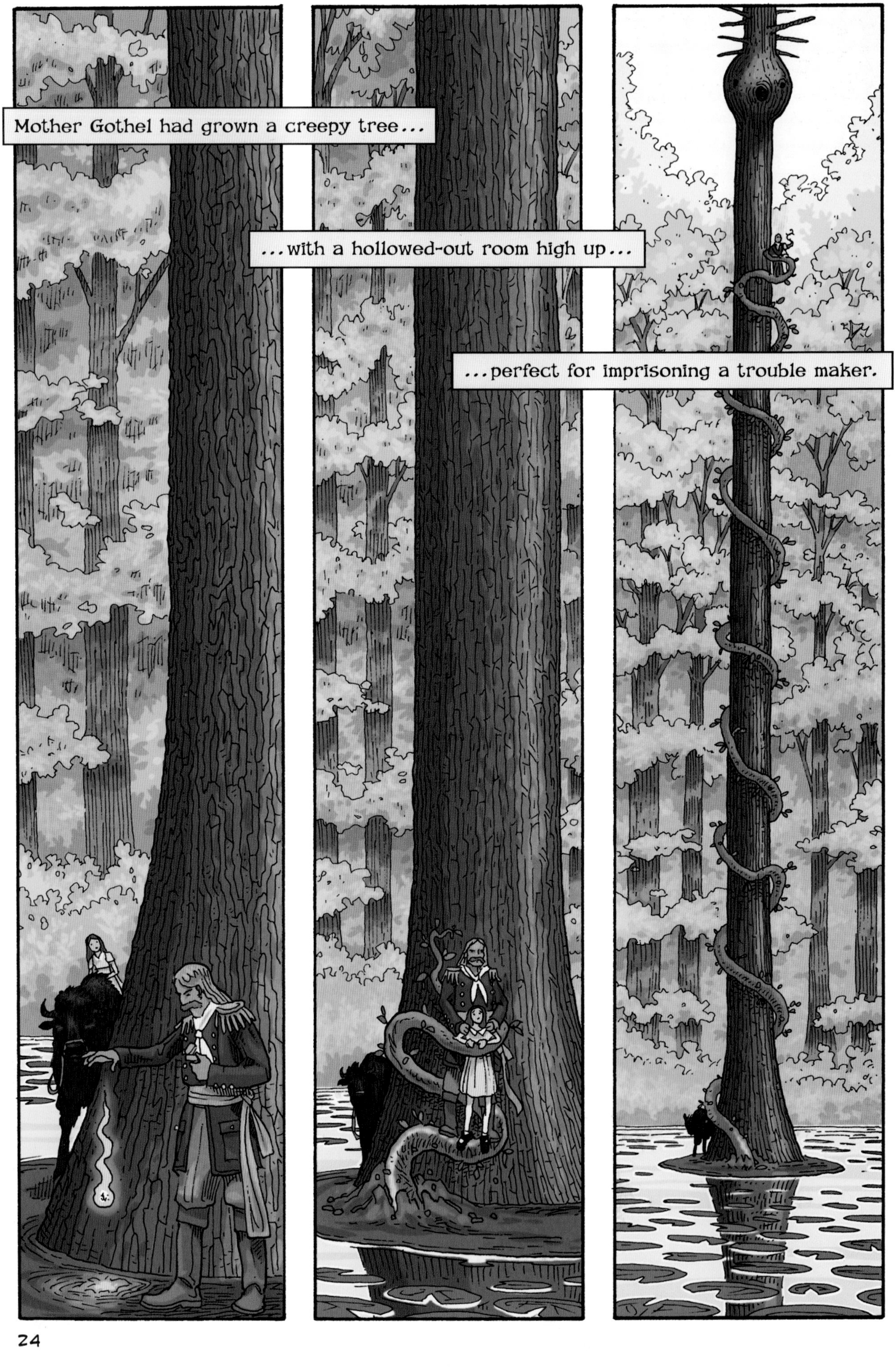
Mother Gothel had grown a creepy tree...
...with a hollowed-out room high up...
...perfect for imprisoning a trouble maker.

PLEASE, BRUTE! DON'T LEAVE ME HERE.

MOTHER GOTHEL SAYS YOU'RE NAUGHTY, SO HERE YOU GO.

I was able to make some helpful observations before he was out of earshot.

They mostly had to do with his odor and bathroom habits.

I hoped he might come right back, that it was just a joke.

But for all I knew, he'd been eaten by a wild boar in the forest.

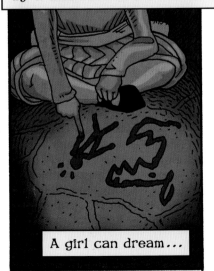

A girl can dream...

So.

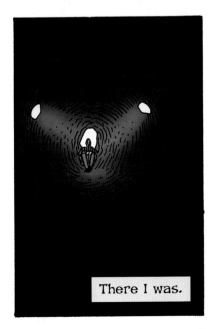

There I was.

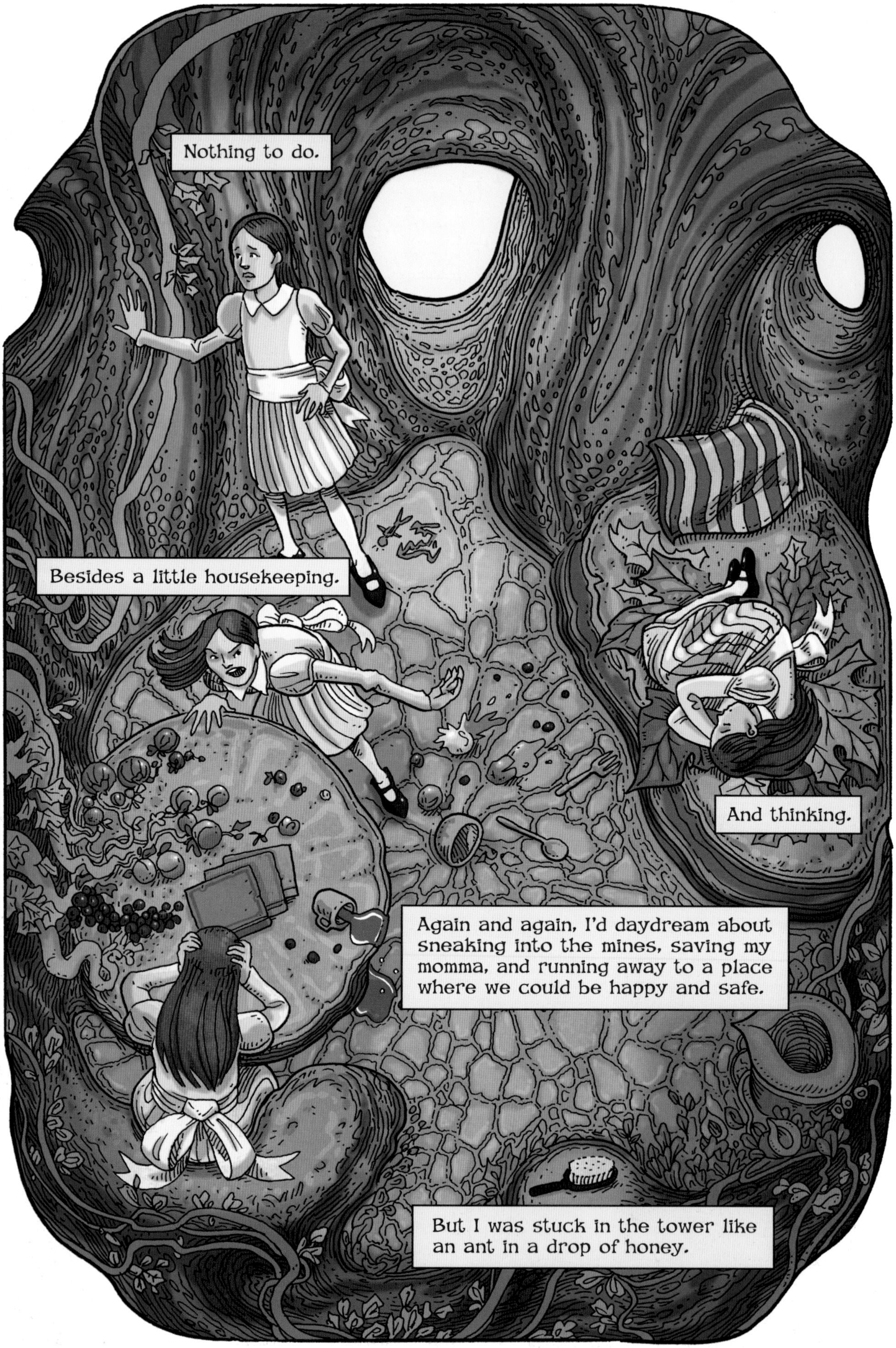
Nothing to do.
Besides a little housekeeping.
And thinking.
Again and again, I'd daydream about sneaking into the mines, saving my momma, and running away to a place where we could be happy and safe.
But I was stuck in the tower like an ant in a drop of honey.

So I did everything I could to keep from thinking.

Winter was the hardest.

Mother Gothel's magic tree sealed up my window tighter to keep in the warmth.

But it kept me in, too.

In the winter all I could do was think.

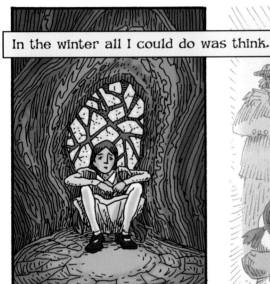

You bet I fantasized about escaping. And saving my mother. And teaching Mother Gothel a lesson.

And I had no idea how to do it.

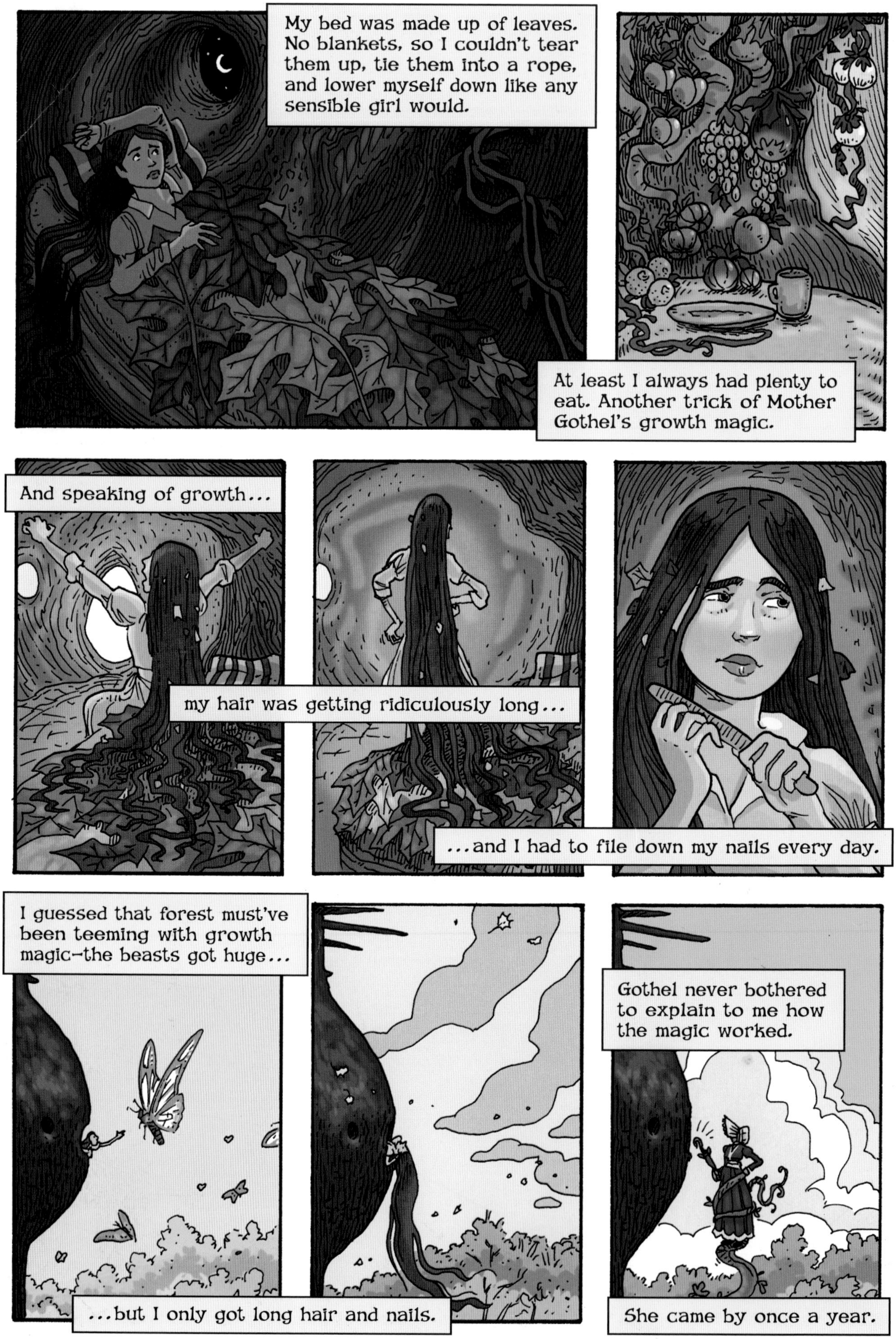
My bed was made up of leaves. No blankets, so I couldn't tear them up, tie them into a rope, and lower myself down like any sensible girl would.
At least I always had plenty to eat. Another trick of Mother Gothel's growth magic.
And speaking of growth...
my hair was getting ridiculously long...
...and I had to file down my nails every day.
I guessed that forest must've been teeming with growth magic—the beasts got huge...
...but I only got long hair and nails.
Gothel never bothered to explain to me how the magic worked.
She came by once a year.

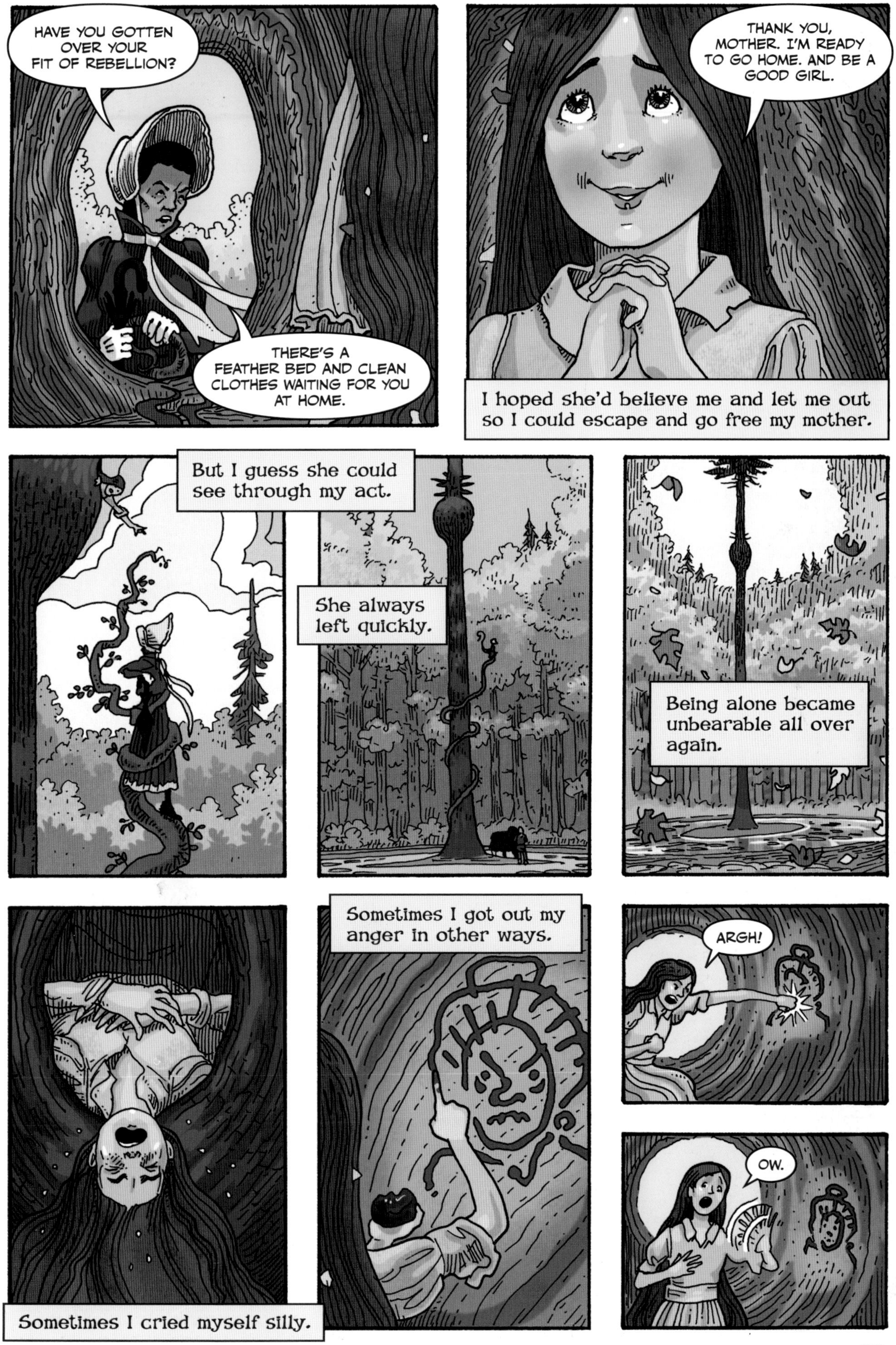
HAVE YOU GOTTEN OVER YOUR FIT OF REBELLION?
THERE'S A FEATHER BED AND CLEAN CLOTHES WAITING FOR YOU AT HOME.
THANK YOU, MOTHER. I'M READY TO GO HOME. AND BE A GOOD GIRL.
I hoped she'd believe me and let me out so I could escape and go free my mother.
But I guess she could see through my act.
She always left quickly.
Being alone became unbearable all over again.
Sometimes I cried myself silly.
Sometimes I got out my anger in other ways.
ARGH!
OW.

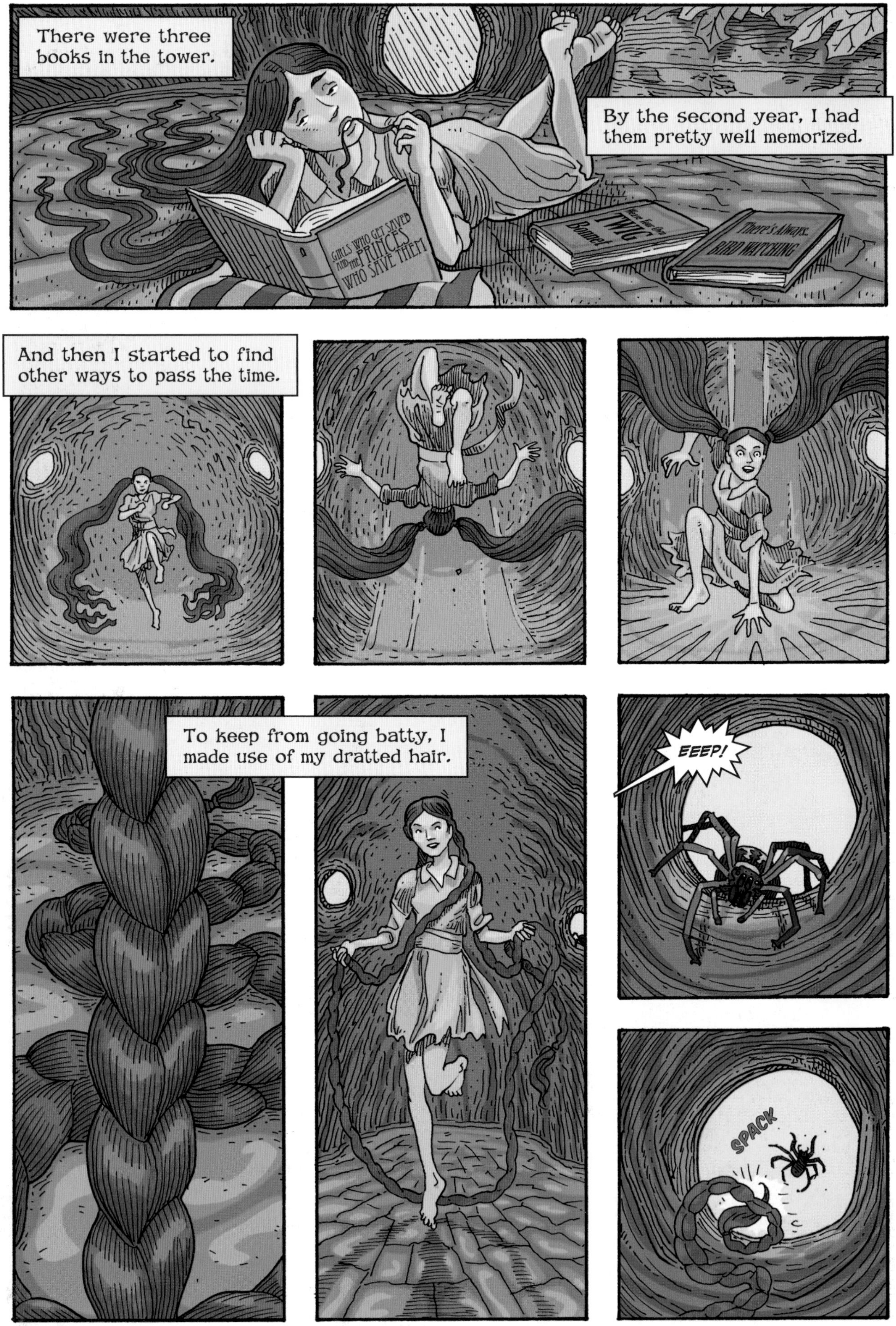
There were three books in the tower.
GIRLS WHO GET SAVED AND THE PRINCES WHO SAVE THEM
Weave Your Own TWIG Bonnet
There's Always... BIRD WATCHING
By the second year, I had them pretty well memorized.
And then I started to find other ways to pass the time.
To keep from going batty, I made use of my dratted hair.
EEEP!
SPACK

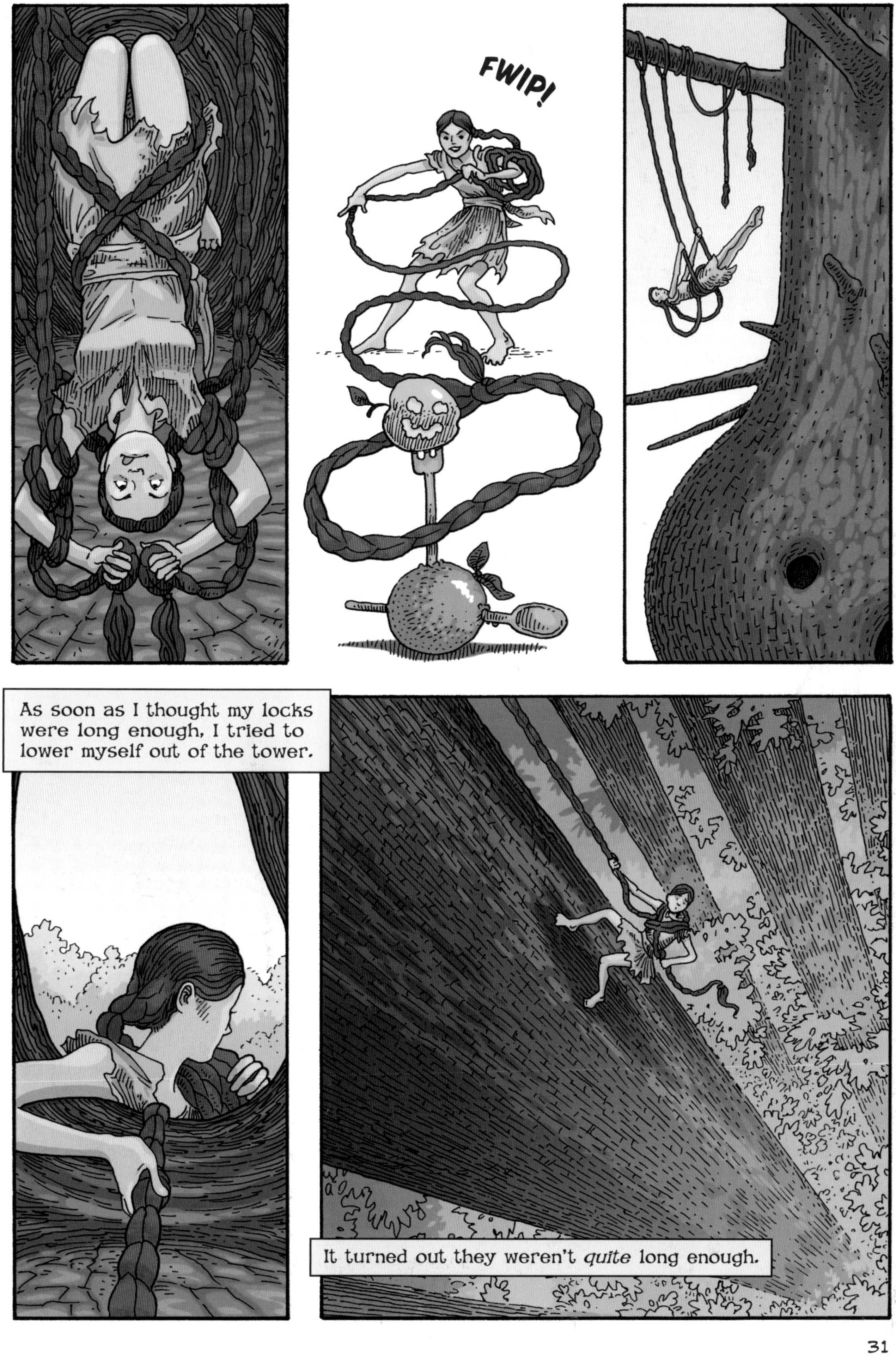
FWIP!
As soon as I thought my locks were long enough, I tried to lower myself out of the tower.
It turned out they weren't *quite* long enough.

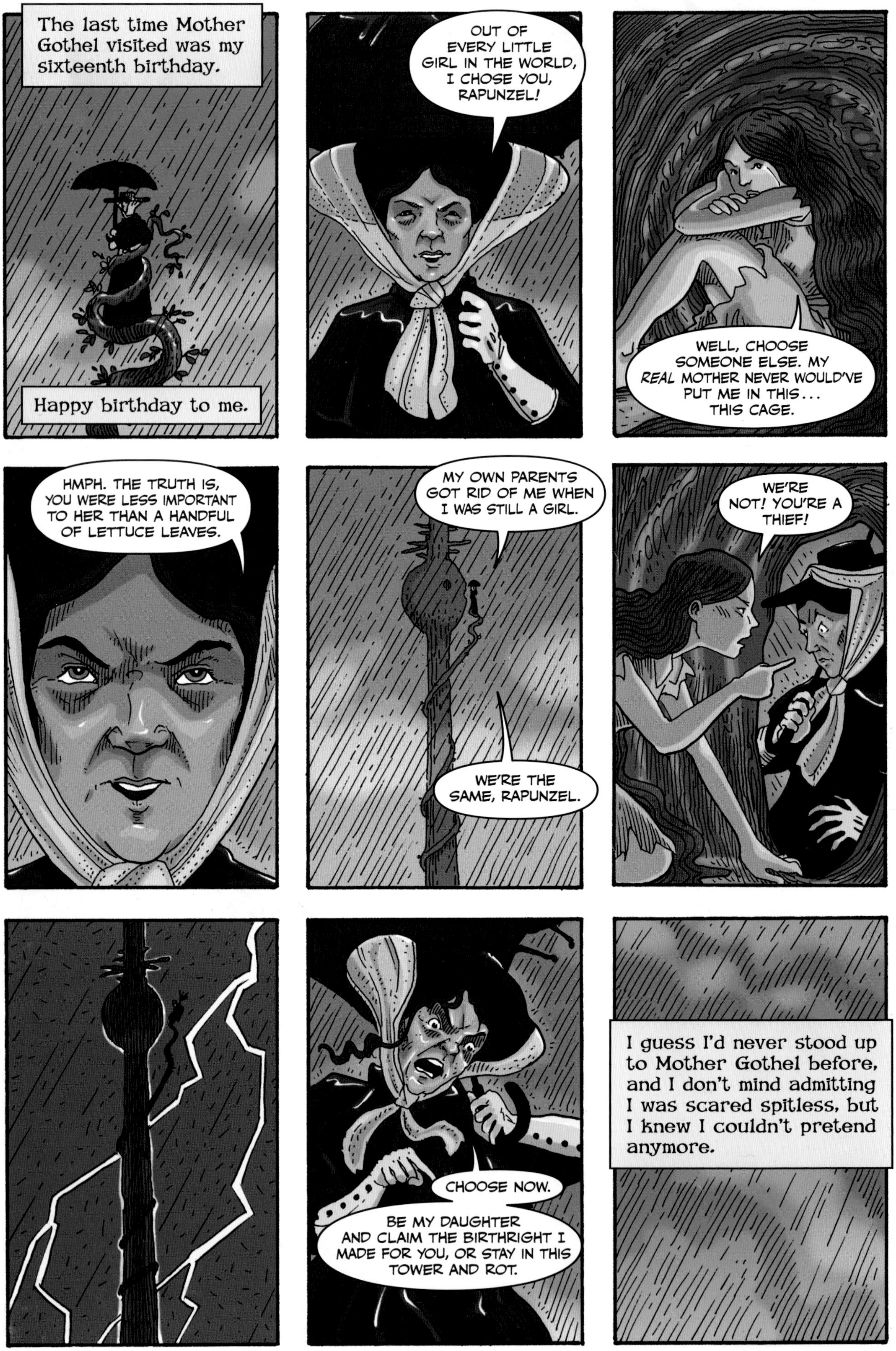
The last time Mother Gothel visited was my sixteenth birthday.
Happy birthday to me.
OUT OF EVERY LITTLE GIRL IN THE WORLD, I CHOSE YOU, RAPUNZEL!
WELL, CHOOSE SOMEONE ELSE. MY REAL MOTHER NEVER WOULD'VE PUT ME IN THIS... THIS CAGE.
HMPH. THE TRUTH IS, YOU WERE LESS IMPORTANT TO HER THAN A HANDFUL OF LETTUCE LEAVES.
MY OWN PARENTS GOT RID OF ME WHEN I WAS STILL A GIRL.
WE'RE THE SAME, RAPUNZEL.
WE'RE NOT! YOU'RE A THIEF!
CHOOSE NOW.
BE MY DAUGHTER AND CLAIM THE BIRTHRIGHT I MADE FOR YOU, OR STAY IN THIS TOWER AND ROT.
I guess I'd never stood up to Mother Gothel before, and I don't mind admitting I was scared spitless, but I knew I couldn't pretend anymore.

So I told her to go to...

...someplace less nice.

In hindsight, that might've been a fairly stupid thing to do.

Fortunately, every day my hair had been growing longer, and the tree outside my window had been growing taller.

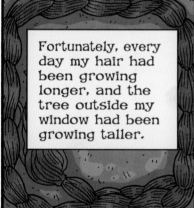

I didn't have much time to practice. As soon as Mother Gothel left, the food stopped coming, and the window seemed to be shrinking with the intent to close forever.

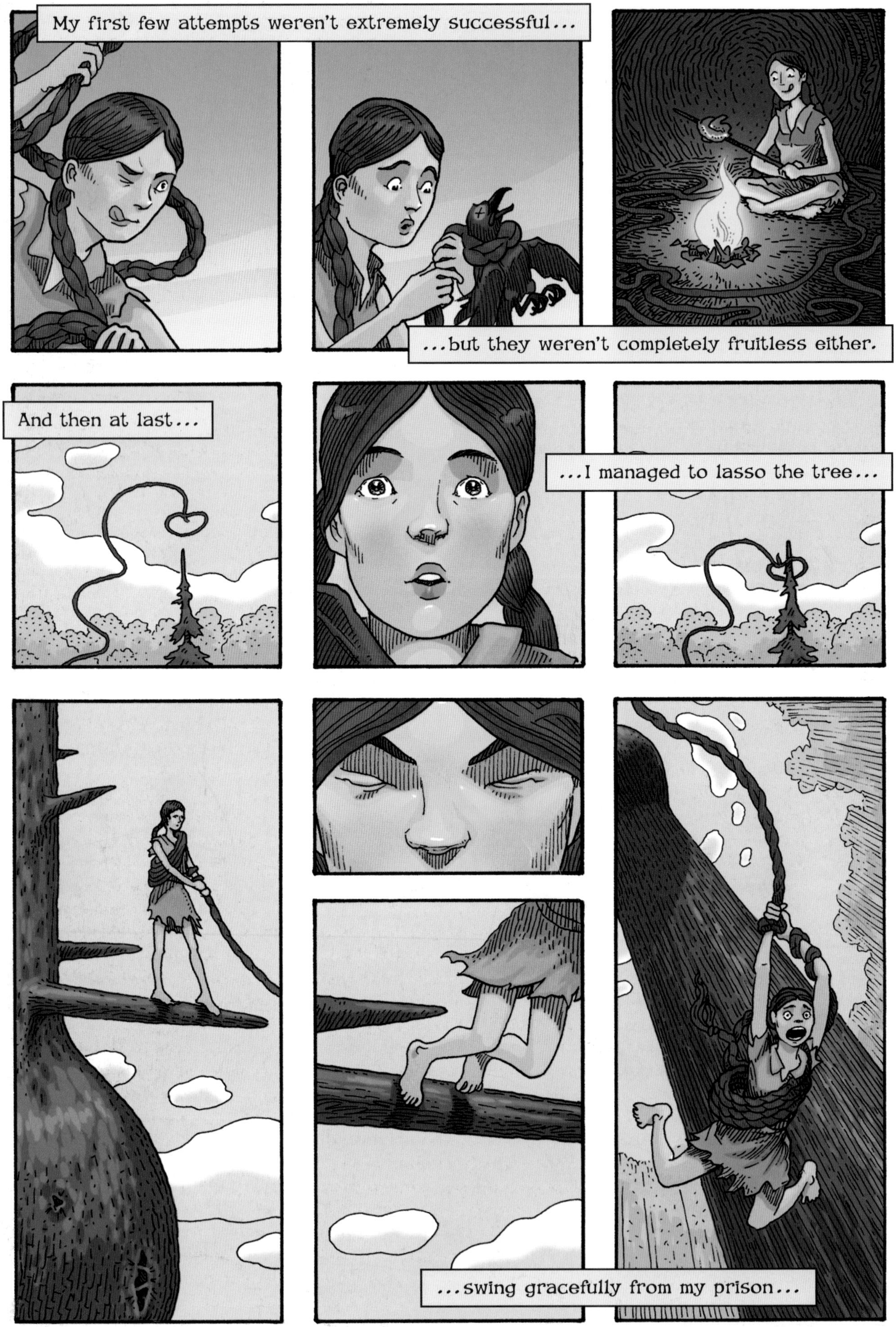

My first few attempts weren't extremely successful...
...but they weren't completely fruitless either.
And then at last...
...I managed to lasso the tree...
...swing gracefully from my prison...

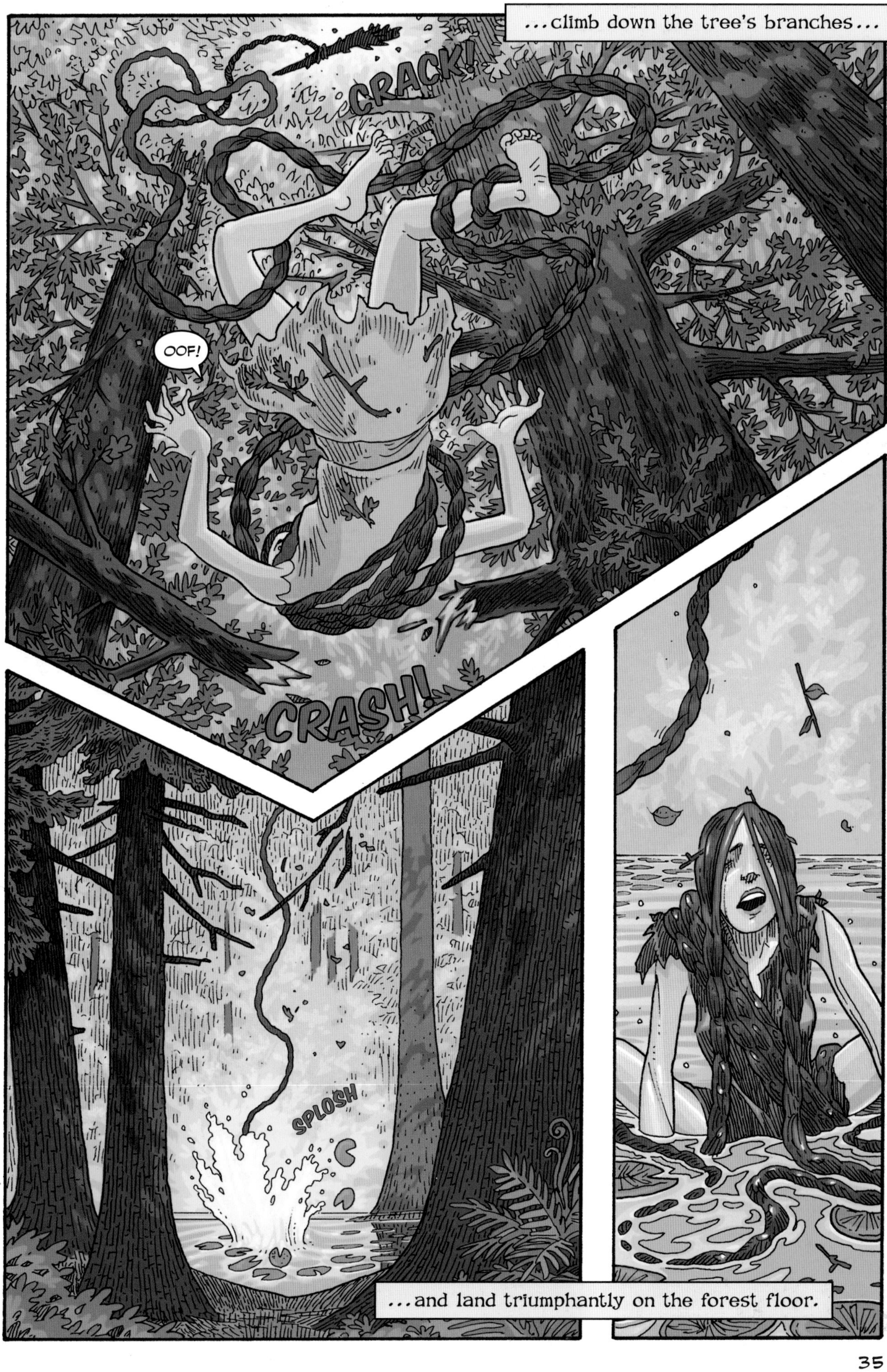
...climb down the tree's branches...
CRACK!
OOF!
CRASH!
SPLOSH
...and land triumphantly on the forest floor.

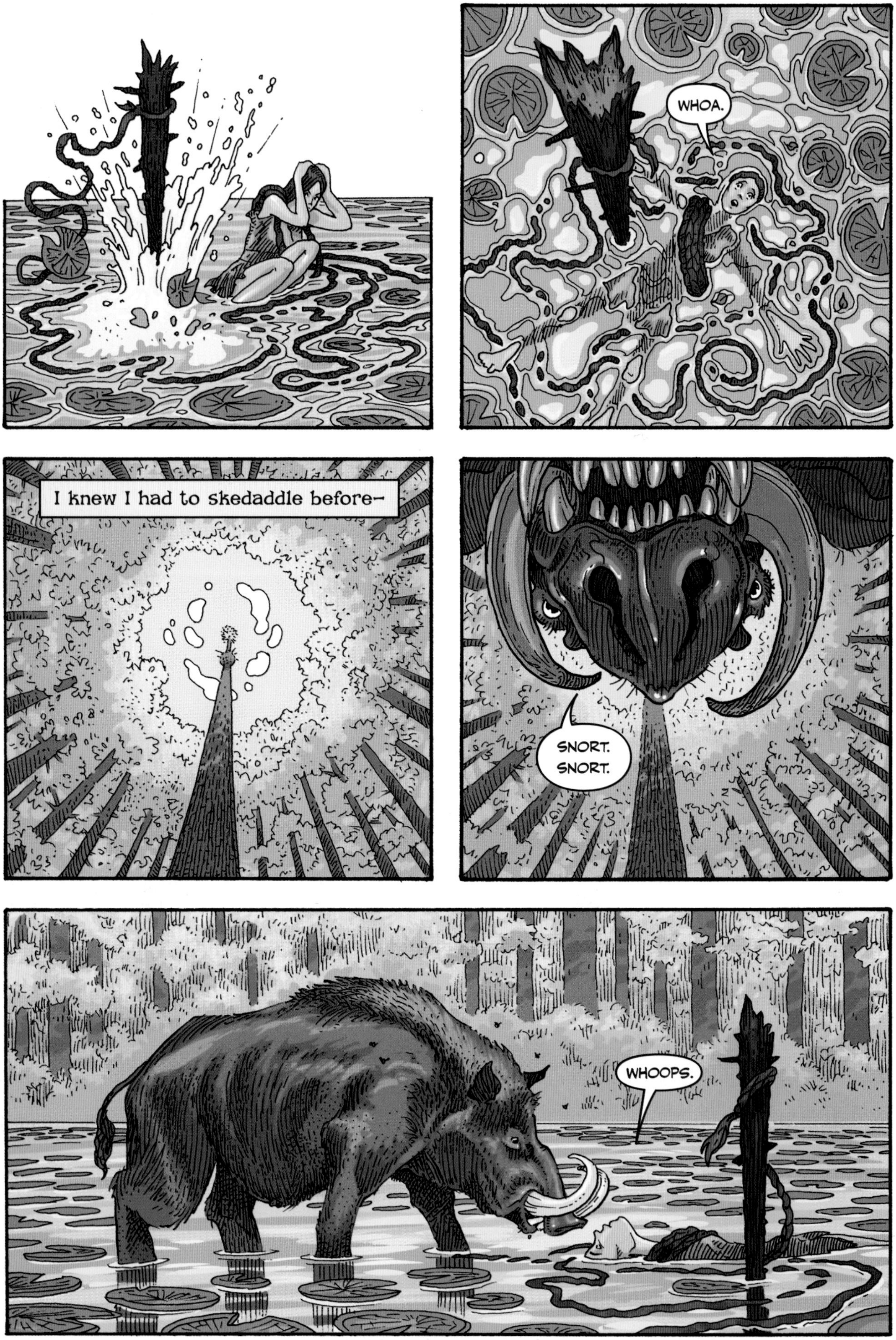
WHOA.
I knew I had to skedaddle before–
SNORT.
SNORT.
WHOOPS.

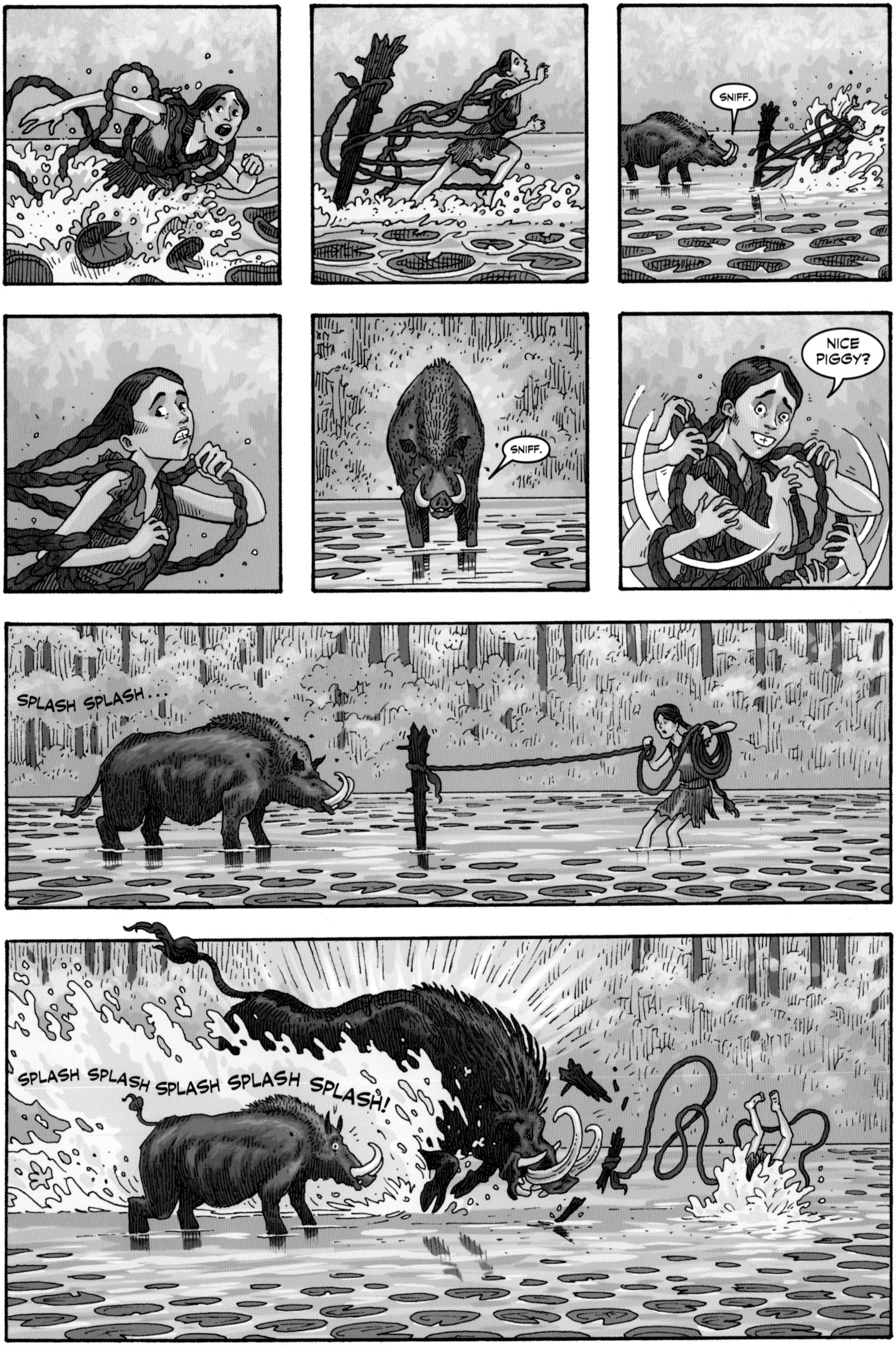
SNIFF.
SNIFF.
NICE PIGGY?
SPLASH SPLASH...
SPLASH SPLASH SPLASH SPLASH SPLASH!

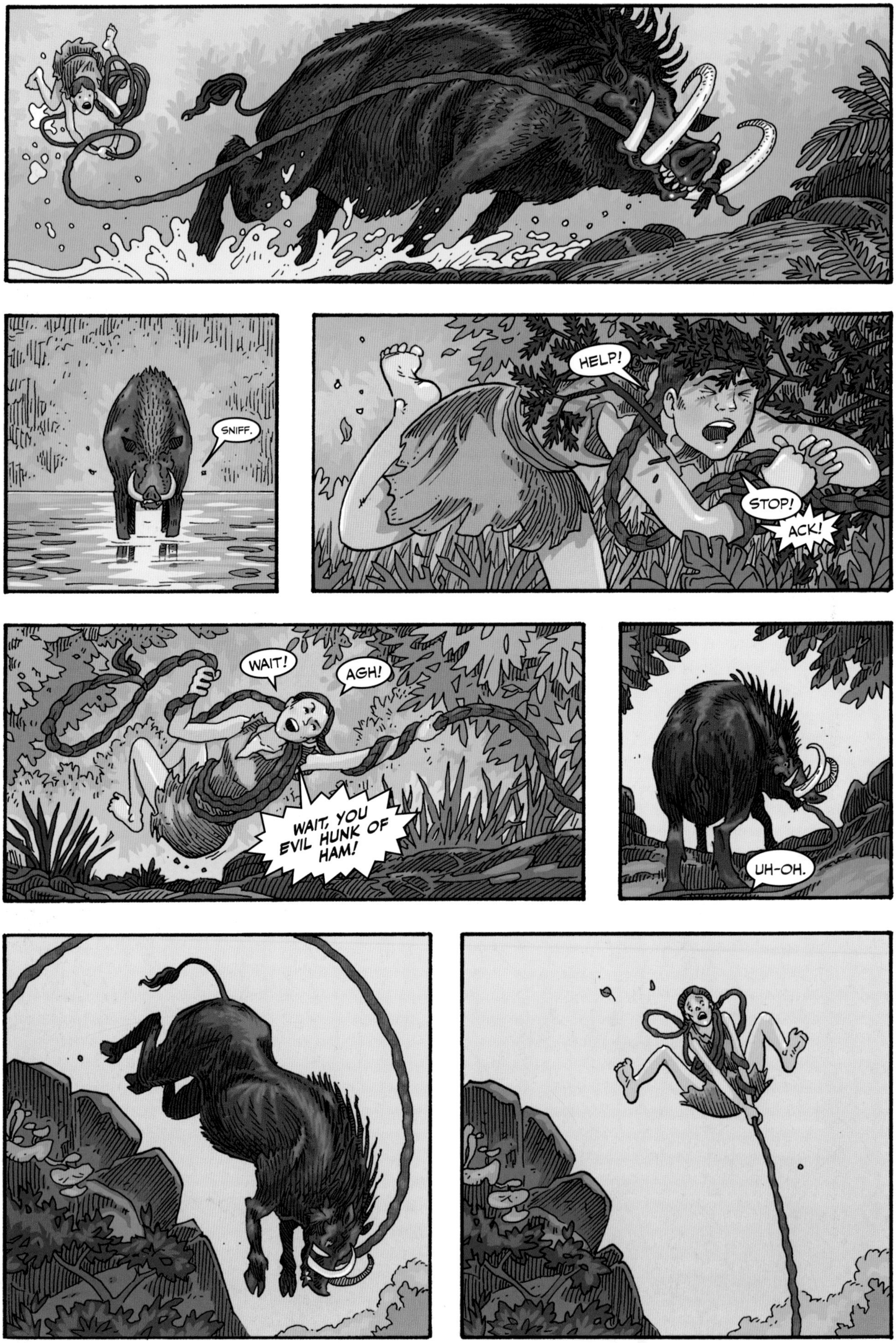
SNIFF.
HELP!
STOP!
ACK!
WAIT!
AGH!
WAIT, YOU EVIL HUNK OF HAM!
UH-OH.

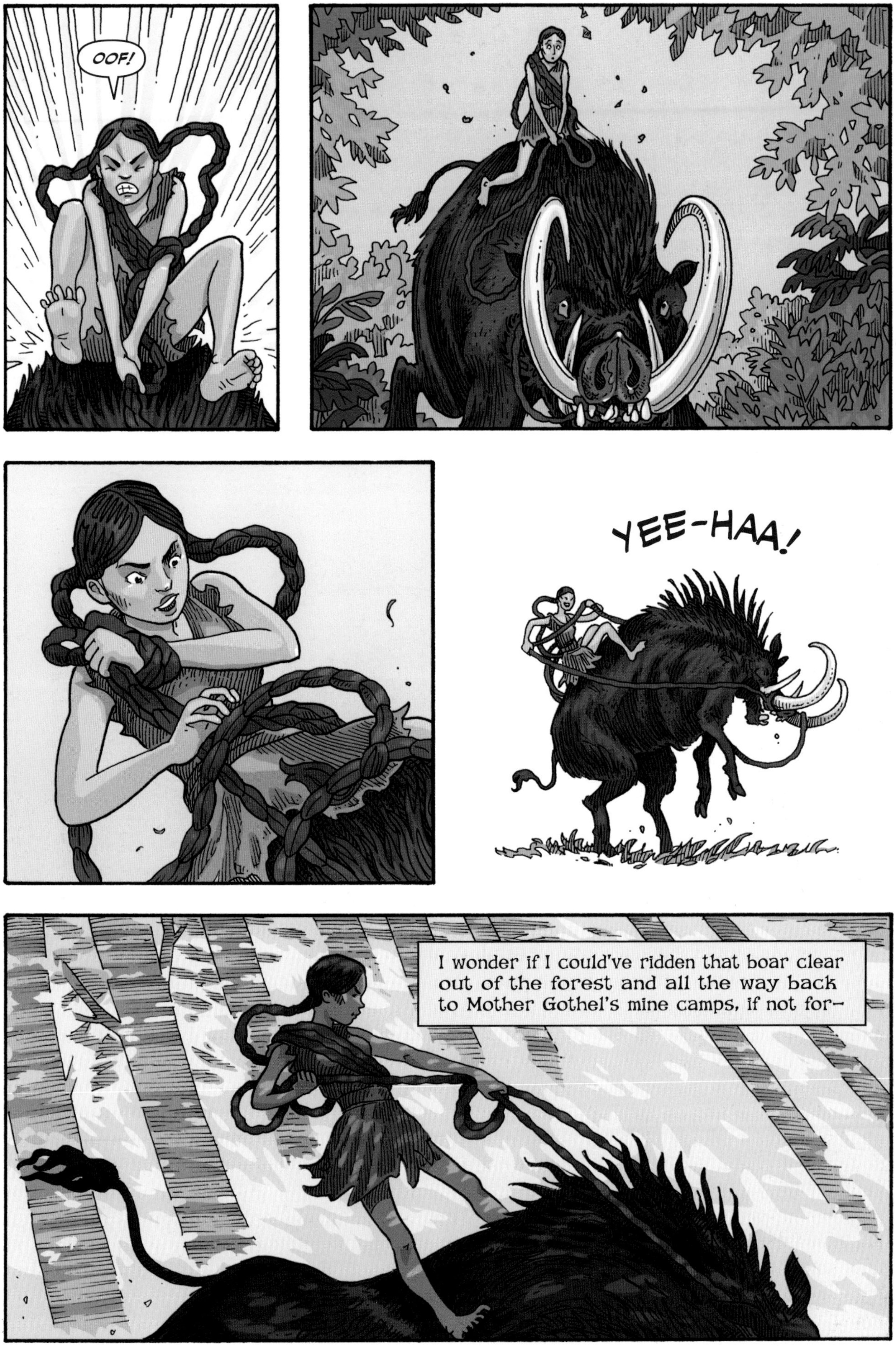
OOF!
YEE-HAA!
I wonder if I could've ridden that boar clear out of the forest and all the way back to Mother Gothel's mine camps, if not for—

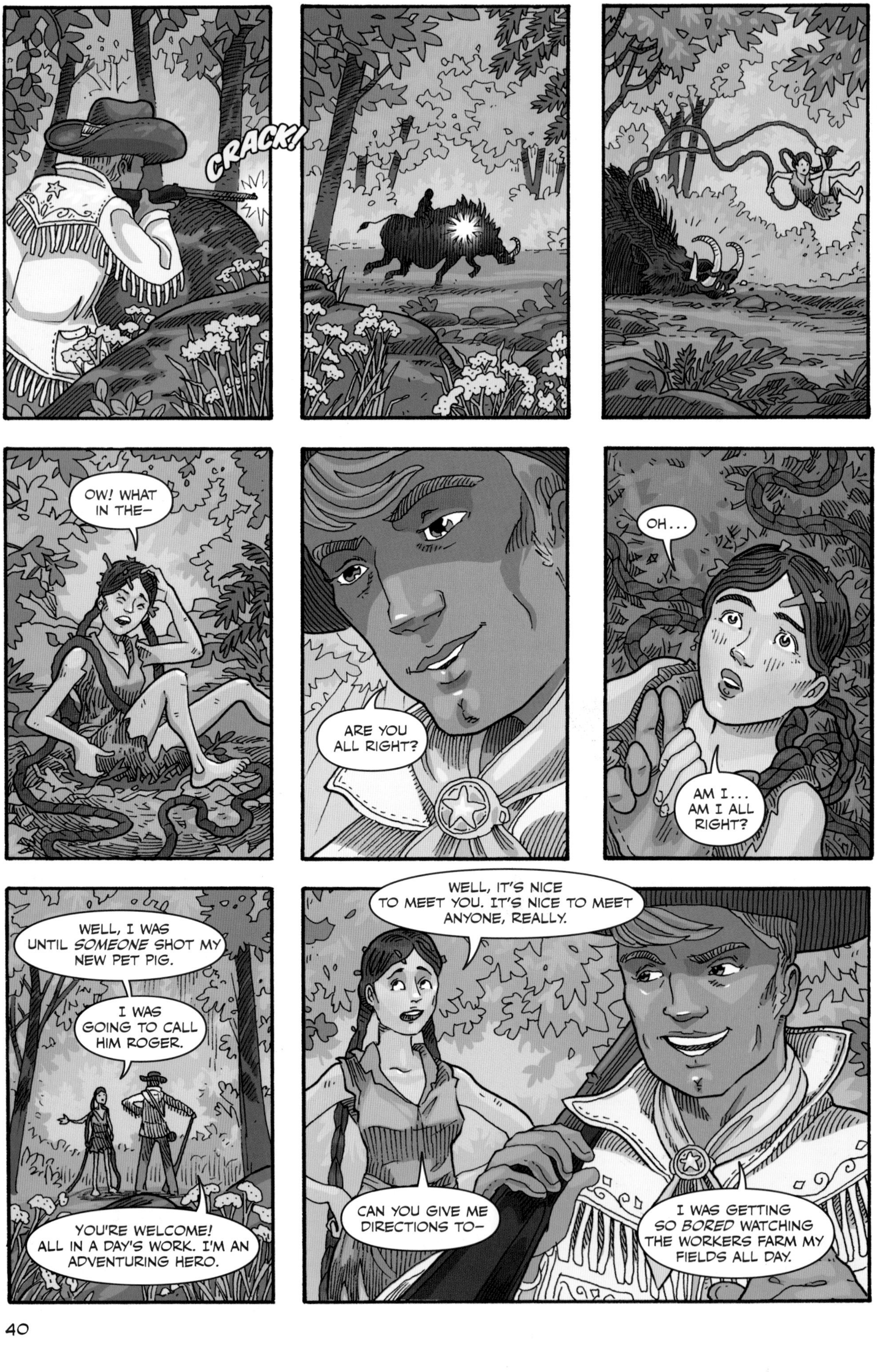
CRACK!
OW! WHAT IN THE–
ARE YOU ALL RIGHT?
OH...
AM I... AM I ALL RIGHT?
WELL, I WAS UNTIL *SOMEONE* SHOT MY NEW PET PIG.
I WAS GOING TO CALL HIM ROGER.
YOU'RE WELCOME! ALL IN A DAY'S WORK. I'M AN ADVENTURING HERO.
WELL, IT'S NICE TO MEET YOU. IT'S NICE TO MEET ANYONE, REALLY.
CAN YOU GIVE ME DIRECTIONS TO–
I WAS GETTING SO *BORED* WATCHING THE WORKERS FARM MY FIELDS ALL DAY.

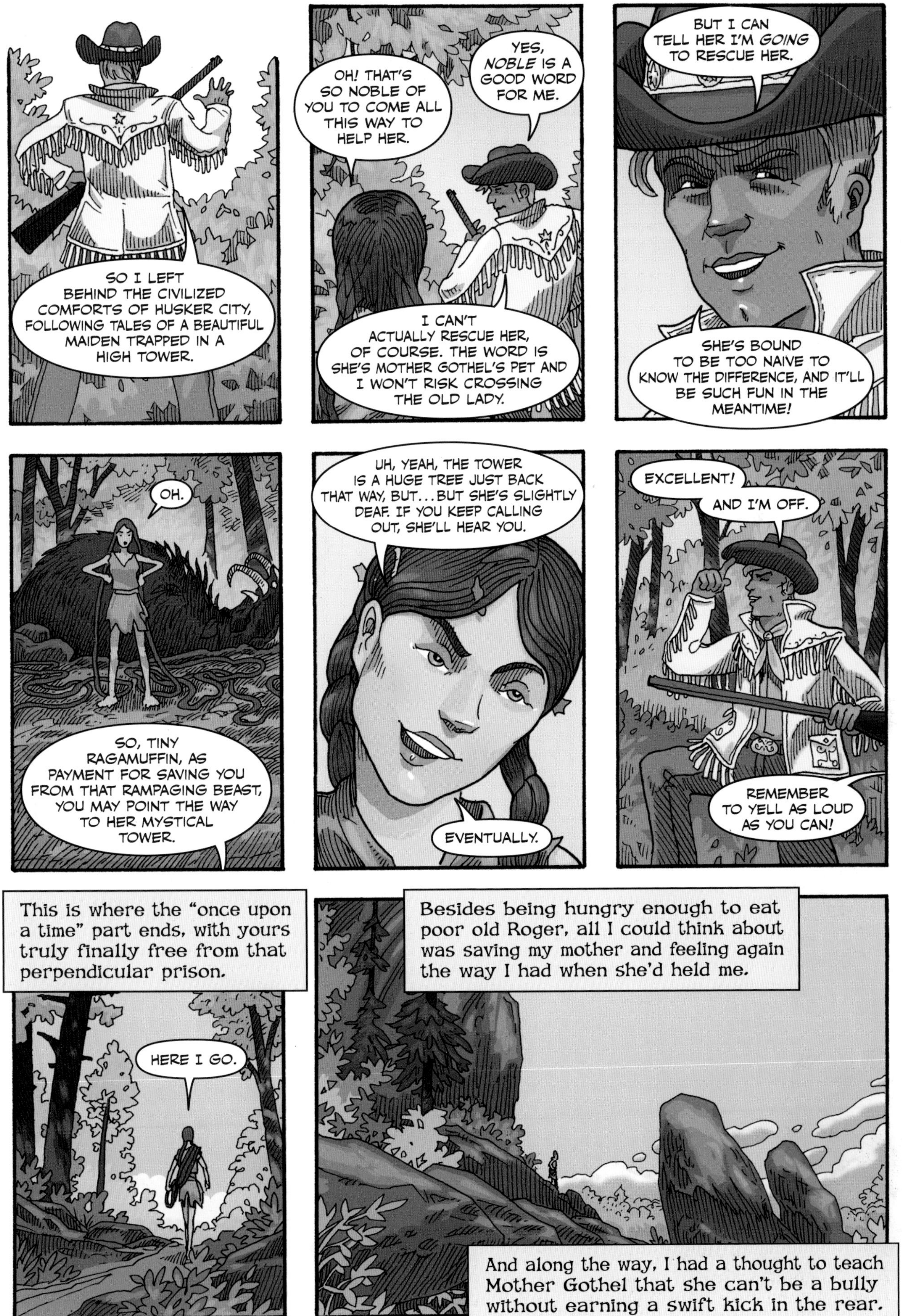

SO I LEFT BEHIND THE CIVILIZED COMFORTS OF HUSKER CITY, FOLLOWING TALES OF A BEAUTIFUL MAIDEN TRAPPED IN A HIGH TOWER.
OH! THAT'S SO NOBLE OF YOU TO COME ALL THIS WAY TO HELP HER.
YES, *NOBLE* IS A GOOD WORD FOR ME.
I CAN'T ACTUALLY RESCUE HER, OF COURSE. THE WORD IS SHE'S MOTHER GOTHEL'S PET AND I WON'T RISK CROSSING THE OLD LADY.
BUT I CAN TELL HER I'M *GOING* TO RESCUE HER.
SHE'S BOUND TO BE TOO NAIVE TO KNOW THE DIFFERENCE, AND IT'LL BE SUCH FUN IN THE MEANTIME!
SO, TINY RAGAMUFFIN, AS PAYMENT FOR SAVING YOU FROM THAT RAMPAGING BEAST, YOU MAY POINT THE WAY TO HER MYSTICAL TOWER.
OH.
UH, YEAH, THE TOWER IS A HUGE TREE JUST BACK THAT WAY, BUT...BUT SHE'S SLIGHTLY DEAF. IF YOU KEEP CALLING OUT, SHE'LL HEAR YOU.
EVENTUALLY.
EXCELLENT!
AND I'M OFF.
REMEMBER TO YELL AS LOUD AS YOU CAN!
This is where the "once upon a time" part ends, with yours truly finally free from that perpendicular prison.
HERE I GO.
Besides being hungry enough to eat poor old Roger, all I could think about was saving my mother and feeling again the way I had when she'd held me.
And along the way, I had a thought to teach Mother Gothel that she can't be a bully without earning a swift kick in the rear.

Part 2: Rustling Up Some Grub

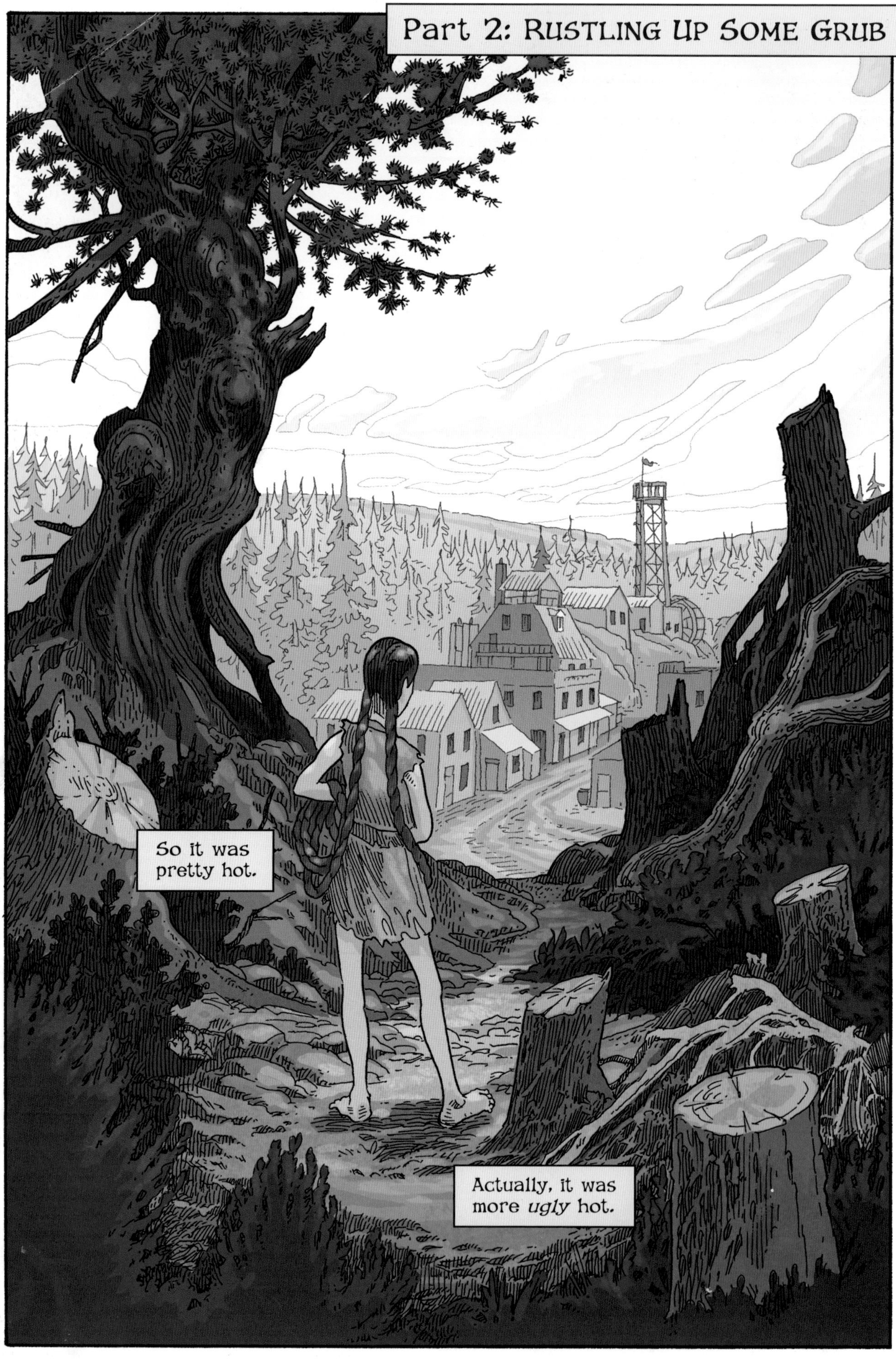
So it was pretty hot.
Actually, it was more *ugly* hot.

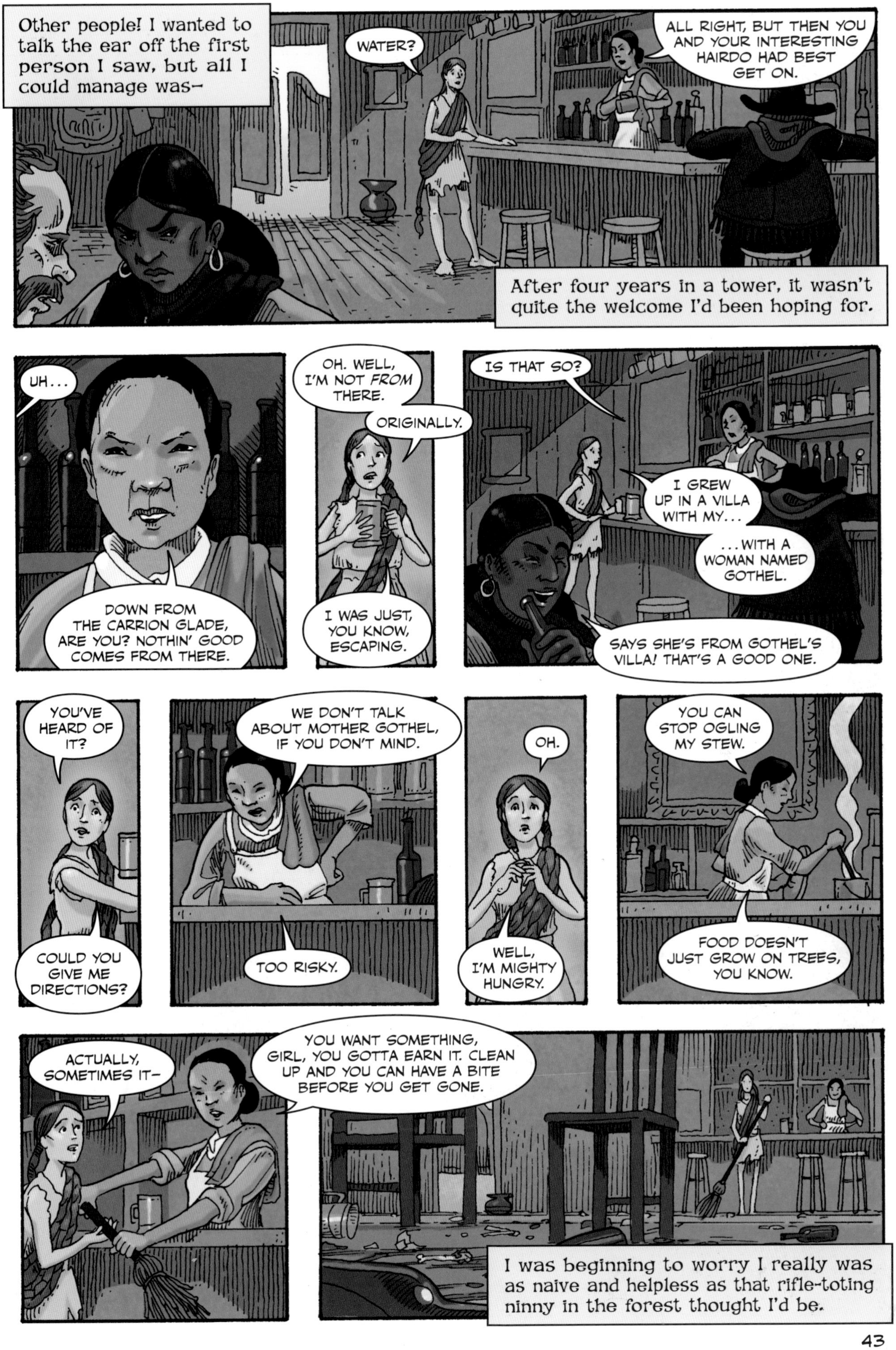

Other people! I wanted to talk the ear off the first person I saw, but all I could manage was—
WATER?
ALL RIGHT, BUT THEN YOU AND YOUR INTERESTING HAIRDO HAD BEST GET ON.
After four years in a tower, it wasn't quite the welcome I'd been hoping for.
UH...
DOWN FROM THE CARRION GLADE, ARE YOU? NOTHIN' GOOD COMES FROM THERE.
OH. WELL, I'M NOT *FROM* THERE.
ORIGINALLY.
I WAS JUST, YOU KNOW, ESCAPING.
IS THAT SO?
I GREW UP IN A VILLA WITH MY...
...WITH A WOMAN NAMED GOTHEL.
SAYS SHE'S FROM GOTHEL'S VILLA! THAT'S A GOOD ONE.
YOU'VE HEARD OF IT?
COULD YOU GIVE ME DIRECTIONS?
WE DON'T TALK ABOUT MOTHER GOTHEL, IF YOU DON'T MIND.
TOO RISKY.
OH.
WELL, I'M MIGHTY HUNGRY.
YOU CAN STOP OGLING MY STEW.
FOOD DOESN'T JUST GROW ON TREES, YOU KNOW.
ACTUALLY, SOMETIMES IT—
YOU WANT SOMETHING, GIRL, YOU GOTTA EARN IT. CLEAN UP AND YOU CAN HAVE A BITE BEFORE YOU GET GONE.
I was beginning to worry I really was as naive and helpless as that rifle-toting ninny in the forest thought I'd be.

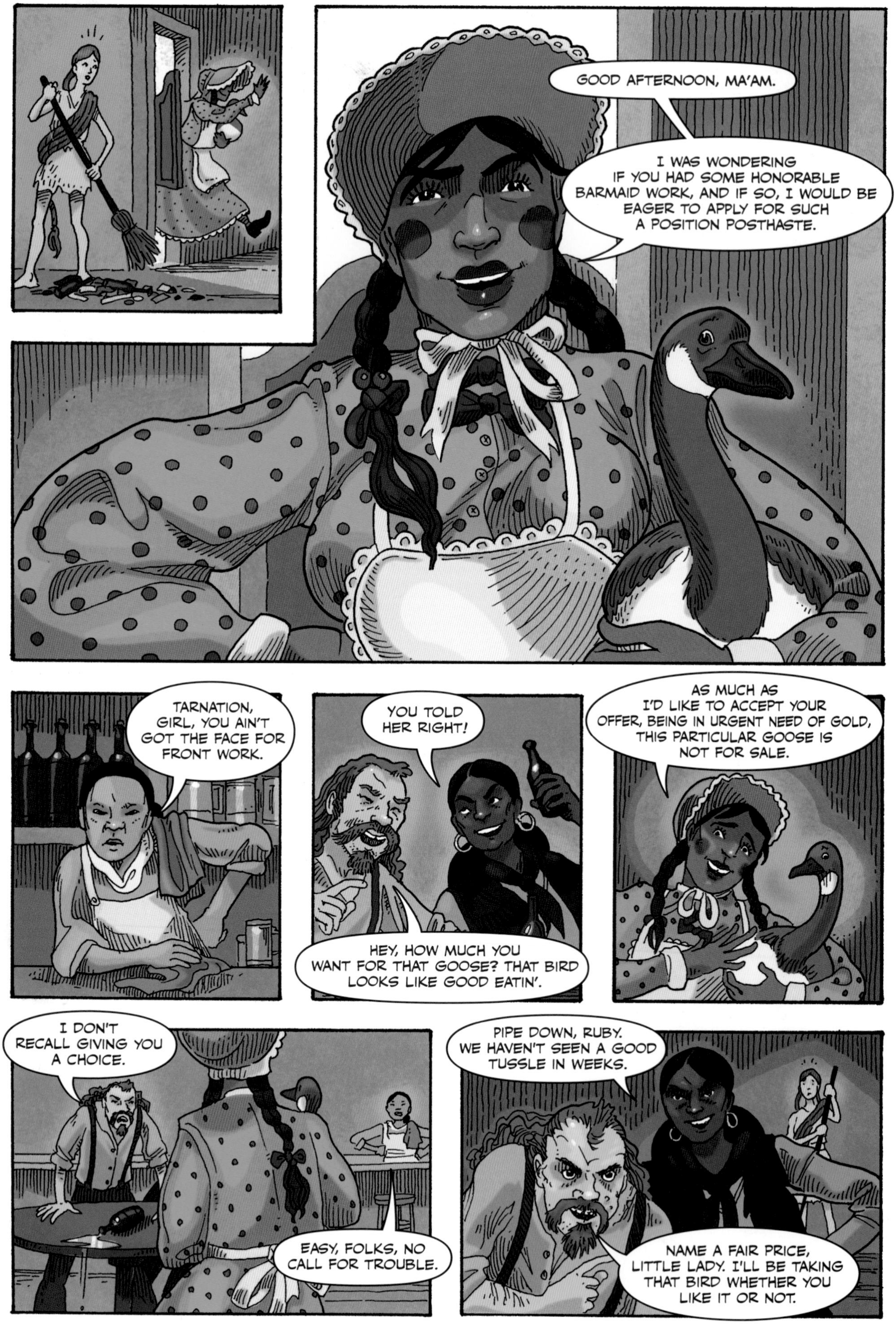
GOOD AFTERNOON, MA'AM.
I WAS WONDERING IF YOU HAD SOME HONORABLE BARMAID WORK, AND IF SO, I WOULD BE EAGER TO APPLY FOR SUCH A POSITION POSTHASTE.
TARNATION, GIRL, YOU AIN'T GOT THE FACE FOR FRONT WORK.
YOU TOLD HER RIGHT!
HEY, HOW MUCH YOU WANT FOR THAT GOOSE? THAT BIRD LOOKS LIKE GOOD EATIN'.
AS MUCH AS I'D LIKE TO ACCEPT YOUR OFFER, BEING IN URGENT NEED OF GOLD, THIS PARTICULAR GOOSE IS NOT FOR SALE.
I DON'T RECALL GIVING YOU A CHOICE.
EASY, FOLKS, NO CALL FOR TROUBLE.
PIPE DOWN, RUBY. WE HAVEN'T SEEN A GOOD TUSSLE IN WEEKS.
NAME A FAIR PRICE, LITTLE LADY. I'LL BE TAKING THAT BIRD WHETHER YOU LIKE IT OR NOT.

SO SORRY TO TREAD UPON YOUR PEACEFUL AFTERNOON, FINE FOLK.

IF YOU'LL BE SO KIND, I'LL JUST TAKE MY EXIT.

NOT SO FAST...

HEY, HOLD THE FORT—THAT'S A BOY!

I used to daydream about the real world.

I imagined happy families...

OOF!

URK.

HONK!

Places where people fell in love and wonderful things happened.

NOW WE GET A LITTLE SUPPER!

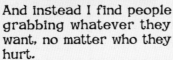

And instead I find people grabbing whatever they want, no matter who they hurt.

NO!

I didn't think twice before pulling out my braid.

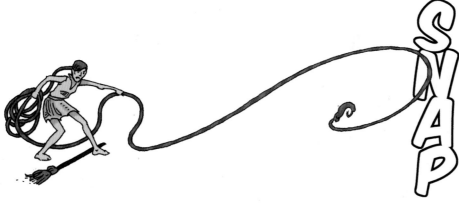

SNAP

OW!

45

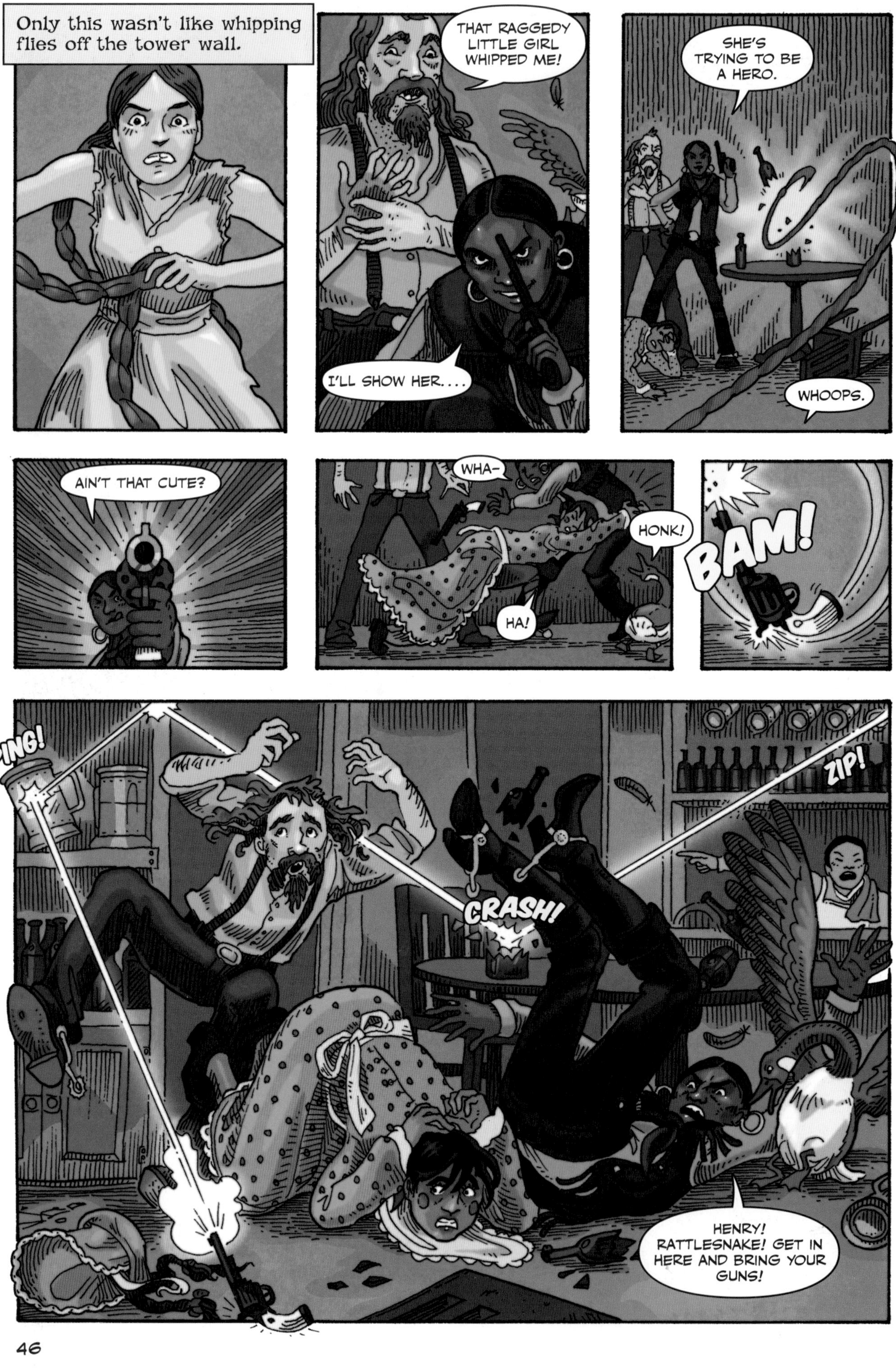

Only this wasn't like whipping flies off the tower wall.
THAT RAGGEDY LITTLE GIRL WHIPPED ME!
I'LL SHOW HER....
SHE'S TRYING TO BE A HERO.
WHOOPS.
AIN'T THAT CUTE?
WHA-
HONK!
HA!
BAM!
PING!
ZIP!
CRASH!
HENRY! RATTLESNAKE! GET IN HERE AND BRING YOUR GUNS!

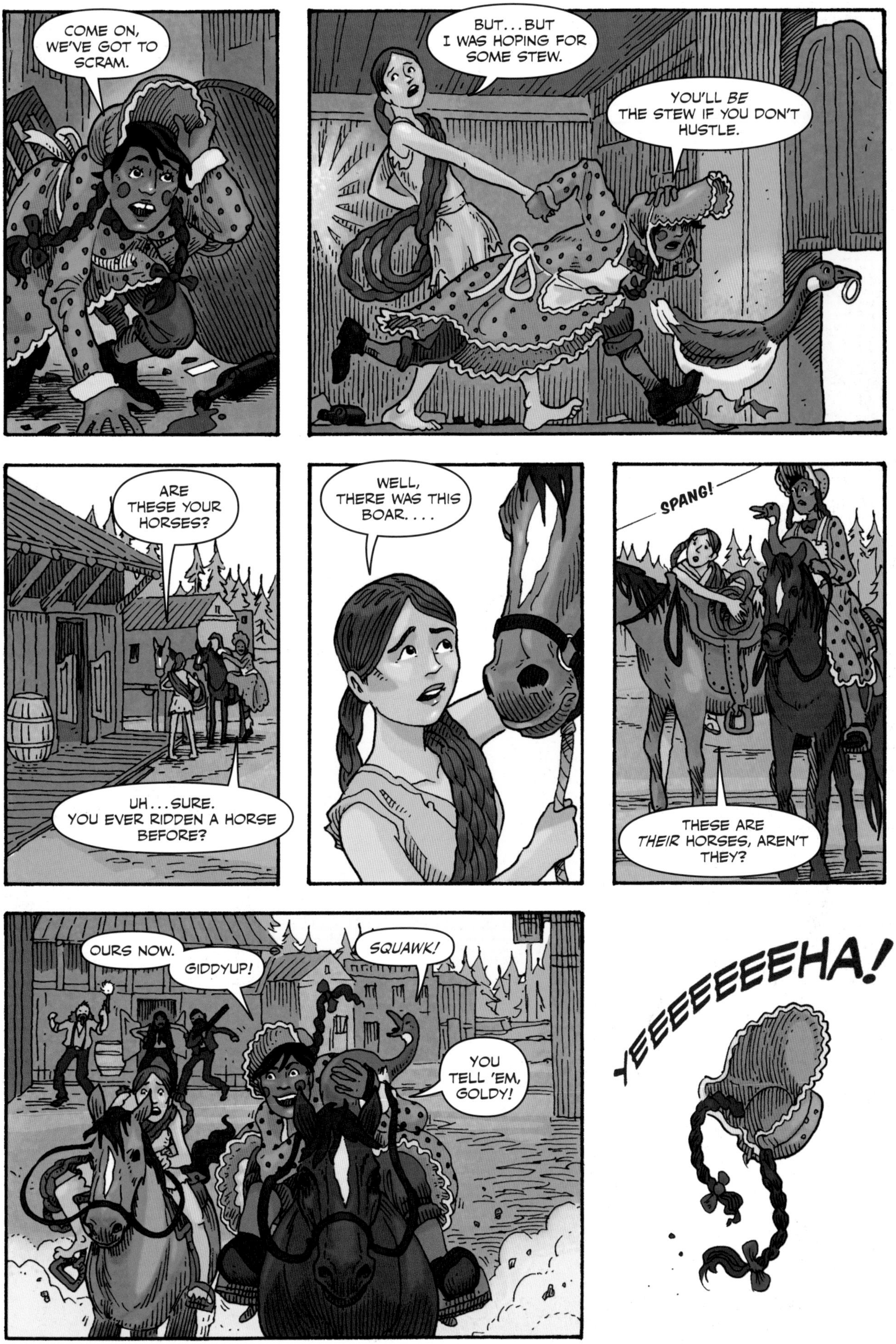
COME ON, WE'VE GOT TO SCRAM.
BUT...BUT I WAS HOPING FOR SOME STEW.
YOU'LL *BE* THE STEW IF YOU DON'T HUSTLE.
ARE THESE YOUR HORSES?
UH...SURE. YOU EVER RIDDEN A HORSE BEFORE?
WELL, THERE WAS THIS BOAR. . . .
SPANG!
THESE ARE *THEIR* HORSES, AREN'T THEY?
OURS NOW.
GIDDYUP!
SQUAWK!
YOU TELL 'EM, GOLDY!
YEEEEEEEEHA!

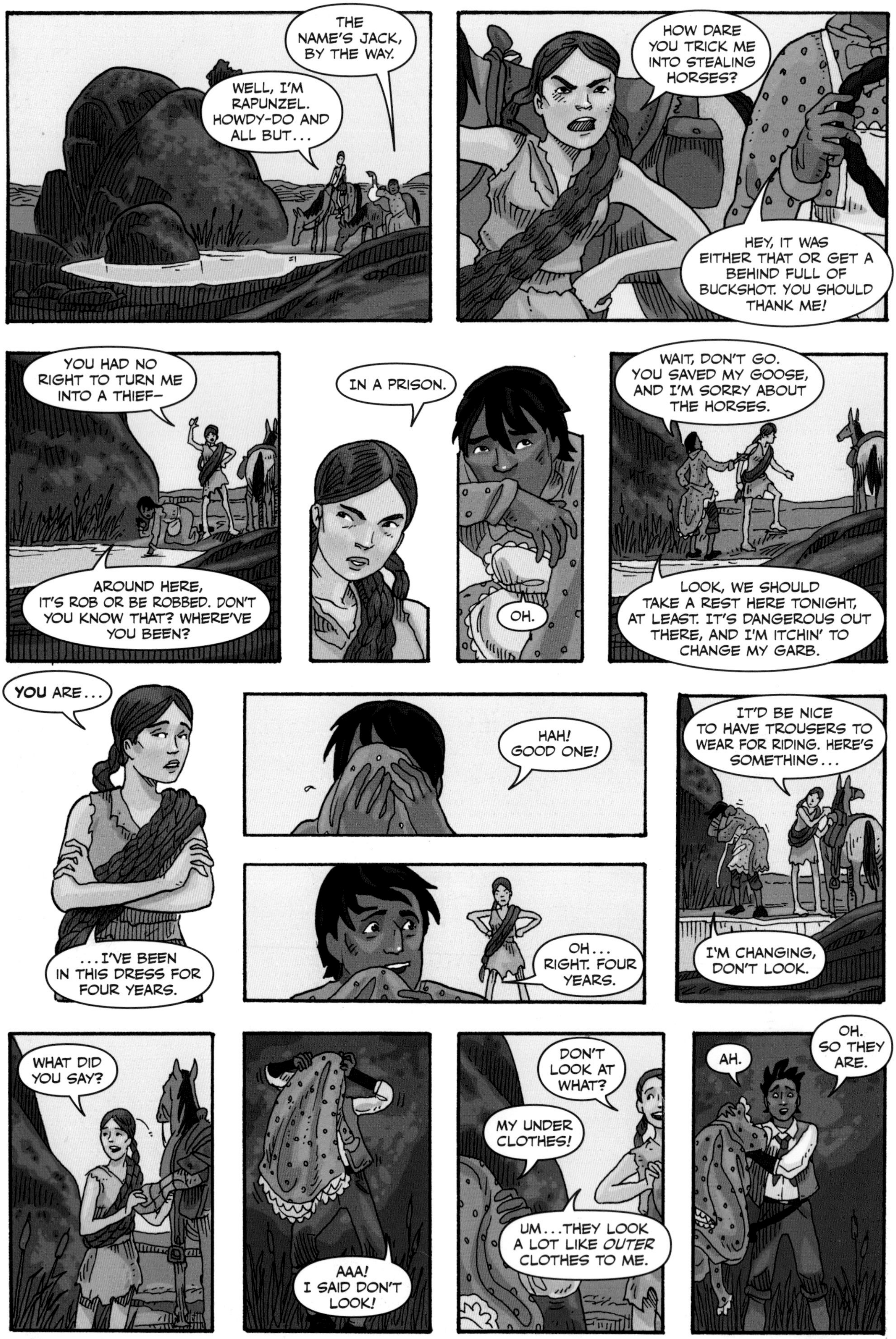
THE NAME'S JACK, BY THE WAY.
WELL, I'M RAPUNZEL. HOWDY-DO AND ALL BUT...
HOW DARE YOU TRICK ME INTO STEALING HORSES?
HEY, IT WAS EITHER THAT OR GET A BEHIND FULL OF BUCKSHOT. YOU SHOULD THANK ME!
YOU HAD NO RIGHT TO TURN ME INTO A THIEF–
AROUND HERE, IT'S ROB OR BE ROBBED. DON'T YOU KNOW THAT? WHERE'VE YOU BEEN?
IN A PRISON.
OH.
WAIT, DON'T GO. YOU SAVED MY GOOSE, AND I'M SORRY ABOUT THE HORSES.
LOOK, WE SHOULD TAKE A REST HERE TONIGHT, AT LEAST. IT'S DANGEROUS OUT THERE, AND I'M ITCHIN' TO CHANGE MY GARB.
YOU ARE...
...I'VE BEEN IN THIS DRESS FOR FOUR YEARS.
HAH! GOOD ONE!
OH... RIGHT. FOUR YEARS.
IT'D BE NICE TO HAVE TROUSERS TO WEAR FOR RIDING. HERE'S SOMETHING...
I'M CHANGING, DON'T LOOK.
WHAT DID YOU SAY?
AAA! I SAID DON'T LOOK!
DON'T LOOK AT WHAT?
MY UNDER CLOTHES!
UM...THEY LOOK A LOT LIKE OUTER CLOTHES TO ME.
AH.
OH. SO THEY ARE.

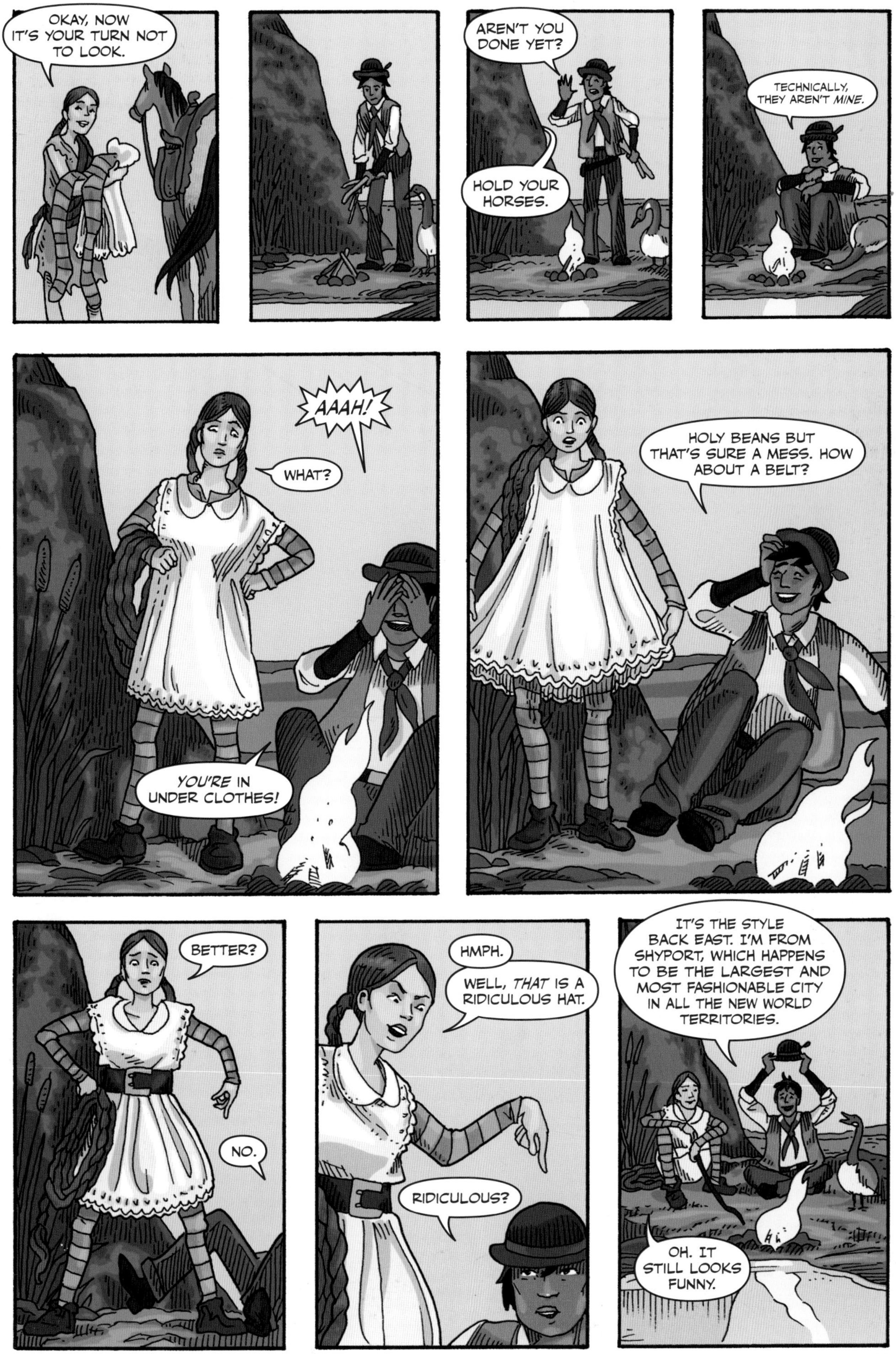

OKAY, NOW IT'S YOUR TURN NOT TO LOOK.
AREN'T YOU DONE YET?
HOLD YOUR HORSES.
TECHNICALLY, THEY AREN'T *MINE.*
AAAH!
WHAT?
YOU'RE IN UNDER CLOTHES!
HOLY BEANS BUT THAT'S SURE A MESS. HOW ABOUT A BELT?
BETTER?
NO.
HMPH.
WELL, *THAT* IS A RIDICULOUS HAT.
RIDICULOUS?
IT'S THE STYLE BACK EAST. I'M FROM SHYPORT, WHICH HAPPENS TO BE THE LARGEST AND MOST FASHIONABLE CITY IN ALL THE NEW WORLD TERRITORIES.
OH. IT STILL LOOKS FUNNY.

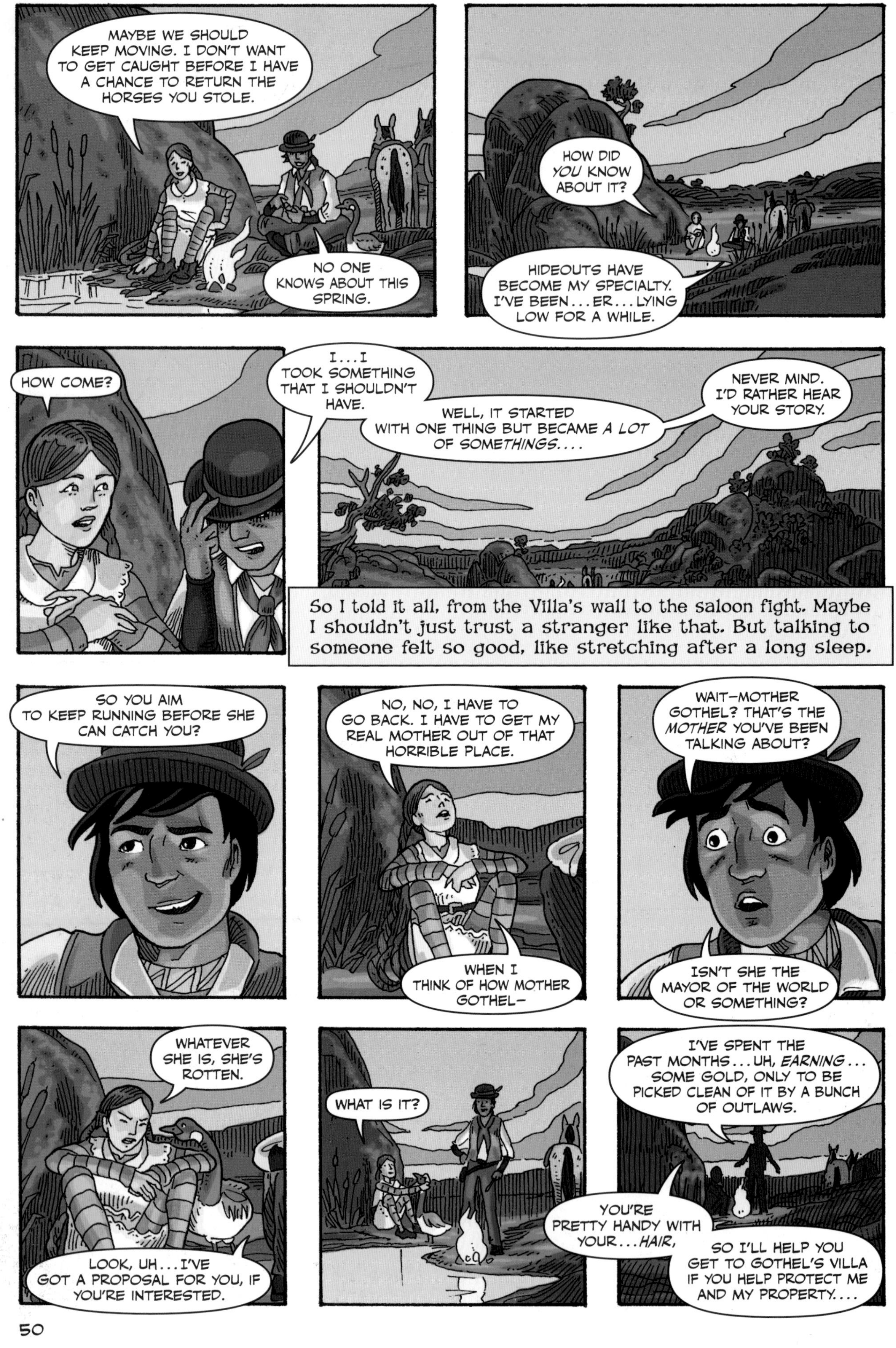
MAYBE WE SHOULD KEEP MOVING. I DON'T WANT TO GET CAUGHT BEFORE I HAVE A CHANCE TO RETURN THE HORSES YOU STOLE.
NO ONE KNOWS ABOUT THIS SPRING.
HOW DID *YOU* KNOW ABOUT IT?
HIDEOUTS HAVE BECOME MY SPECIALTY. I'VE BEEN...ER...LYING LOW FOR A WHILE.
HOW COME?
I...I TOOK SOMETHING THAT I SHOULDN'T HAVE.
WELL, IT STARTED WITH ONE THING BUT BECAME *A LOT* OF SOME*THINGS*....
NEVER MIND. I'D RATHER HEAR YOUR STORY.
So I told it all, from the Villa's wall to the saloon fight. Maybe I shouldn't just trust a stranger like that. But talking to someone felt so good, like stretching after a long sleep.
SO YOU AIM TO KEEP RUNNING BEFORE SHE CAN CATCH YOU?
NO, NO, I HAVE TO GO BACK. I HAVE TO GET MY REAL MOTHER OUT OF THAT HORRIBLE PLACE.
WHEN I THINK OF HOW MOTHER GOTHEL—
WAIT—MOTHER GOTHEL? THAT'S THE *MOTHER* YOU'VE BEEN TALKING ABOUT?
ISN'T SHE THE MAYOR OF THE WORLD OR SOMETHING?
WHATEVER SHE IS, SHE'S ROTTEN.
LOOK, UH...I'VE GOT A PROPOSAL FOR YOU, IF YOU'RE INTERESTED.
WHAT IS IT?
I'VE SPENT THE PAST MONTHS...UH, *EARNING*... SOME GOLD, ONLY TO BE PICKED CLEAN OF IT BY A BUNCH OF OUTLAWS.
YOU'RE PRETTY HANDY WITH YOUR...*HAIR*,
SO I'LL HELP YOU GET TO GOTHEL'S VILLA IF YOU HELP PROTECT ME AND MY PROPERTY....

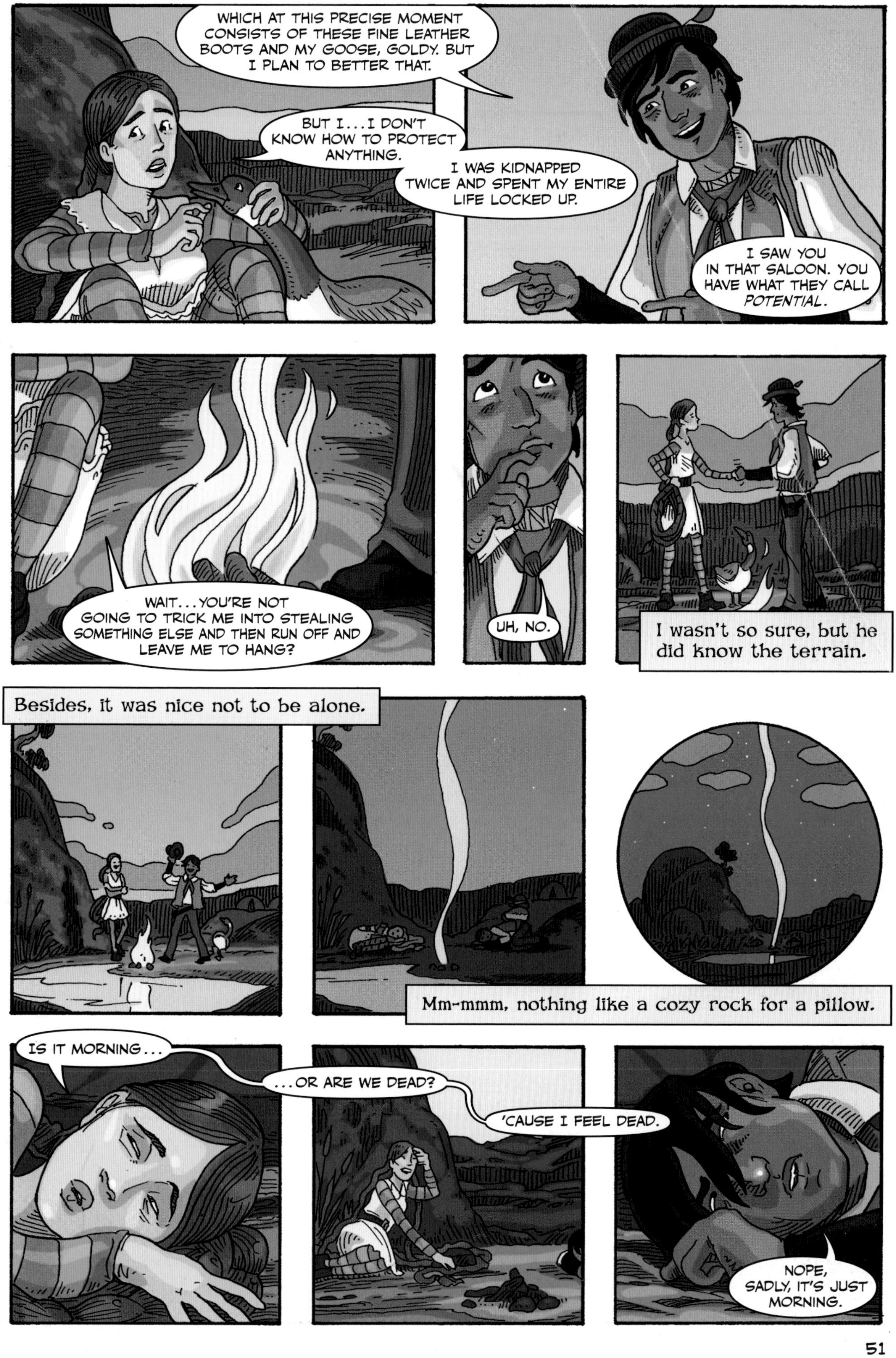
WHICH AT THIS PRECISE MOMENT CONSISTS OF THESE FINE LEATHER BOOTS AND MY GOOSE, GOLDY. BUT I PLAN TO BETTER THAT.
BUT I... I DON'T KNOW HOW TO PROTECT ANYTHING.
I WAS KIDNAPPED TWICE AND SPENT MY ENTIRE LIFE LOCKED UP.
I SAW YOU IN THAT SALOON. YOU HAVE WHAT THEY CALL *POTENTIAL*.
WAIT... YOU'RE NOT GOING TO TRICK ME INTO STEALING SOMETHING ELSE AND THEN RUN OFF AND LEAVE ME TO HANG?
UH, NO.
I wasn't so sure, but he did know the terrain.
Besides, it was nice not to be alone.
Mm-mmm, nothing like a cozy rock for a pillow.
IS IT MORNING...
...OR ARE WE DEAD?
'CAUSE I FEEL DEAD.
NOPE, SADLY, IT'S JUST MORNING.

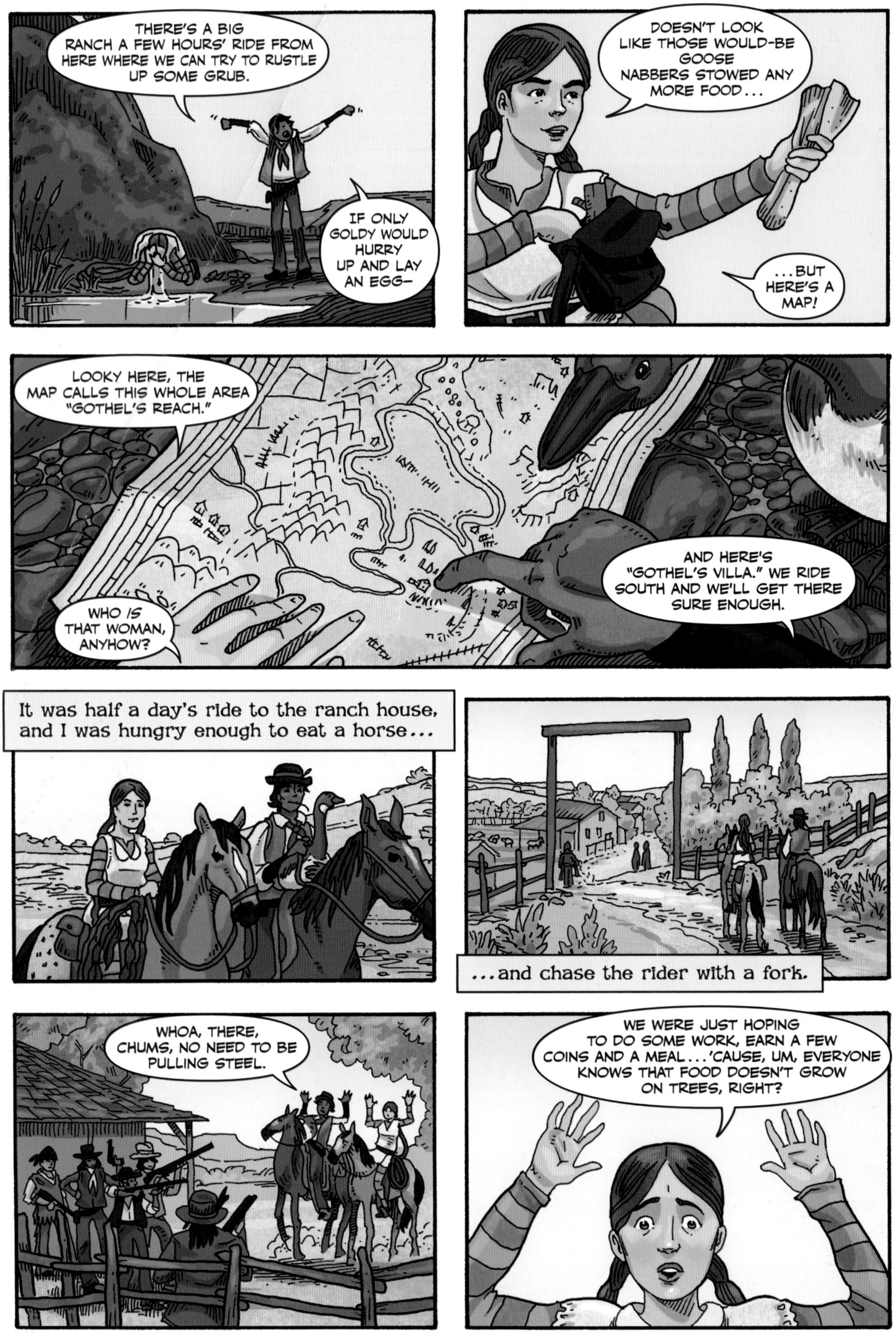
THERE'S A BIG RANCH A FEW HOURS' RIDE FROM HERE WHERE WE CAN TRY TO RUSTLE UP SOME GRUB.
IF ONLY GOLDY WOULD HURRY UP AND LAY AN EGG–
DOESN'T LOOK LIKE THOSE WOULD-BE GOOSE NABBERS STOWED ANY MORE FOOD...
...BUT HERE'S A MAP!
LOOKY HERE, THE MAP CALLS THIS WHOLE AREA "GOTHEL'S REACH."
AND HERE'S "GOTHEL'S VILLA." WE RIDE SOUTH AND WE'LL GET THERE SURE ENOUGH.
WHO *IS* THAT WOMAN, ANYHOW?
It was half a day's ride to the ranch house, and I was hungry enough to eat a horse...
...and chase the rider with a fork.
WHOA, THERE, CHUMS, NO NEED TO BE PULLING STEEL.
WE WERE JUST HOPING TO DO SOME WORK, EARN A FEW COINS AND A MEAL...'CAUSE, UM, EVERYONE KNOWS THAT FOOD DOESN'T GROW ON TREES, RIGHT?

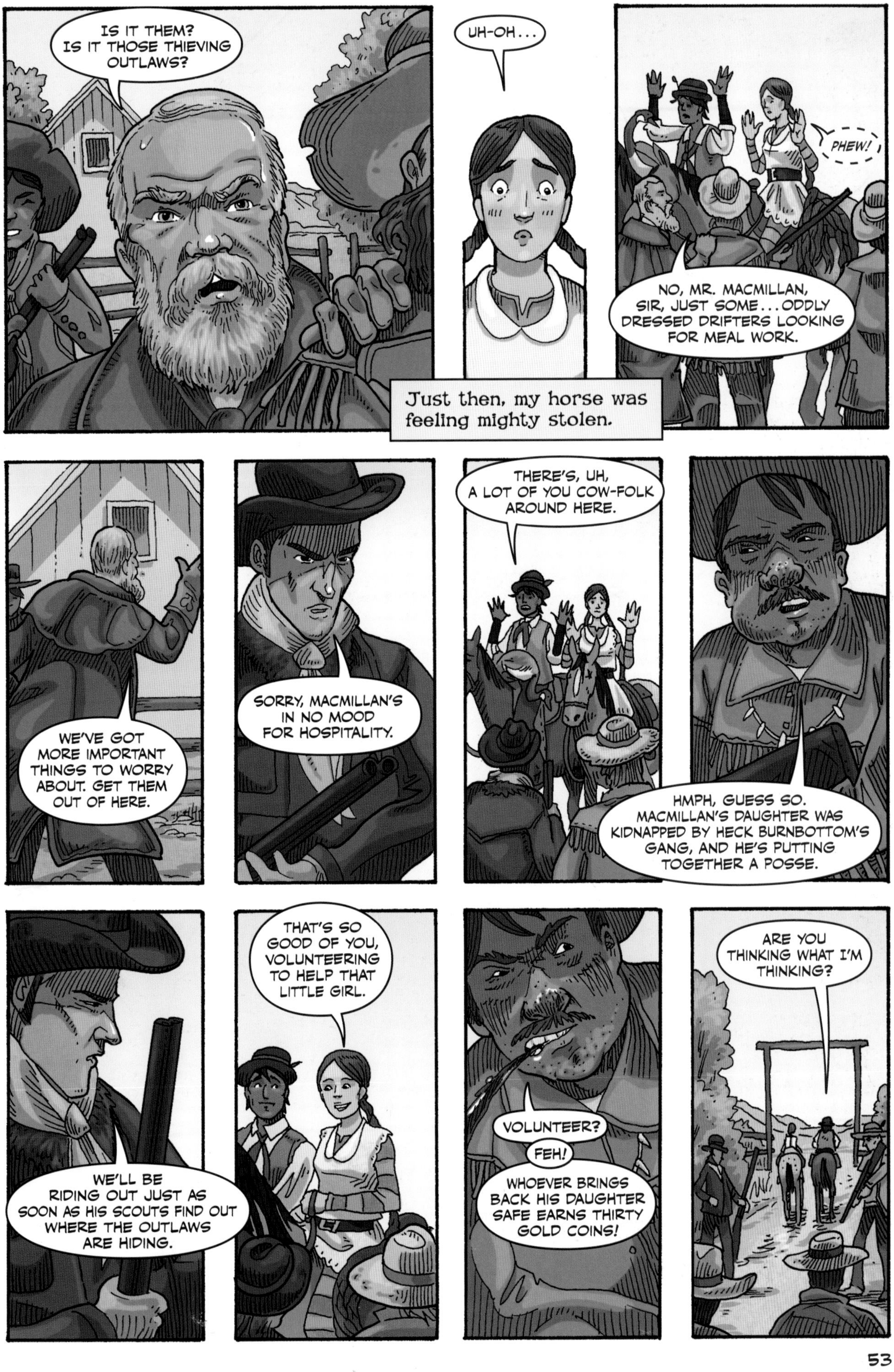
IS IT THEM? IS IT THOSE THIEVING OUTLAWS?
UH-OH...
NO, MR. MACMILLAN, SIR, JUST SOME... ODDLY DRESSED DRIFTERS LOOKING FOR MEAL WORK.
PHEW!
Just then, my horse was feeling mighty stolen.
WE'VE GOT MORE IMPORTANT THINGS TO WORRY ABOUT. GET THEM OUT OF HERE.
SORRY, MACMILLAN'S IN NO MOOD FOR HOSPITALITY.
THERE'S, UH, A LOT OF YOU COW-FOLK AROUND HERE.
HMPH, GUESS SO. MACMILLAN'S DAUGHTER WAS KIDNAPPED BY HECK BURNBOTTOM'S GANG, AND HE'S PUTTING TOGETHER A POSSE.
WE'LL BE RIDING OUT JUST AS SOON AS HIS SCOUTS FIND OUT WHERE THE OUTLAWS ARE HIDING.
THAT'S SO GOOD OF YOU, VOLUNTEERING TO HELP THAT LITTLE GIRL.
VOLUNTEER?
FEH!
WHOEVER BRINGS BACK HIS DAUGHTER SAFE EARNS THIRTY GOLD COINS!
ARE YOU THINKING WHAT I'M THINKING?

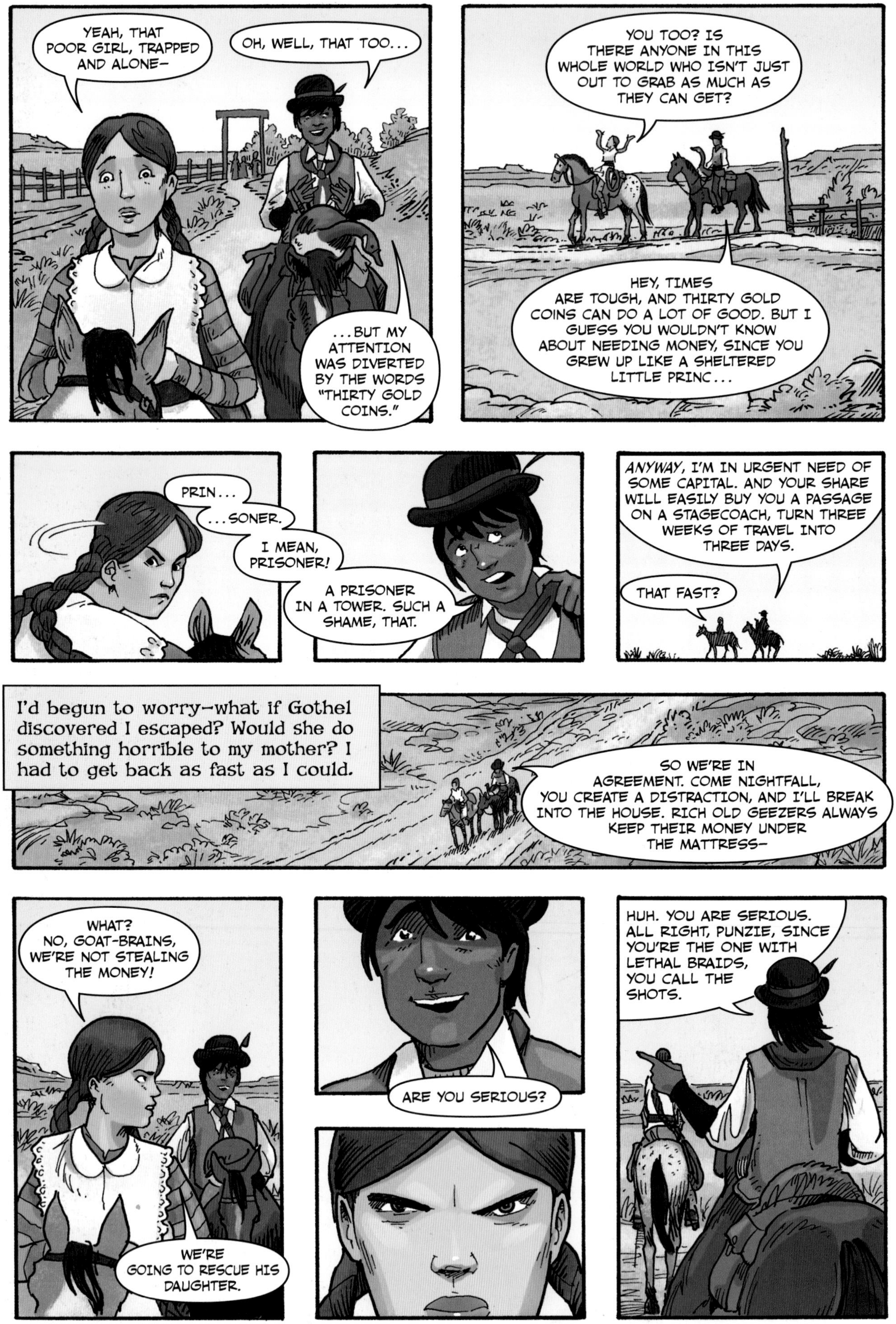
YEAH, THAT POOR GIRL, TRAPPED AND ALONE–
OH, WELL, THAT TOO...
...BUT MY ATTENTION WAS DIVERTED BY THE WORDS "THIRTY GOLD COINS."
YOU TOO? IS THERE ANYONE IN THIS WHOLE WORLD WHO ISN'T JUST OUT TO GRAB AS MUCH AS THEY CAN GET?
HEY, TIMES ARE TOUGH, AND THIRTY GOLD COINS CAN DO A LOT OF GOOD. BUT I GUESS YOU WOULDN'T KNOW ABOUT NEEDING MONEY, SINCE YOU GREW UP LIKE A SHELTERED LITTLE PRINC...
PRIN...
...SONER.
I MEAN, PRISONER!
A PRISONER IN A TOWER. SUCH A SHAME, THAT.
ANYWAY, I'M IN URGENT NEED OF SOME CAPITAL. AND YOUR SHARE WILL EASILY BUY YOU A PASSAGE ON A STAGECOACH, TURN THREE WEEKS OF TRAVEL INTO THREE DAYS.
THAT FAST?
I'd begun to worry–what if Gothel discovered I escaped? Would she do something horrible to my mother? I had to get back as fast as I could.
SO WE'RE IN AGREEMENT. COME NIGHTFALL, YOU CREATE A DISTRACTION, AND I'LL BREAK INTO THE HOUSE. RICH OLD GEEZERS ALWAYS KEEP THEIR MONEY UNDER THE MATTRESS–
WHAT? NO, GOAT-BRAINS, WE'RE NOT STEALING THE MONEY!
WE'RE GOING TO RESCUE HIS DAUGHTER.
ARE YOU SERIOUS?
HUH. YOU ARE SERIOUS. ALL RIGHT, PUNZIE, SINCE YOU'RE THE ONE WITH LETHAL BRAIDS, YOU CALL THE SHOTS.

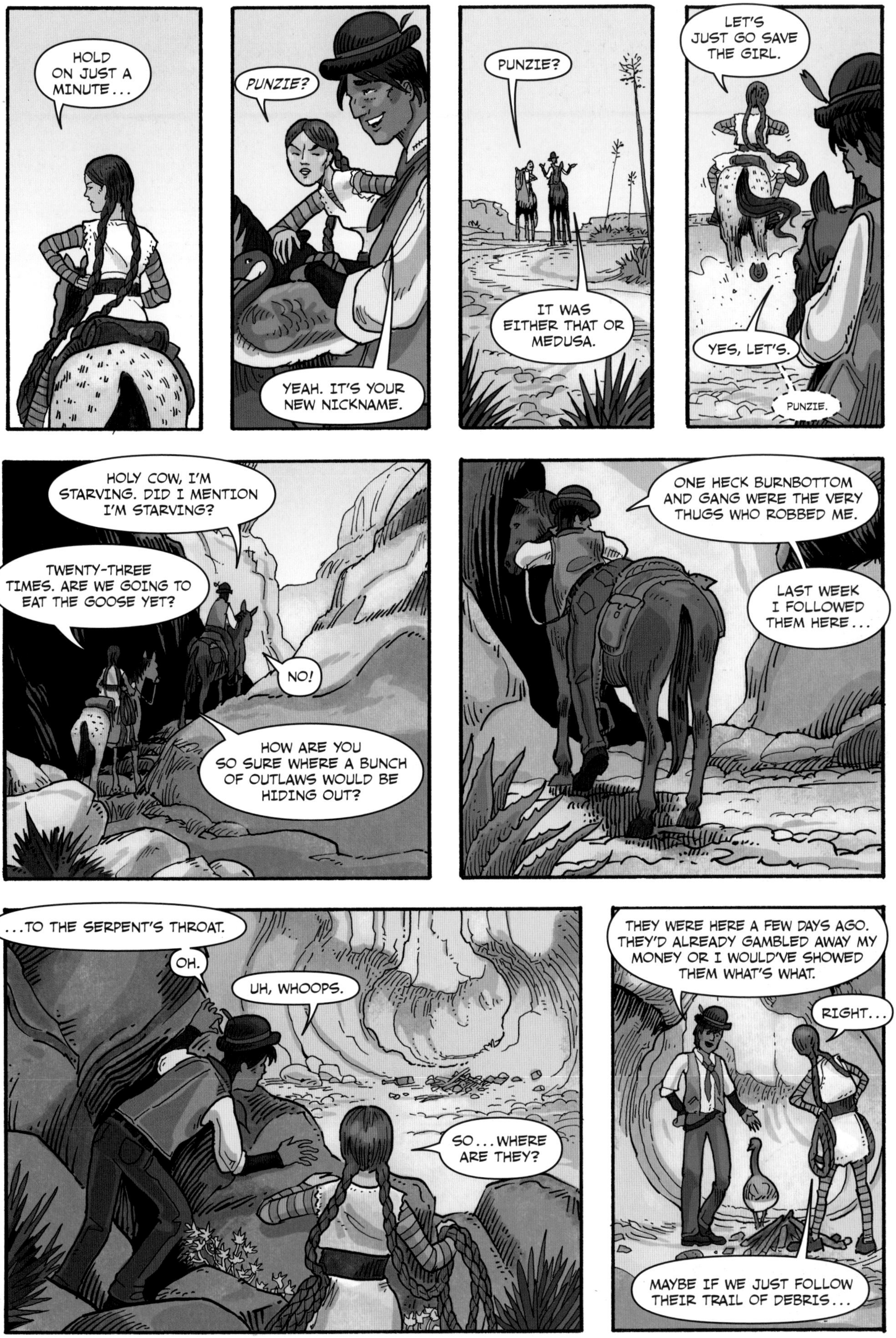
HOLD ON JUST A MINUTE...
PUNZIE?
YEAH. IT'S YOUR NEW NICKNAME.
PUNZIE?
IT WAS EITHER THAT OR MEDUSA.
LET'S JUST GO SAVE THE GIRL.
YES, LET'S.
PUNZIE.
HOLY COW, I'M STARVING. DID I MENTION I'M STARVING?
TWENTY-THREE TIMES. ARE WE GOING TO EAT THE GOOSE YET?
NO!
HOW ARE YOU SO SURE WHERE A BUNCH OF OUTLAWS WOULD BE HIDING OUT?
ONE HECK BURNBOTTOM AND GANG WERE THE VERY THUGS WHO ROBBED ME.
LAST WEEK I FOLLOWED THEM HERE...
...TO THE SERPENT'S THROAT.
OH.
UH, WHOOPS.
SO...WHERE ARE THEY?
THEY WERE HERE A FEW DAYS AGO. THEY'D ALREADY GAMBLED AWAY MY MONEY OR I WOULD'VE SHOWED THEM WHAT'S WHAT.
RIGHT...
MAYBE IF WE JUST FOLLOW THEIR TRAIL OF DEBRIS...

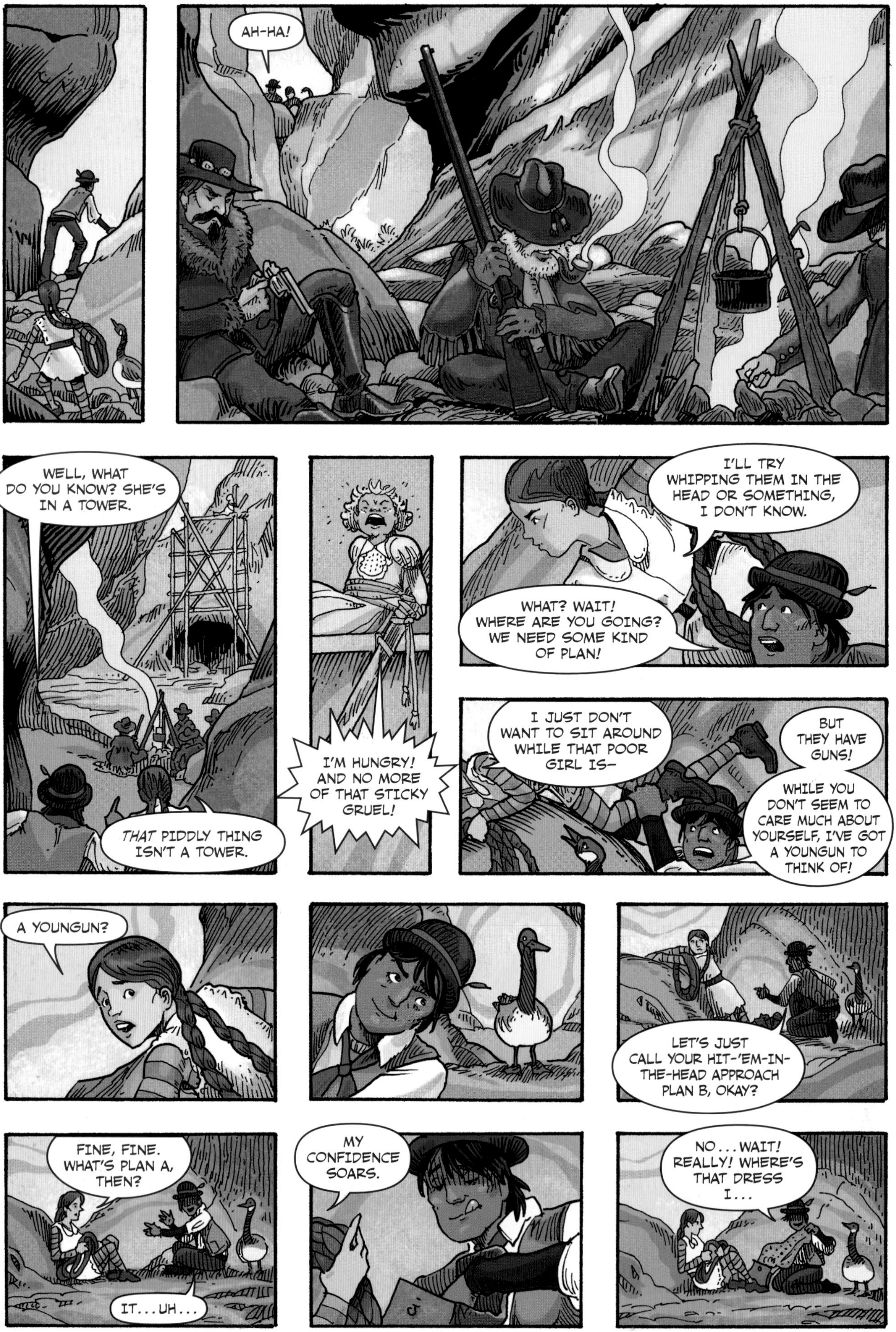
AH-HA!
WELL, WHAT DO YOU KNOW? SHE'S IN A TOWER.
THAT PIDDLY THING ISN'T A TOWER.
I'M HUNGRY! AND NO MORE OF THAT STICKY GRUEL!
I'LL TRY WHIPPING THEM IN THE HEAD OR SOMETHING, I DON'T KNOW.
WHAT? WAIT! WHERE ARE YOU GOING? WE NEED SOME KIND OF PLAN!
I JUST DON'T WANT TO SIT AROUND WHILE THAT POOR GIRL IS—
BUT THEY HAVE GUNS!
WHILE YOU DON'T SEEM TO CARE MUCH ABOUT YOURSELF, I'VE GOT A YOUNGUN TO THINK OF!
A YOUNGUN?
LET'S JUST CALL YOUR HIT-'EM-IN-THE-HEAD APPROACH PLAN B, OKAY?
FINE, FINE. WHAT'S PLAN A, THEN?
IT... UH...
MY CONFIDENCE SOARS.
NO... WAIT! REALLY! WHERE'S THAT DRESS I...

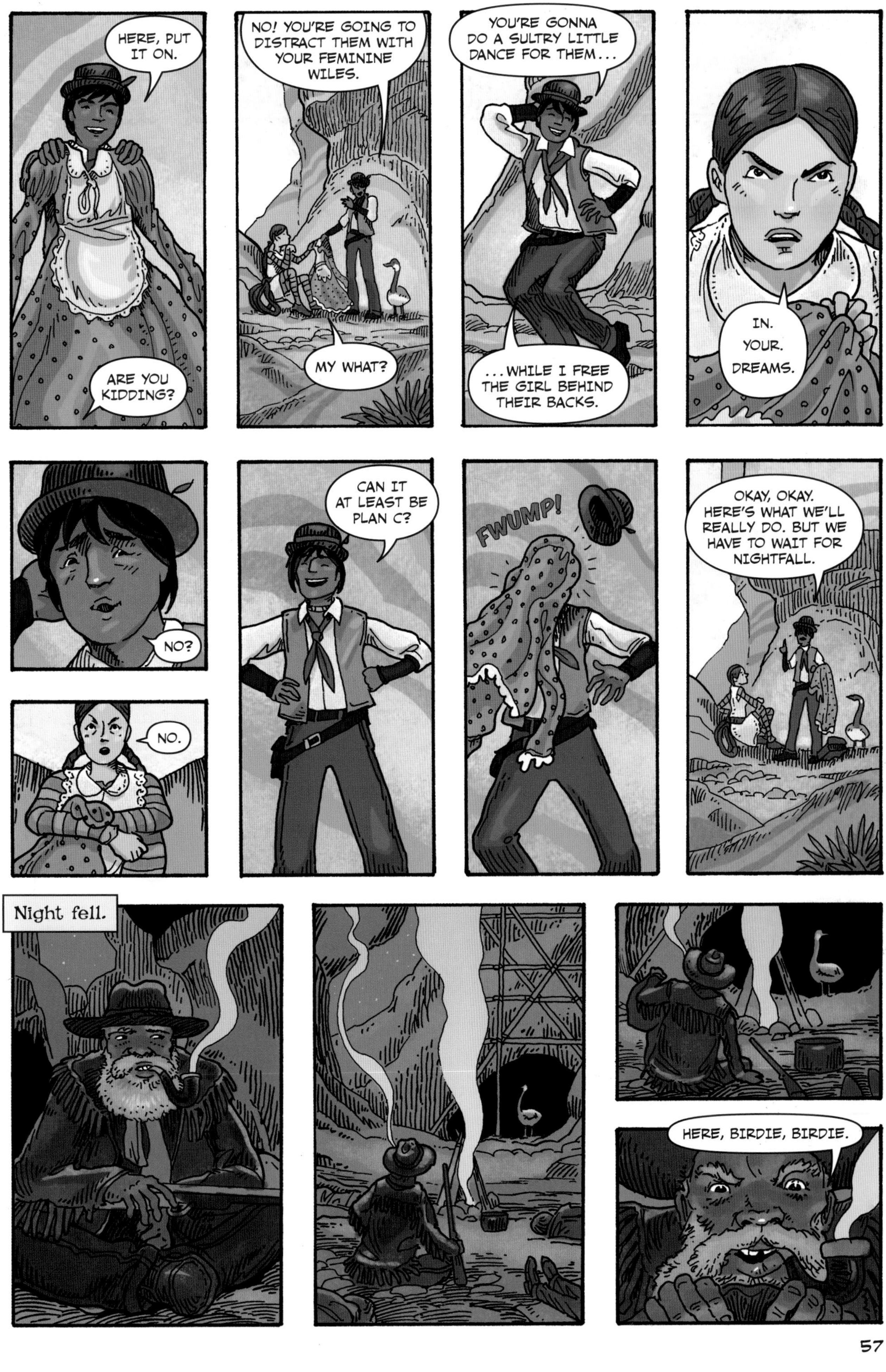
HERE, PUT IT ON.
ARE YOU KIDDING?
NO! YOU'RE GOING TO DISTRACT THEM WITH YOUR FEMININE WILES.
MY WHAT?
YOU'RE GONNA DO A SULTRY LITTLE DANCE FOR THEM...
...WHILE I FREE THE GIRL BEHIND THEIR BACKS.
IN. YOUR. DREAMS.
NO?
NO.
CAN IT AT LEAST BE PLAN C?
FWUMP!
OKAY, OKAY. HERE'S WHAT WE'LL REALLY DO. BUT WE HAVE TO WAIT FOR NIGHTFALL.
Night fell.
HERE, BIRDIE, BIRDIE.

GURK.

JACK! GIMME THE GAG! JACK!

Jack was supposed to be right there.

UGH...

ELMER! LOUIE!

WE GOT—

OOOF!

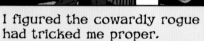

I figured the cowardly rogue had tricked me proper.

Served me right for trusting anybody.

UH-OH.

One was out cold, but three more were coming at me. I was pickled for sure. If only they didn't have guns.

WHAT THE...WHERE'S MY—?

HA-HA! I'VE GOT YOUR GUNS!

I'VE GOT YOUR GUNS! HA-HA!

LOUIE! GORDO! GET THAT WEASEL!

I'LL TAKE CARE OF LITTLE MISSY HERE.

NOW THEN, YOU DESERVE A BEATING FOR THAT OUTFIT ALONE.

ARRH!

SPACK!

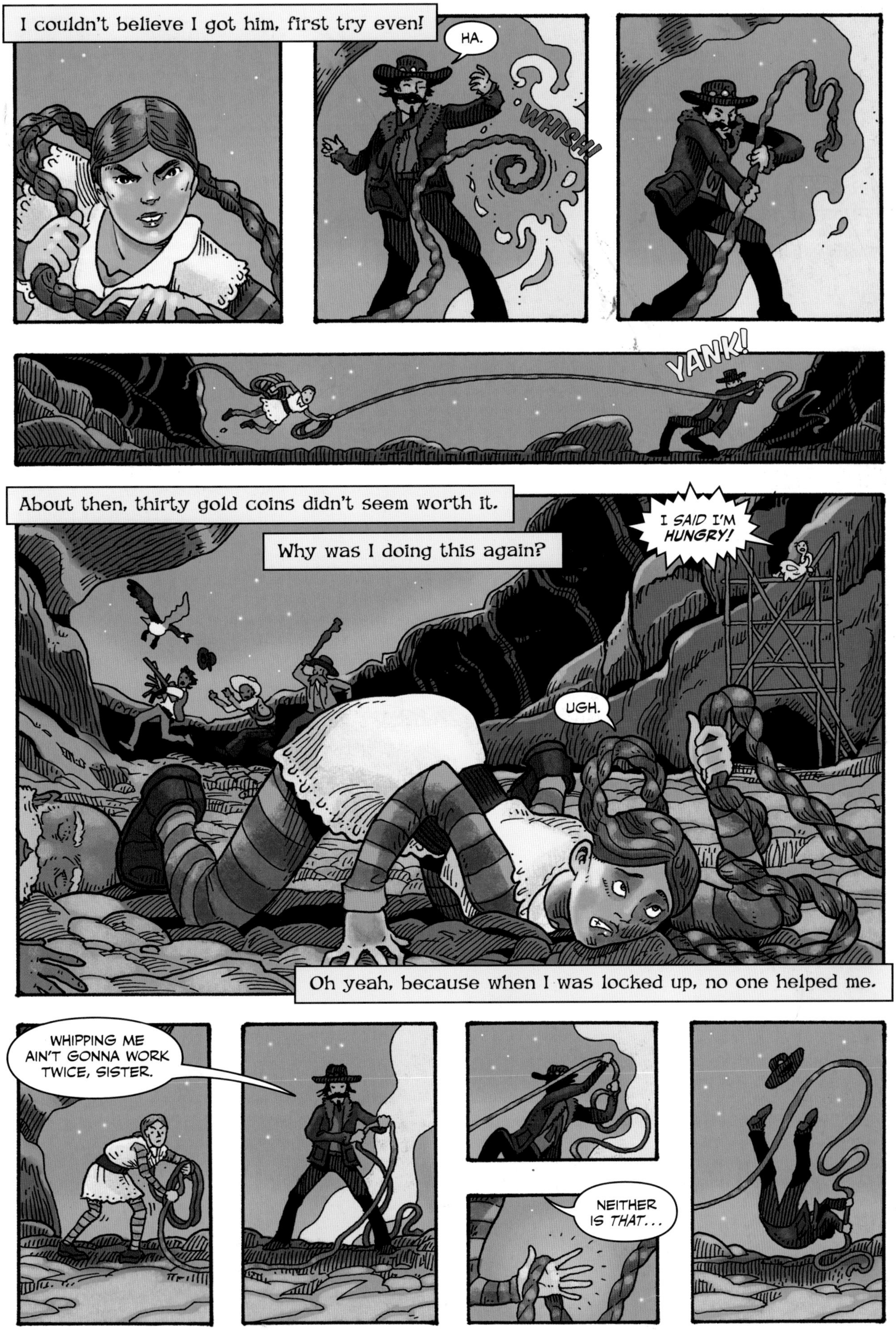
I couldn't believe I got him, first try even!
HA.
WHISH!
YANK!
About then, thirty gold coins didn't seem worth it.
Why was I doing this again?
I SAID I'M HUNGRY!
UGH.
Oh yeah, because when I was locked up, no one helped me.
WHIPPING ME AIN'T GONNA WORK TWICE, SISTER.
NEITHER IS THAT...

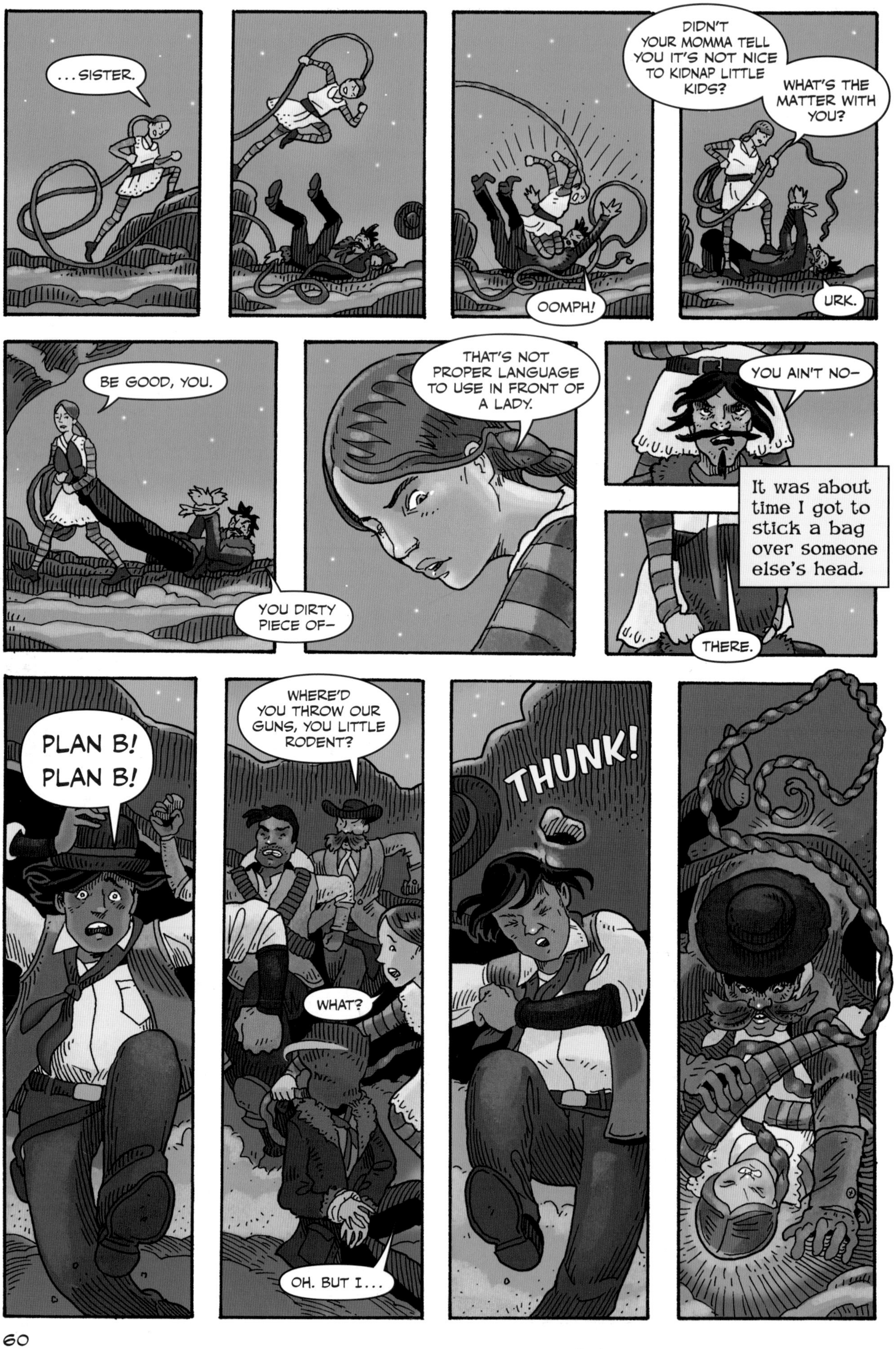
. . . SISTER.
DIDN'T YOUR MOMMA TELL YOU IT'S NOT NICE TO KIDNAP LITTLE KIDS?
OOMPH!
WHAT'S THE MATTER WITH YOU?
URK.
BE GOOD, YOU.
YOU DIRTY PIECE OF–
THAT'S NOT PROPER LANGUAGE TO USE IN FRONT OF A LADY.
YOU AIN'T NO–
It was about time I got to stick a bag over someone else's head.
THERE.
PLAN B! PLAN B!
WHERE'D YOU THROW OUR GUNS, YOU LITTLE RODENT?
WHAT?
OH. BUT I . . .
THUNK!

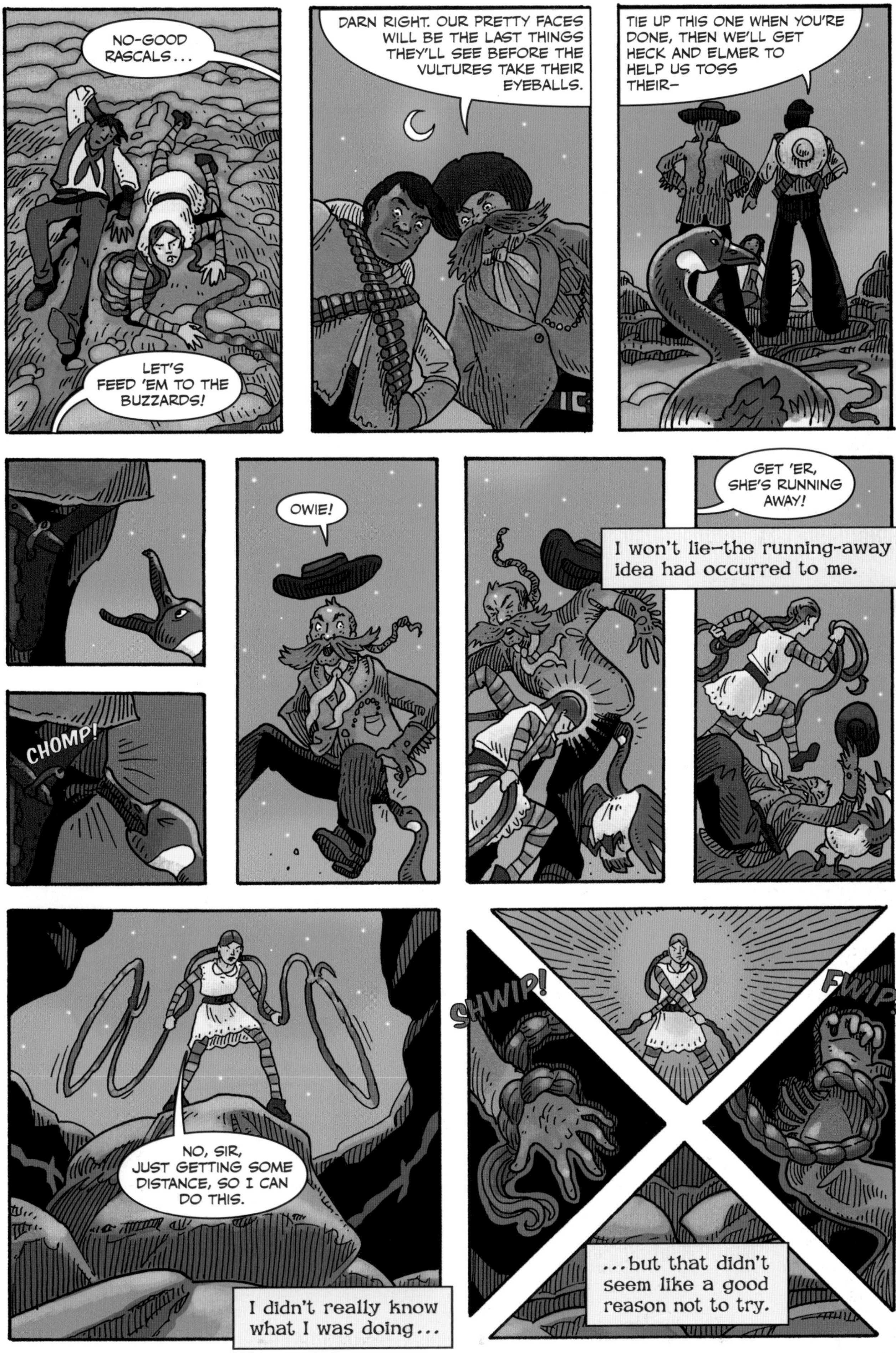
NO-GOOD RASCALS...
LET'S FEED 'EM TO THE BUZZARDS!
DARN RIGHT. OUR PRETTY FACES WILL BE THE LAST THINGS THEY'LL SEE BEFORE THE VULTURES TAKE THEIR EYEBALLS.
TIE UP THIS ONE WHEN YOU'RE DONE, THEN WE'LL GET HECK AND ELMER TO HELP US TOSS THEIR–
CHOMP!
OWIE!
I won't lie–the running-away idea had occurred to me.
GET 'ER, SHE'S RUNNING AWAY!
NO, SIR, JUST GETTING SOME DISTANCE, SO I CAN DO THIS.
I didn't really know what I was doing...
SHWIP!
FWIP!
...but that didn't seem like a good reason not to try.

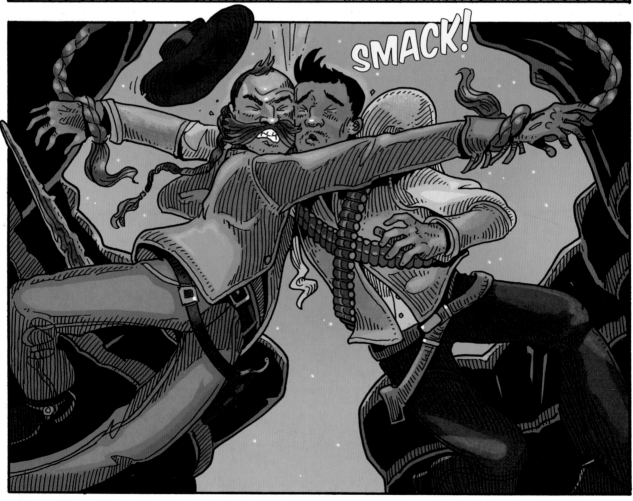

SMACK!

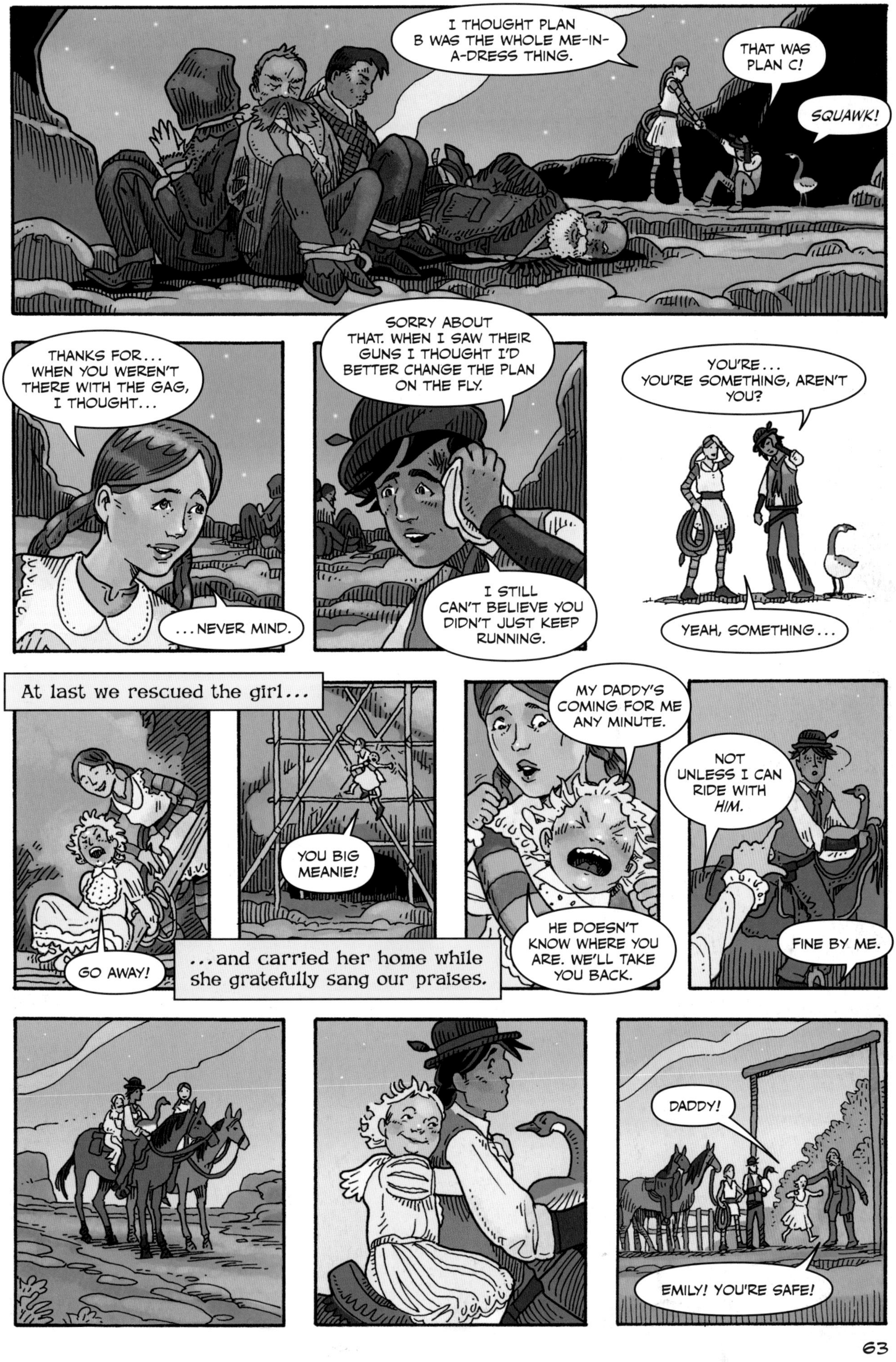
I THOUGHT PLAN B WAS THE WHOLE ME-IN-A-DRESS THING.
THAT WAS PLAN C!
SQUAWK!
THANKS FOR... WHEN YOU WEREN'T THERE WITH THE GAG, I THOUGHT...
...NEVER MIND.
SORRY ABOUT THAT. WHEN I SAW THEIR GUNS I THOUGHT I'D BETTER CHANGE THE PLAN ON THE FLY.
I STILL CAN'T BELIEVE YOU DIDN'T JUST KEEP RUNNING.
YOU'RE... YOU'RE SOMETHING, AREN'T YOU?
YEAH, SOMETHING...
At last we rescued the girl...
GO AWAY!
YOU BIG MEANIE!
...and carried her home while she gratefully sang our praises.
MY DADDY'S COMING FOR ME ANY MINUTE.
HE DOESN'T KNOW WHERE YOU ARE. WE'LL TAKE YOU BACK.
NOT UNLESS I CAN RIDE WITH HIM.
FINE BY ME.
DADDY!
EMILY! YOU'RE SAFE!

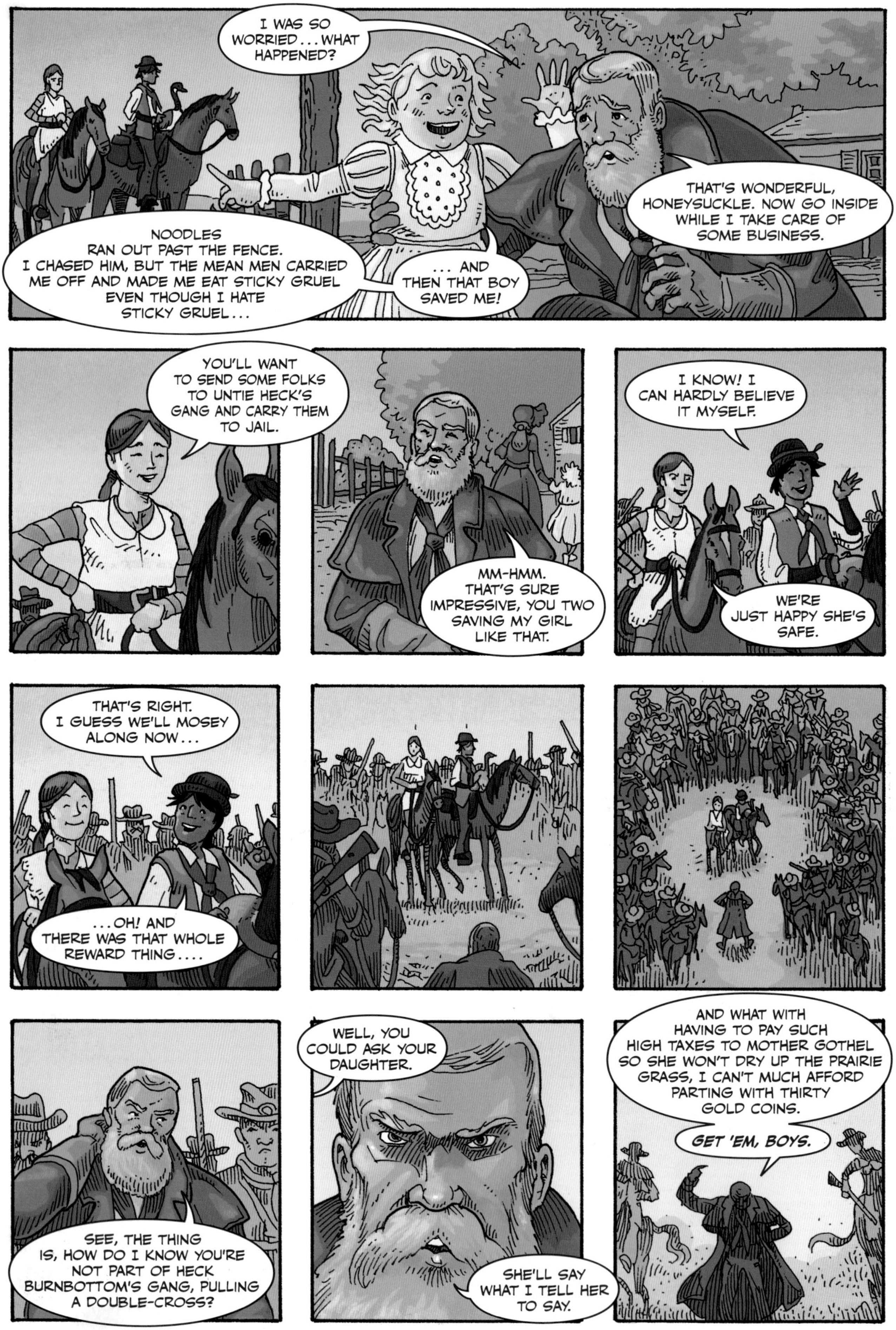
I WAS SO WORRIED... WHAT HAPPENED?
NOODLES RAN OUT PAST THE FENCE. I CHASED HIM, BUT THE MEAN MEN CARRIED ME OFF AND MADE ME EAT STICKY GRUEL EVEN THOUGH I HATE STICKY GRUEL...
... AND THEN THAT BOY SAVED ME!
THAT'S WONDERFUL, HONEYSUCKLE. NOW GO INSIDE WHILE I TAKE CARE OF SOME BUSINESS.
YOU'LL WANT TO SEND SOME FOLKS TO UNTIE HECK'S GANG AND CARRY THEM TO JAIL.
MM-HMM. THAT'S SURE IMPRESSIVE, YOU TWO SAVING MY GIRL LIKE THAT.
I KNOW! I CAN HARDLY BELIEVE IT MYSELF.
WE'RE JUST HAPPY SHE'S SAFE.
THAT'S RIGHT. I GUESS WE'LL MOSEY ALONG NOW...
...OH! AND THERE WAS THAT WHOLE REWARD THING....
SEE, THE THING IS, HOW DO I KNOW YOU'RE NOT PART OF HECK BURNBOTTOM'S GANG, PULLING A DOUBLE-CROSS?
WELL, YOU COULD ASK YOUR DAUGHTER.
SHE'LL SAY WHAT I TELL HER TO SAY.
AND WHAT WITH HAVING TO PAY SUCH HIGH TAXES TO MOTHER GOTHEL SO SHE WON'T DRY UP THE PRAIRIE GRASS, I CAN'T MUCH AFFORD PARTING WITH THIRTY GOLD COINS.
GET 'EM, BOYS.

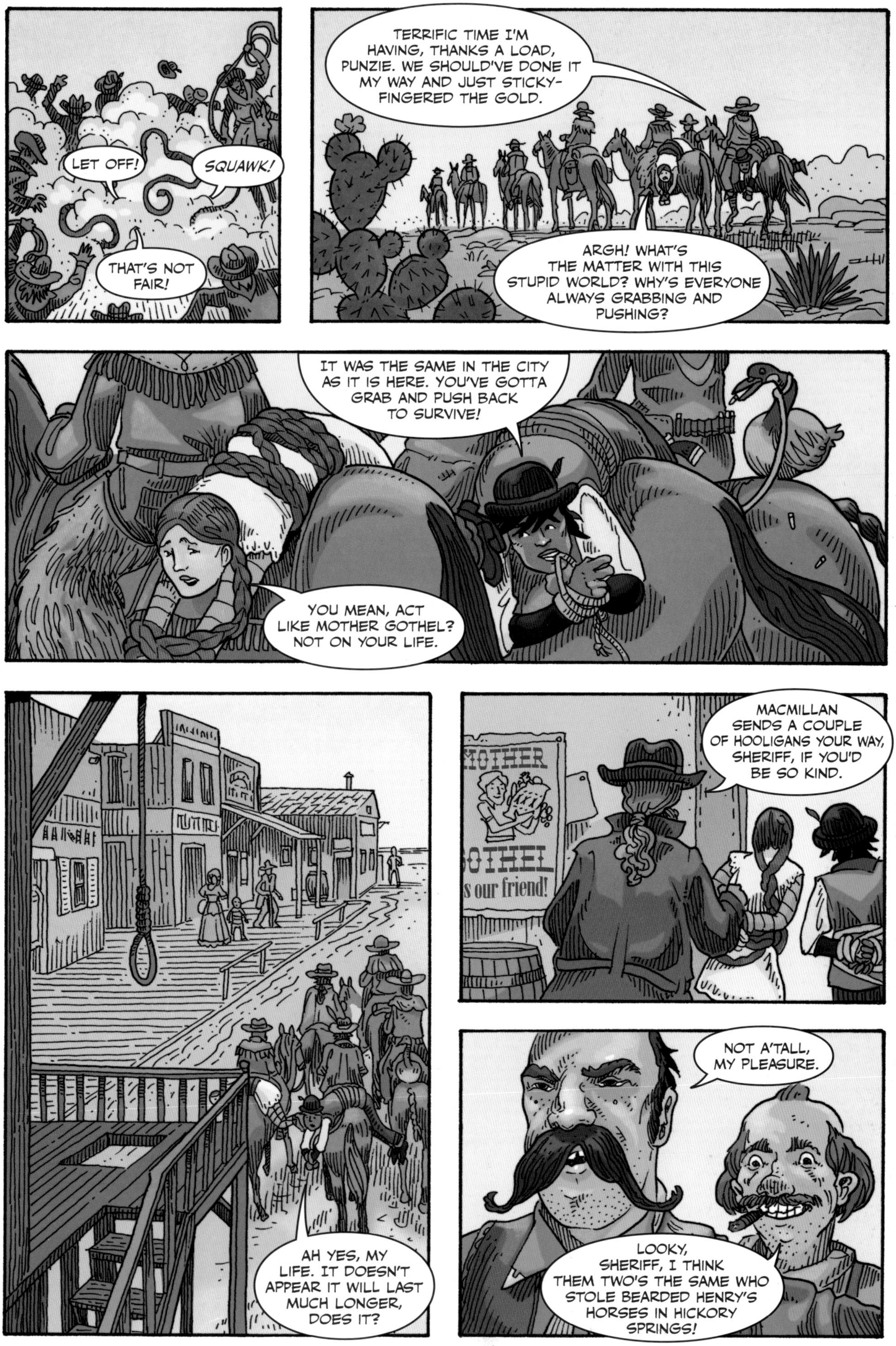
LET OFF!
SQUAWK!
THAT'S NOT FAIR!
TERRIFIC TIME I'M HAVING, THANKS A LOAD, PUNZIE. WE SHOULD'VE DONE IT MY WAY AND JUST STICKY-FINGERED THE GOLD.
ARGH! WHAT'S THE MATTER WITH THIS STUPID WORLD? WHY'S EVERYONE ALWAYS GRABBING AND PUSHING?
IT WAS THE SAME IN THE CITY AS IT IS HERE. YOU'VE GOTTA GRAB AND PUSH BACK TO SURVIVE!
YOU MEAN, ACT LIKE MOTHER GOTHEL? NOT ON YOUR LIFE.
AH YES, MY LIFE. IT DOESN'T APPEAR IT WILL LAST MUCH LONGER, DOES IT?
MOTHER GOTHEL is our friend!
MACMILLAN SENDS A COUPLE OF HOOLIGANS YOUR WAY, SHERIFF, IF YOU'D BE SO KIND.
NOT A'TALL, MY PLEASURE.
LOOKY, SHERIFF, I THINK THEM TWO'S THE SAME WHO STOLE BEARDED HENRY'S HORSES IN HICKORY SPRINGS!

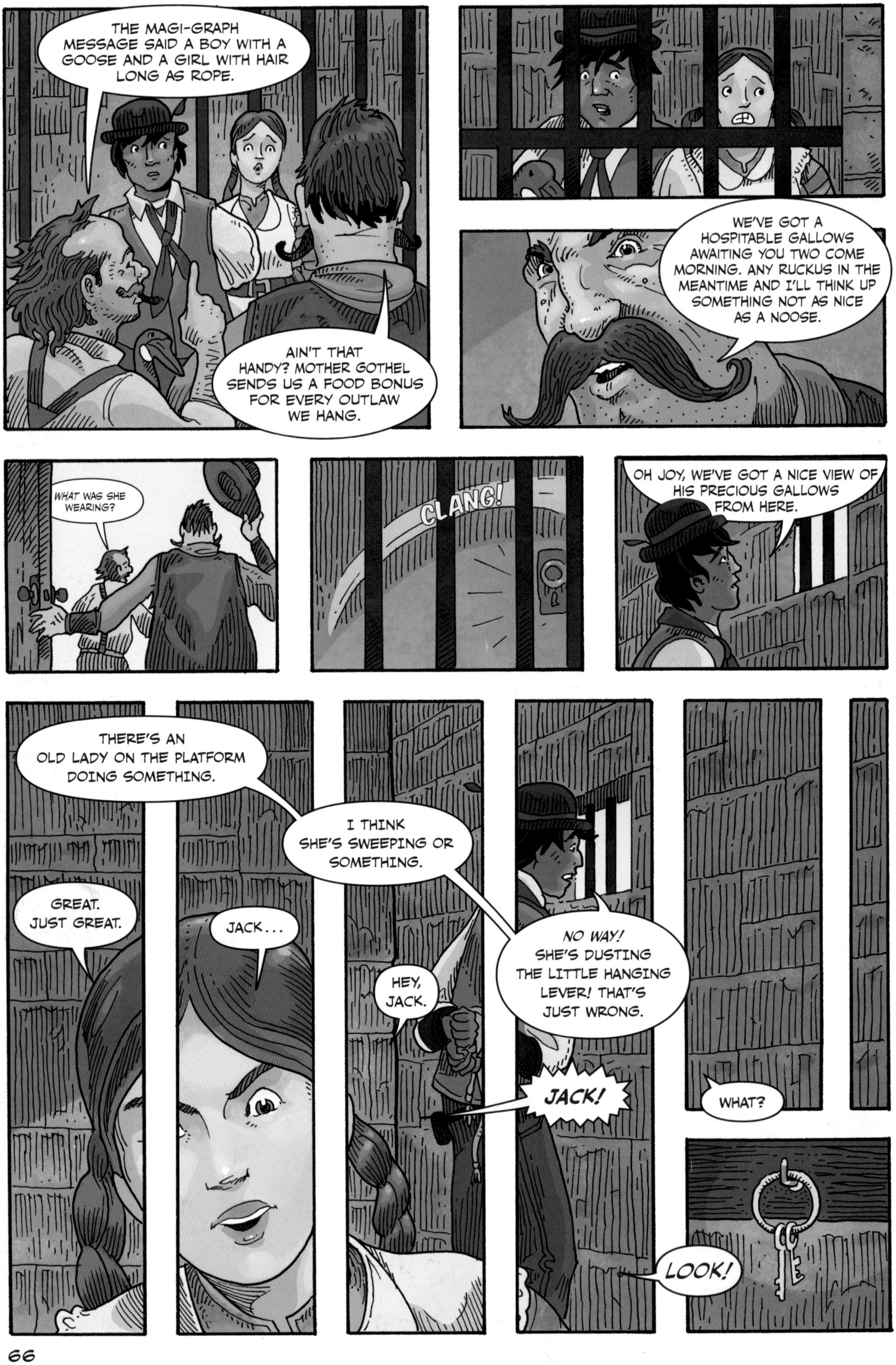
THE MAGI-GRAPH MESSAGE SAID A BOY WITH A GOOSE AND A GIRL WITH HAIR LONG AS ROPE.
AIN'T THAT HANDY? MOTHER GOTHEL SENDS US A FOOD BONUS FOR EVERY OUTLAW WE HANG.
WE'VE GOT A HOSPITABLE GALLOWS AWAITING YOU TWO COME MORNING. ANY RUCKUS IN THE MEANTIME AND I'LL THINK UP SOMETHING NOT AS NICE AS A NOOSE.
WHAT WAS SHE WEARING?
CLANG!
OH JOY, WE'VE GOT A NICE VIEW OF HIS PRECIOUS GALLOWS FROM HERE.
THERE'S AN OLD LADY ON THE PLATFORM DOING SOMETHING.
I THINK SHE'S SWEEPING OR SOMETHING.
GREAT. JUST GREAT.
JACK...
HEY, JACK.
NO WAY! SHE'S DUSTING THE LITTLE HANGING LEVER*!* THAT'S JUST WRONG.
JACK!
WHAT?
LOOK!

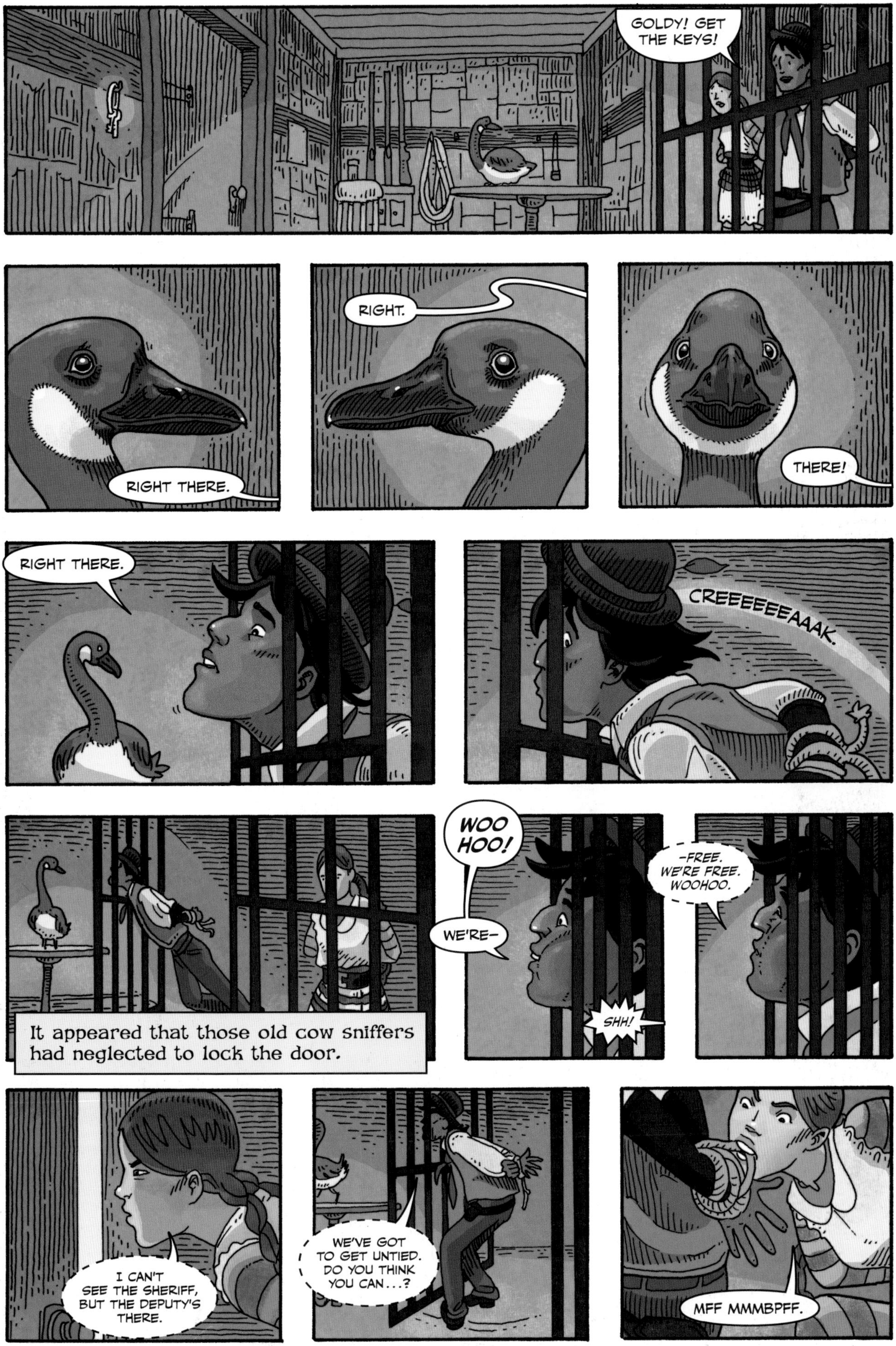
GOLDY! GET THE KEYS!
RIGHT THERE.
RIGHT.
THERE!
RIGHT THERE.
CREEEEEEAAAK.
It appeared that those old cow sniffers had neglected to lock the door.
WOO HOO!
WE'RE-
SHH!
-FREE. WE'RE FREE. WOOHOO.
I CAN'T SEE THE SHERIFF, BUT THE DEPUTY'S THERE.
WE'VE GOT TO GET UNTIED. DO YOU THINK YOU CAN...?
MFF MMMBPFF.

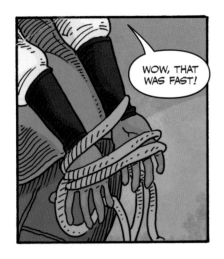

WOW, THAT WAS FAST!

YOU MUST HAVE TEETH LIKE A HORSE!

GEE, THANKS.

OKAY, OKAY. IF WE CAN LURE THE DEPUTY IN HERE, AND...

HONK! HONK! HONK!

WHAT'S GOIN' ON IN THERE?

SOUNDS LIKE YER STRANGLIN' A GOAT!

IT WAS JUST OUR FINE GOOSE.

EH? OH, YER BIRD. I WOULDN'T MIND A LITTLE ROAST GOOSE, COME TO THINK OF IT.

I'D BE HAPPY TO GIVE HER TO YOU, BUT ALAS, SHE'S GOT THE POX.

EW. SHAME THAT.

HERE'S YOUR POXY BIRD THEN.

HEY... WEREN'T YOU TIED UP?

ARE YOU TRAINED IN THE FINE ART OF SKULL THUMPING, THEN?

YOU SEEM TO FAVOR IT.

WELL, MY OPTIONS WERE SOMEWHAT LIMITED, WHAT WITH MY *HANDS BEING TIED....*

OH. ER...RIGHT. LET ME TAKE CARE OF THAT. SORRY.

And so, after cleverly discovering the weakness in our captor's prison...

...and pausing for a bit of nourishment...

...we were on our way to freedom.

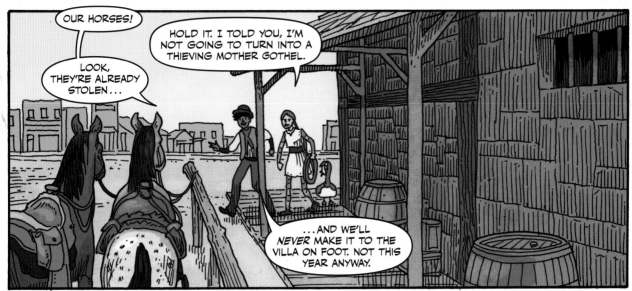
OUR HORSES!

LOOK, THEY'RE ALREADY STOLEN...

HOLD IT. I TOLD YOU, I'M NOT GOING TO TURN INTO A THIEVING MOTHER GOTHEL.

...AND WE'LL *NEVER* MAKE IT TO THE VILLA ON FOOT. NOT THIS YEAR ANYWAY.

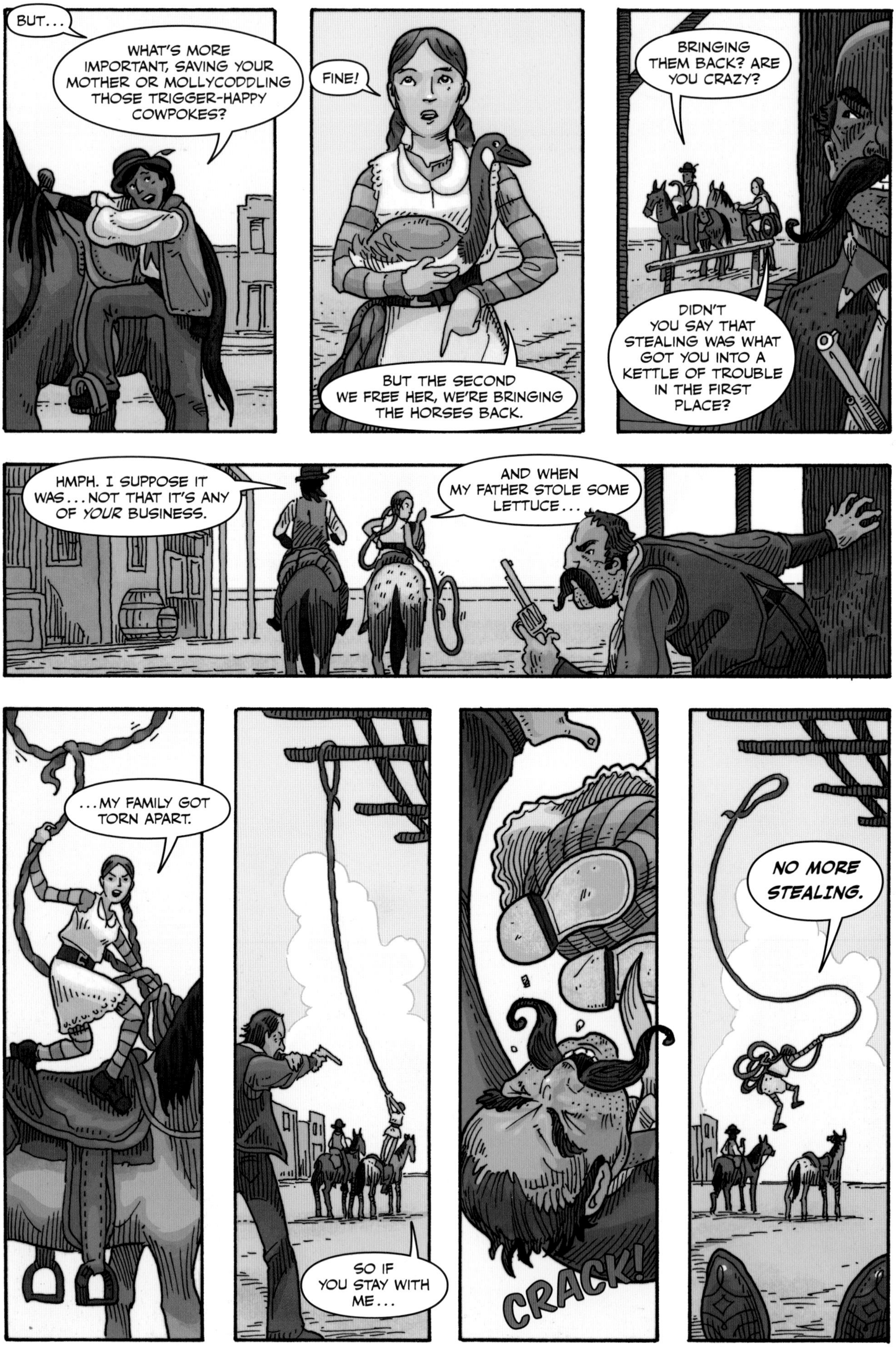
BUT...
WHAT'S MORE IMPORTANT, SAVING YOUR MOTHER OR MOLLYCODDLING THOSE TRIGGER-HAPPY COWPOKES?
FINE!
BUT THE SECOND WE FREE HER, WE'RE BRINGING THE HORSES BACK.
BRINGING THEM BACK? ARE YOU CRAZY?
DIDN'T YOU SAY THAT STEALING WAS WHAT GOT YOU INTO A KETTLE OF TROUBLE IN THE FIRST PLACE?
HMPH. I SUPPOSE IT WAS... NOT THAT IT'S ANY OF *YOUR* BUSINESS.
AND WHEN MY FATHER STOLE SOME LETTUCE...
...MY FAMILY GOT TORN APART.
SO IF YOU STAY WITH ME...
CRACK!
NO MORE STEALING.

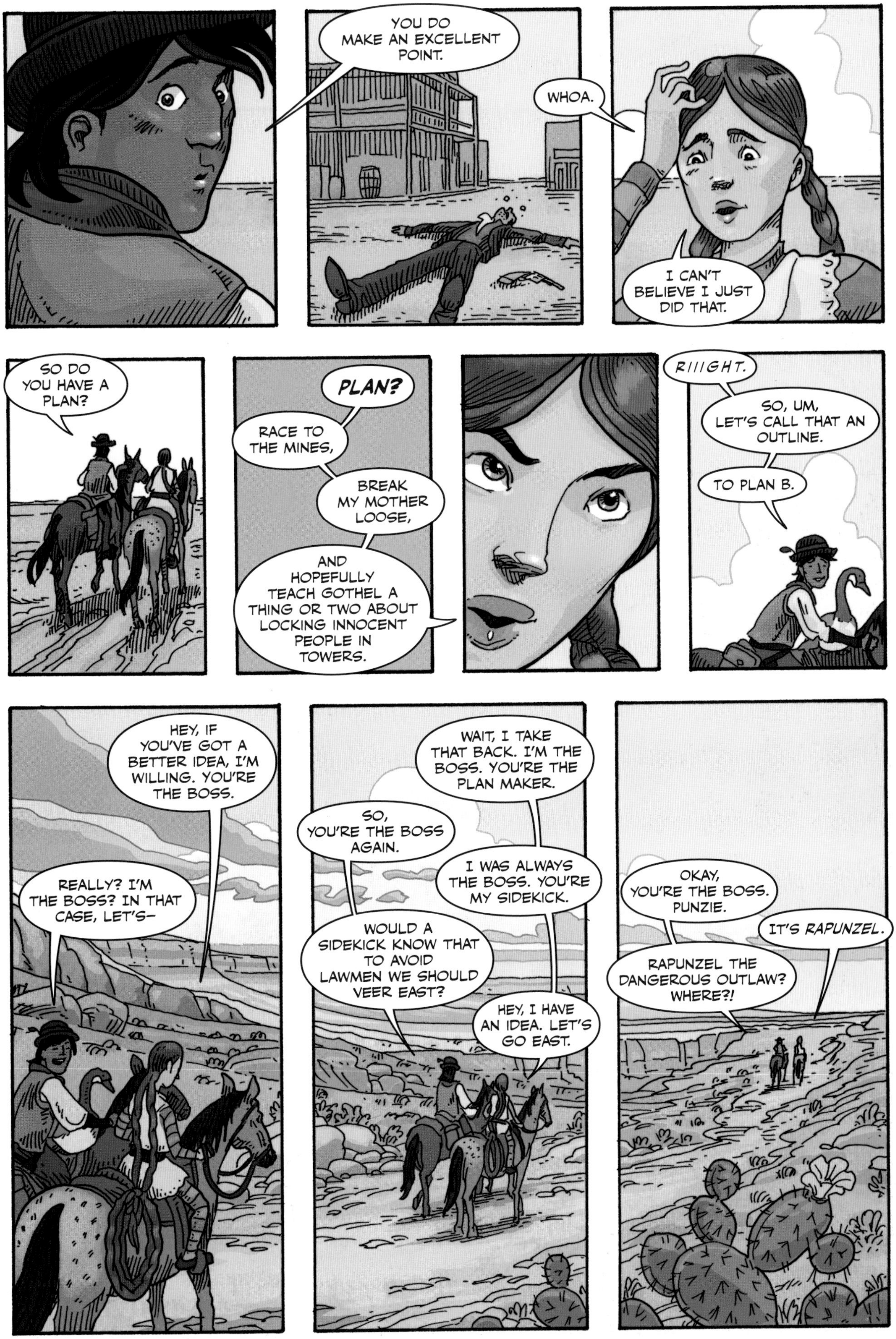
YOU DO MAKE AN EXCELLENT POINT.
WHOA.
I CAN'T BELIEVE I JUST DID THAT.
SO DO YOU HAVE A PLAN?
PLAN?
RACE TO THE MINES,
BREAK MY MOTHER LOOSE,
AND HOPEFULLY TEACH GOTHEL A THING OR TWO ABOUT LOCKING INNOCENT PEOPLE IN TOWERS.
RIIIGHT.
SO, UM, LET'S CALL THAT AN OUTLINE.
TO PLAN B.
HEY, IF YOU'VE GOT A BETTER IDEA, I'M WILLING. YOU'RE THE BOSS.
REALLY? I'M THE BOSS? IN THAT CASE, LET'S–
WAIT, I TAKE THAT BACK. I'M THE BOSS. YOU'RE THE PLAN MAKER.
SO, YOU'RE THE BOSS AGAIN.
I WAS ALWAYS THE BOSS. YOU'RE MY SIDEKICK.
WOULD A SIDEKICK KNOW THAT TO AVOID LAWMEN WE SHOULD VEER EAST?
HEY, I HAVE AN IDEA. LET'S GO EAST.
OKAY, YOU'RE THE BOSS. PUNZIE.
IT'S *RAPUNZEL*.
RAPUNZEL THE DANGEROUS OUTLAW? WHERE?!

Part 3: Banditry in the Badlands

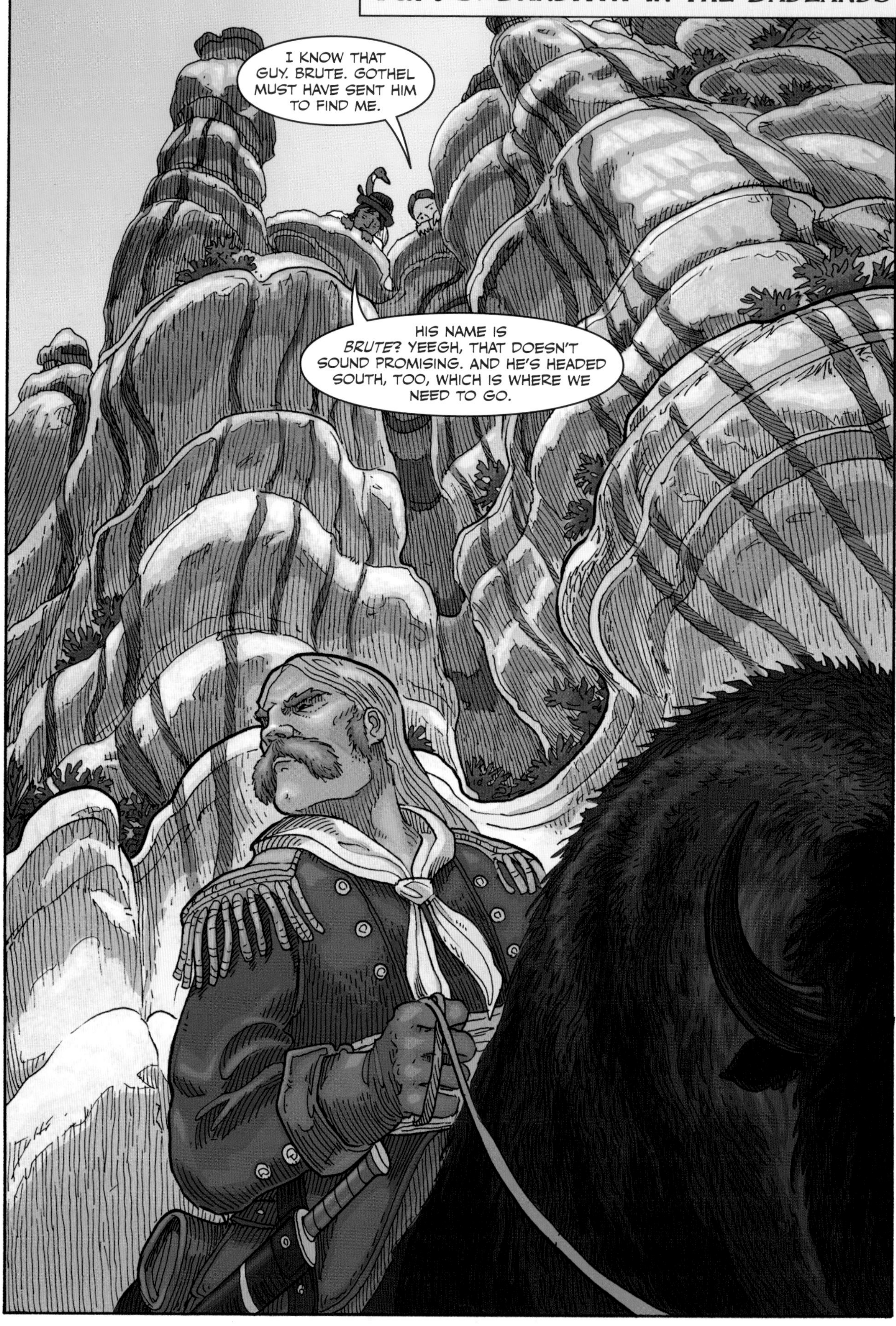
I KNOW THAT GUY. BRUTE. GOTHEL MUST HAVE SENT HIM TO FIND ME.
HIS NAME IS *BRUTE*? YEEGH, THAT DOESN'T SOUND PROMISING. AND HE'S HEADED SOUTH, TOO, WHICH IS WHERE WE NEED TO GO.

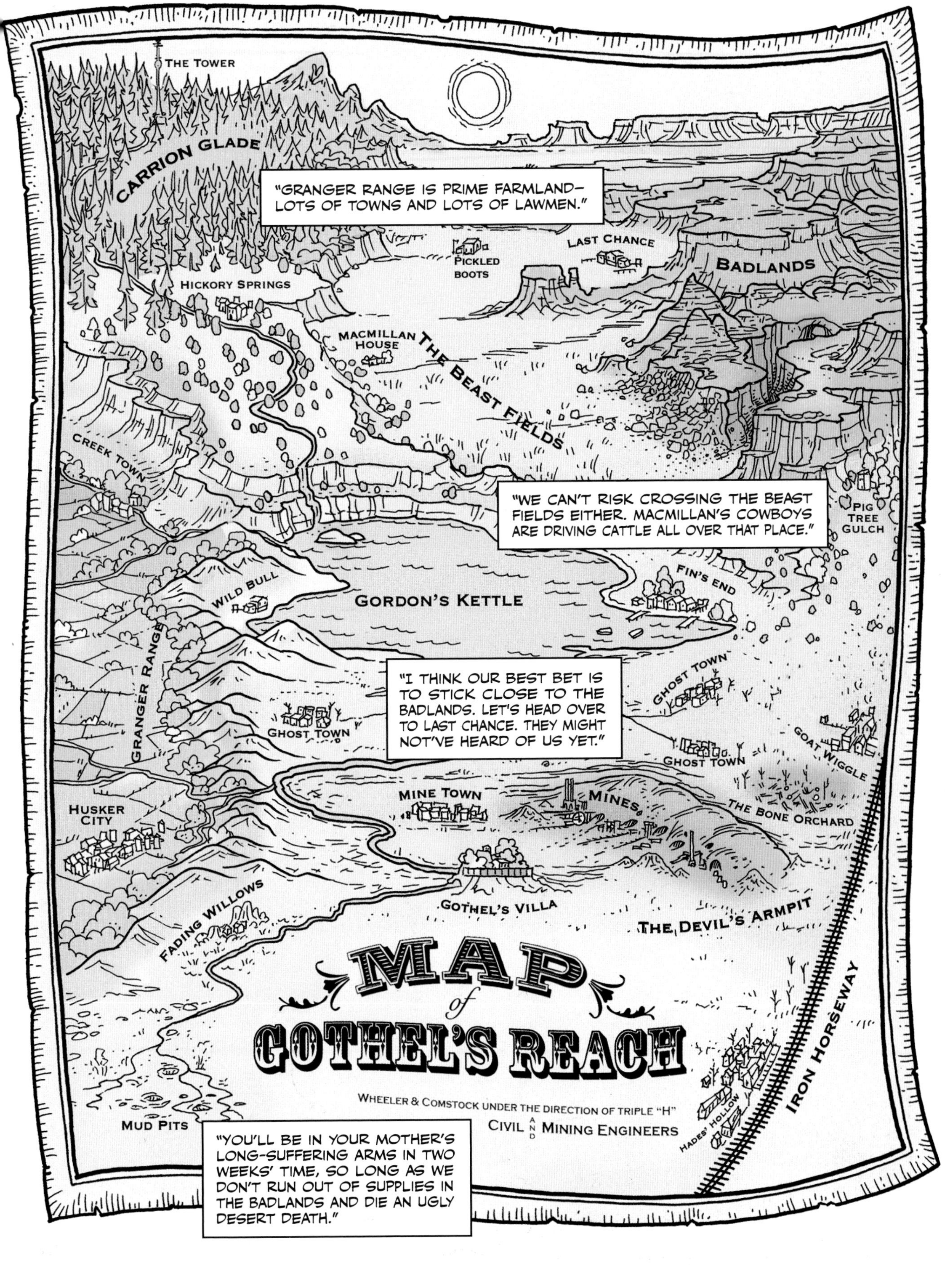

THE TOWER
CARRION GLADE
"GRANGER RANGE IS PRIME FARMLAND—LOTS OF TOWNS AND LOTS OF LAWMEN."
PICKLED BOOTS
LAST CHANCE
BADLANDS
HICKORY SPRINGS
MACMILLAN HOUSE
THE BEAST FIELDS
CREEK TOWN
"WE CAN'T RISK CROSSING THE BEAST FIELDS EITHER. MACMILLAN'S COWBOYS ARE DRIVING CATTLE ALL OVER THAT PLACE."
PIG TREE GULCH
FIN'S END
WILD BULL
GORDON'S KETTLE
GRANGER RANGE
"I THINK OUR BEST BET IS TO STICK CLOSE TO THE BADLANDS. LET'S HEAD OVER TO LAST CHANCE. THEY MIGHT NOT'VE HEARD OF US YET."
GHOST TOWN
GHOST TOWN
GHOST TOWN
GOAT WIGGLE
MINE TOWN
MINES
THE BONE ORCHARD
HUSKER CITY
GOTHEL'S VILLA
FADING WILLOWS
THE DEVIL'S ARMPIT
MAP of GOTHEL'S REACH
IRON HORSEWAY
WHEELER & COMSTOCK UNDER THE DIRECTION OF TRIPLE "H"
CIVIL AND MINING ENGINEERS
HADES' HOLLOW
MUD PITS
"YOU'LL BE IN YOUR MOTHER'S LONG-SUFFERING ARMS IN TWO WEEKS' TIME, SO LONG AS WE DON'T RUN OUT OF SUPPLIES IN THE BADLANDS AND DIE AN UGLY DESERT DEATH."

THEN WE'D BETTER HOPE THERE'S WORK IN LAST CHANCE SO WE CAN EARN SUPPLIES.
IF NOT FOR CERTAIN PROMISES REGARDING, UM, CREATIVE BORROWING, WE WOULDN'T HAVE TO EARN THEM.
HMPH. I DON'T SUPPOSE YOUR STICKY FINGERS PICKED UP ANY FOOD FOR US BEFORE YOU TOOK THE OATH OF HONESTY.
I MIGHT HAVE A CRUMB OF SOMETHING LEFT IN MY PACK.
IS THIS WHAT YOU MEANT—A SINGLE BEAN?
GIVE IT HERE! THAT'S MY LUCKY BEAN.
YOU'VE GOT A *LUCKY BEAN*?
YOU'VE GOT *TWENTY FEET OF HAIR?*
IS THERE AN INN AT LAST CHANCE? WHAT I WOULDN'T GIVE FOR JUST ONE NIGHT ON A MATTRESS.
WIMP.
ME, WIMP? YOU TRY HAULING AROUND *TWENTY FEET OF HAIR*. IT'S LIKELY TO BREAK MY NECK.
SO . . . IS IT STILL HARD SOMETIMES TO THINK ABOUT WHAT MOTHER GOTHEL DID TO YOU?
I CALLED HER *MOTHER* FOR MOST OF MY LIFE, AND ALL THE WHILE SHE HAD MY *REAL* MOTHER IN HER SLAVE MINES.
NO, NO, NOT THAT. I MEANT HOW SHE, YOU KNOW, NAMED YOU AFTER *LETTUCE*.
OW.

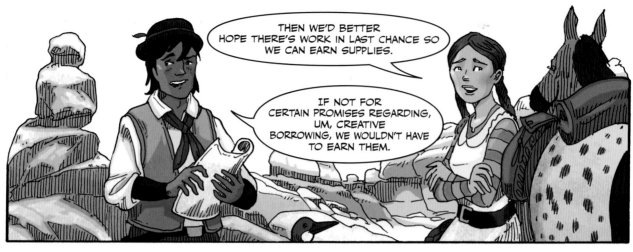

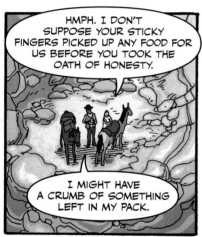

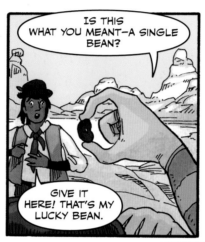

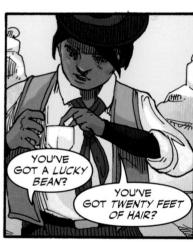

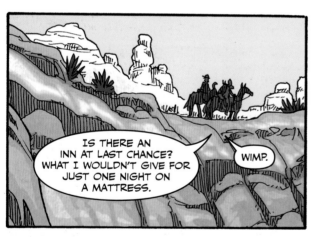

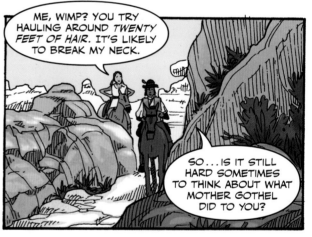

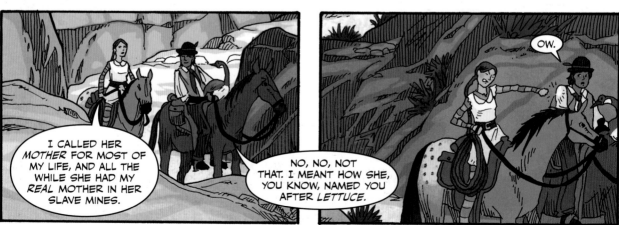

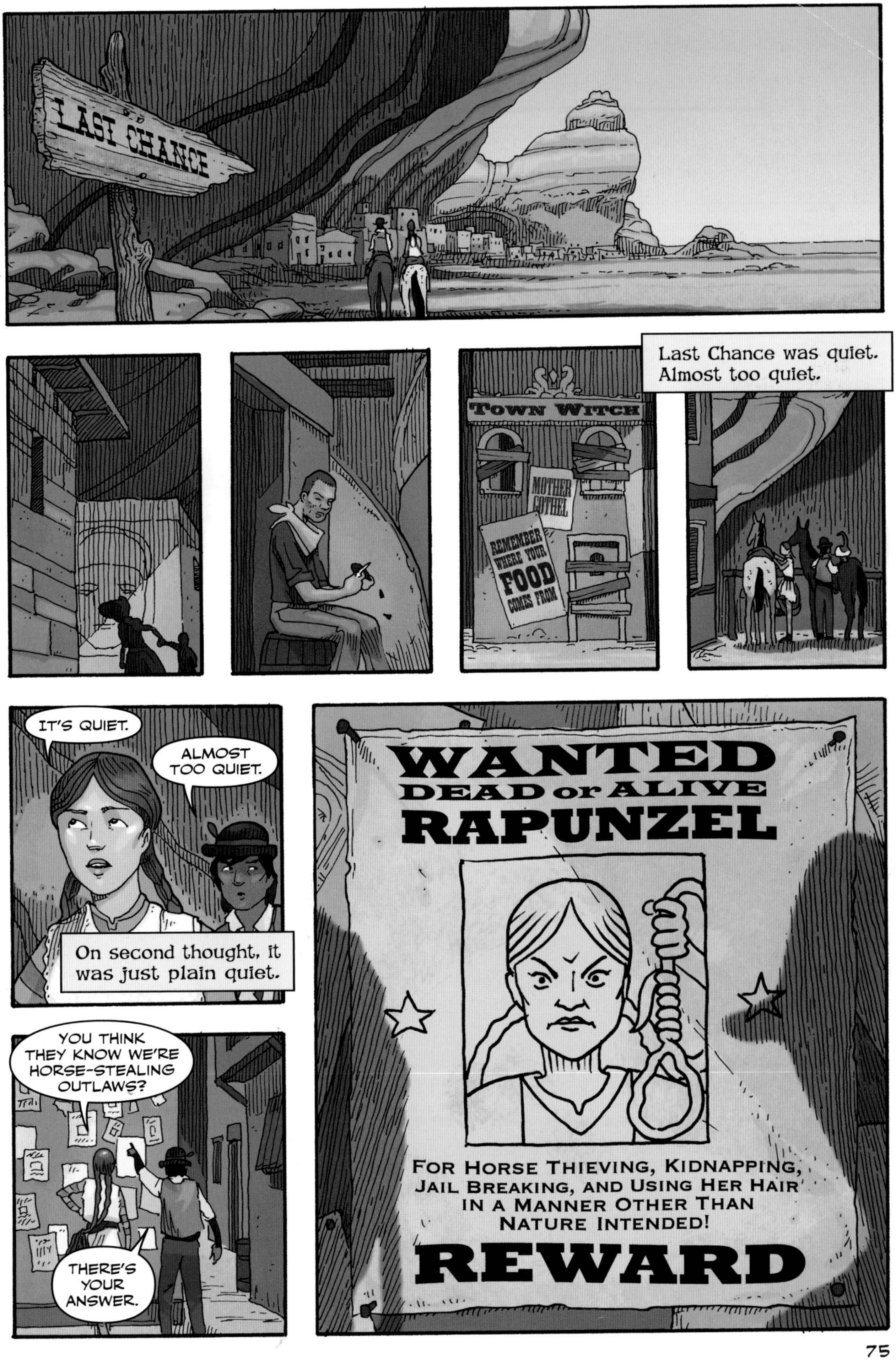
LAST CHANCE
Last Chance was quiet. Almost too quiet.
TOWN WITCH
MOTHER GOTHEL
REMEMBER WHERE YOUR FOOD COMES FROM
IT'S QUIET.
ALMOST TOO QUIET.
On second thought, it was just plain quiet.
YOU THINK THEY KNOW WE'RE HORSE-STEALING OUTLAWS?
THERE'S YOUR ANSWER.
WANTED
DEAD or ALIVE
RAPUNZEL
FOR HORSE THIEVING, KIDNAPPING, JAIL BREAKING, AND USING HER HAIR IN A MANNER OTHER THAN NATURE INTENDED!
REWARD

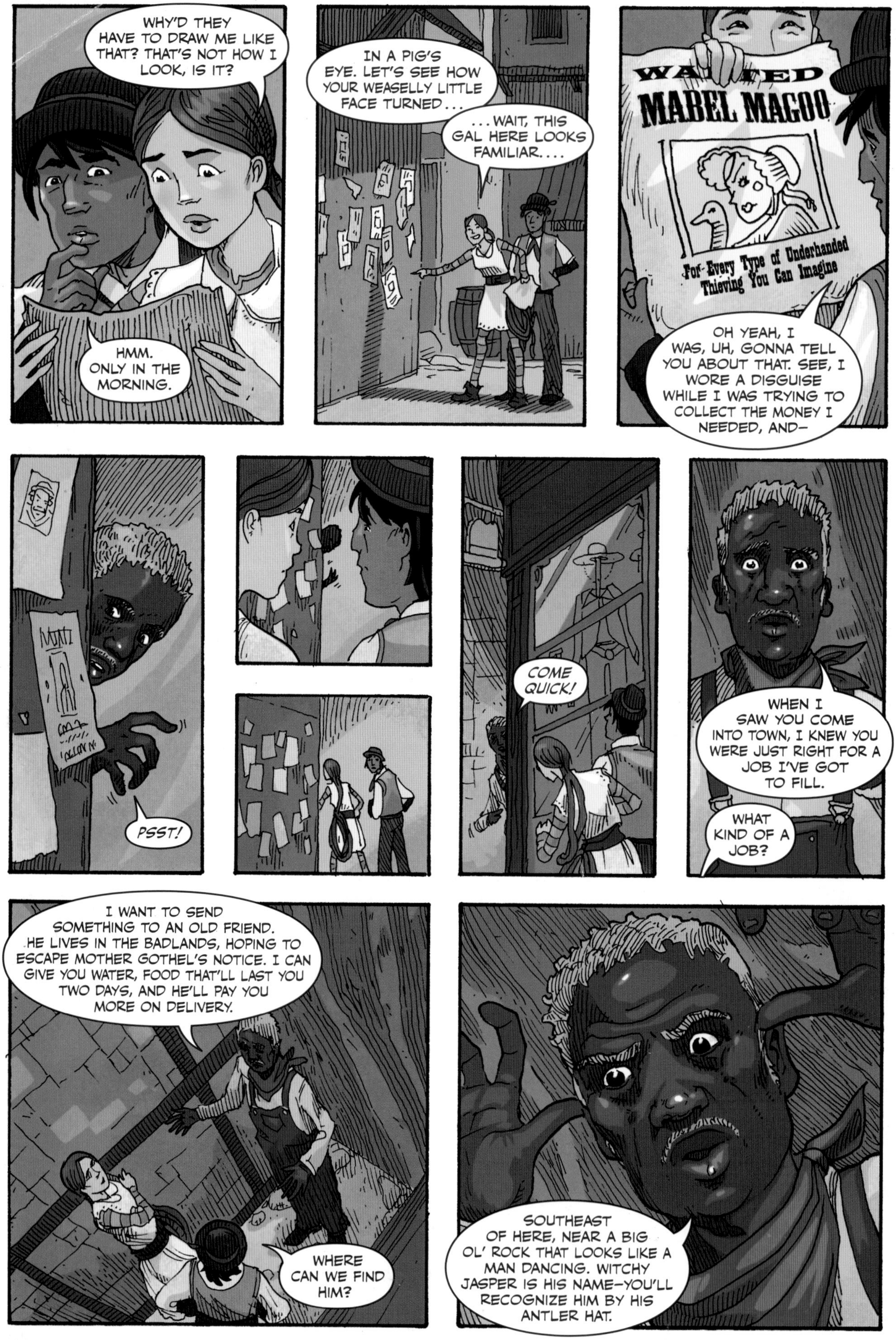
WHY'D THEY HAVE TO DRAW ME LIKE THAT? THAT'S NOT HOW I LOOK, IS IT?
HMM. ONLY IN THE MORNING.
IN A PIG'S EYE. LET'S SEE HOW YOUR WEASELLY LITTLE FACE TURNED...
...WAIT, THIS GAL HERE LOOKS FAMILIAR....
WANTED
MABEL MAGOO
For Every Type of Underhanded Thieving You Can Imagine
OH YEAH, I WAS, UH, GONNA TELL YOU ABOUT THAT. SEE, I WORE A DISGUISE WHILE I WAS TRYING TO COLLECT THE MONEY I NEEDED, AND–
PSST!
COME QUICK!
WHEN I SAW YOU COME INTO TOWN, I KNEW YOU WERE JUST RIGHT FOR A JOB I'VE GOT TO FILL.
WHAT KIND OF A JOB?
I WANT TO SEND SOMETHING TO AN OLD FRIEND. HE LIVES IN THE BADLANDS, HOPING TO ESCAPE MOTHER GOTHEL'S NOTICE. I CAN GIVE YOU WATER, FOOD THAT'LL LAST YOU TWO DAYS, AND HE'LL PAY YOU MORE ON DELIVERY.
WHERE CAN WE FIND HIM?
SOUTHEAST OF HERE, NEAR A BIG OL' ROCK THAT LOOKS LIKE A MAN DANCING. WITCHY JASPER IS HIS NAME–YOU'LL RECOGNIZE HIM BY HIS ANTLER HAT.

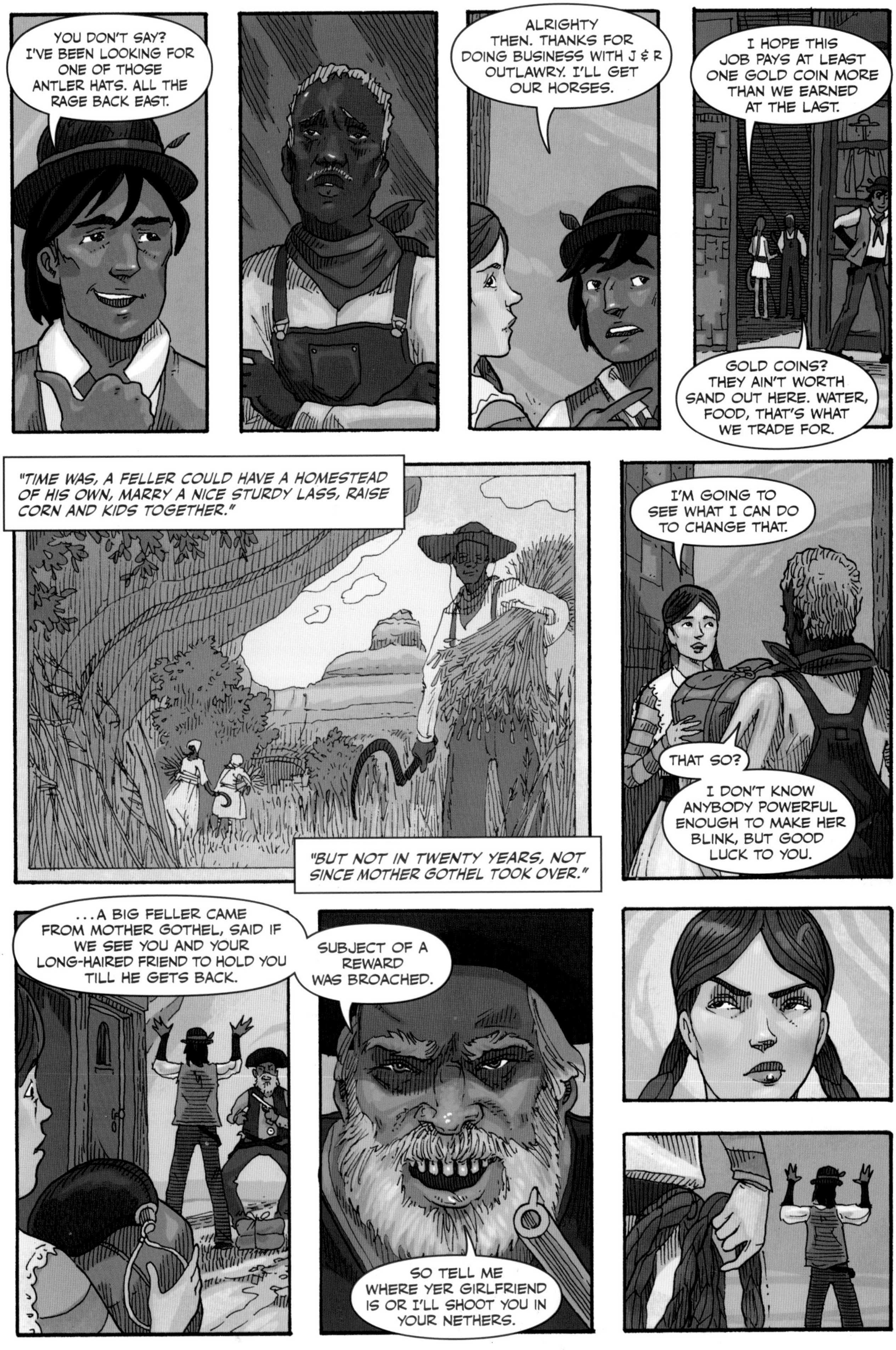
YOU DON'T SAY? I'VE BEEN LOOKING FOR ONE OF THOSE ANTLER HATS. ALL THE RAGE BACK EAST.
ALRIGHTY THEN. THANKS FOR DOING BUSINESS WITH J & R OUTLAWRY. I'LL GET OUR HORSES.
I HOPE THIS JOB PAYS AT LEAST ONE GOLD COIN MORE THAN WE EARNED AT THE LAST.
GOLD COINS? THEY AIN'T WORTH SAND OUT HERE. WATER, FOOD, THAT'S WHAT WE TRADE FOR.
"TIME WAS, A FELLER COULD HAVE A HOMESTEAD OF HIS OWN, MARRY A NICE STURDY LASS, RAISE CORN AND KIDS TOGETHER."
"BUT NOT IN TWENTY YEARS, NOT SINCE MOTHER GOTHEL TOOK OVER."
I'M GOING TO SEE WHAT I CAN DO TO CHANGE THAT.
THAT SO?
I DON'T KNOW ANYBODY POWERFUL ENOUGH TO MAKE HER BLINK, BUT GOOD LUCK TO YOU.
. . . A BIG FELLER CAME FROM MOTHER GOTHEL, SAID IF WE SEE YOU AND YOUR LONG-HAIRED FRIEND TO HOLD YOU TILL HE GETS BACK.
SUBJECT OF A REWARD WAS BROACHED.
SO TELL ME WHERE YER GIRLFRIEND IS OR I'LL SHOOT YOU IN YOUR NETHERS.

 CLICK!

 CLICK!

 WHAT THE— YANK!

 SNAP!

 CRASH! DAG-NABIT!

I was noticing how without guns in their hands...

Made me realize I'd never seen Jack touch a gun except to throw it away.

I JUST...HE MADE ME MAD, AND I THOUGHT HE WAS GOING TO SHOOT YOU.

I DIDN'T MEAN TO.

 I RECKON YOU'D BETTER LEAVE MY FRIEND ALONE.

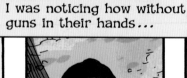 ...most folk around here turned pale.

 WOW. I MEAN, WOW.

 PUNZIE, I CAN'T WAIT TO SEE WHAT YOU'LL DO WHEN YOU ACTUALLY MEAN TO.

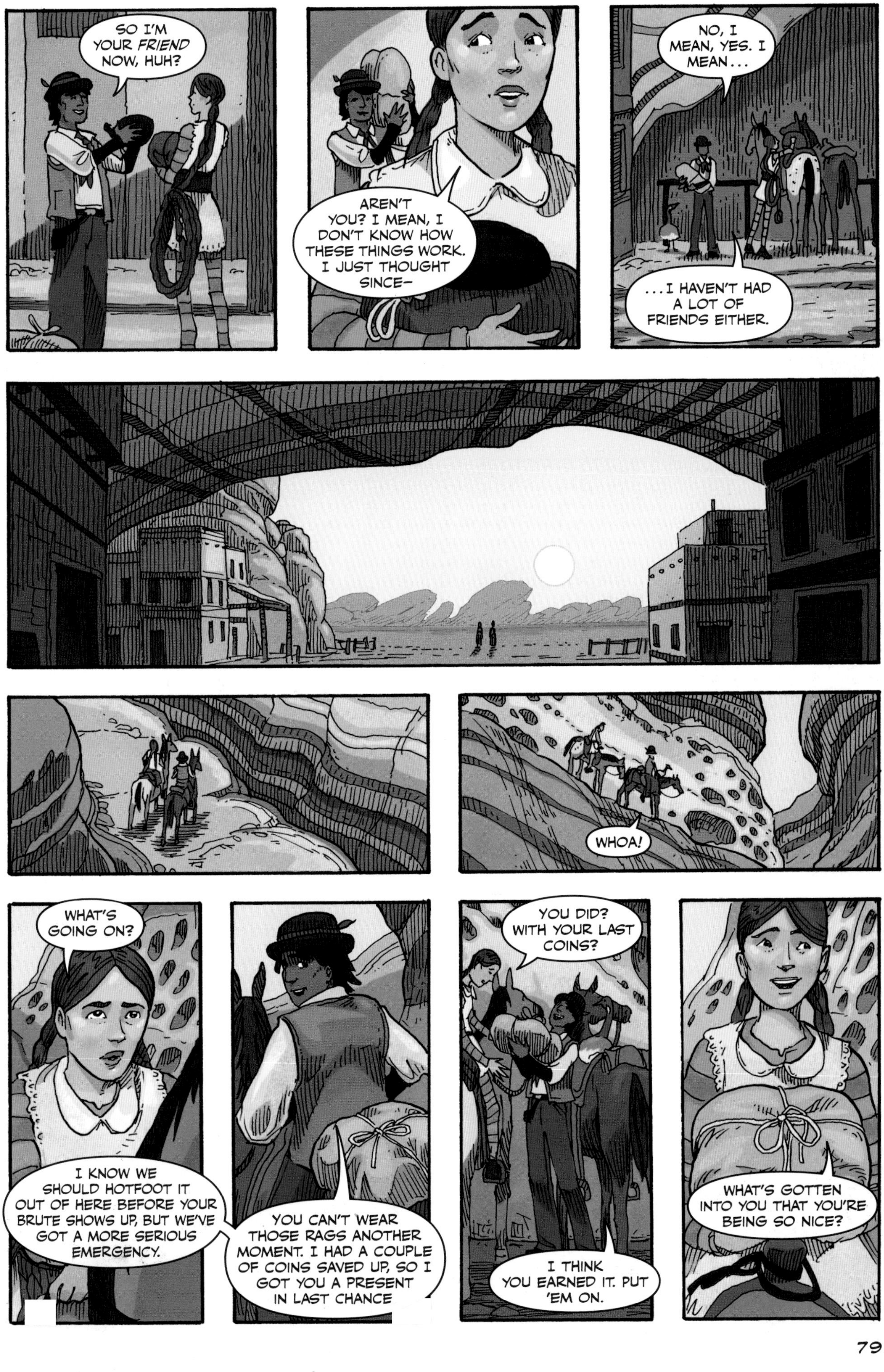
SO I'M YOUR *FRIEND* NOW, HUH?
AREN'T YOU? I MEAN, I DON'T KNOW HOW THESE THINGS WORK. I JUST THOUGHT SINCE–
NO, I MEAN, YES. I MEAN...
...I HAVEN'T HAD A LOT OF FRIENDS EITHER.
WHOA!
WHAT'S GOING ON?
I KNOW WE SHOULD HOTFOOT IT OUT OF HERE BEFORE YOUR BRUTE SHOWS UP, BUT WE'VE GOT A MORE SERIOUS EMERGENCY.
YOU CAN'T WEAR THOSE RAGS ANOTHER MOMENT. I HAD A COUPLE OF COINS SAVED UP, SO I GOT YOU A PRESENT IN LAST CHANCE
YOU DID? WITH YOUR LAST COINS?
I THINK YOU EARNED IT. PUT 'EM ON.
WHAT'S GOTTEN INTO YOU THAT YOU'RE BEING SO NICE?

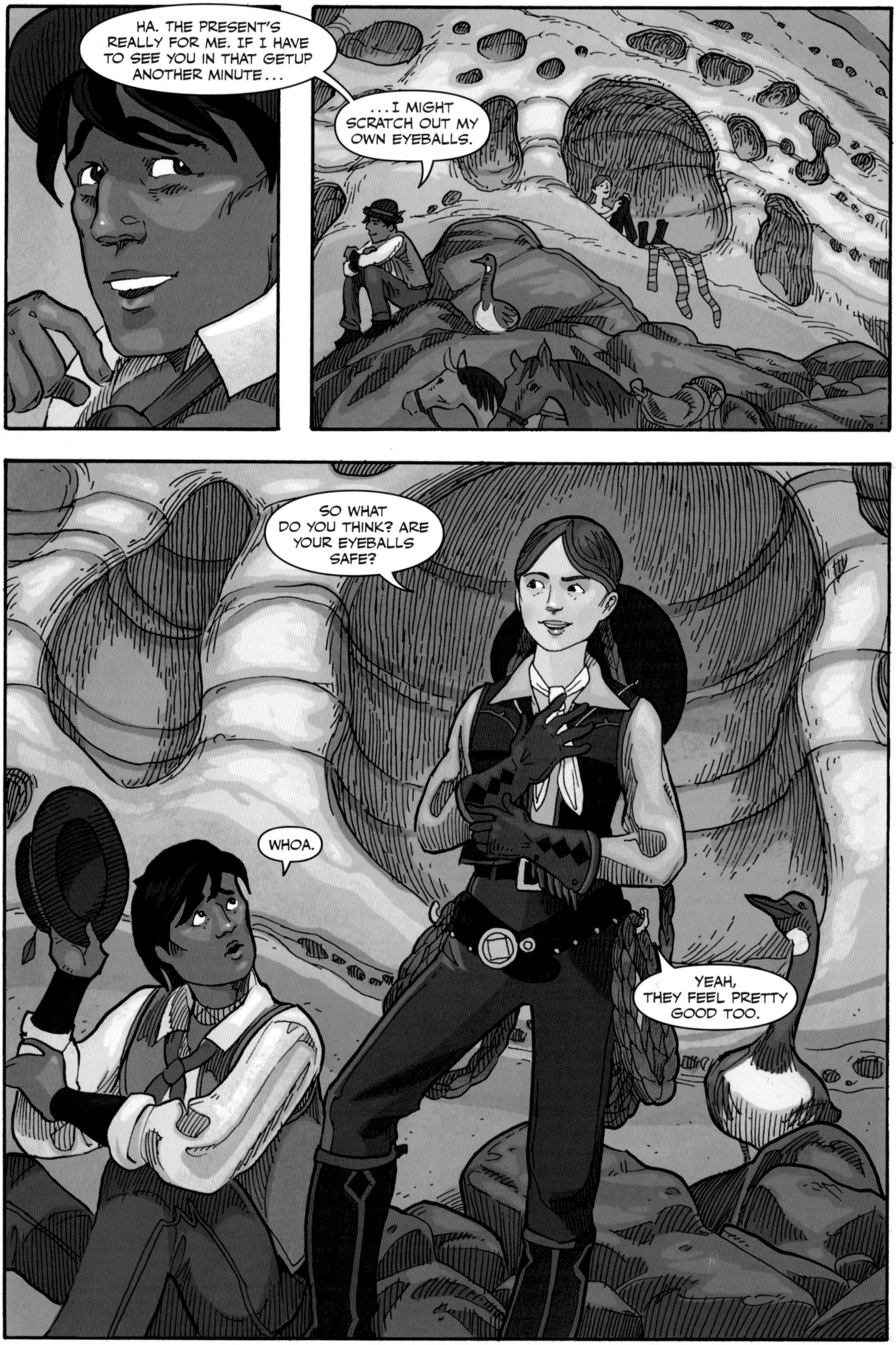
HA. THE PRESENT'S REALLY FOR ME. IF I HAVE TO SEE YOU IN THAT GETUP ANOTHER MINUTE...
...I MIGHT SCRATCH OUT MY OWN EYEBALLS.
SO WHAT DO YOU THINK? ARE YOUR EYEBALLS SAFE?
WHOA.
YEAH, THEY FEEL PRETTY GOOD TOO.

Two days later, we came upon Dancing Man Rock.

THAT'S NOT ANY KIND OF DANCING I'VE EVER SEEN.

CLOSE ENOUGH. THIS MUST BE THE PLACE.

HELLO?

MR. ANTLER-MAN, SIR?

YOU HERE?

WHAT WAS THAT NOISE?

JUST GAS. IT'LL PASS.

NO, NOT THAT! JUST... SHH, FOR A SECOND!

EEEEEEEEEEEEEEEEEEEEEEEEE

EEEYAAA!

OOF!

YAH!

HEE!

HEY!

STOP IT!

WHAT?

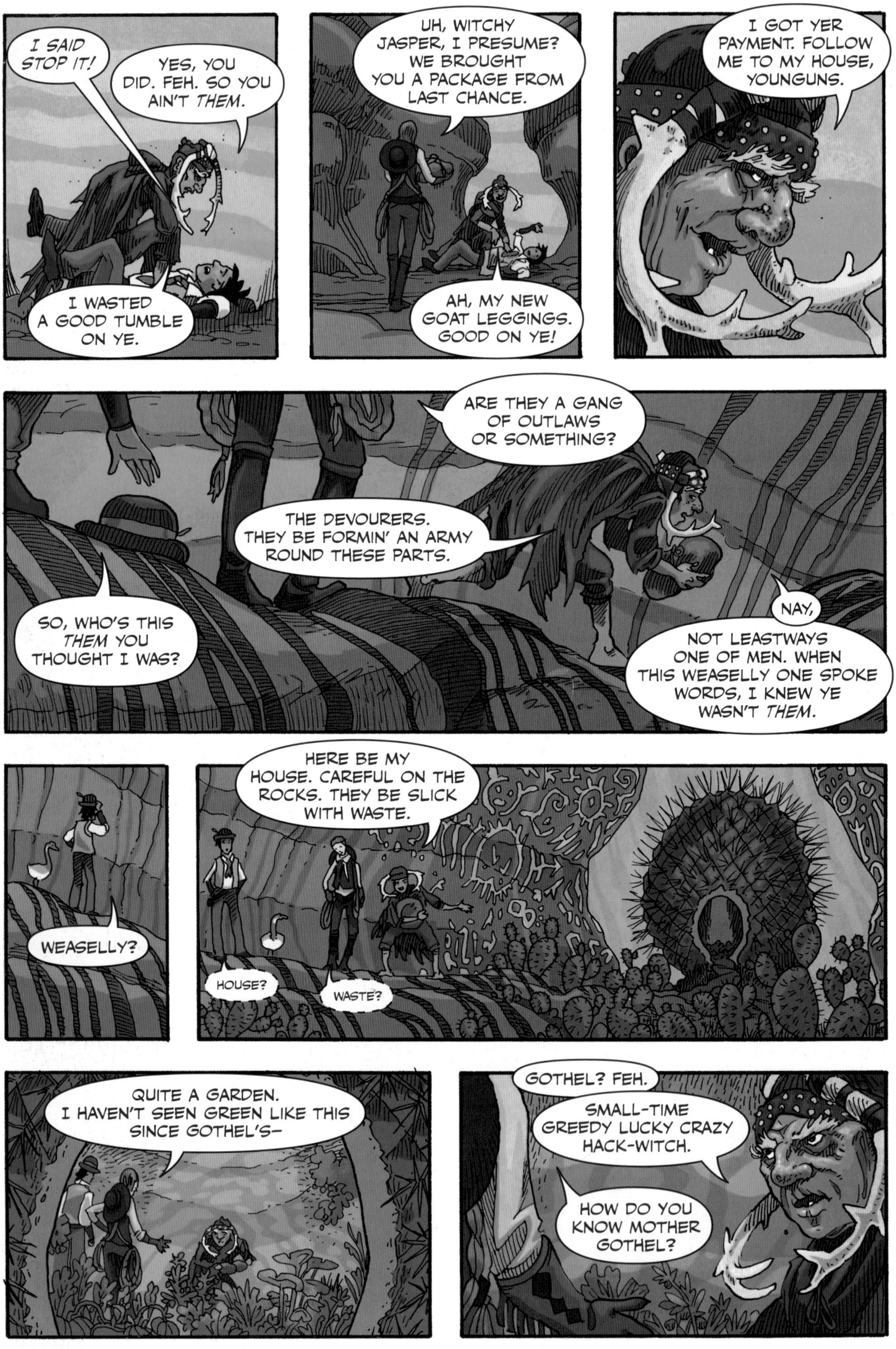

I SAID STOP IT!
YES, YOU DID. FEH. SO YOU AIN'T *THEM*.
I WASTED A GOOD TUMBLE ON YE.
UH, WITCHY JASPER, I PRESUME? WE BROUGHT YOU A PACKAGE FROM LAST CHANCE.
AH, MY NEW GOAT LEGGINGS. GOOD ON YE!
I GOT YER PAYMENT. FOLLOW ME TO MY HOUSE, YOUNGUNS.
SO, WHO'S THIS *THEM* YOU THOUGHT I WAS?
ARE THEY A GANG OF OUTLAWS OR SOMETHING?
THE DEVOURERS. THEY BE FORMIN' AN ARMY ROUND THESE PARTS.
NAY,
NOT LEASTWAYS ONE OF MEN. WHEN THIS WEASELLY ONE SPOKE WORDS, I KNEW YE WASN'T *THEM*.
WEASELLY?
HERE BE MY HOUSE. CAREFUL ON THE ROCKS. THEY BE SLICK WITH WASTE.
HOUSE?
WASTE?
QUITE A GARDEN. I HAVEN'T SEEN GREEN LIKE THIS SINCE GOTHEL'S–
GOTHEL? FEH.
SMALL-TIME GREEDY LUCKY CRAZY HACK-WITCH.
HOW DO YOU KNOW MOTHER GOTHEL?

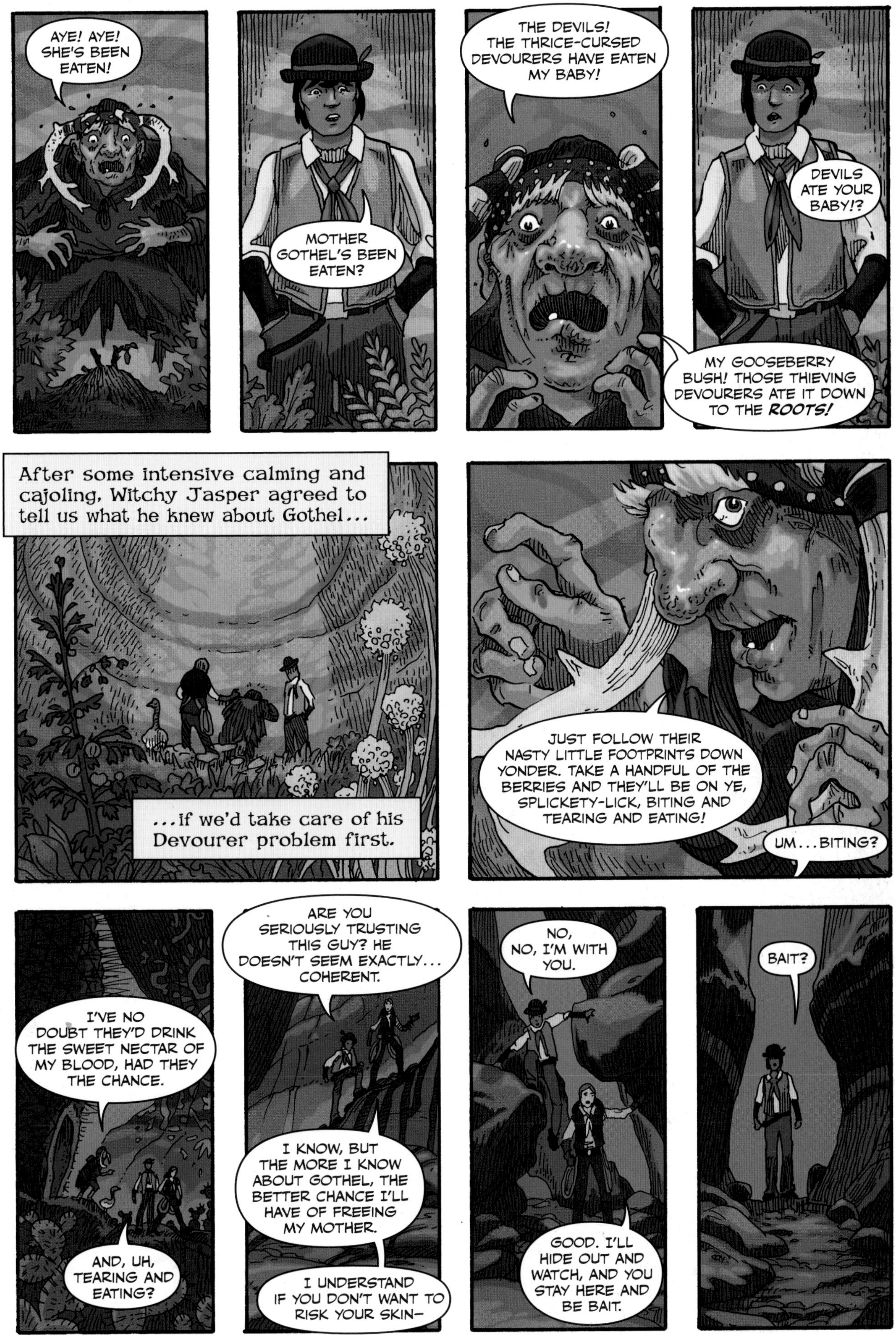
AYE! AYE! SHE'S BEEN EATEN!
MOTHER GOTHEL'S BEEN EATEN?
THE DEVILS! THE THRICE-CURSED DEVOURERS HAVE EATEN MY BABY!
DEVILS ATE YOUR BABY!?
MY GOOSEBERRY BUSH! THOSE THIEVING DEVOURERS ATE IT DOWN TO THE ROOTS!
After some intensive calming and cajoling, Witchy Jasper agreed to tell us what he knew about Gothel...
...if we'd take care of his Devourer problem first.
JUST FOLLOW THEIR NASTY LITTLE FOOTPRINTS DOWN YONDER. TAKE A HANDFUL OF THE BERRIES AND THEY'LL BE ON YE, SPLICKETY-LICK, BITING AND TEARING AND EATING!
UM...BITING?
I'VE NO DOUBT THEY'D DRINK THE SWEET NECTAR OF MY BLOOD, HAD THEY THE CHANCE.
AND, UH, TEARING AND EATING?
ARE YOU SERIOUSLY TRUSTING THIS GUY? HE DOESN'T SEEM EXACTLY... COHERENT.
I KNOW, BUT THE MORE I KNOW ABOUT GOTHEL, THE BETTER CHANCE I'LL HAVE OF FREEING MY MOTHER.
I UNDERSTAND IF YOU DON'T WANT TO RISK YOUR SKIN–
NO, NO, I'M WITH YOU.
GOOD. I'LL HIDE OUT AND WATCH, AND YOU STAY HERE AND BE BAIT.
BAIT?

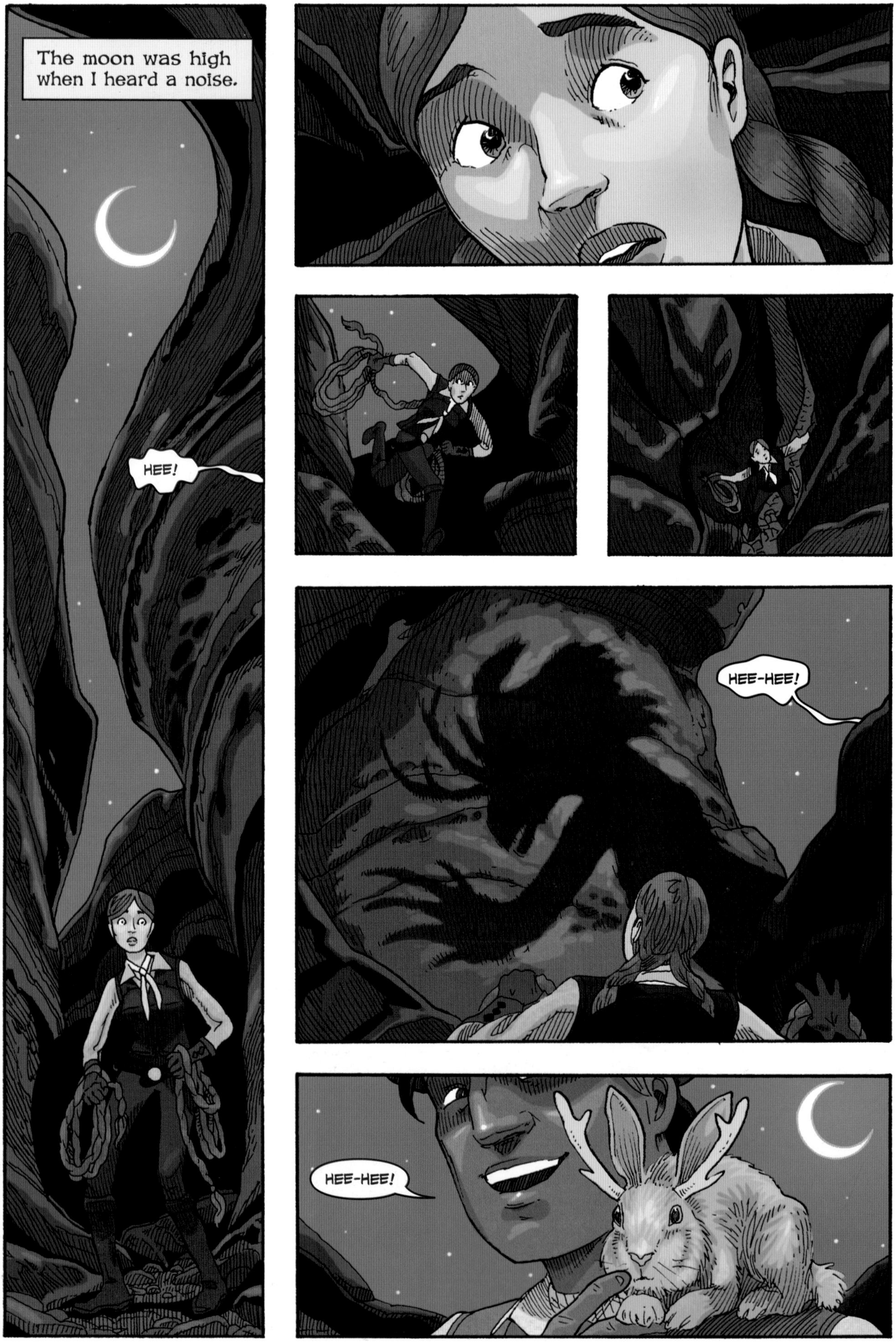
The moon was high when I heard a noise.
HEE!
HEE-HEE!
HEE-HEE!

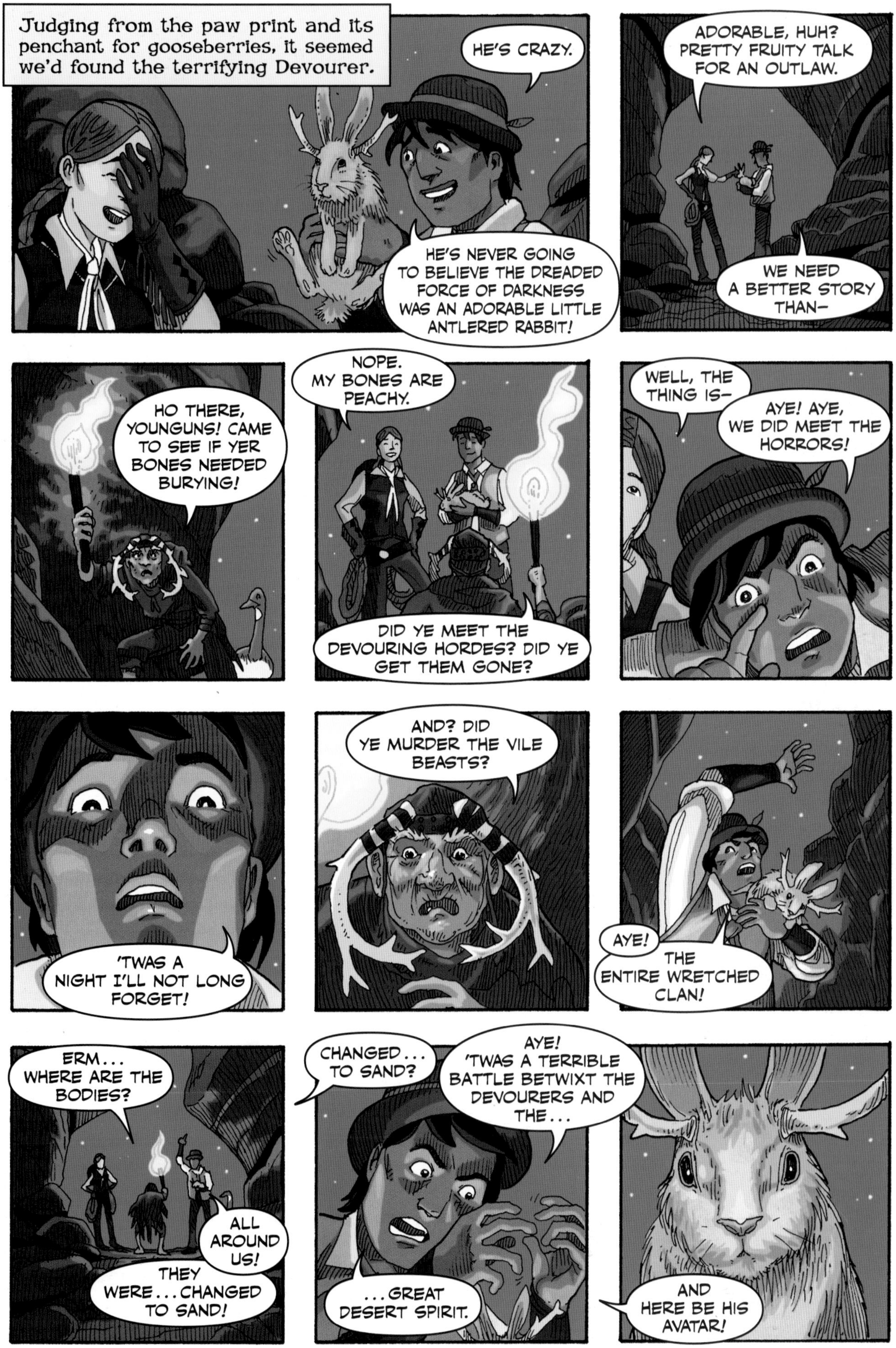
Judging from the paw print and its penchant for gooseberries, it seemed we'd found the terrifying Devourer.
HE'S CRAZY.
HE'S NEVER GOING TO BELIEVE THE DREADED FORCE OF DARKNESS WAS AN ADORABLE LITTLE ANTLERED RABBIT!
ADORABLE, HUH? PRETTY FRUITY TALK FOR AN OUTLAW.
WE NEED A BETTER STORY THAN–
HO THERE, YOUNGUNS! CAME TO SEE IF YER BONES NEEDED BURYING!
NOPE. MY BONES ARE PEACHY.
DID YE MEET THE DEVOURING HORDES? DID YE GET THEM GONE?
WELL, THE THING IS–
AYE! AYE, WE DID MEET THE HORRORS!
'TWAS A NIGHT I'LL NOT LONG FORGET!
AND? DID YE MURDER THE VILE BEASTS?
AYE!
THE ENTIRE WRETCHED CLAN!
ERM... WHERE ARE THE BODIES?
ALL AROUND US!
THEY WERE... CHANGED TO SAND!
CHANGED... TO SAND?
AYE! 'TWAS A TERRIBLE BATTLE BETWIXT THE DEVOURERS AND THE...
...GREAT DESERT SPIRIT.
AND HERE BE HIS AVATAR!

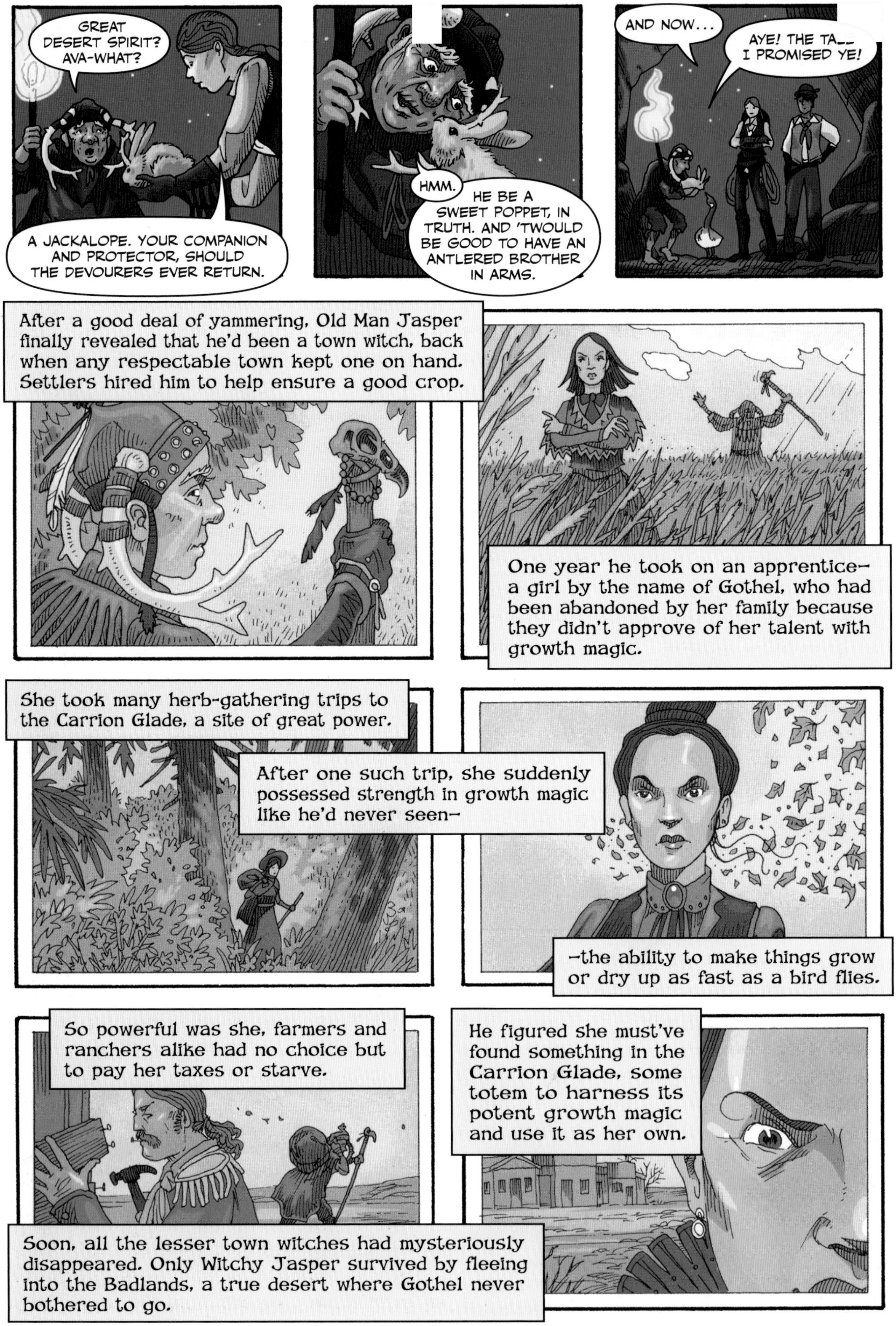
GREAT DESERT SPIRIT? AVA-WHAT?
A JACKALOPE. YOUR COMPANION AND PROTECTOR, SHOULD THE DEVOURERS EVER RETURN.
HMM.
HE BE A SWEET POPPET, IN TRUTH. AND 'TWOULD BE GOOD TO HAVE AN ANTLERED BROTHER IN ARMS.
AND NOW...
AYE! THE TA
I PROMISED YE!
After a good deal of yammering, Old Man Jasper finally revealed that he'd been a town witch, back when any respectable town kept one on hand. Settlers hired him to help ensure a good crop.
One year he took on an apprentice— a girl by the name of Gothel, who had been abandoned by her family because they didn't approve of her talent with growth magic.
She took many herb-gathering trips to the Carrion Glade, a site of great power.
After one such trip, she suddenly possessed strength in growth magic like he'd never seen—
—the ability to make things grow or dry up as fast as a bird flies.
So powerful was she, farmers and ranchers alike had no choice but to pay her taxes or starve.
He figured she must've found something in the Carrion Glade, some totem to harness its potent growth magic and use it as her own.
Soon, all the lesser town witches had mysteriously disappeared. Only Witchy Jasper survived by fleeing into the Badlands, a true desert where Gothel never bothered to go.

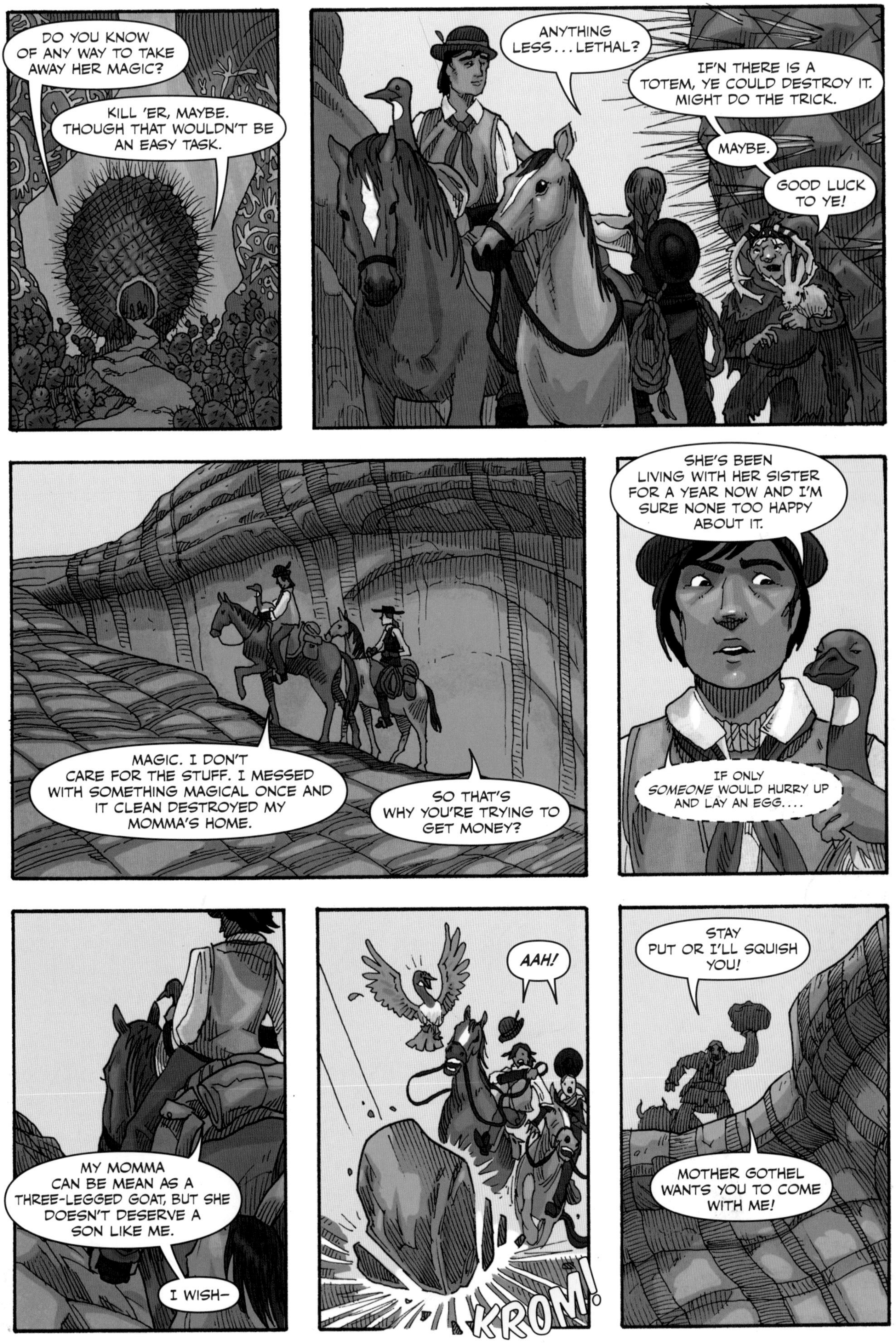
DO YOU KNOW OF ANY WAY TO TAKE AWAY HER MAGIC?
KILL 'ER, MAYBE. THOUGH THAT WOULDN'T BE AN EASY TASK.
ANYTHING LESS... LETHAL?
IF'N THERE IS A TOTEM, YE COULD DESTROY IT. MIGHT DO THE TRICK.
MAYBE.
GOOD LUCK TO YE!
MAGIC. I DON'T CARE FOR THE STUFF. I MESSED WITH SOMETHING MAGICAL ONCE AND IT CLEAN DESTROYED MY MOMMA'S HOME.
SO THAT'S WHY YOU'RE TRYING TO GET MONEY?
SHE'S BEEN LIVING WITH HER SISTER FOR A YEAR NOW AND I'M SURE NONE TOO HAPPY ABOUT IT.
IF ONLY *SOMEONE* WOULD HURRY UP AND LAY AN EGG....
MY MOMMA CAN BE MEAN AS A THREE-LEGGED GOAT, BUT SHE DOESN'T DESERVE A SON LIKE ME.
I WISH–
AAH!
KROM!
STAY PUT OR I'LL SQUISH YOU!
MOTHER GOTHEL WANTS YOU TO COME WITH ME!

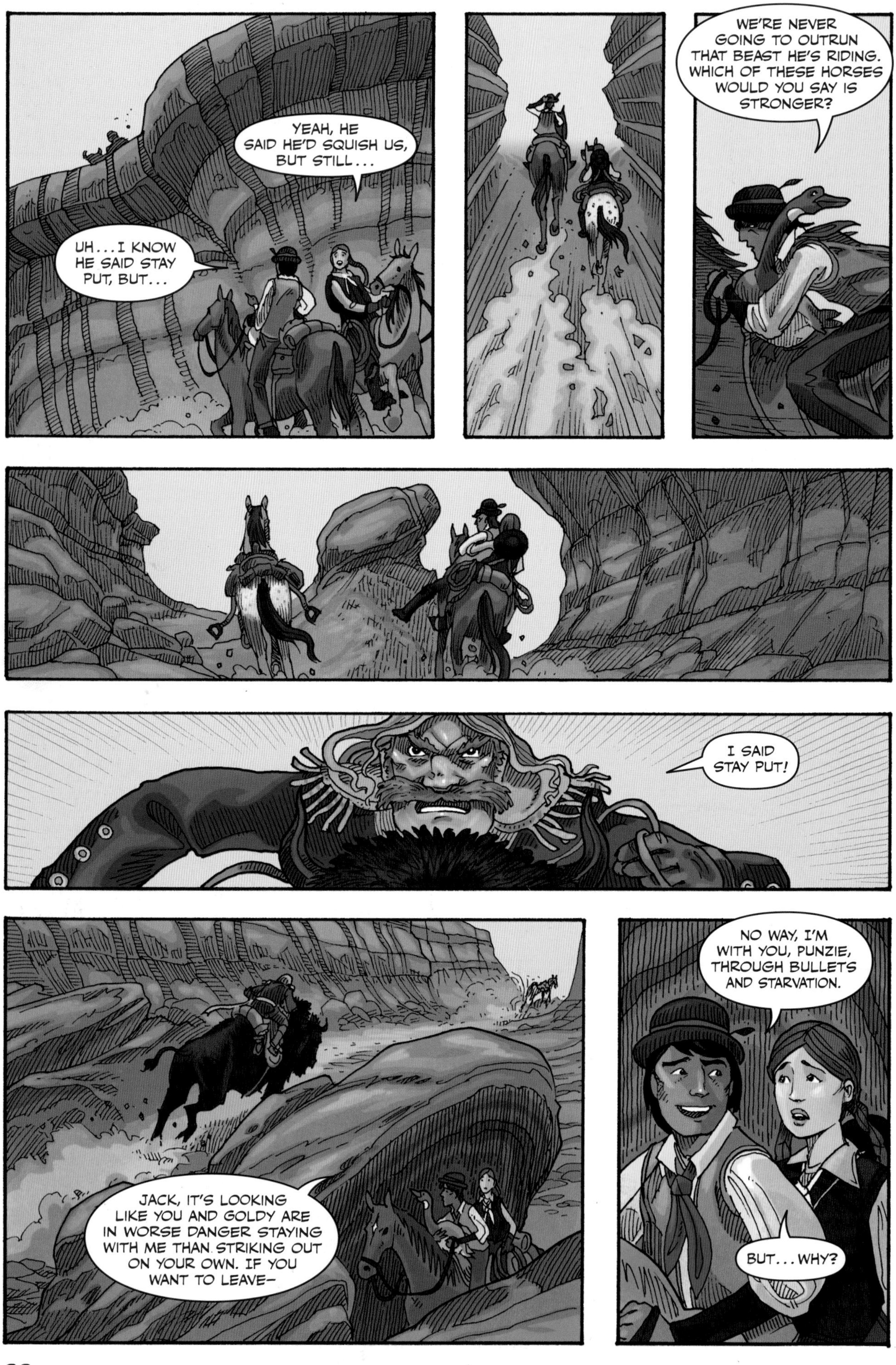
YEAH, HE SAID HE'D SQUISH US, BUT STILL...
UH...I KNOW HE SAID STAY PUT, BUT...
WE'RE NEVER GOING TO OUTRUN THAT BEAST HE'S RIDING. WHICH OF THESE HORSES WOULD YOU SAY IS STRONGER?
I SAID STAY PUT!
JACK, IT'S LOOKING LIKE YOU AND GOLDY ARE IN WORSE DANGER STAYING WITH ME THAN STRIKING OUT ON YOUR OWN. IF YOU WANT TO LEAVE–
NO WAY, I'M WITH YOU, PUNZIE, THROUGH BULLETS AND STARVATION.
BUT...WHY?

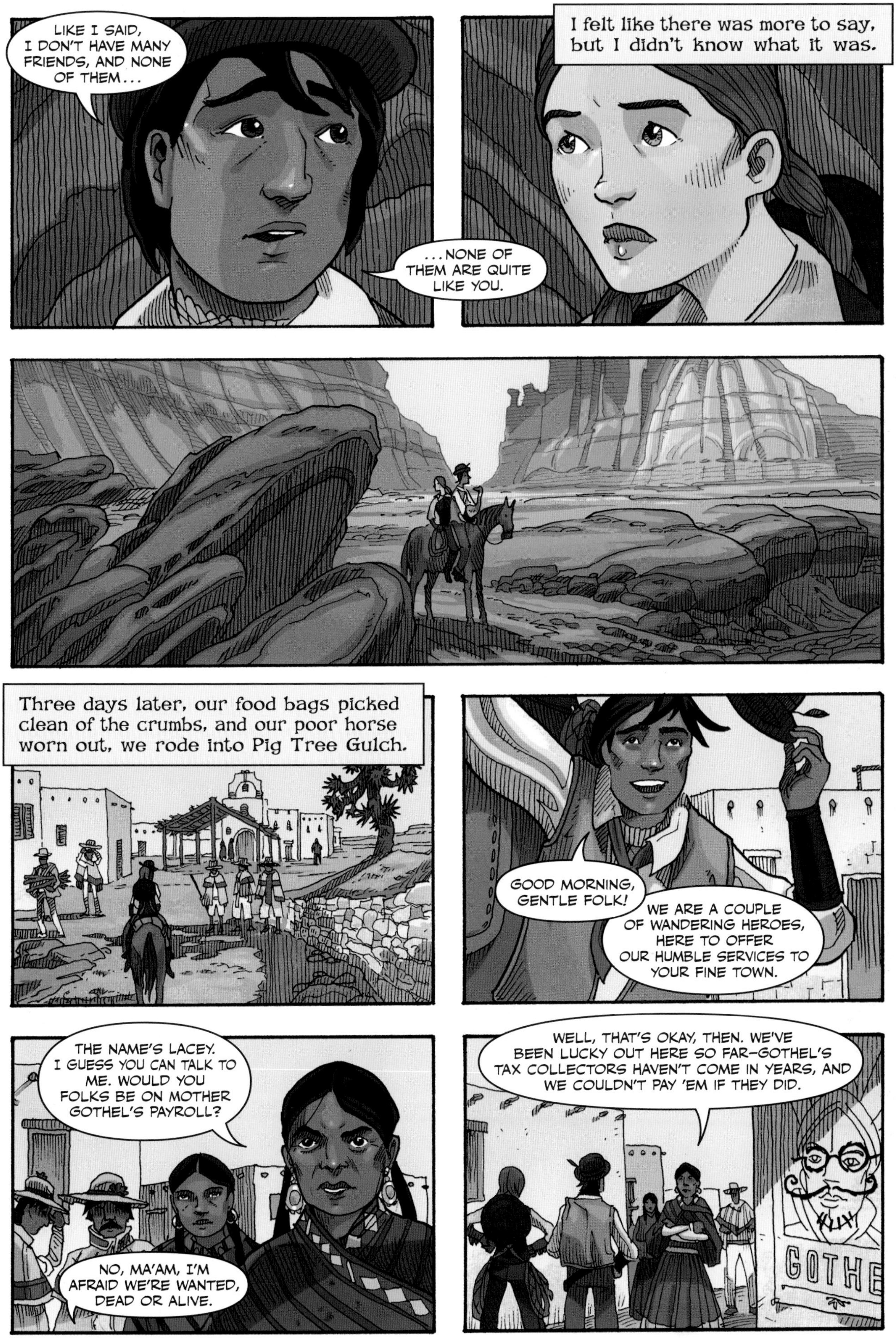
LIKE I SAID, I DON'T HAVE MANY FRIENDS, AND NONE OF THEM...
...NONE OF THEM ARE QUITE LIKE YOU.
I felt like there was more to say, but I didn't know what it was.
Three days later, our food bags picked clean of the crumbs, and our poor horse worn out, we rode into Pig Tree Gulch.
GOOD MORNING, GENTLE FOLK!
WE ARE A COUPLE OF WANDERING HEROES, HERE TO OFFER OUR HUMBLE SERVICES TO YOUR FINE TOWN.
THE NAME'S LACEY. I GUESS YOU CAN TALK TO ME. WOULD YOU FOLKS BE ON MOTHER GOTHEL'S PAYROLL?
NO, MA'AM, I'M AFRAID WE'RE WANTED, DEAD OR ALIVE.
WELL, THAT'S OKAY, THEN. WE'VE BEEN LUCKY OUT HERE SO FAR—GOTHEL'S TAX COLLECTORS HAVEN'T COME IN YEARS, AND WE COULDN'T PAY 'EM IF THEY DID.
GOTHE

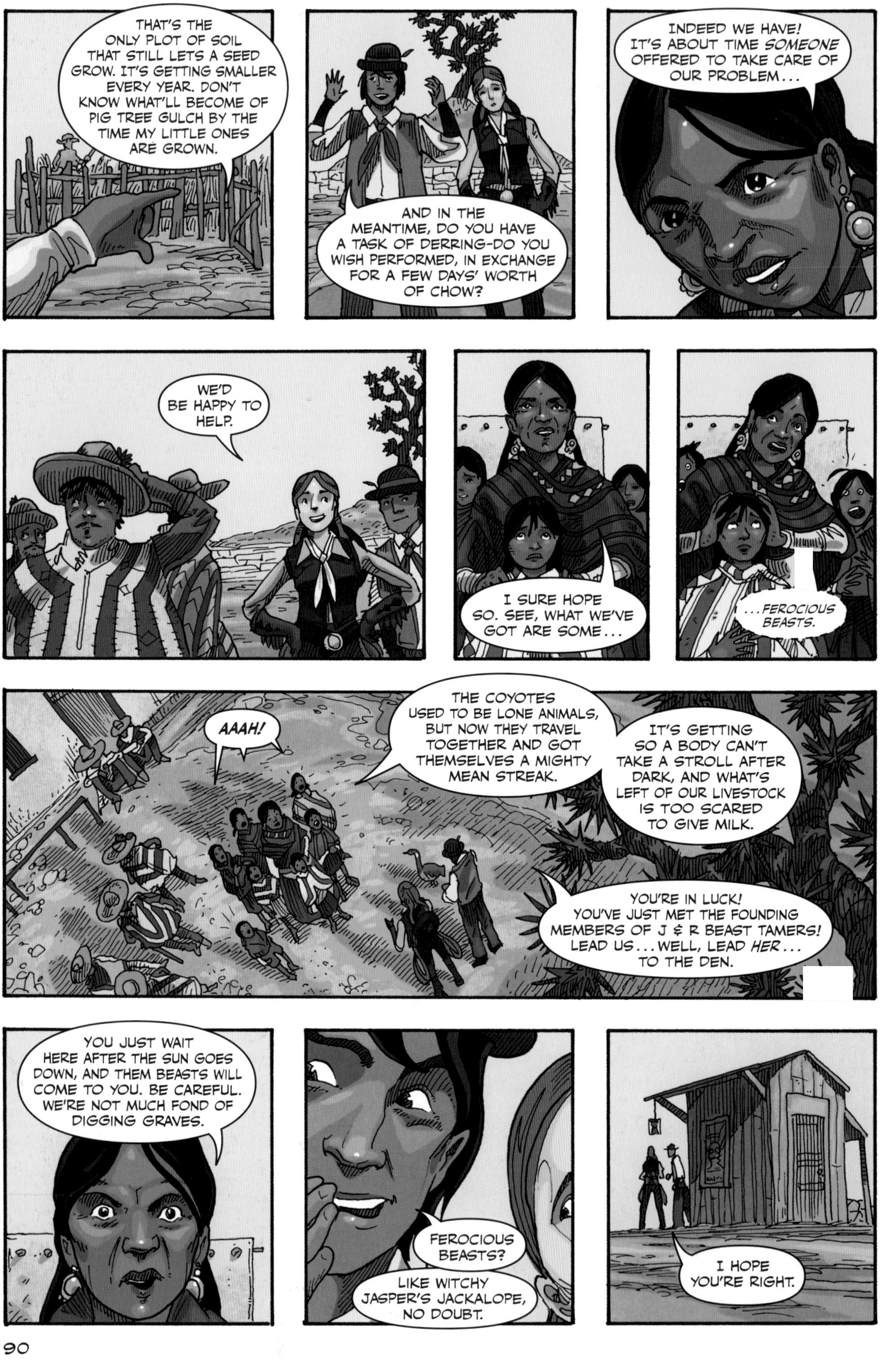
THAT'S THE ONLY PLOT OF SOIL THAT STILL LETS A SEED GROW. IT'S GETTING SMALLER EVERY YEAR. DON'T KNOW WHAT'LL BECOME OF PIG TREE GULCH BY THE TIME MY LITTLE ONES ARE GROWN.
AND IN THE MEANTIME, DO YOU HAVE A TASK OF DERRING-DO YOU WISH PERFORMED, IN EXCHANGE FOR A FEW DAYS' WORTH OF CHOW?
INDEED WE HAVE! IT'S ABOUT TIME *SOMEONE* OFFERED TO TAKE CARE OF OUR PROBLEM...
WE'D BE HAPPY TO HELP.
I SURE HOPE SO. SEE, WHAT WE'VE GOT ARE SOME...
...*FEROCIOUS BEASTS.*
AAAH!
THE COYOTES USED TO BE LONE ANIMALS, BUT NOW THEY TRAVEL TOGETHER AND GOT THEMSELVES A MIGHTY MEAN STREAK.
IT'S GETTING SO A BODY CAN'T TAKE A STROLL AFTER DARK, AND WHAT'S LEFT OF OUR LIVESTOCK IS TOO SCARED TO GIVE MILK.
YOU'RE IN LUCK! YOU'VE JUST MET THE FOUNDING MEMBERS OF J & R BEAST TAMERS! LEAD US...WELL, LEAD *HER*... TO THE DEN.
YOU JUST WAIT HERE AFTER THE SUN GOES DOWN, AND THEM BEASTS WILL COME TO YOU. BE CAREFUL. WE'RE NOT MUCH FOND OF DIGGING GRAVES.
FEROCIOUS BEASTS?
LIKE WITCHY JASPER'S JACKALOPE, NO DOUBT.
I HOPE YOU'RE RIGHT.

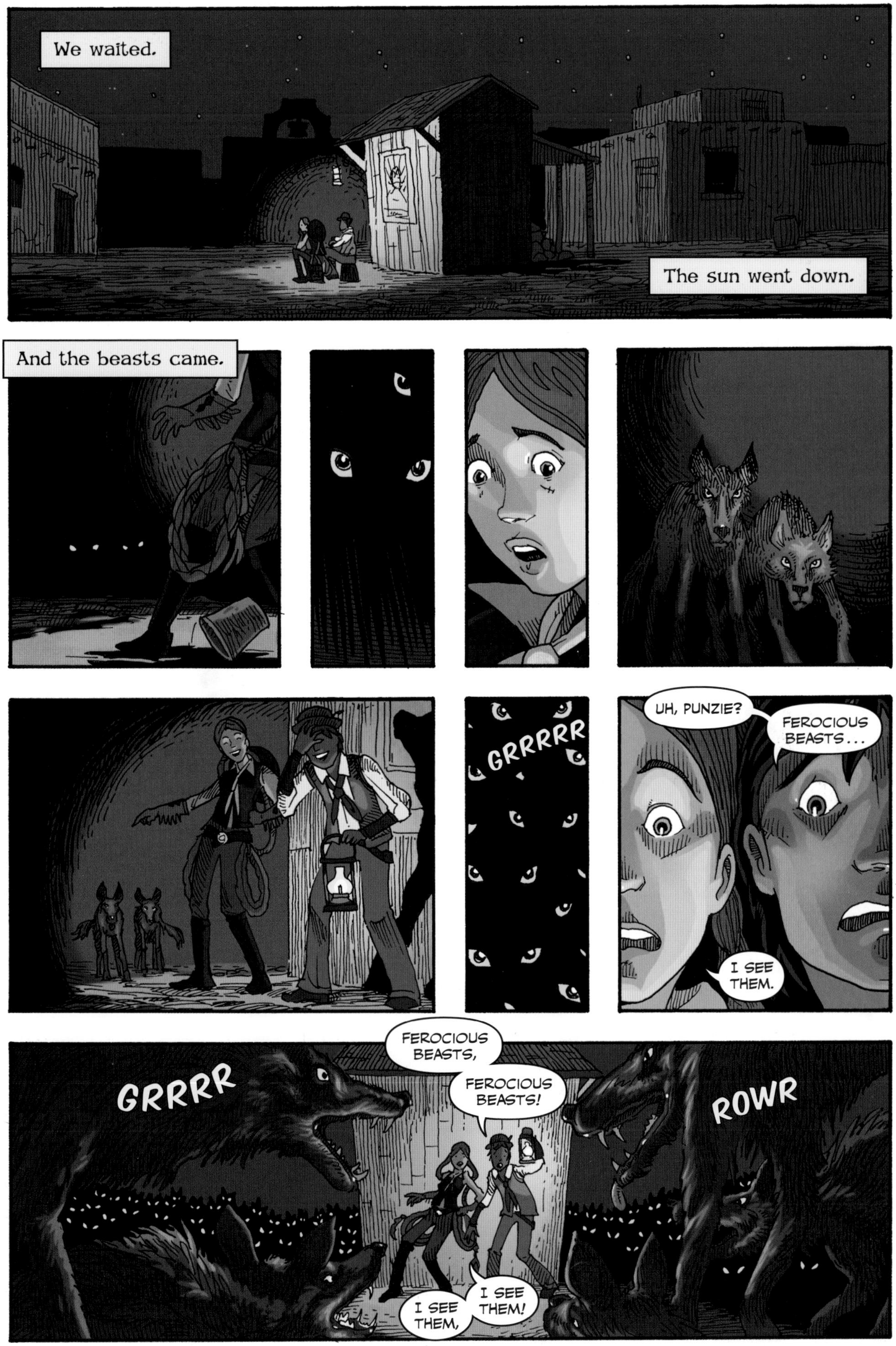
We waited.
The sun went down.
And the beasts came.
GRRRRR
UH, PUNZIE?
FEROCIOUS BEASTS...
I SEE THEM.
GRRRR
FEROCIOUS BEASTS,
FEROCIOUS BEASTS!
ROWR
I SEE THEM,
I SEE THEM!

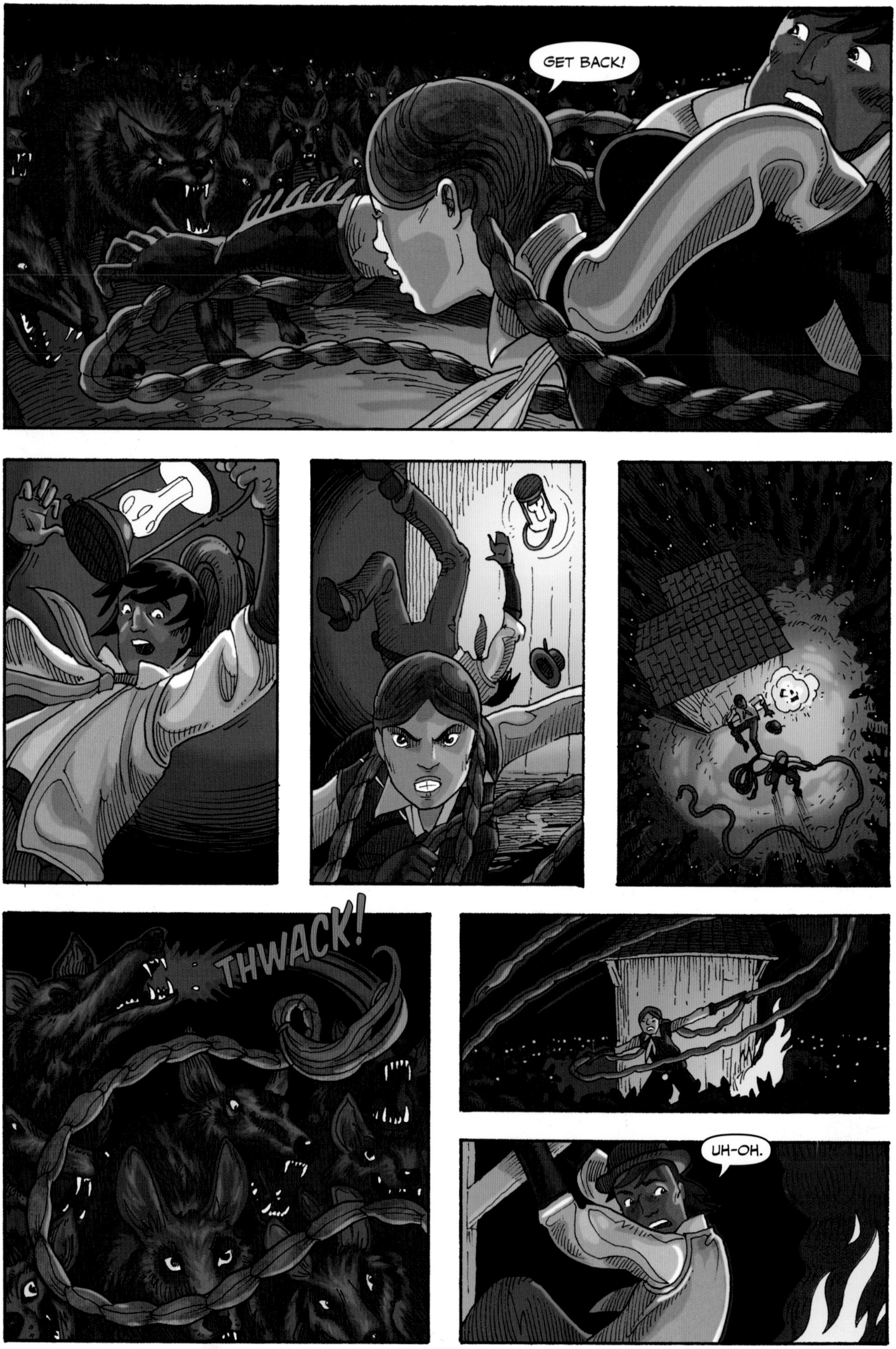
GET BACK!
THWACK!
UH-OH.

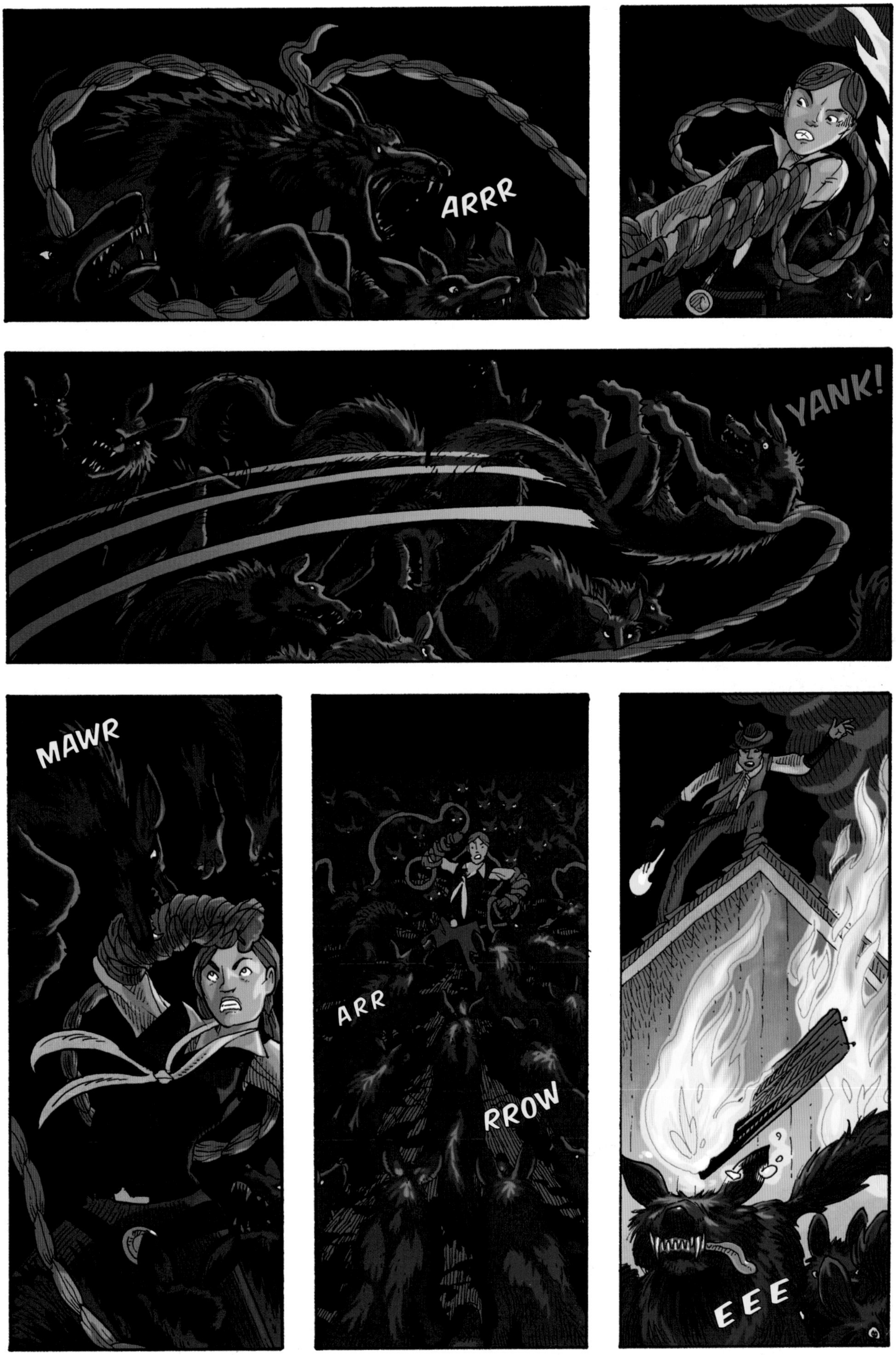
ARRR
YANK!
MAWR
ARR
RROW
EEE

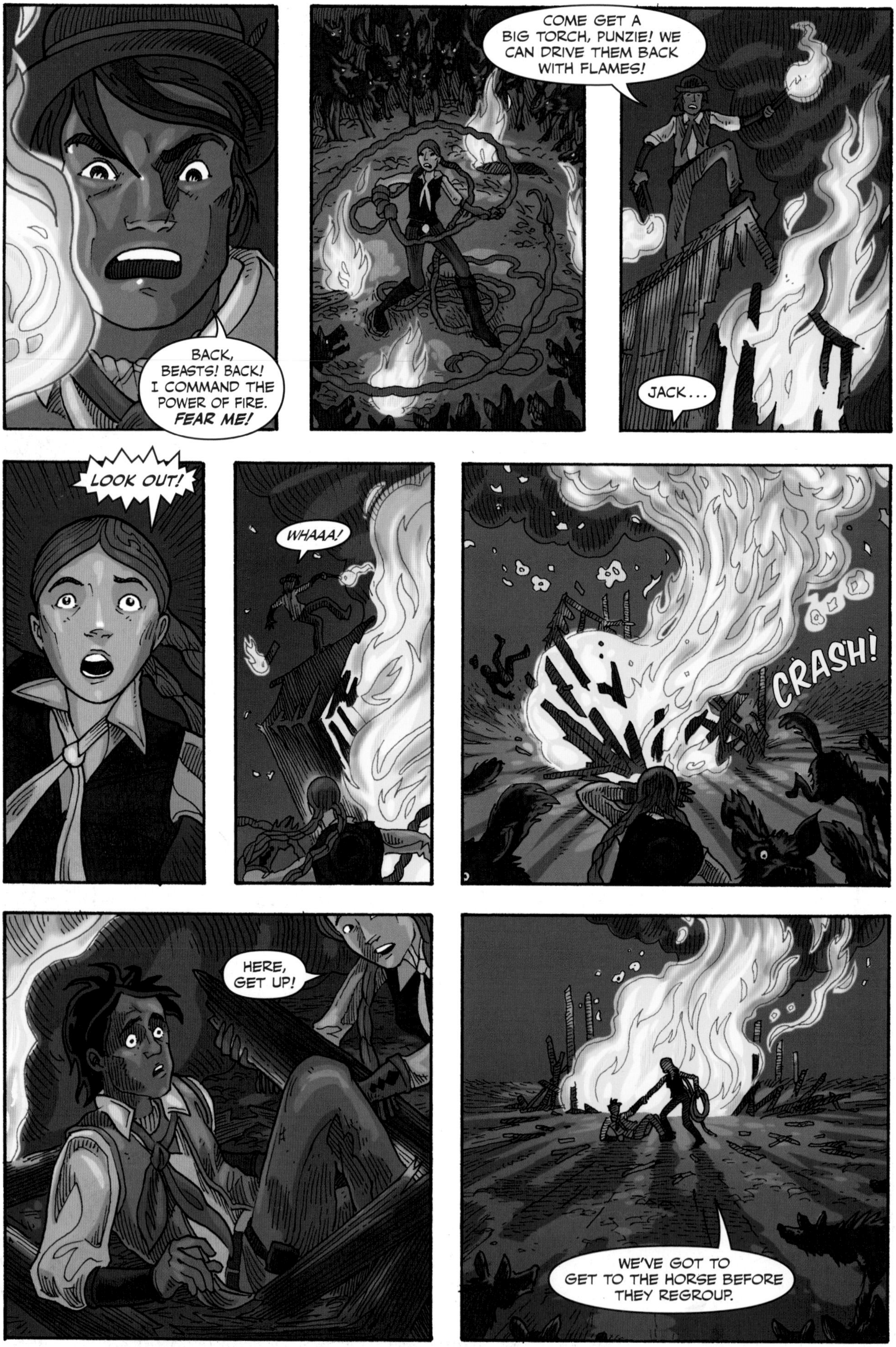
BACK, BEASTS! BACK! I COMMAND THE POWER OF FIRE. FEAR ME!
COME GET A BIG TORCH, PUNZIE! WE CAN DRIVE THEM BACK WITH FLAMES!
JACK...
LOOK OUT!
WHAAA!
CRASH!
HERE, GET UP!
WE'VE GOT TO GET TO THE HORSE BEFORE THEY REGROUP.

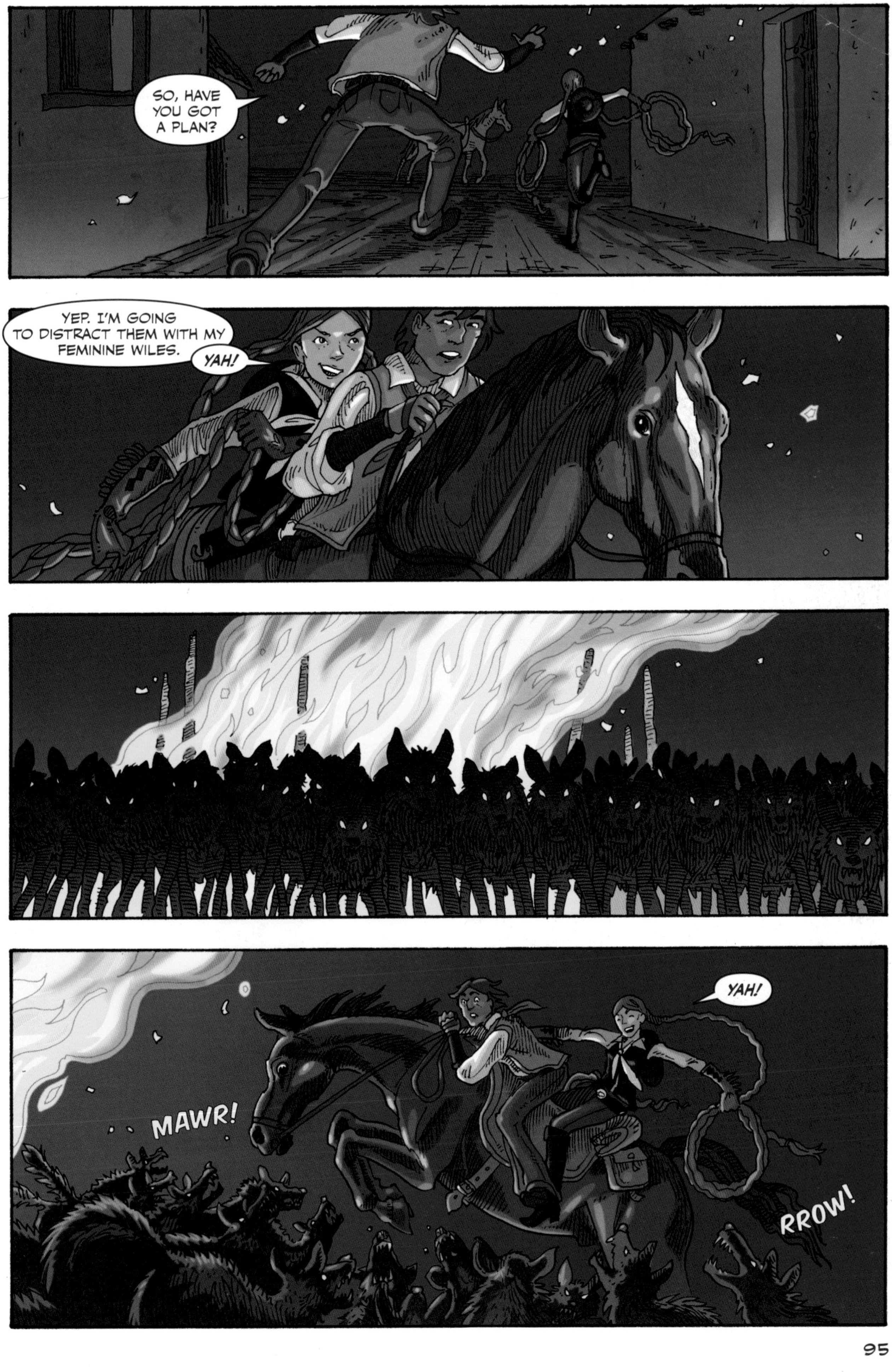
SO, HAVE YOU GOT A PLAN?
YEP. I'M GOING TO DISTRACT THEM WITH MY FEMININE WILES.
YAH!
YAH!
MAWR!
RROW!

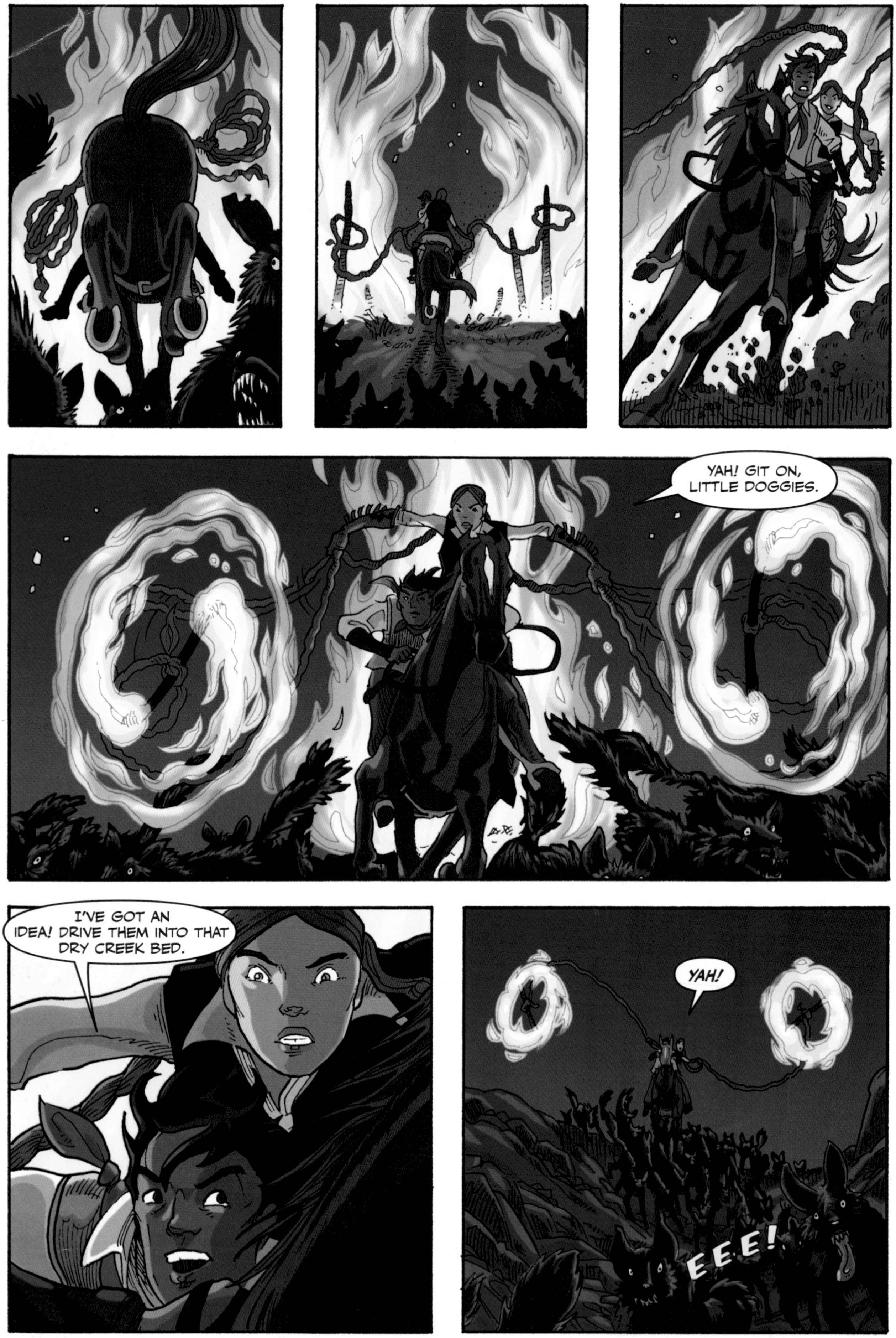
YAH! GIT ON, LITTLE DOGGIES.
I'VE GOT AN IDEA! DRIVE THEM INTO THAT DRY CREEK BED.
YAH!
EEE!

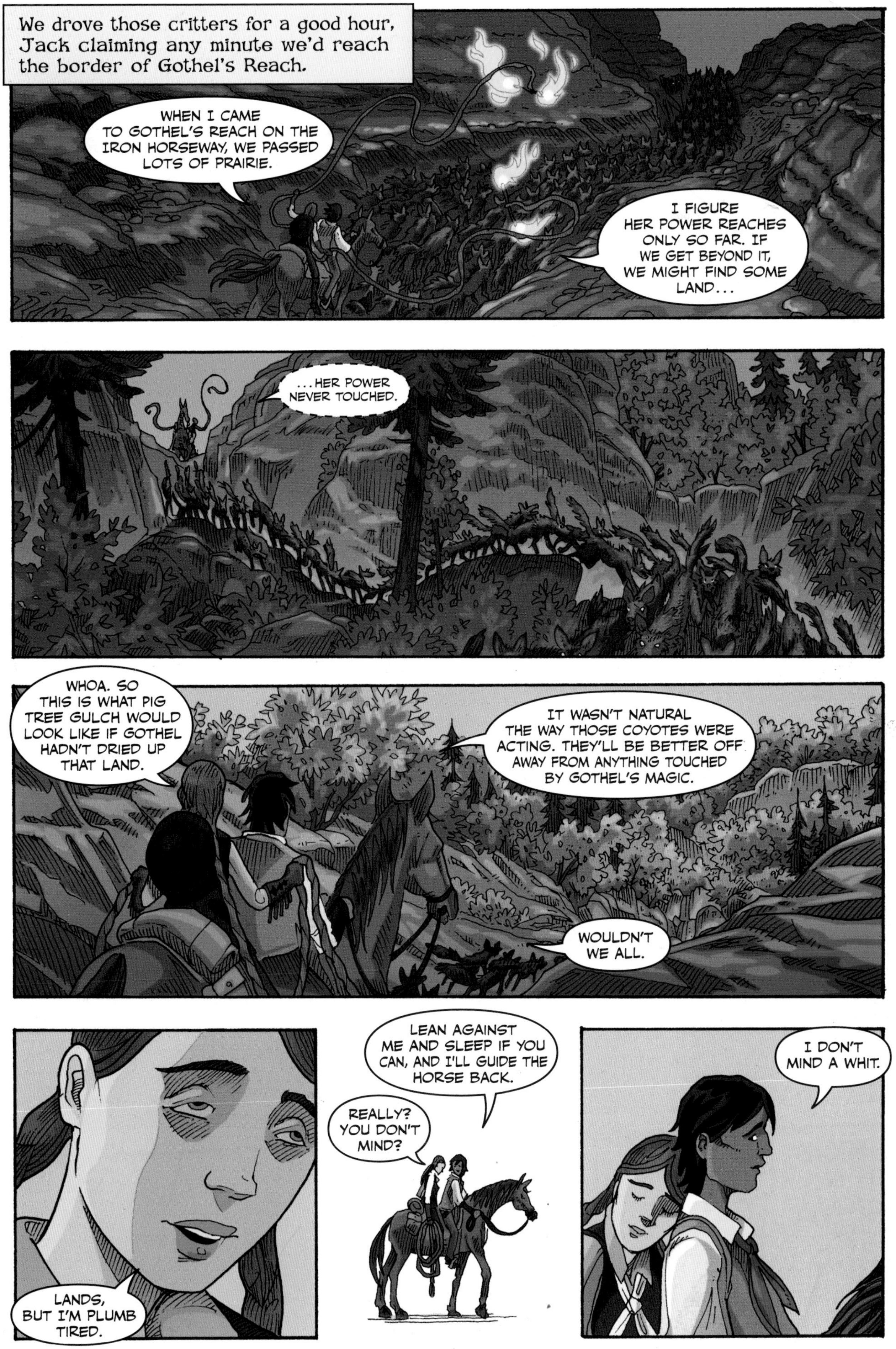
We drove those critters for a good hour, Jack claiming any minute we'd reach the border of Gothel's Reach.
WHEN I CAME TO GOTHEL'S REACH ON THE IRON HORSEWAY, WE PASSED LOTS OF PRAIRIE.
I FIGURE HER POWER REACHES ONLY SO FAR. IF WE GET BEYOND IT, WE MIGHT FIND SOME LAND...
...HER POWER NEVER TOUCHED.
WHOA. SO THIS IS WHAT PIG TREE GULCH WOULD LOOK LIKE IF GOTHEL HADN'T DRIED UP THAT LAND.
IT WASN'T NATURAL THE WAY THOSE COYOTES WERE ACTING. THEY'LL BE BETTER OFF AWAY FROM ANYTHING TOUCHED BY GOTHEL'S MAGIC.
WOULDN'T WE ALL.
LANDS, BUT I'M PLUMB TIRED.
LEAN AGAINST ME AND SLEEP IF YOU CAN, AND I'LL GUIDE THE HORSE BACK.
REALLY? YOU DON'T MIND?
I DON'T MIND A WHIT.

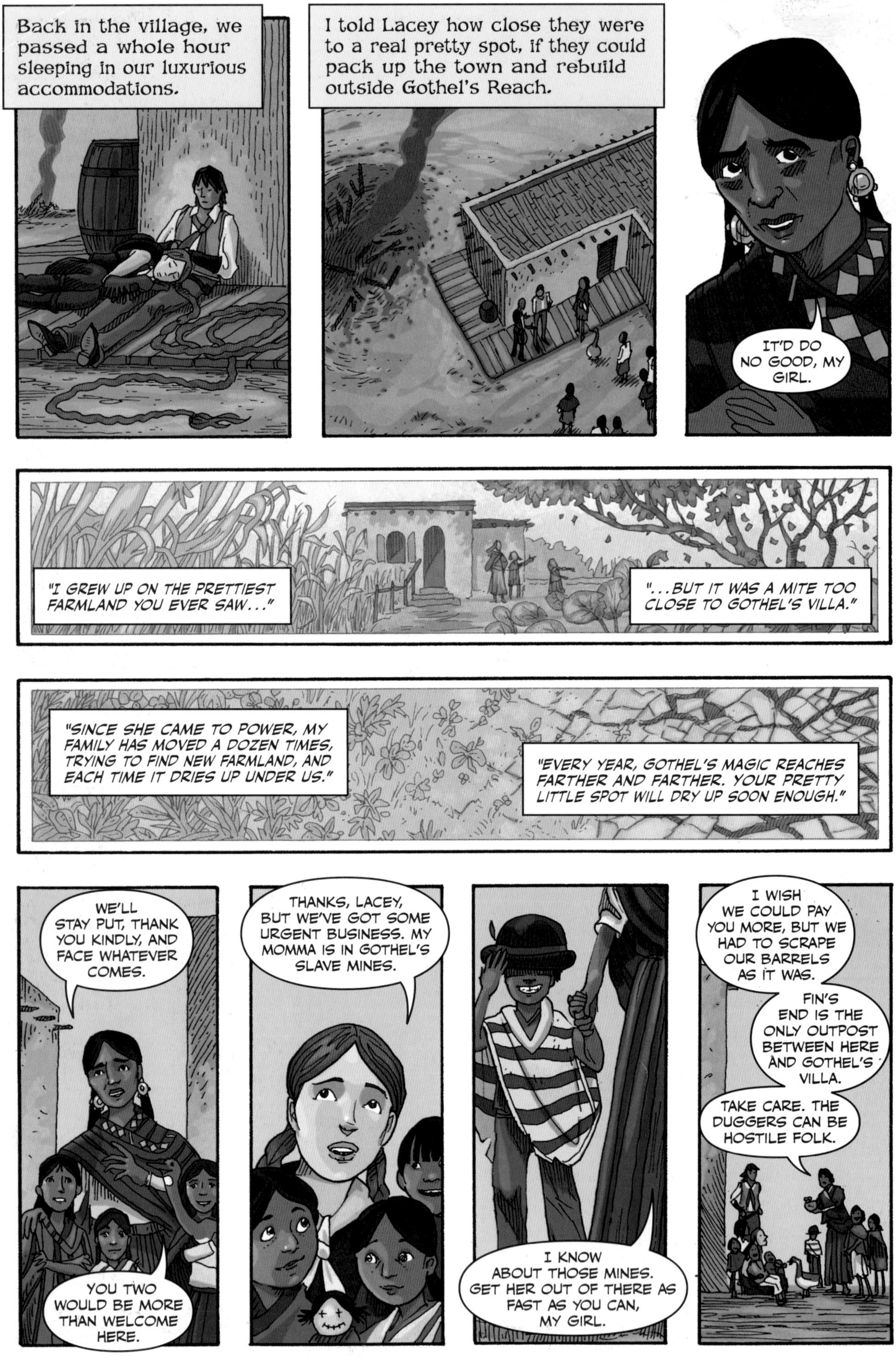
Back in the village, we passed a whole hour sleeping in our luxurious accommodations.
I told Lacey how close they were to a real pretty spot, if they could pack up the town and rebuild outside Gothel's Reach.
IT'D DO NO GOOD, MY GIRL.
"I GREW UP ON THE PRETTIEST FARMLAND YOU EVER SAW..."
"...BUT IT WAS A MITE TOO CLOSE TO GOTHEL'S VILLA."
"SINCE SHE CAME TO POWER, MY FAMILY HAS MOVED A DOZEN TIMES, TRYING TO FIND NEW FARMLAND, AND EACH TIME IT DRIES UP UNDER US."
"EVERY YEAR, GOTHEL'S MAGIC REACHES FARTHER AND FARTHER. YOUR PRETTY LITTLE SPOT WILL DRY UP SOON ENOUGH."
WE'LL STAY PUT, THANK YOU KINDLY, AND FACE WHATEVER COMES.
YOU TWO WOULD BE MORE THAN WELCOME HERE.
THANKS, LACEY, BUT WE'VE GOT SOME URGENT BUSINESS. MY MOMMA IS IN GOTHEL'S SLAVE MINES.
I KNOW ABOUT THOSE MINES. GET HER OUT OF THERE AS FAST AS YOU CAN, MY GIRL.
I WISH WE COULD PAY YOU MORE, BUT WE HAD TO SCRAPE OUR BARRELS AS IT WAS.
FIN'S END IS THE ONLY OUTPOST BETWEEN HERE AND GOTHEL'S VILLA.
TAKE CARE. THE DUGGERS CAN BE HOSTILE FOLK.

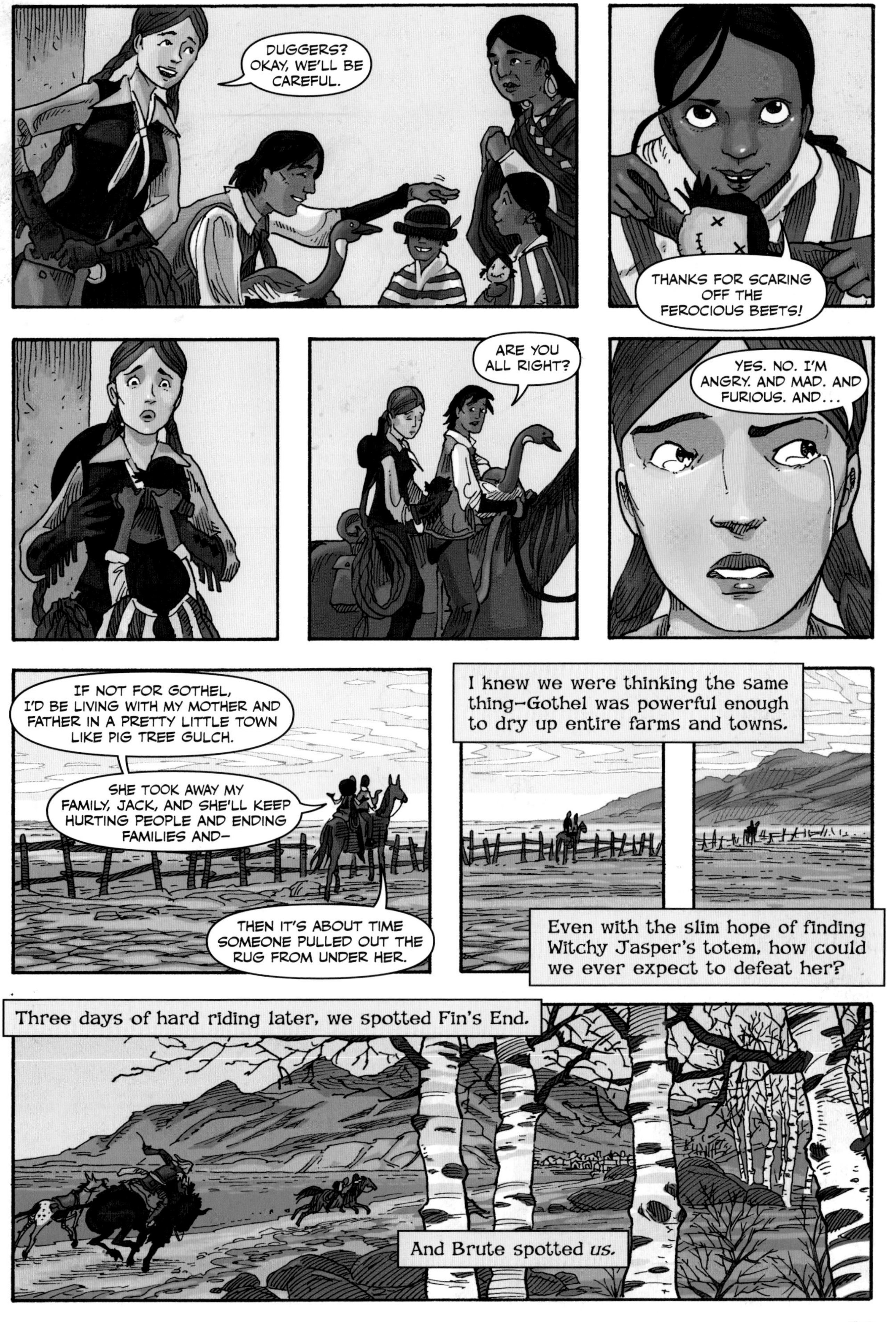
DUGGERS? OKAY, WE'LL BE CAREFUL.
THANKS FOR SCARING OFF THE FEROCIOUS BEETS!
ARE YOU ALL RIGHT?
YES. NO. I'M ANGRY. AND MAD. AND FURIOUS. AND...
IF NOT FOR GOTHEL, I'D BE LIVING WITH MY MOTHER AND FATHER IN A PRETTY LITTLE TOWN LIKE PIG TREE GULCH.
SHE TOOK AWAY MY FAMILY, JACK, AND SHE'LL KEEP HURTING PEOPLE AND ENDING FAMILIES AND–
THEN IT'S ABOUT TIME SOMEONE PULLED OUT THE RUG FROM UNDER HER.
I knew we were thinking the same thing–Gothel was powerful enough to dry up entire farms and towns.
Even with the slim hope of finding Witchy Jasper's totem, how could we ever expect to defeat her?
Three days of hard riding later, we spotted Fin's End.
And Brute spotted *us.*

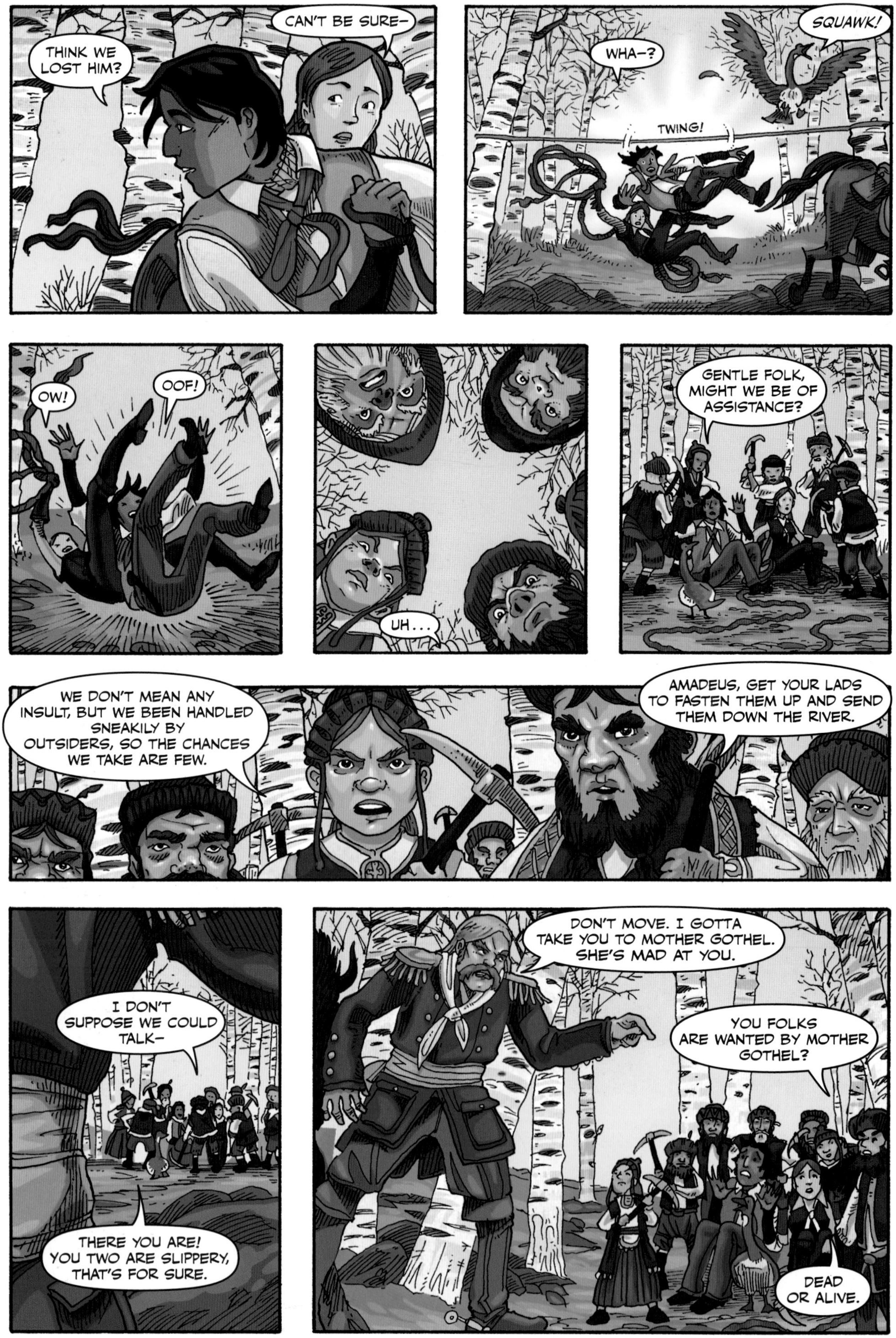
THINK WE LOST HIM?
CAN'T BE SURE–
WHA–?
SQUAWK!
TWING!
OW!
OOF!
UH...
GENTLE FOLK, MIGHT WE BE OF ASSISTANCE?
WE DON'T MEAN ANY INSULT, BUT WE BEEN HANDLED SNEAKILY BY OUTSIDERS, SO THE CHANCES WE TAKE ARE FEW.
AMADEUS, GET YOUR LADS TO FASTEN THEM UP AND SEND THEM DOWN THE RIVER.
I DON'T SUPPOSE WE COULD TALK–
THERE YOU ARE! YOU TWO ARE SLIPPERY, THAT'S FOR SURE.
DON'T MOVE. I GOTTA TAKE YOU TO MOTHER GOTHEL. SHE'S MAD AT YOU.
YOU FOLKS ARE WANTED BY MOTHER GOTHEL?
DEAD OR ALIVE.

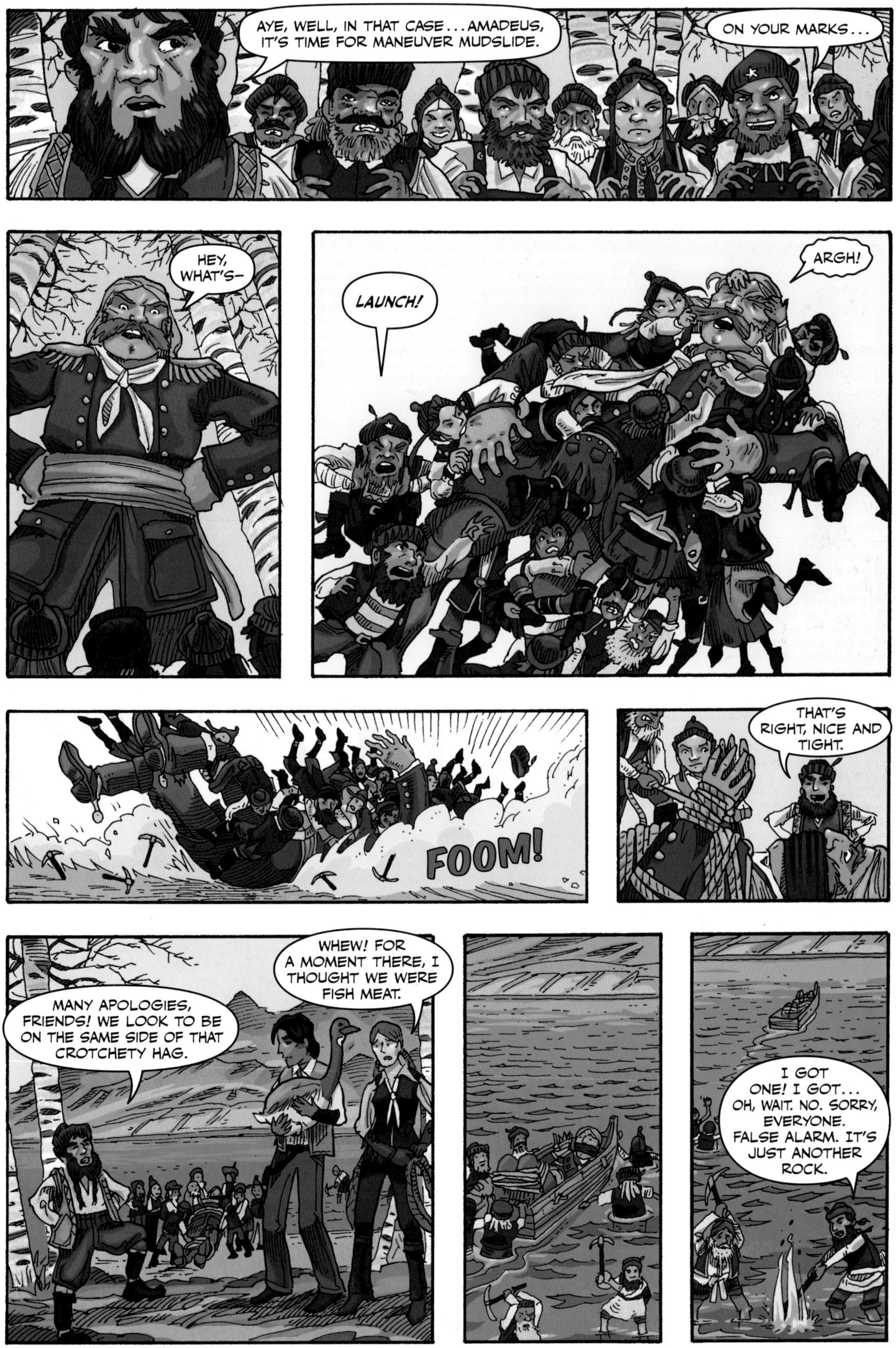
AYE, WELL, IN THAT CASE... AMADEUS, IT'S TIME FOR MANEUVER MUDSLIDE.
ON YOUR MARKS...
HEY, WHAT'S-
LAUNCH!
ARGH!
FOOM!
THAT'S RIGHT, NICE AND TIGHT.
WHEW! FOR A MOMENT THERE, I THOUGHT WE WERE FISH MEAT.
MANY APOLOGIES, FRIENDS! WE LOOK TO BE ON THE SAME SIDE OF THAT CROTCHETY HAG.
I GOT ONE! I GOT... OH, WAIT. NO. SORRY, EVERYONE. FALSE ALARM. IT'S JUST ANOTHER ROCK.

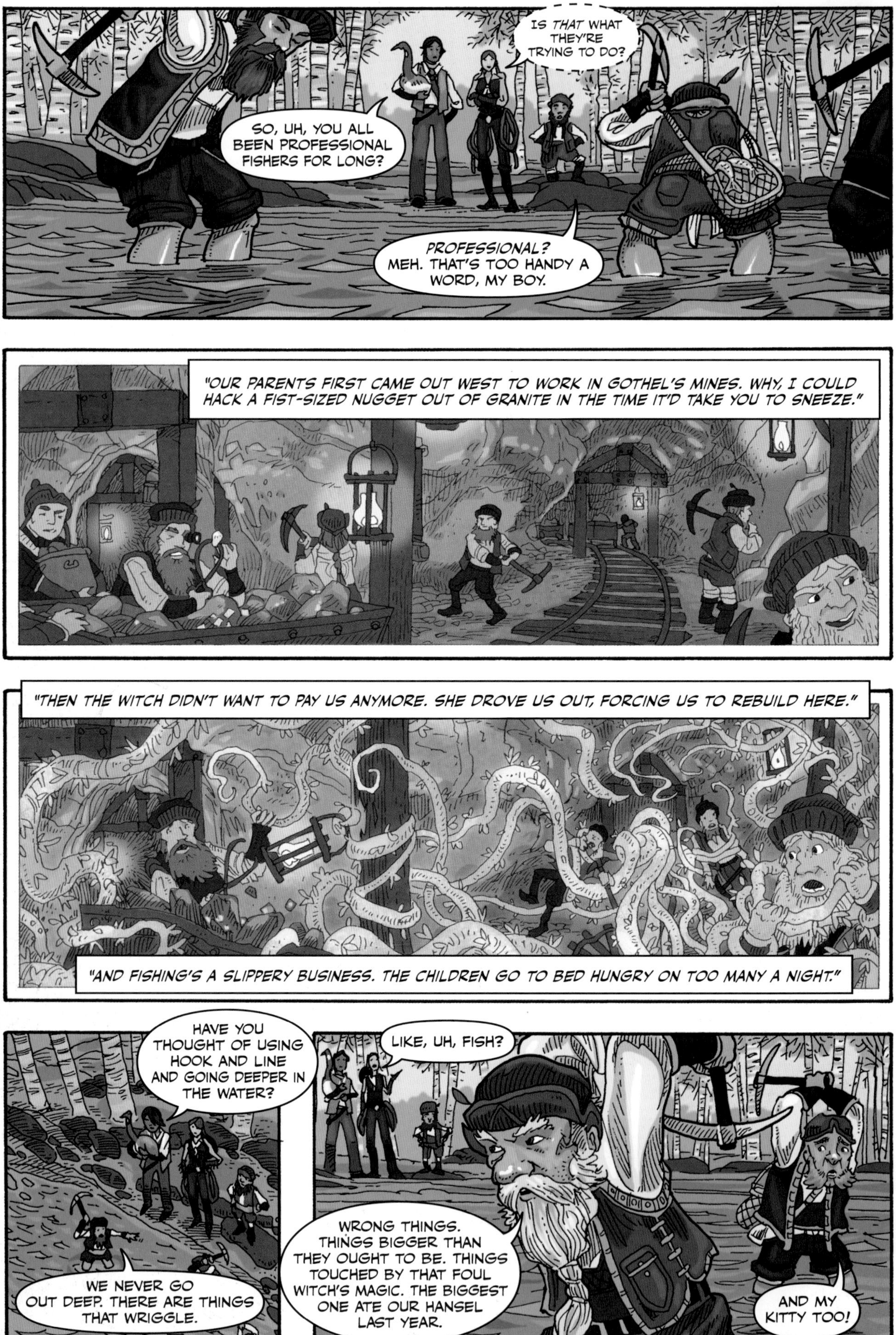

SO, UH, YOU ALL BEEN PROFESSIONAL FISHERS FOR LONG?
IS *THAT* WHAT THEY'RE TRYING TO DO?
PROFESSIONAL? MEH. THAT'S TOO HANDY A WORD, MY BOY.
"OUR PARENTS FIRST CAME OUT WEST TO WORK IN GOTHEL'S MINES. WHY, I COULD HACK A FIST-SIZED NUGGET OUT OF GRANITE IN THE TIME IT'D TAKE YOU TO SNEEZE."
"THEN THE WITCH DIDN'T WANT TO PAY US ANYMORE. SHE DROVE US OUT, FORCING US TO REBUILD HERE."
"AND FISHING'S A SLIPPERY BUSINESS. THE CHILDREN GO TO BED HUNGRY ON TOO MANY A NIGHT."
HAVE YOU THOUGHT OF USING HOOK AND LINE AND GOING DEEPER IN THE WATER?
WE NEVER GO OUT DEEP. THERE ARE THINGS THAT WRIGGLE.
LIKE, UH, FISH?
WRONG THINGS. THINGS BIGGER THAN THEY OUGHT TO BE. THINGS TOUCHED BY THAT FOUL WITCH'S MAGIC. THE BIGGEST ONE ATE OUR HANSEL LAST YEAR.
AND MY KITTY TOO!

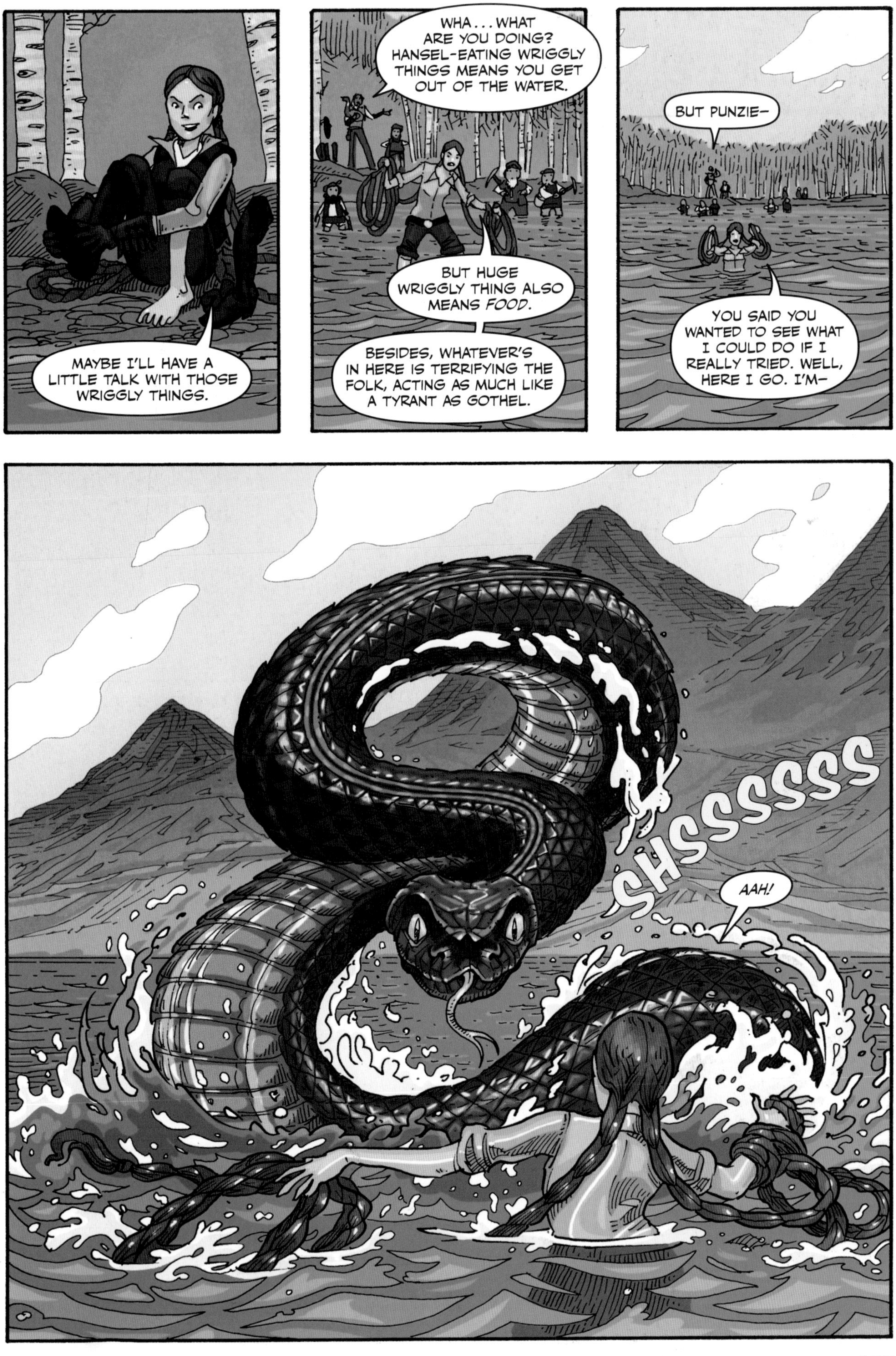
MAYBE I'LL HAVE A LITTLE TALK WITH THOSE WRIGGLY THINGS.
WHA... WHAT ARE YOU DOING? HANSEL-EATING WRIGGLY THINGS MEANS YOU GET OUT OF THE WATER.
BUT HUGE WRIGGLY THING ALSO MEANS *FOOD*.
BESIDES, WHATEVER'S IN HERE IS TERRIFYING THE FOLK, ACTING AS MUCH LIKE A TYRANT AS GOTHEL.
BUT PUNZIE–
YOU SAID YOU WANTED TO SEE WHAT I COULD DO IF I REALLY TRIED. WELL, HERE I GO. I'M–
SHSSSSSS
AAH!

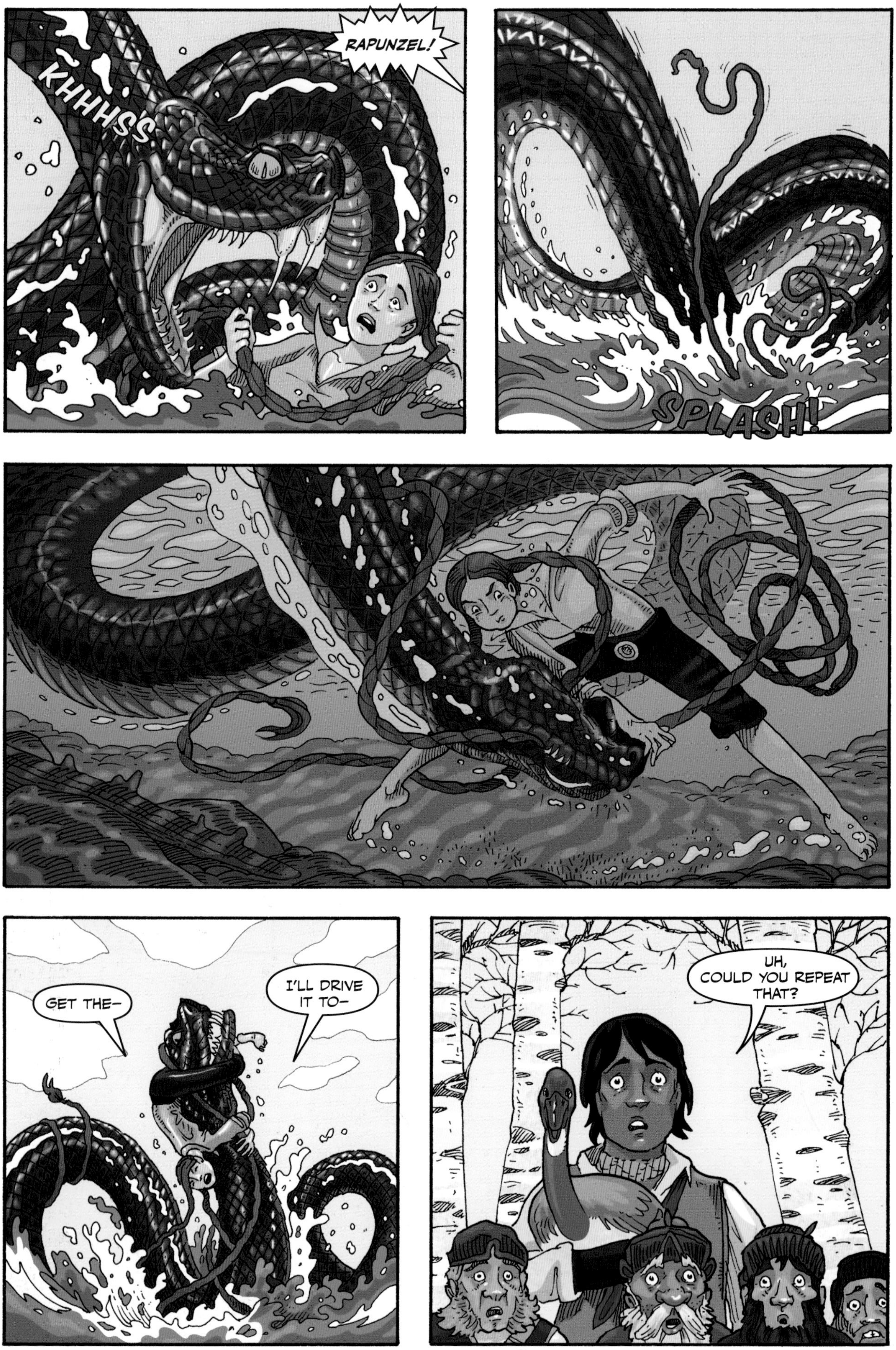
RAPUNZEL!
KHHHSS
SPLASH!
GET THE–
I'LL DRIVE IT TO–
UH, COULD YOU REPEAT THAT?

PICKAXES! SHE NEEDS BACKUP.

HOP TO IT, LADS AND LASSIES!

WITH YOUR PERMISSION, CAPTAIN, GIVE ME A LINE ONSHORE.

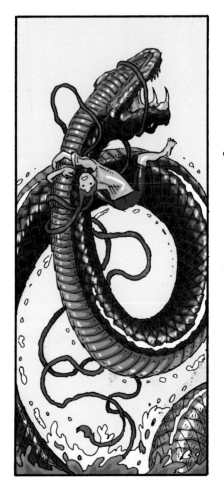

KHAAA

SPLISH

105

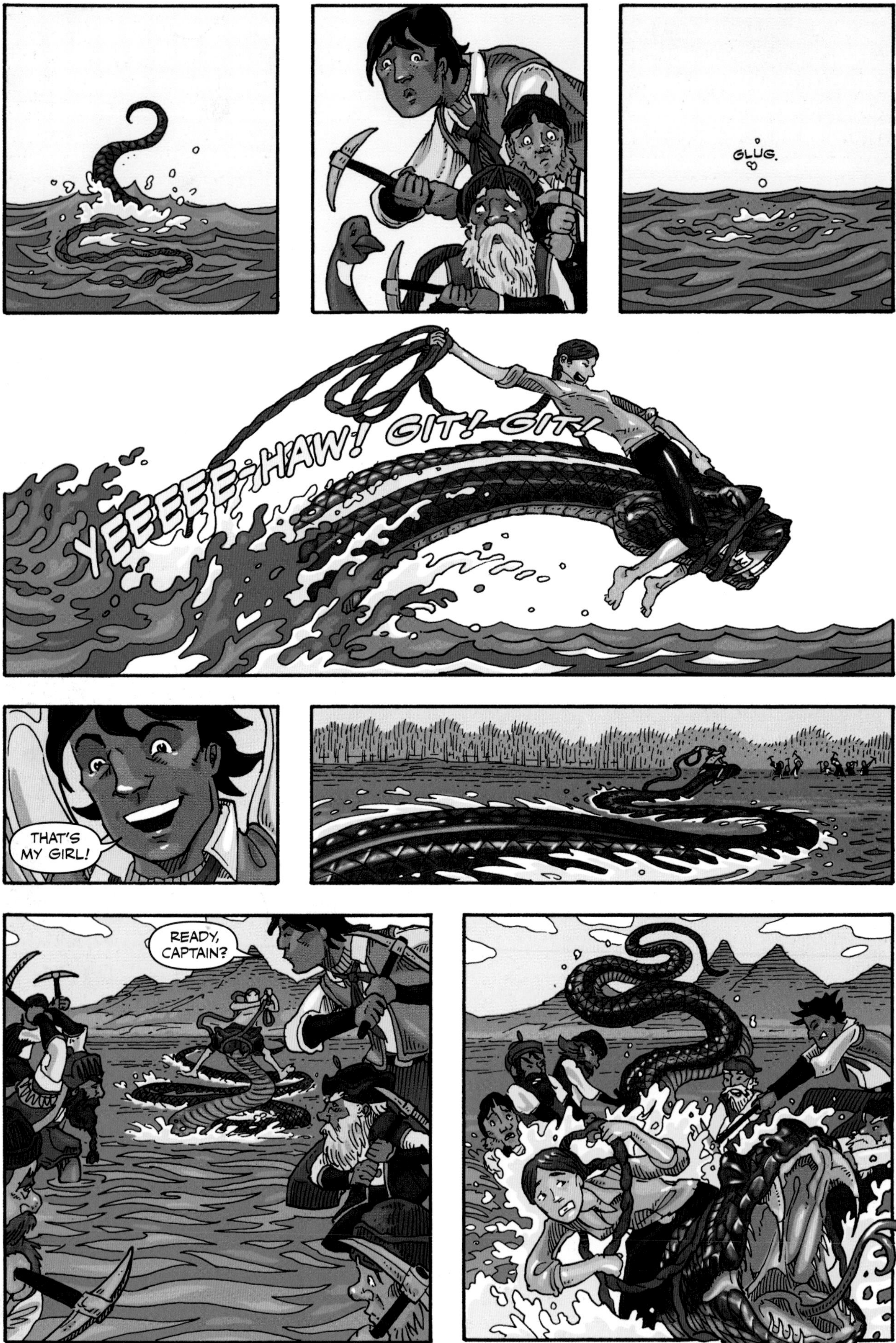
GLUG.
YEEEEEE-HAW! GIT! GIT!
THAT'S MY GIRL!
READY, CAPTAIN?

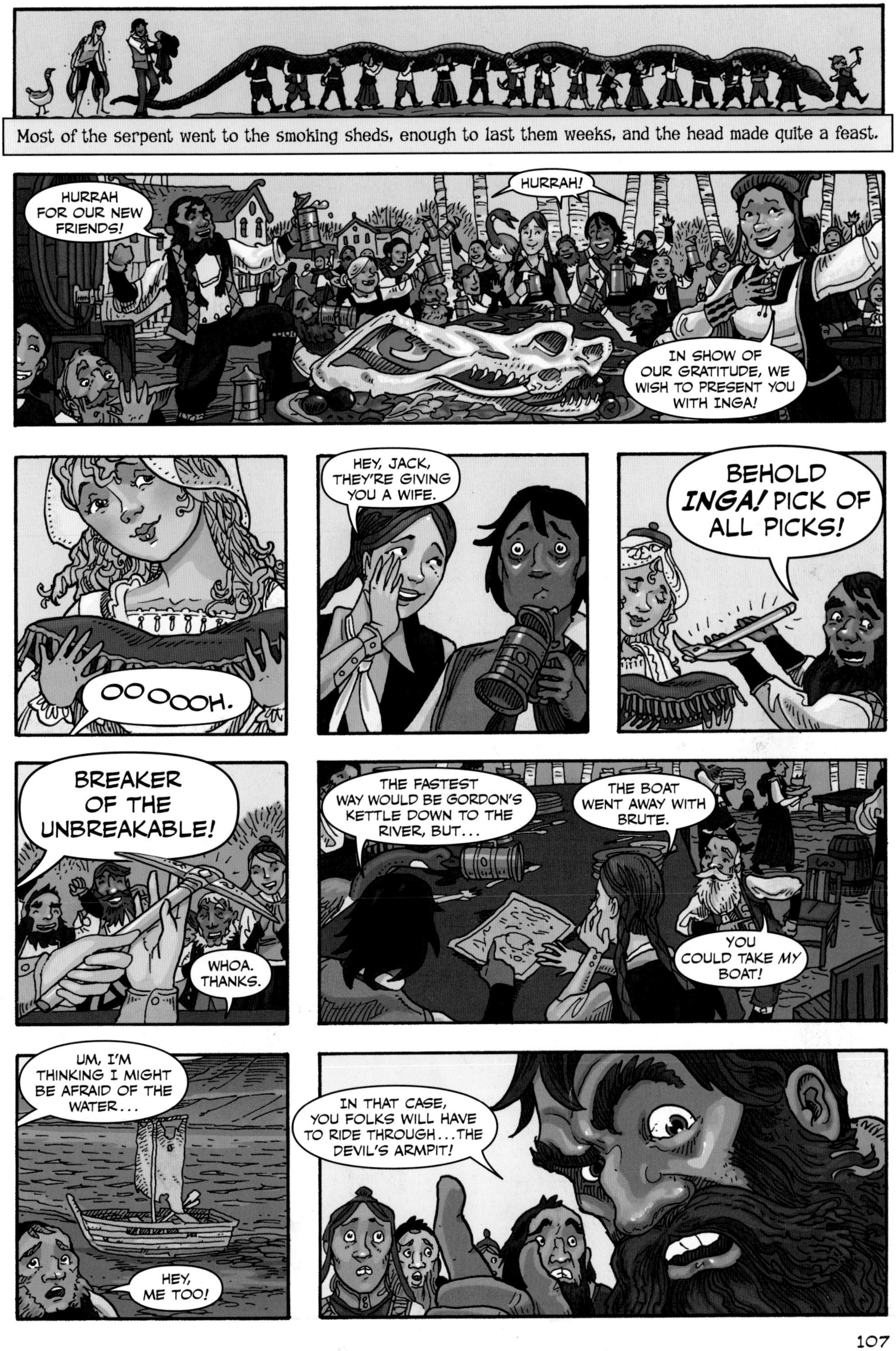
Most of the serpent went to the smoking sheds, enough to last them weeks, and the head made quite a feast.
HURRAH FOR OUR NEW FRIENDS!
HURRAH!
IN SHOW OF OUR GRATITUDE, WE WISH TO PRESENT YOU WITH INGA!
OOOOOH.
HEY, JACK, THEY'RE GIVING YOU A WIFE.
BEHOLD *INGA!* PICK OF ALL PICKS!
BREAKER OF THE UNBREAKABLE!
WHOA. THANKS.
THE FASTEST WAY WOULD BE GORDON'S KETTLE DOWN TO THE RIVER, BUT...
THE BOAT WENT AWAY WITH BRUTE.
YOU COULD TAKE *MY* BOAT!
UM, I'M THINKING I MIGHT BE AFRAID OF THE WATER...
HEY, ME TOO!
IN THAT CASE, YOU FOLKS WILL HAVE TO RIDE THROUGH...THE DEVIL'S ARMPIT!

Part 4: The Shindig

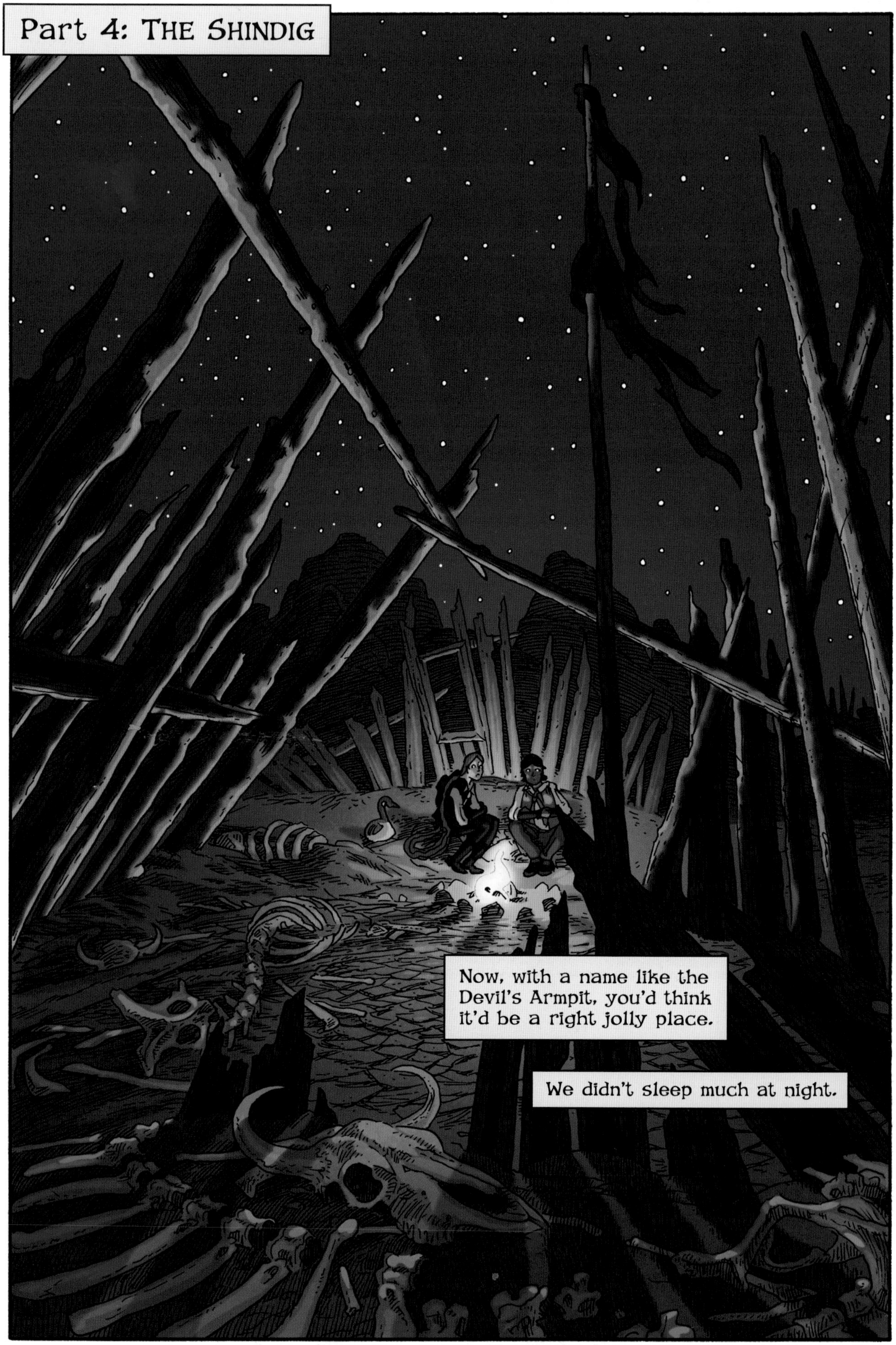
Now, with a name like the Devil's Armpit, you'd think it'd be a right jolly place.
We didn't sleep much at night.

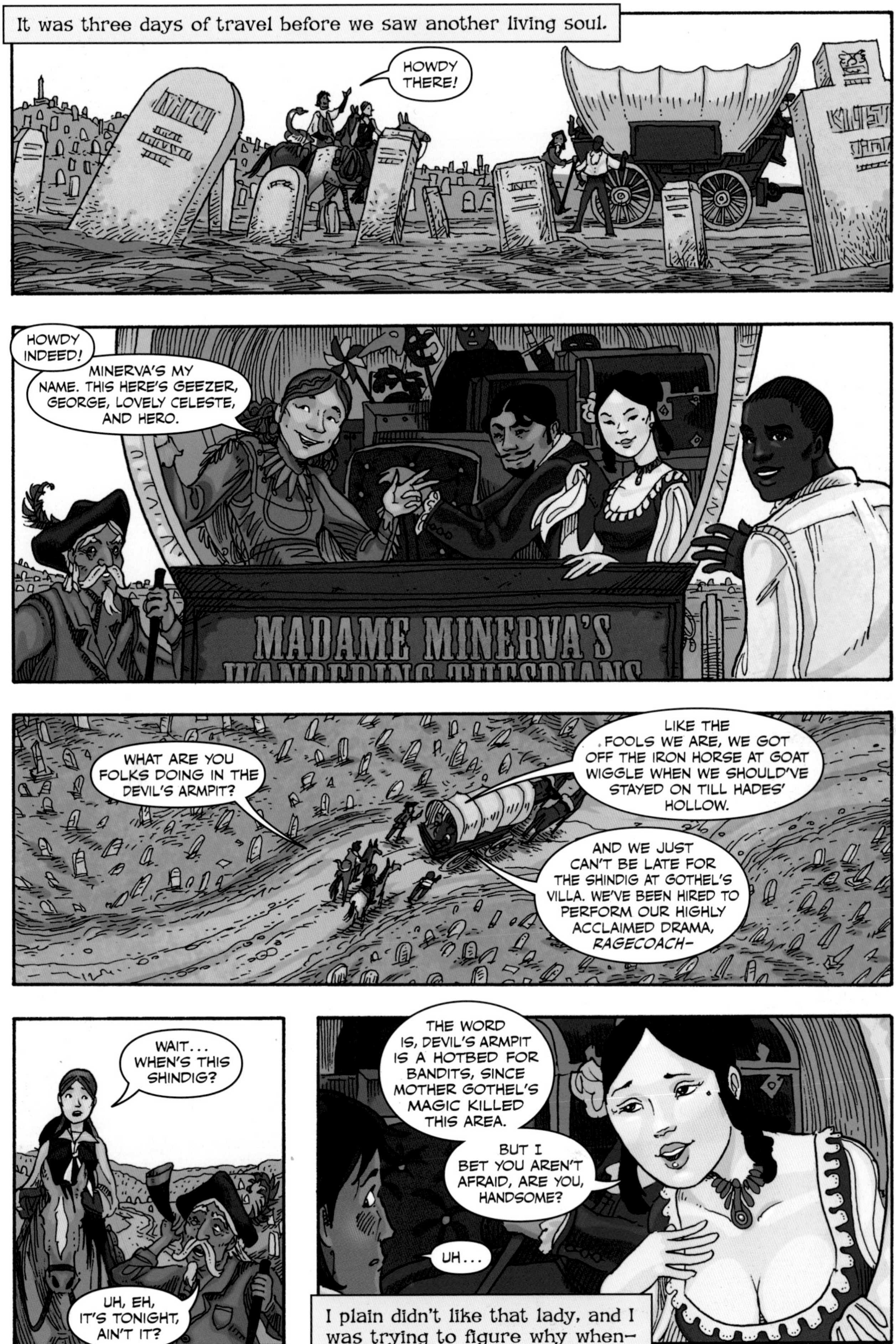

It was three days of travel before we saw another living soul.
HOWDY THERE!
HOWDY INDEED!
MINERVA'S MY NAME. THIS HERE'S GEEZER, GEORGE, LOVELY CELESTE, AND HERO.
MADAME MINERVA'S
WHAT ARE YOU FOLKS DOING IN THE DEVIL'S ARMPIT?
LIKE THE FOOLS WE ARE, WE GOT OFF THE IRON HORSE AT GOAT WIGGLE WHEN WE SHOULD'VE STAYED ON TILL HADES' HOLLOW.
AND WE JUST CAN'T BE LATE FOR THE SHINDIG AT GOTHEL'S VILLA. WE'VE BEEN HIRED TO PERFORM OUR HIGHLY ACCLAIMED DRAMA, *RAGECOACH*–
WAIT... WHEN'S THIS SHINDIG?
UH, EH, IT'S TONIGHT, AIN'T IT?
THE WORD IS, DEVIL'S ARMPIT IS A HOTBED FOR BANDITS, SINCE MOTHER GOTHEL'S MAGIC KILLED THIS AREA.
BUT I BET YOU AREN'T AFRAID, ARE YOU, HANDSOME?
UH...
I plain didn't like that lady, and I was trying to figure why when–

SOMEONE CALL FOR TROUBLE?

THAT HAPPENS TO BE THE SPECIALTY OF TINA'S TERRIBLE TRIO.

ARRRH!

BEEFEATER, YOU AND YOKUM KEEP YOUR GUNS POINTED AT ANYTHING THAT MOVES, AND I'LL JUST HAVE A LOOK-SEE IN THAT WAGON.

HOLD IT THERE, ER...*TINA*. WE'RE PROTECTING THIS CONVOY OF ENTERTAINMENT.

WELL, *SHE* IS ANYWAY.

IGNORE 'EM, BOYS. THEY'RE NOT EVEN ARMED.

There was a time when I might have been scared of those clowns.

But since tussling with a rampaging boar...

WHACK!

CRACK!

...a pack of outlaw kidnappers...

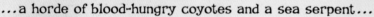

...a horde of blood-hungry coyotes and a sea serpent...

ZIP!

WE'RE OUT-WOMANED, FELLAS! BACK TO THE LAIR!

...well, Tina's Terrible Trio just didn't raise my hackles.

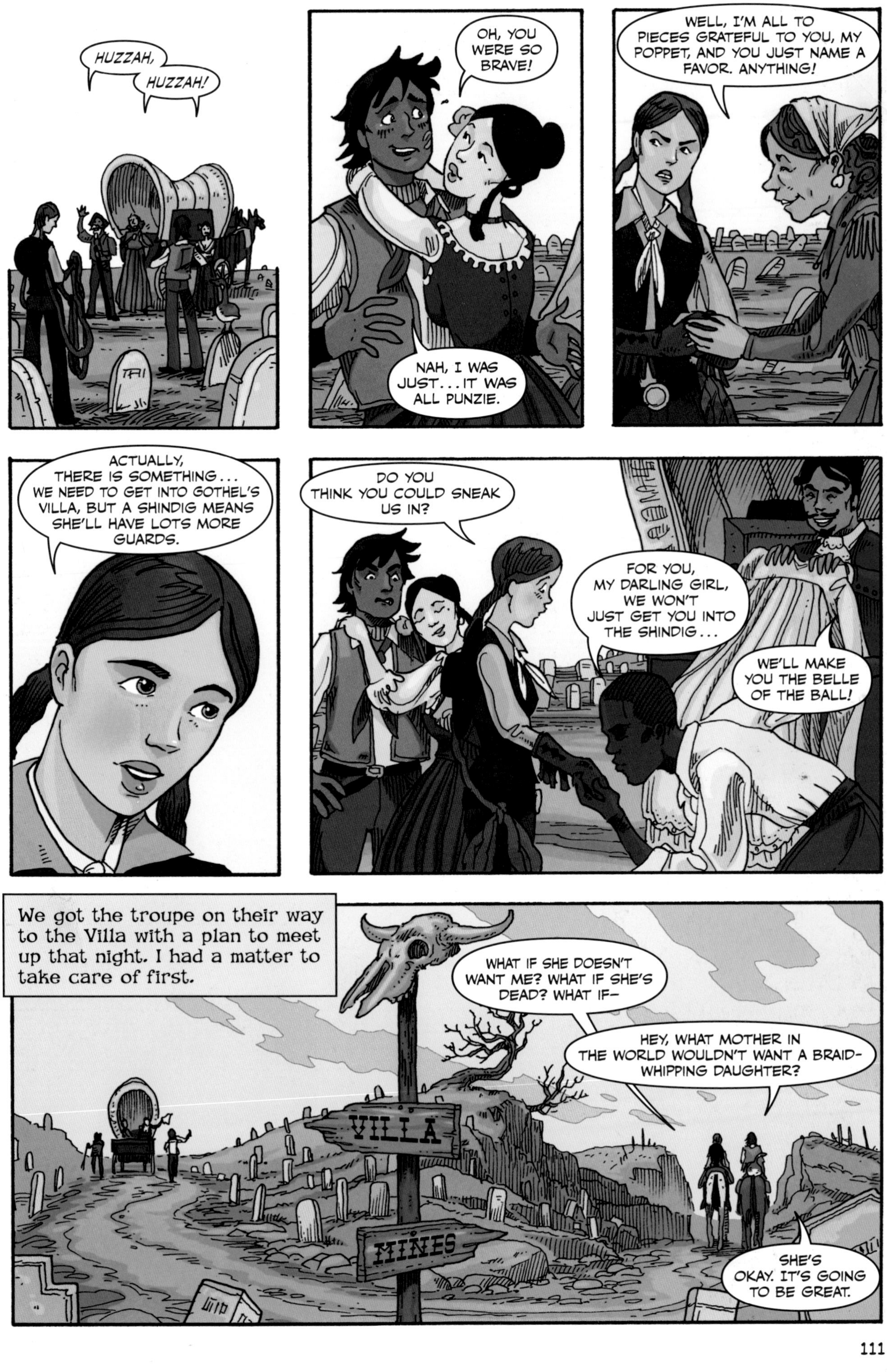
HUZZAH,
HUZZAH!
OH, YOU WERE SO BRAVE!
NAH, I WAS JUST... IT WAS ALL PUNZIE.
WELL, I'M ALL TO PIECES GRATEFUL TO YOU, MY POPPET, AND YOU JUST NAME A FAVOR. ANYTHING!
ACTUALLY, THERE IS SOMETHING... WE NEED TO GET INTO GOTHEL'S VILLA, BUT A SHINDIG MEANS SHE'LL HAVE LOTS MORE GUARDS.
DO YOU THINK YOU COULD SNEAK US IN?
FOR YOU, MY DARLING GIRL, WE WON'T JUST GET YOU INTO THE SHINDIG...
WE'LL MAKE YOU THE BELLE OF THE BALL!
We got the troupe on their way to the Villa with a plan to meet up that night. I had a matter to take care of first.
VILLA
MINES
WHAT IF SHE DOESN'T WANT ME? WHAT IF SHE'S DEAD? WHAT IF–
HEY, WHAT MOTHER IN THE WORLD WOULDN'T WANT A BRAID-WHIPPING DAUGHTER?
SHE'S OKAY. IT'S GOING TO BE GREAT.

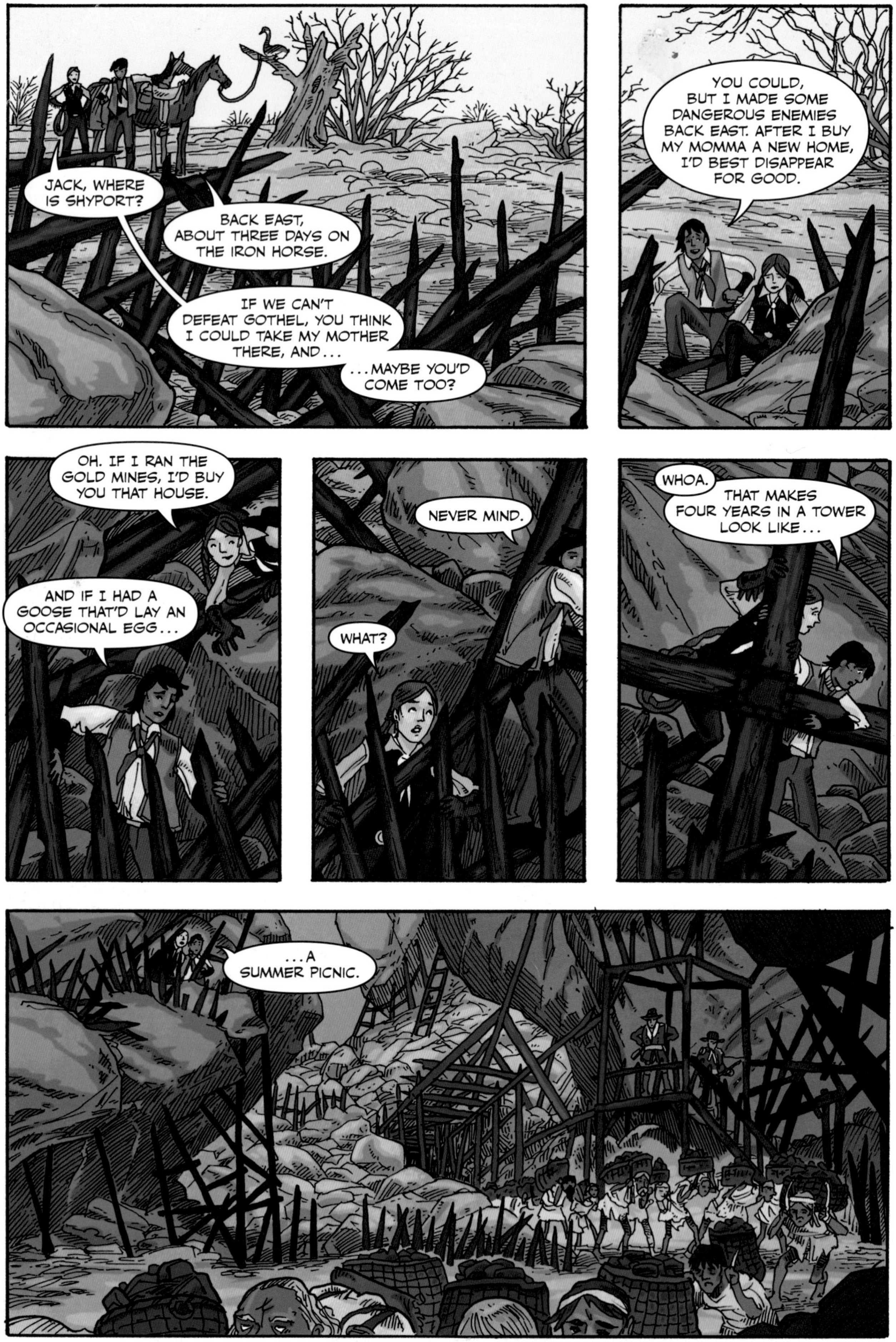
JACK, WHERE IS SHYPORT?
BACK EAST, ABOUT THREE DAYS ON THE IRON HORSE.
IF WE CAN'T DEFEAT GOTHEL, YOU THINK I COULD TAKE MY MOTHER THERE, AND...
...MAYBE YOU'D COME TOO?
YOU COULD, BUT I MADE SOME DANGEROUS ENEMIES BACK EAST. AFTER I BUY MY MOMMA A NEW HOME, I'D BEST DISAPPEAR FOR GOOD.
OH. IF I RAN THE GOLD MINES, I'D BUY YOU THAT HOUSE.
AND IF I HAD A GOOSE THAT'D LAY AN OCCASIONAL EGG...
NEVER MIND.
WHAT?
WHOA.
THAT MAKES FOUR YEARS IN A TOWER LOOK LIKE...
...A SUMMER PICNIC.

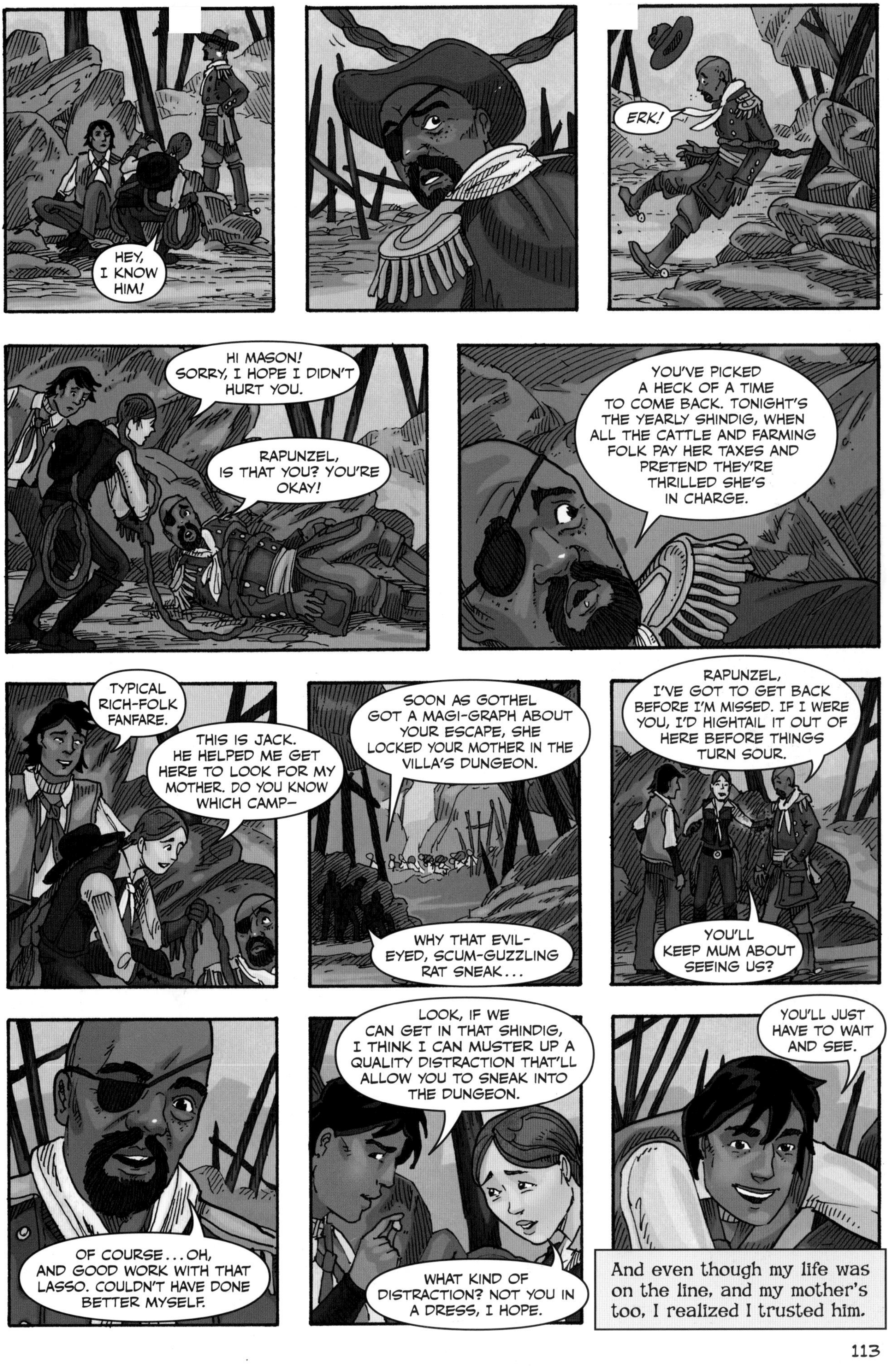
HEY, I KNOW HIM!
ERK!
HI MASON! SORRY, I HOPE I DIDN'T HURT YOU.
RAPUNZEL, IS THAT YOU? YOU'RE OKAY!
YOU'VE PICKED A HECK OF A TIME TO COME BACK. TONIGHT'S THE YEARLY SHINDIG, WHEN ALL THE CATTLE AND FARMING FOLK PAY HER TAXES AND PRETEND THEY'RE THRILLED SHE'S IN CHARGE.
TYPICAL RICH-FOLK FANFARE.
THIS IS JACK. HE HELPED ME GET HERE TO LOOK FOR MY MOTHER. DO YOU KNOW WHICH CAMP–
SOON AS GOTHEL GOT A MAGI-GRAPH ABOUT YOUR ESCAPE, SHE LOCKED YOUR MOTHER IN THE VILLA'S DUNGEON.
WHY THAT EVIL-EYED, SCUM-GUZZLING RAT SNEAK...
RAPUNZEL, I'VE GOT TO GET BACK BEFORE I'M MISSED. IF I WERE YOU, I'D HIGHTAIL IT OUT OF HERE BEFORE THINGS TURN SOUR.
YOU'LL KEEP MUM ABOUT SEEING US?
OF COURSE... OH, AND GOOD WORK WITH THAT LASSO. COULDN'T HAVE DONE BETTER MYSELF.
LOOK, IF WE CAN GET IN THAT SHINDIG, I THINK I CAN MUSTER UP A QUALITY DISTRACTION THAT'LL ALLOW YOU TO SNEAK INTO THE DUNGEON.
WHAT KIND OF DISTRACTION? NOT YOU IN A DRESS, I HOPE.
YOU'LL JUST HAVE TO WAIT AND SEE.
And even though my life was on the line, and my mother's too, I realized I trusted him.

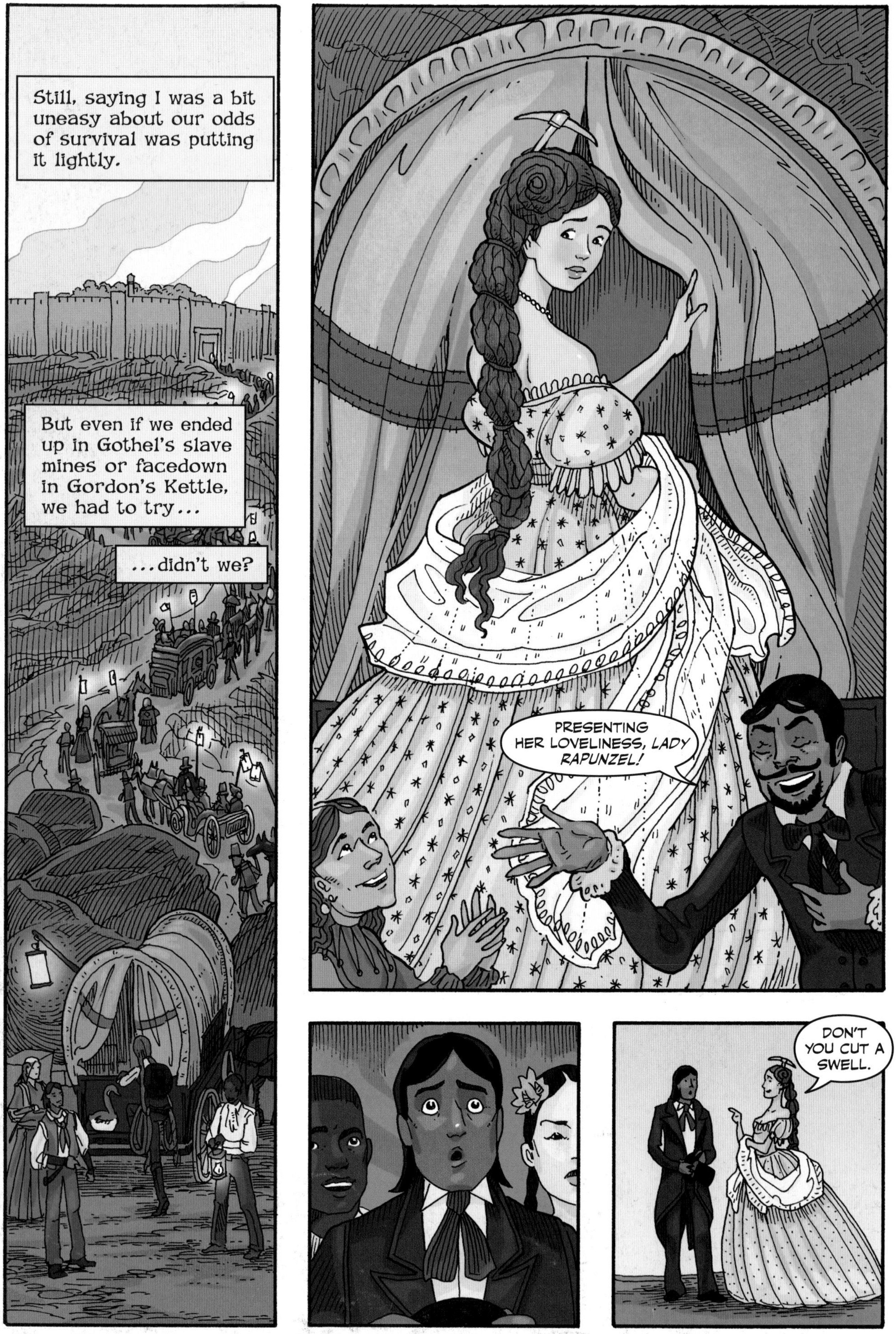
Still, saying I was a bit uneasy about our odds of survival was putting it lightly.
But even if we ended up in Gothel's slave mines or facedown in Gordon's Kettle, we had to try...
...didn't we?
PRESENTING HER LOVELINESS, *LADY RAPUNZEL!*
DON'T YOU CUT A SWELL.

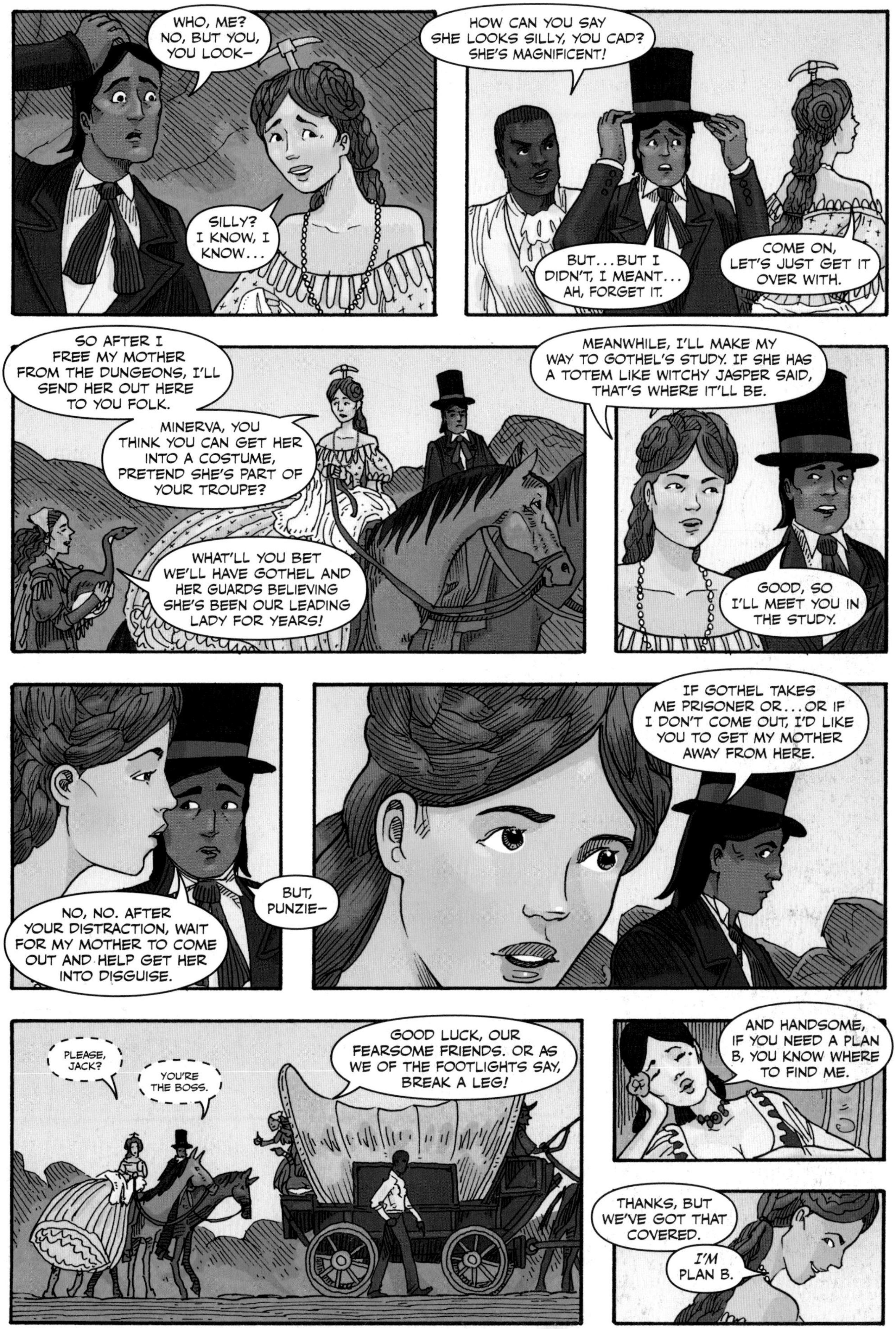
WHO, ME? NO, BUT YOU, YOU LOOK–
SILLY? I KNOW, I KNOW...
HOW CAN YOU SAY SHE LOOKS SILLY, YOU CAD? SHE'S MAGNIFICENT!
BUT...BUT I DIDN'T, I MEANT... AH, FORGET IT.
COME ON, LET'S JUST GET IT OVER WITH.
SO AFTER I FREE MY MOTHER FROM THE DUNGEONS, I'LL SEND HER OUT HERE TO YOU FOLK.
MINERVA, YOU THINK YOU CAN GET HER INTO A COSTUME, PRETEND SHE'S PART OF YOUR TROUPE?
WHAT'LL YOU BET WE'LL HAVE GOTHEL AND HER GUARDS BELIEVING SHE'S BEEN OUR LEADING LADY FOR YEARS!
MEANWHILE, I'LL MAKE MY WAY TO GOTHEL'S STUDY. IF SHE HAS A TOTEM LIKE WITCHY JASPER SAID, THAT'S WHERE IT'LL BE.
GOOD, SO I'LL MEET YOU IN THE STUDY.
NO, NO. AFTER YOUR DISTRACTION, WAIT FOR MY MOTHER TO COME OUT AND HELP GET HER INTO DISGUISE.
BUT, PUNZIE–
IF GOTHEL TAKES ME PRISONER OR...OR IF I DON'T COME OUT, I'D LIKE YOU TO GET MY MOTHER AWAY FROM HERE.
PLEASE, JACK?
YOU'RE THE BOSS.
GOOD LUCK, OUR FEARSOME FRIENDS. OR AS WE OF THE FOOTLIGHTS SAY, BREAK A LEG!
AND HANDSOME, IF YOU NEED A PLAN B, YOU KNOW WHERE TO FIND ME.
THANKS, BUT WE'VE GOT THAT COVERED.
I'M PLAN B.

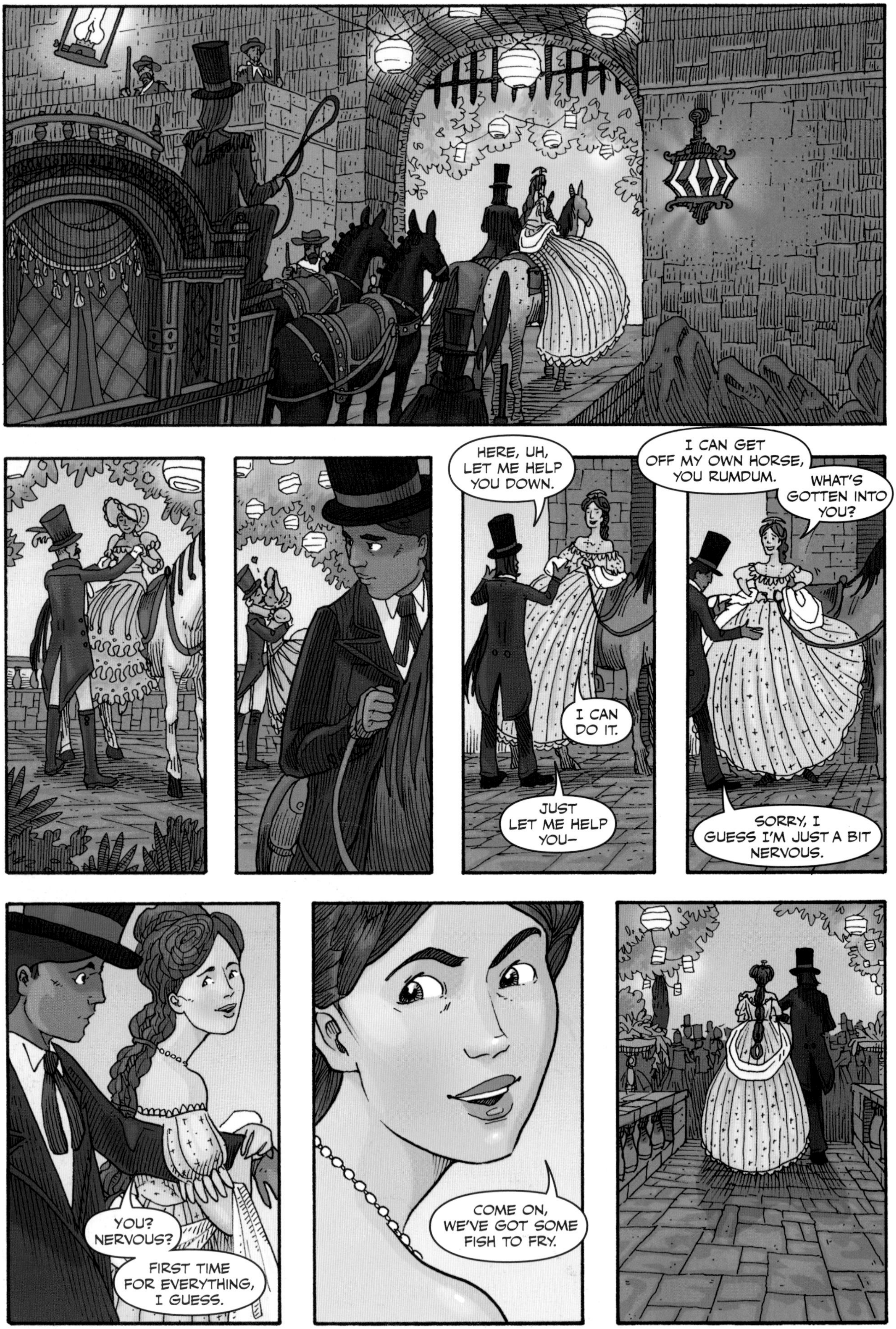
HERE, UH, LET ME HELP YOU DOWN.
I CAN DO IT.
JUST LET ME HELP YOU–
I CAN GET OFF MY OWN HORSE, YOU RUMDUM.
WHAT'S GOTTEN INTO YOU?
SORRY, I GUESS I'M JUST A BIT NERVOUS.
YOU? NERVOUS?
FIRST TIME FOR EVERYTHING, I GUESS.
COME ON, WE'VE GOT SOME FISH TO FRY.

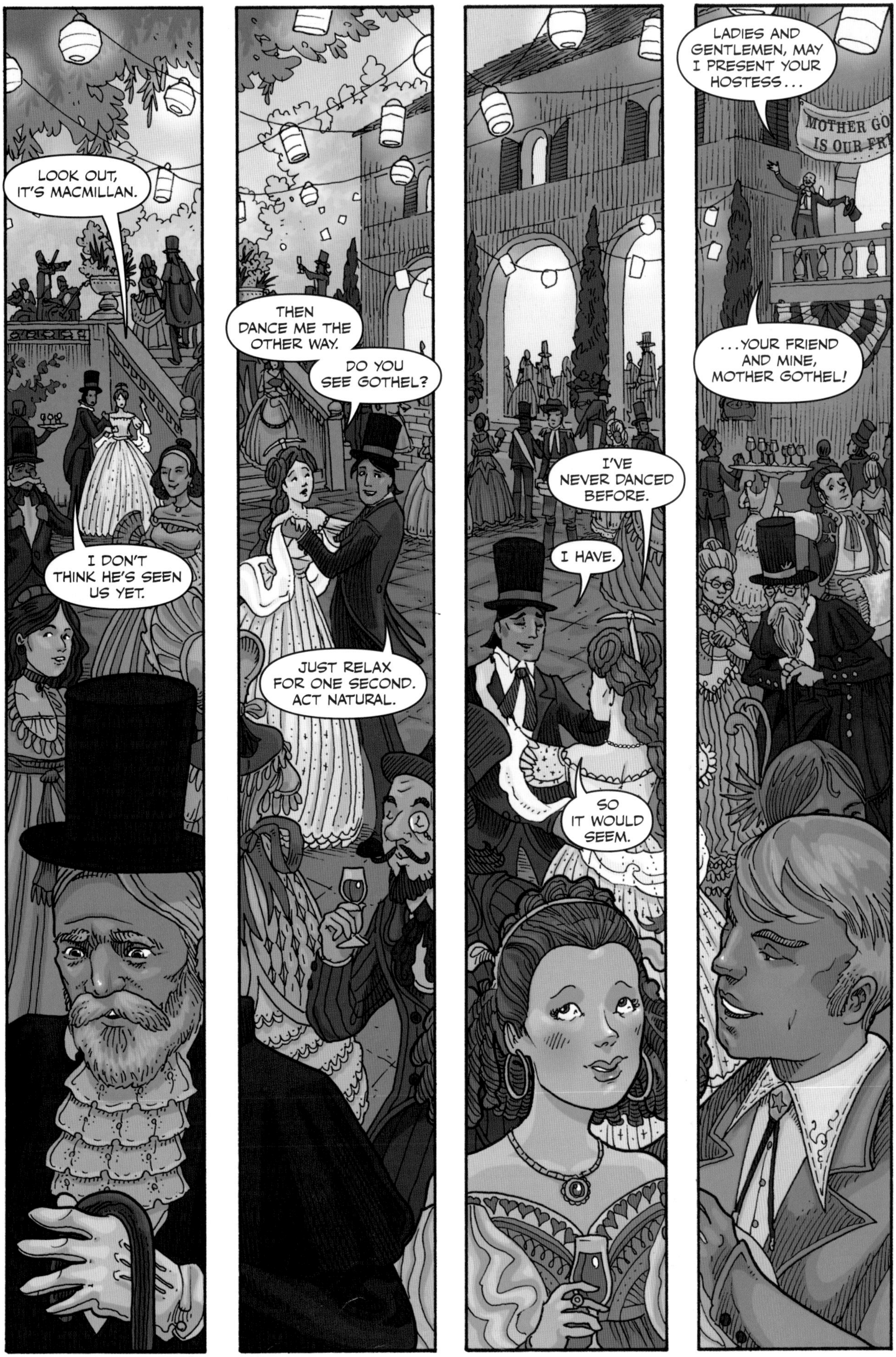
LOOK OUT, IT'S MACMILLAN.
I DON'T THINK HE'S SEEN US YET.
THEN DANCE ME THE OTHER WAY.
DO YOU SEE GOTHEL?
JUST RELAX FOR ONE SECOND. ACT NATURAL.
I'VE NEVER DANCED BEFORE.
I HAVE.
SO IT WOULD SEEM.
LADIES AND GENTLEMEN, MAY I PRESENT YOUR HOSTESS...
...YOUR FRIEND AND MINE, MOTHER GOTHEL!

GOOD EVENING, FRIENDS.

ANOTHER PROFITABLE YEAR IN CATTLE, MINES, AND FARMS. WHEN MOTHER GOTHEL DOES WELL, YOU DO WELL.

MOTHER GOTHEL IS OUR FRIEND

NOW MIGHT BE A GOOD TIME FOR THAT DISTRACTION...

I'M ON IT. HEY, BE CAREFUL, OKAY?

YOU BE CAREFUL.

MOTHER GOTHEL IS OUR FRIEND

HURRY, JACK, PLEASE...

I started wondering, could Jack have left me? If the price were right, would he betray me? And should I run before it was too late?

No, I thought. He wouldn't. There are good people in this world. And Jack's good people. I was as sure of that as my braids were long.

SHUDDA SHUDDA SHUDDA SHUDDA SHUDDA SHUDDA SHUDDA SHUDDA SHUDDA SHUDDA SHUDDA SHUDDA S

DDA SHUDDA SHUDDA SHUDDA SHUDDA SHUDDA SHU

HELLO THERE, JACK'S DISTRACTION.

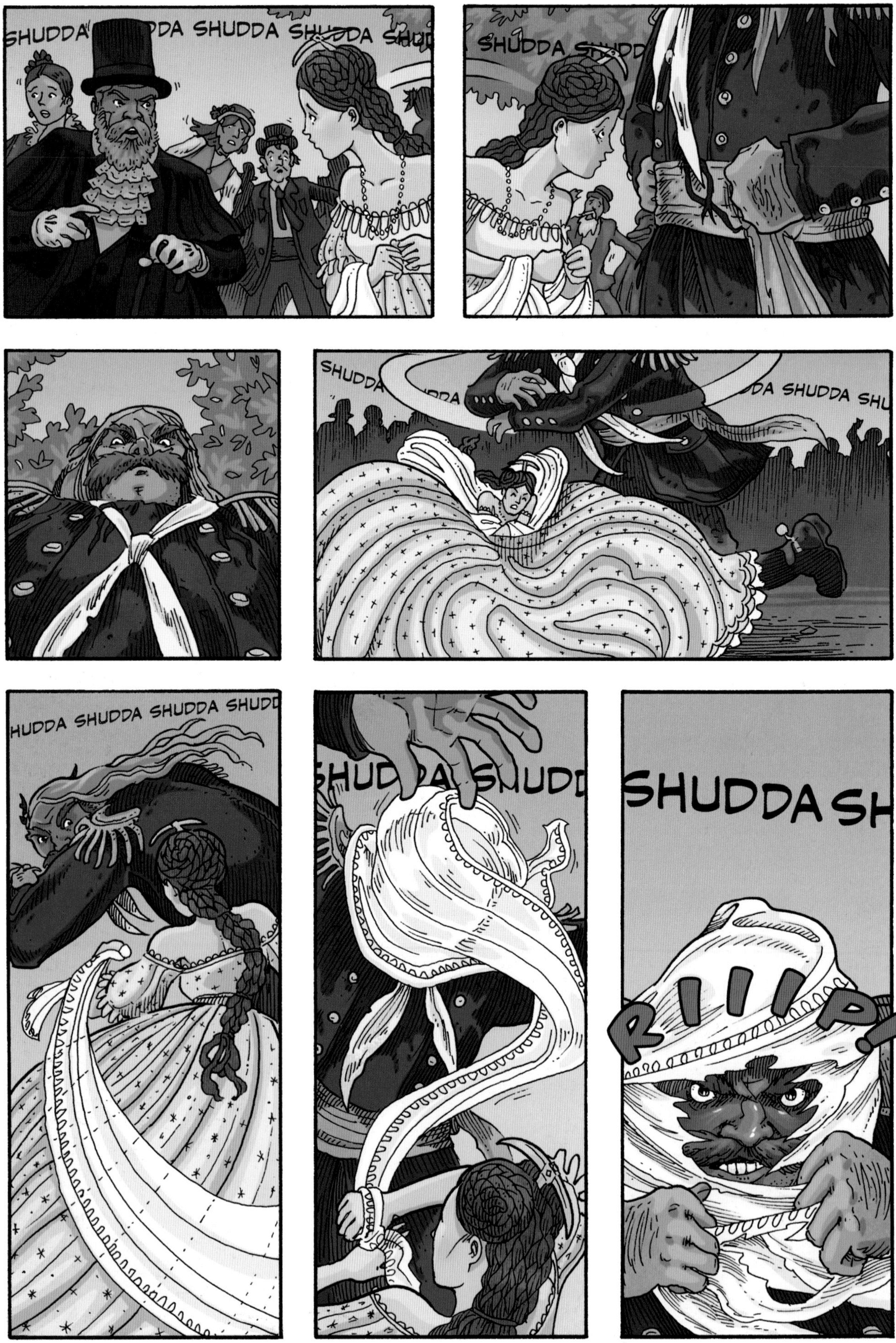
SHUDDA SHUDDA SHUDDA SHUDDA SHUDDA
SHUDDA SHUDDA
SHUDDA SHUDDA SHUDDA SHUDDA SHU
SHUDDA SHUDDA SHUDDA SHUDD
SHUDDA SHUDD
SHUDDA SH
RIIIP!

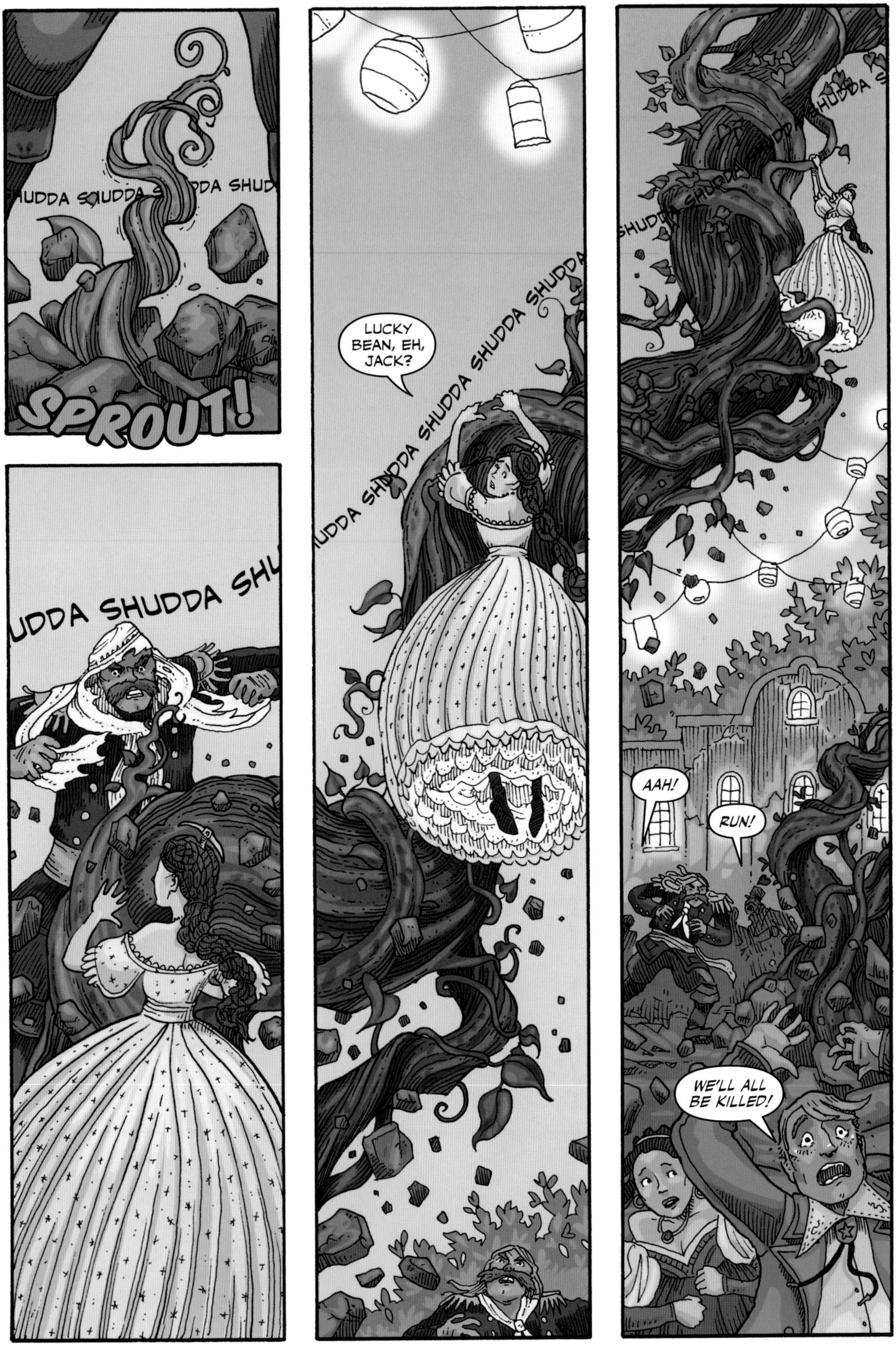
SHUDDA SHUDDA SHUDDA SHUD
SPROUT!
UDDA SHUDDA SH
SHUDDA SHUDDA SHUDDA SHUDDA
LUCKY BEAN, EH, JACK?
SHUDDA SHUDDA SHUDDA SHUDDA
AAH!
RUN!
WE'LL ALL BE KILLED!

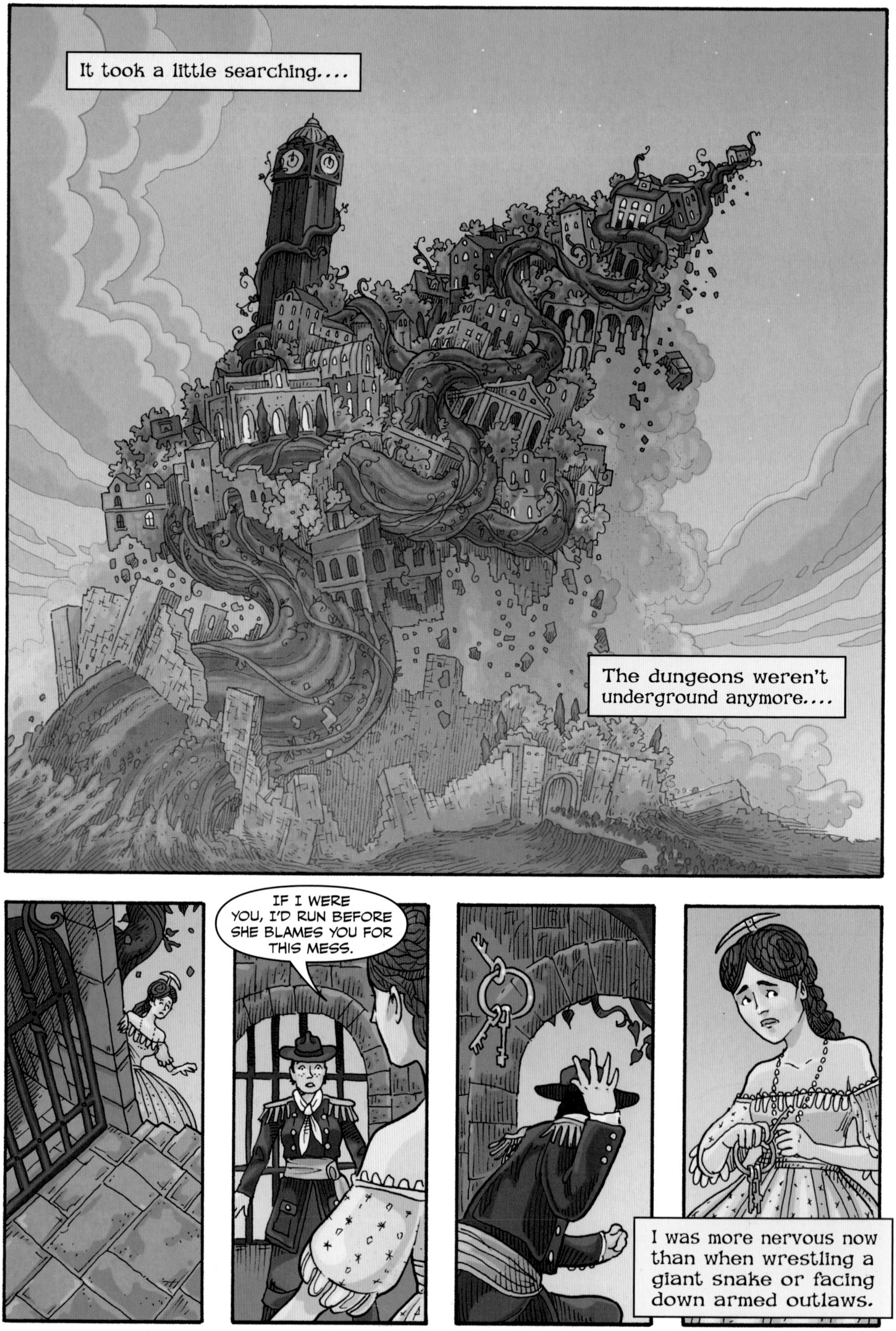
It took a little searching....
The dungeons weren't underground anymore....
IF I WERE YOU, I'D RUN BEFORE SHE BLAMES YOU FOR THIS MESS.
I was more nervous now than when wrestling a giant snake or facing down armed outlaws.

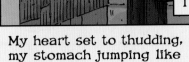

My heart set to thudding, my stomach jumping like a jackalope.

I hadn't planned on what to say.

HI.

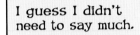

I guess I didn't need to say much.

ALL THESE YEARS LOST....

WE'RE NOT GOING TO LOSE ANOTHER DAY.

BUT YOU BETTER GET A WIGGLE ON BEFORE GOTHEL FINDS US. MY FRIEND JACK IS WAITING FOR YOU IN THE COURTYARD BELOW.

BUT YOU'RE COMING TOO, RIGHT?

I'LL JOIN YOU SOON. I JUST... GOTHEL'S POWER HAS DESTROYED SO MUCH, AND I NEED TO TRY AND STOP HER.

PLEASE BE CAREFUL. I DON'T THINK I COULD STAND TO LOSE YOU AGAIN.

DON'T WORRY ABOUT ME, MOMMA. I'LL BE RIGHT AS RAIN!

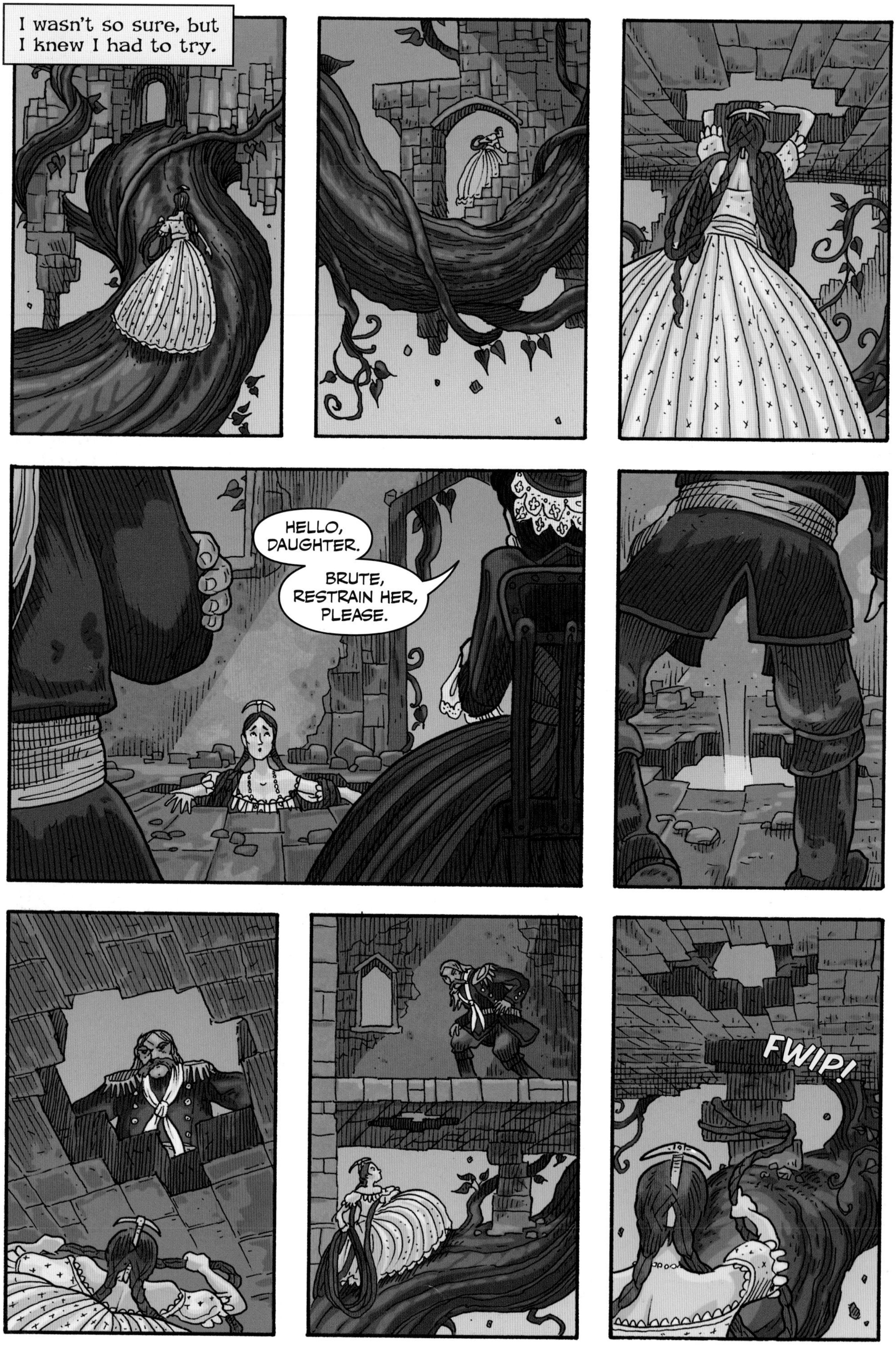
I wasn't so sure, but I knew I had to try.
HELLO, DAUGHTER.
BRUTE, RESTRAIN HER, PLEASE.
FWIP!

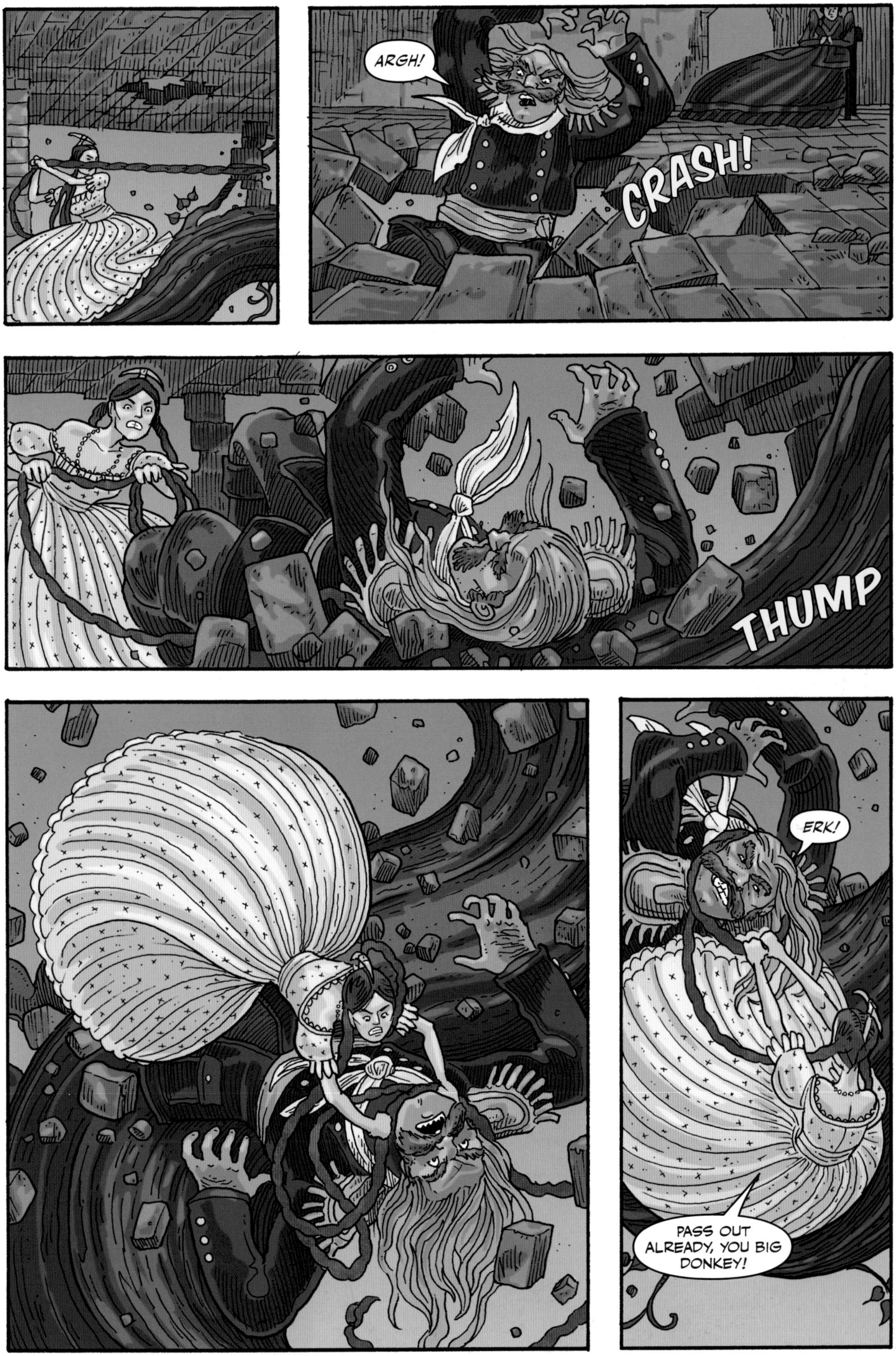
ARGH!
CRASH!
THUMP
ERK!
PASS OUT ALREADY, YOU BIG DONKEY!

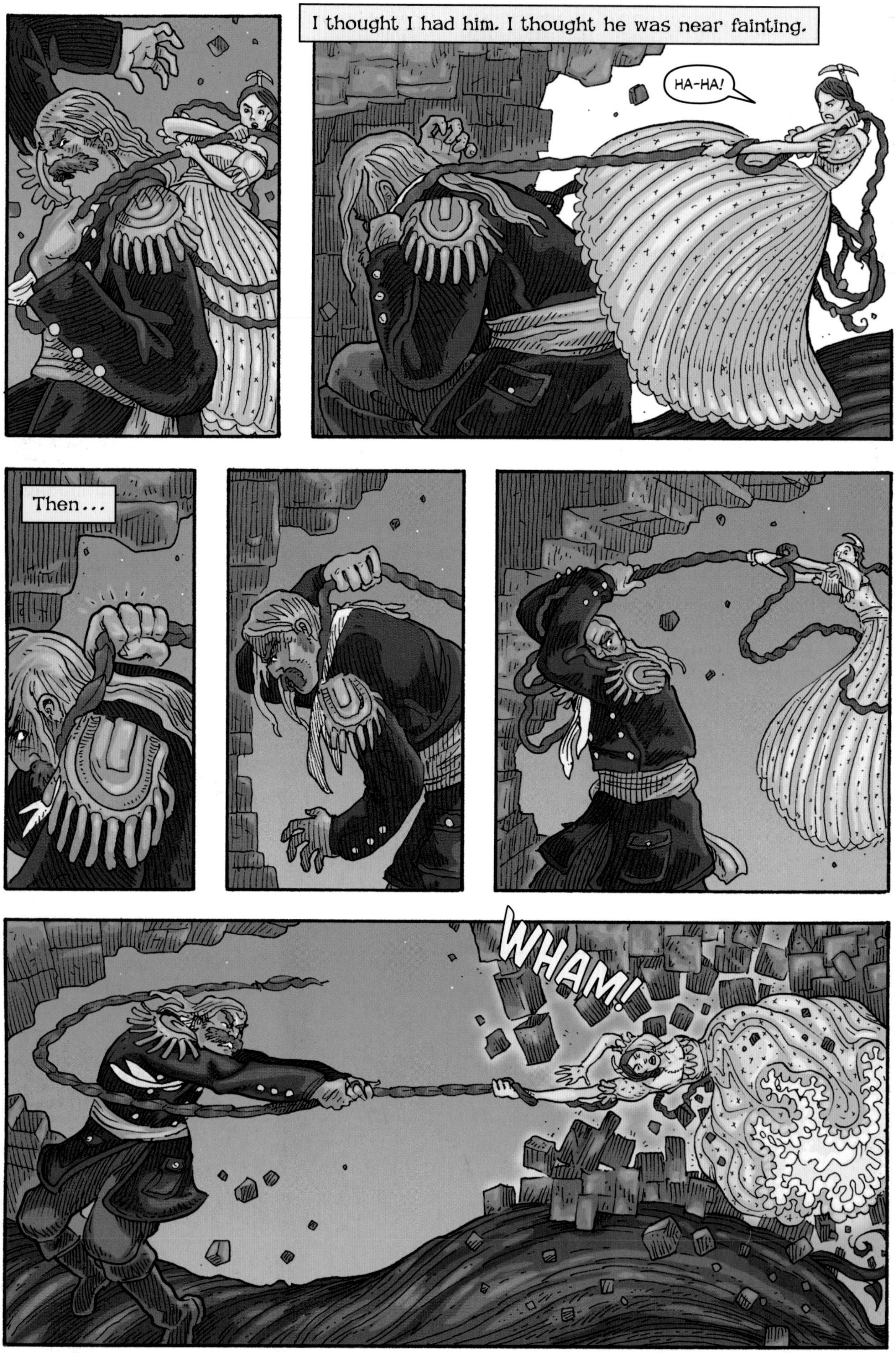
I thought I had him. I thought he was near fainting.
HA-HA!
Then...
WHAM!

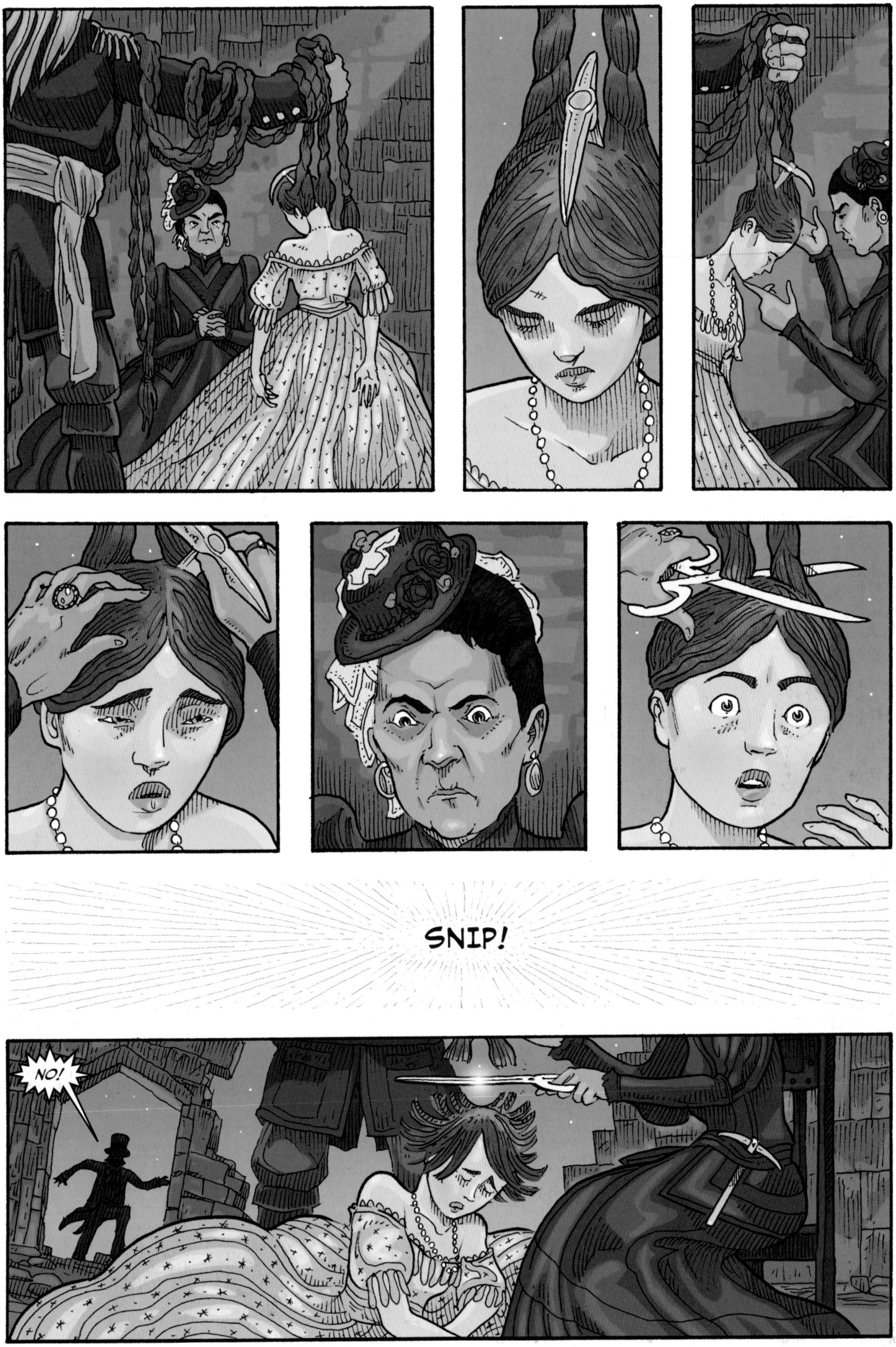
SNIP!
NO!

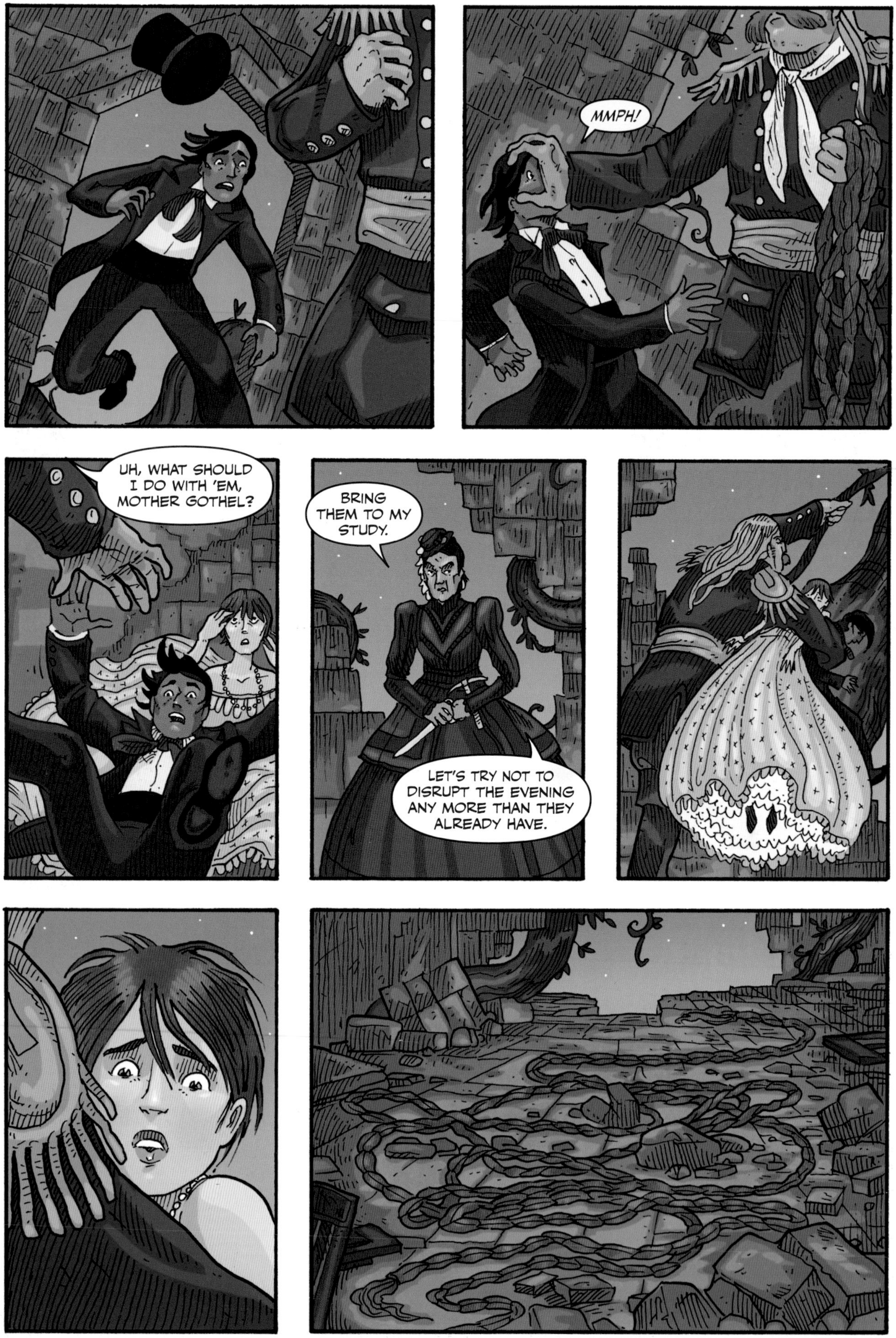
MMPH!
UH, WHAT SHOULD I DO WITH 'EM, MOTHER GOTHEL?
BRING THEM TO MY STUDY.
LET'S TRY NOT TO DISRUPT THE EVENING ANY MORE THAN THEY ALREADY HAVE.

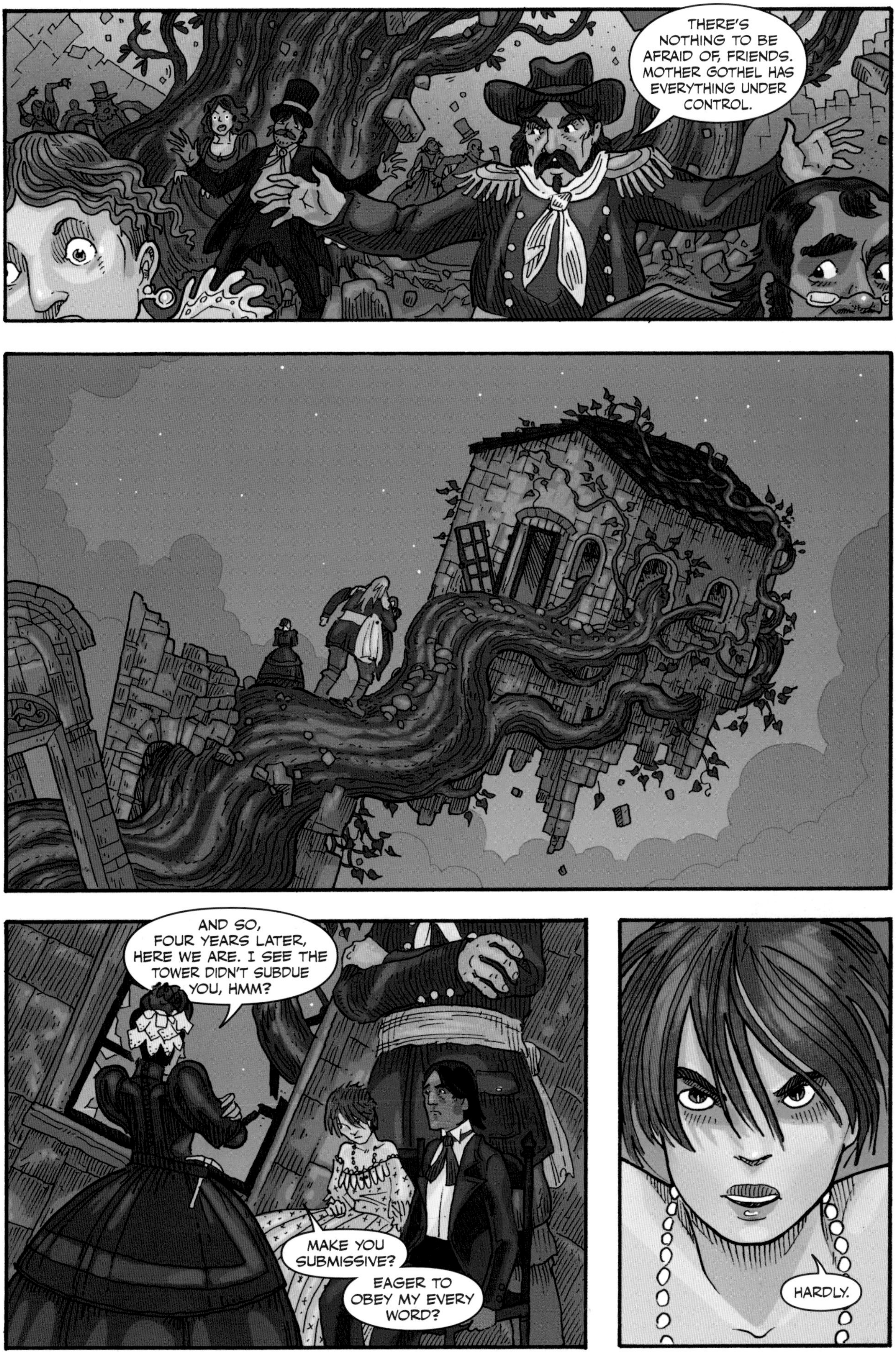
THERE'S NOTHING TO BE AFRAID OF, FRIENDS. MOTHER GOTHEL HAS EVERYTHING UNDER CONTROL.
AND SO, FOUR YEARS LATER, HERE WE ARE. I SEE THE TOWER DIDN'T SUBDUE YOU, HMM?
MAKE YOU SUBMISSIVE?
EAGER TO OBEY MY EVERY WORD?
HARDLY.

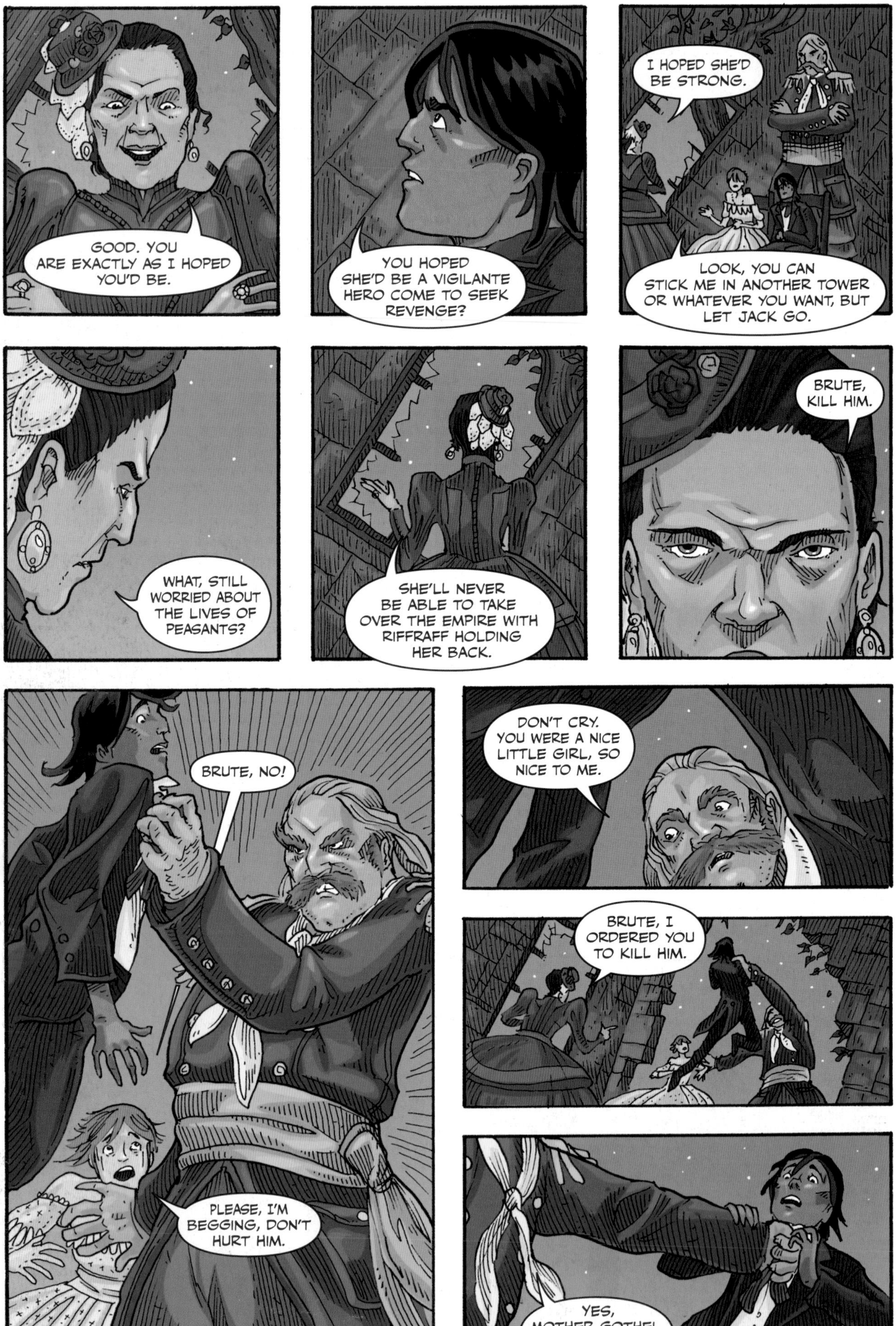
GOOD. YOU ARE EXACTLY AS I HOPED YOU'D BE.
YOU HOPED SHE'D BE A VIGILANTE HERO COME TO SEEK REVENGE?
I HOPED SHE'D BE STRONG.
LOOK, YOU CAN STICK ME IN ANOTHER TOWER OR WHATEVER YOU WANT, BUT LET JACK GO.
WHAT, STILL WORRIED ABOUT THE LIVES OF PEASANTS?
SHE'LL NEVER BE ABLE TO TAKE OVER THE EMPIRE WITH RIFFRAFF HOLDING HER BACK.
BRUTE, KILL HIM.
BRUTE, NO!
PLEASE, I'M BEGGING, DON'T HURT HIM.
DON'T CRY. YOU WERE A NICE LITTLE GIRL, SO NICE TO ME.
BRUTE, I ORDERED YOU TO KILL HIM.
YES, MOTHER GOTHEL.

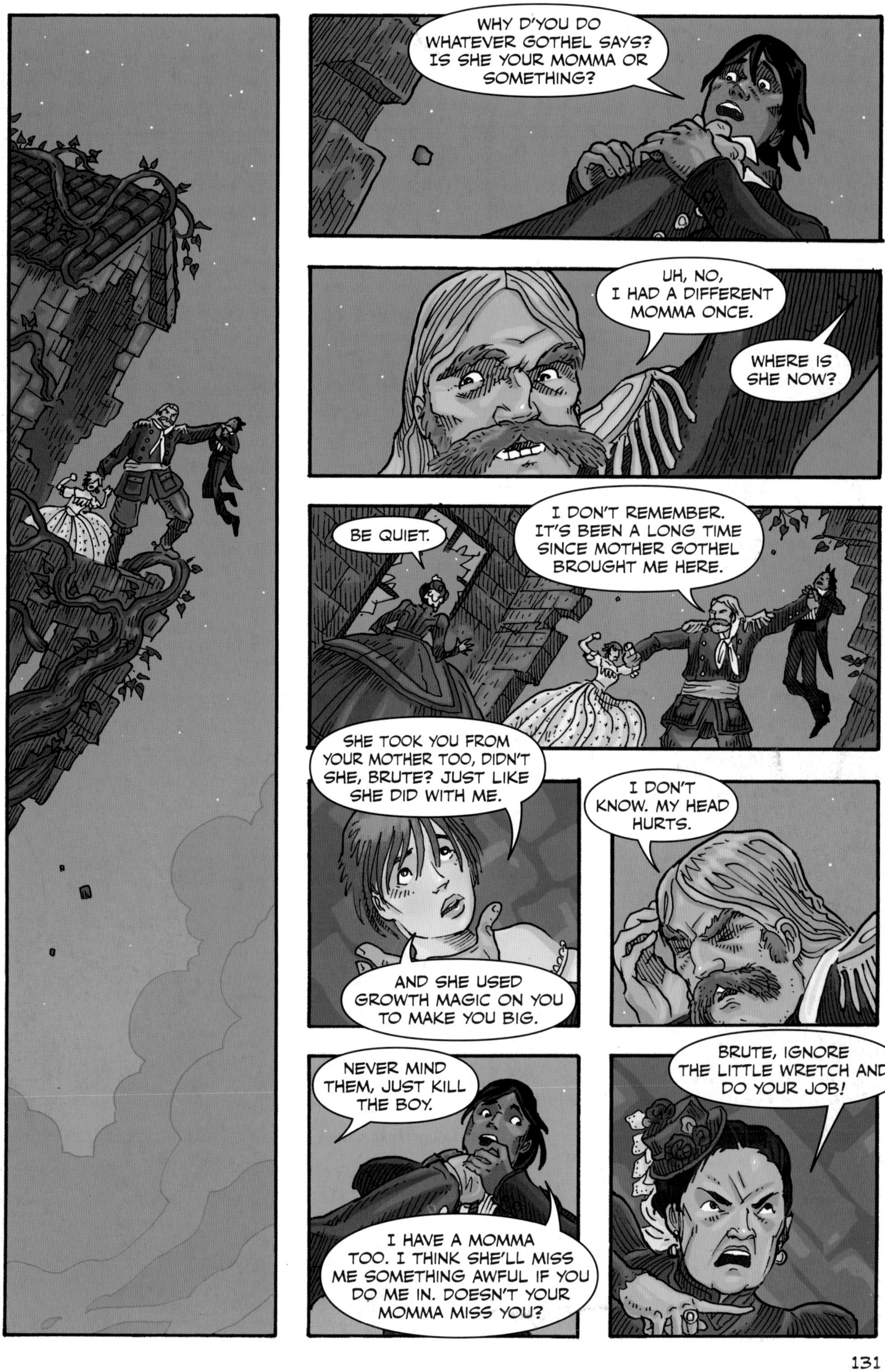
WHY D'YOU DO WHATEVER GOTHEL SAYS? IS SHE YOUR MOMMA OR SOMETHING?
UH, NO, I HAD A DIFFERENT MOMMA ONCE.
WHERE IS SHE NOW?
I DON'T REMEMBER. IT'S BEEN A LONG TIME SINCE MOTHER GOTHEL BROUGHT ME HERE.
BE QUIET.
SHE TOOK YOU FROM YOUR MOTHER TOO, DIDN'T SHE, BRUTE? JUST LIKE SHE DID WITH ME.
AND SHE USED GROWTH MAGIC ON YOU TO MAKE YOU BIG.
I DON'T KNOW. MY HEAD HURTS.
NEVER MIND THEM, JUST KILL THE BOY.
I HAVE A MOMMA TOO. I THINK SHE'LL MISS ME SOMETHING AWFUL IF YOU DO ME IN. DOESN'T YOUR MOMMA MISS YOU?
BRUTE, IGNORE THE LITTLE WRETCH AND DO YOUR JOB!

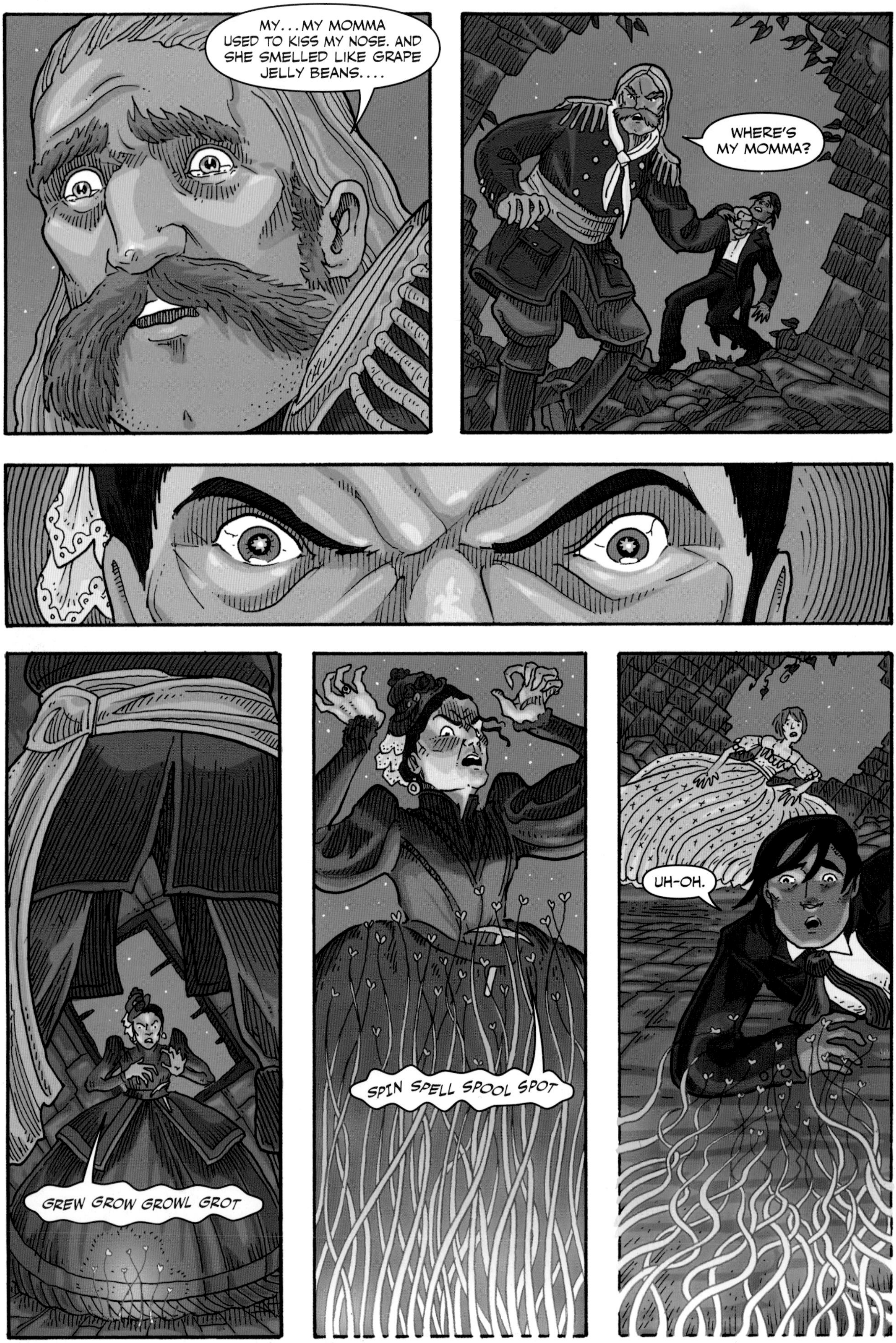
MY...MY MOMMA USED TO KISS MY NOSE. AND SHE SMELLED LIKE GRAPE JELLY BEANS....
WHERE'S MY MOMMA?
GREW GROW GROWL GROT
SPIN SPELL SPOOL SPOT
UH-OH.

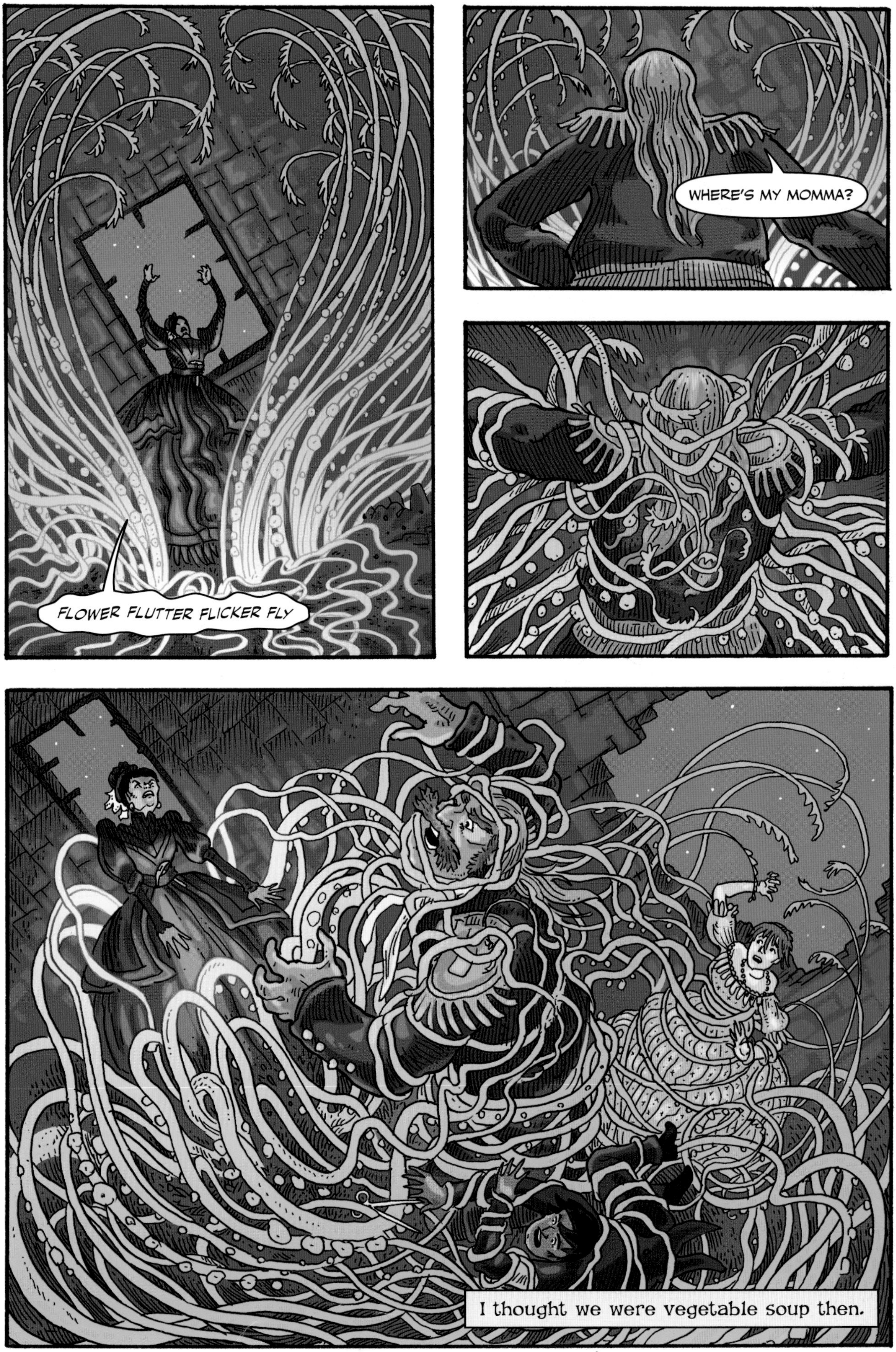
FLOWER FLUTTER FLICKER FLY
WHERE'S MY MOMMA?
I thought we were vegetable soup then.

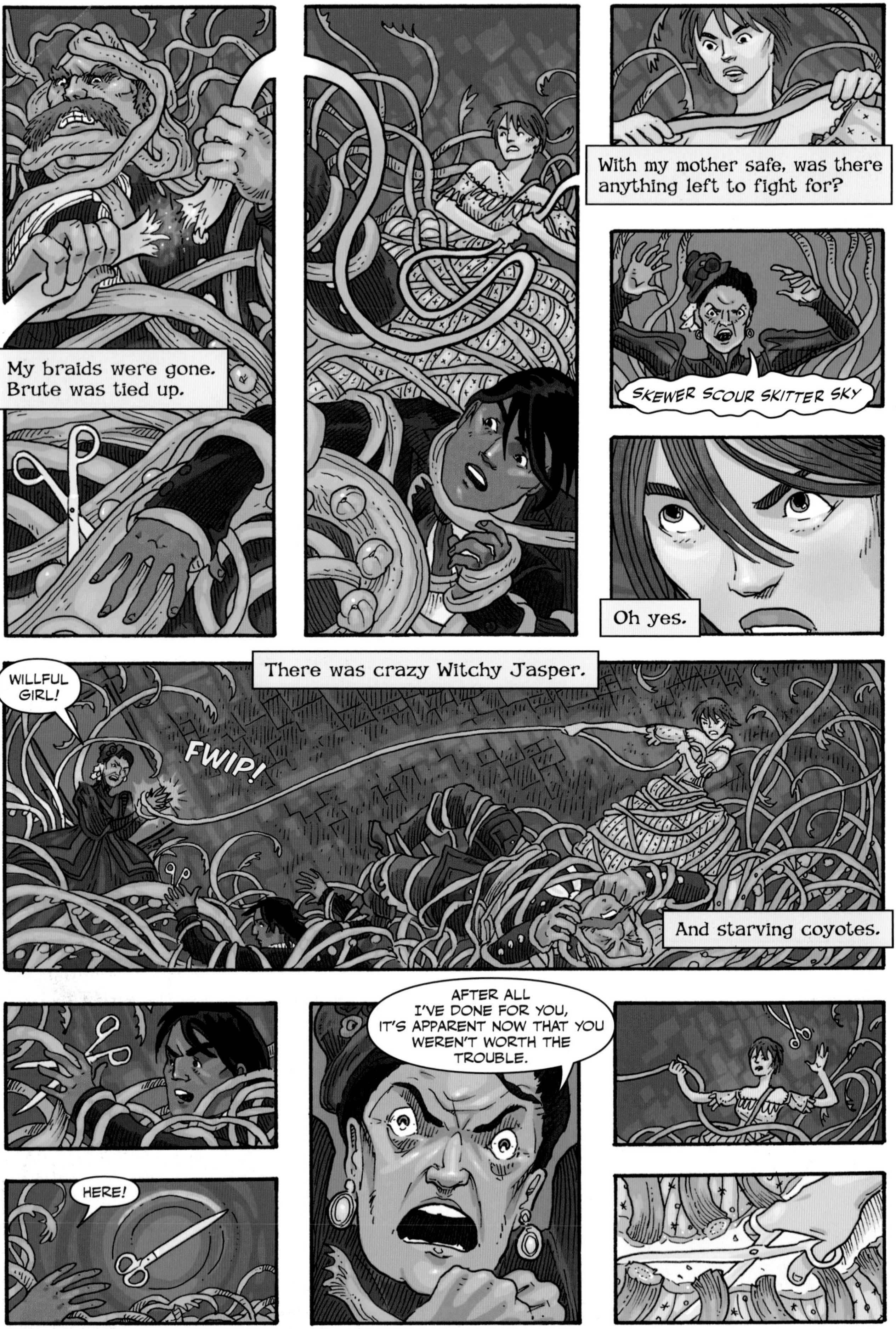
My braids were gone.
Brute was tied up.
With my mother safe, was there anything left to fight for?
SKEWER SCOUR SKITTER SKY
Oh yes.
There was crazy Witchy Jasper.
WILLFUL GIRL!
FWIP!
And starving coyotes.
AFTER ALL I'VE DONE FOR YOU, IT'S APPARENT NOW THAT YOU WEREN'T WORTH THE TROUBLE.
HERE!

That little girl from Pig Tree Gulch.

Duggers fishing with pickaxes.

TEMPER TIMBER... SPLAT!

HA!

SPLUT SPLURT

...TANTRUM TURN

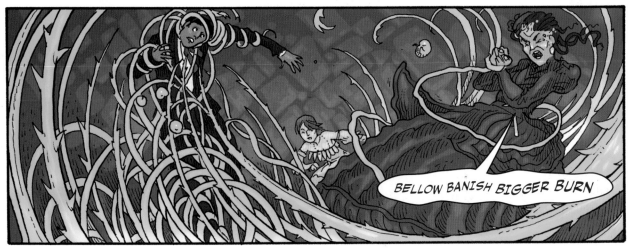

BELLOW BANISH BIGGER BURN

135

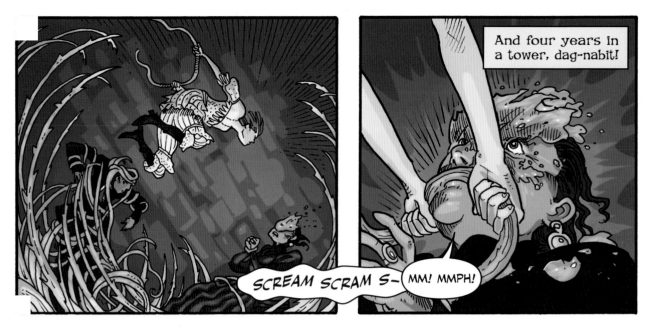

And four years in a tower, dag-nabit!

SCREAM SCRAM S— MM! MMPH!

IF YOU WANT TO STOP THE WATER, PLUG UP THE SPIGOT.

QUICK, SEE IF YOU CAN FIND SOMETHING THAT MIGHT BE HER TOTEM, BEFORE SHE HAS A CHANCE TO GET WITCHY AGAIN.

HELLO, THERE. THIS LOOKS PROMISING.

THERE WERE TREES THIS COLOR IN CARRION GLADE, BUT THEY WERE LOTS BIGGER.

DO YOU KNOW WHAT THIS IS, BRUTE?

NO, BUT WHENEVER THERE'S A FULL MOON, I GUARD THE DOOR AND SHE GETS THE LITTLE TREE OUT.

SNIP, SNIP, SHE TRIMS THE TINY BRANCHES THEN PUTS IT BACK IN THE GLASS CASE. MAGIC GLASS, SEE?

THEN HOW DOES SHE GET IT OPEN?

MAGIC.

SHEESH, WE MIGHT BE DOOMED.

HANG ON, SOUNDS LIKE IT'S *UNBREAKABLE*, DOESN'T IT?

WHERE'S INGA?

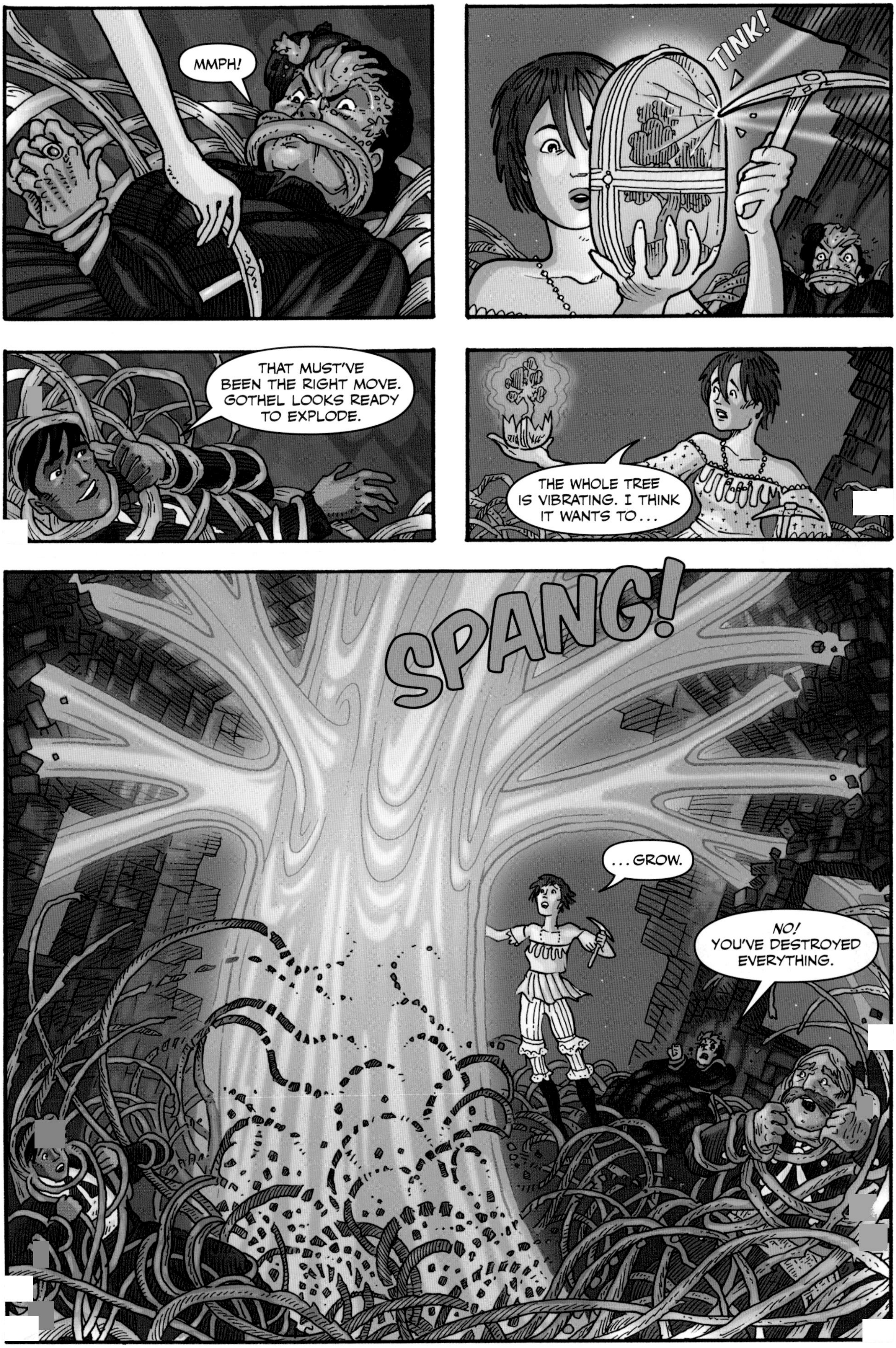
MMPH!
TINK!
THAT MUST'VE BEEN THE RIGHT MOVE. GOTHEL LOOKS READY TO EXPLODE.
THE WHOLE TREE IS VIBRATING. I THINK IT WANTS TO . . .
SPANG!
. . . GROW.
NO! YOU'VE DESTROYED EVERYTHING.

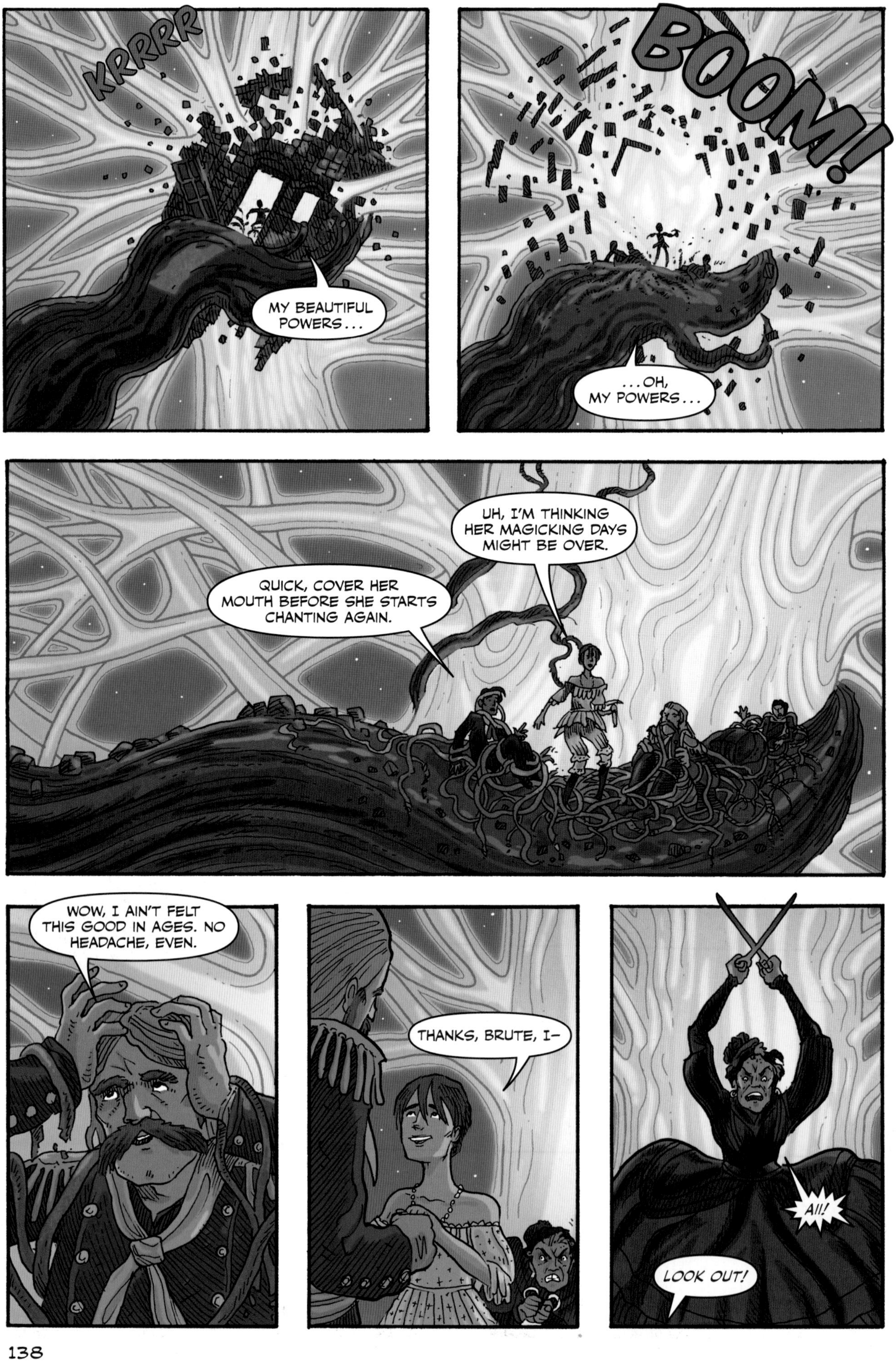
KRRRR
MY BEAUTIFUL POWERS...
BOOM!
...OH, MY POWERS...
QUICK, COVER HER MOUTH BEFORE SHE STARTS CHANTING AGAIN.
UH, I'M THINKING HER MAGICKING DAYS MIGHT BE OVER.
WOW, I AIN'T FELT THIS GOOD IN AGES. NO HEADACHE, EVEN.
THANKS, BRUTE, I–
AII!
LOOK OUT!

NO!

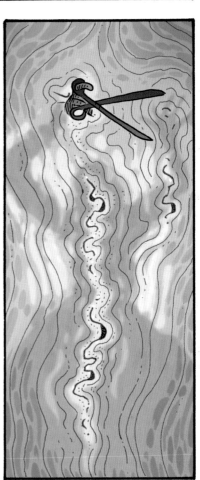

CLINK

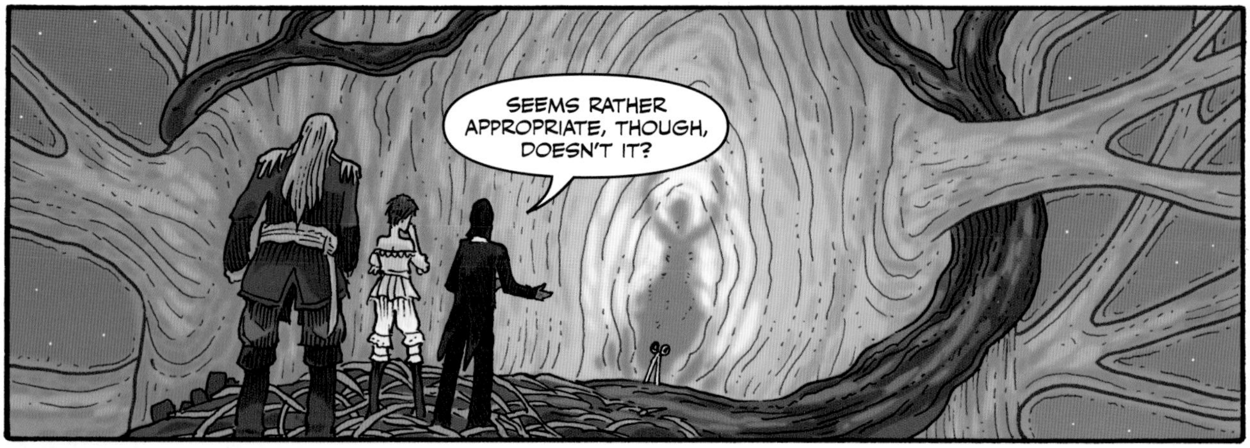
SEEMS RATHER APPROPRIATE, THOUGH, DOESN'T IT?

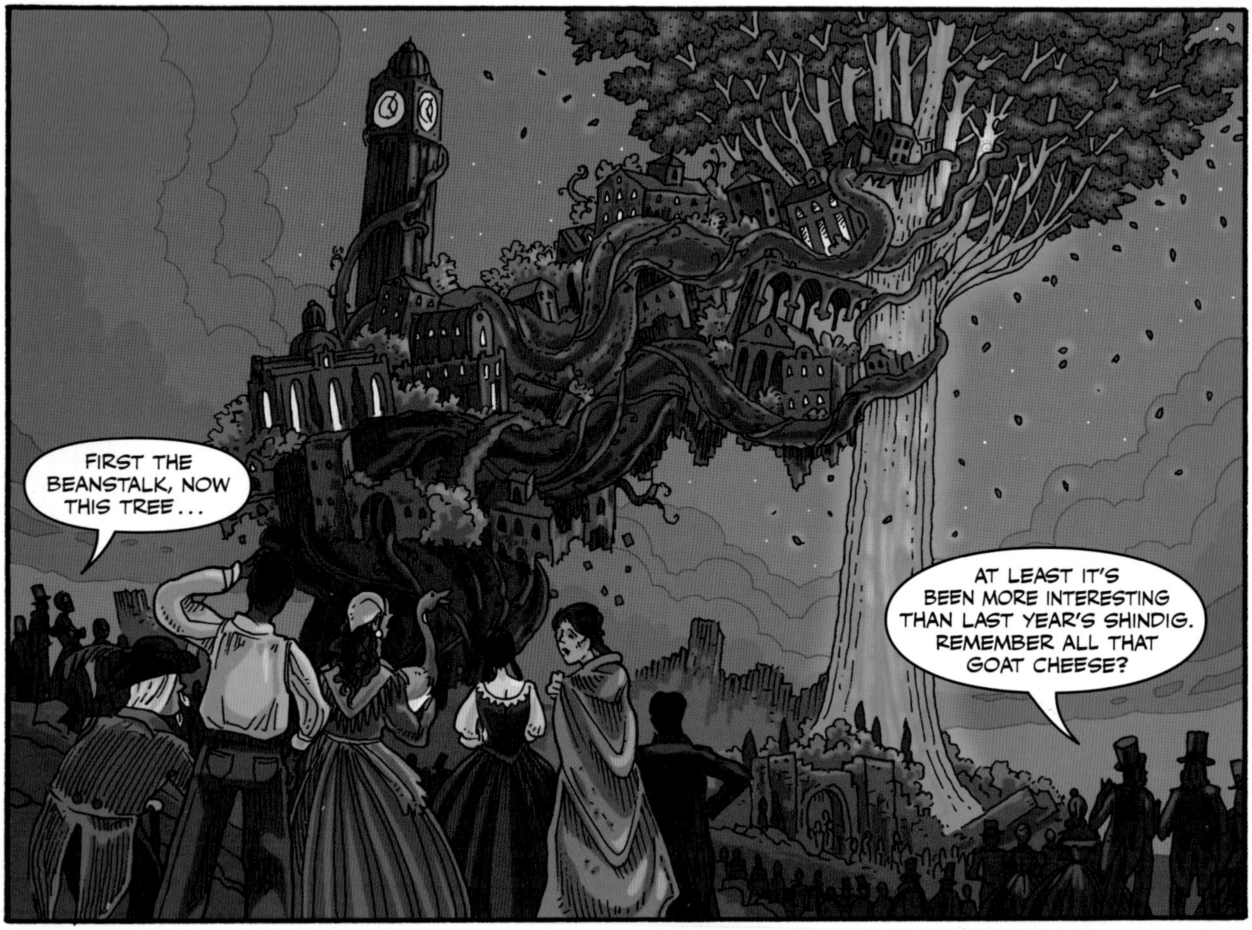
FIRST THE BEANSTALK, NOW THIS TREE . . .
AT LEAST IT'S BEEN MORE INTERESTING THAN LAST YEAR'S SHINDIG. REMEMBER ALL THAT GOAT CHEESE?

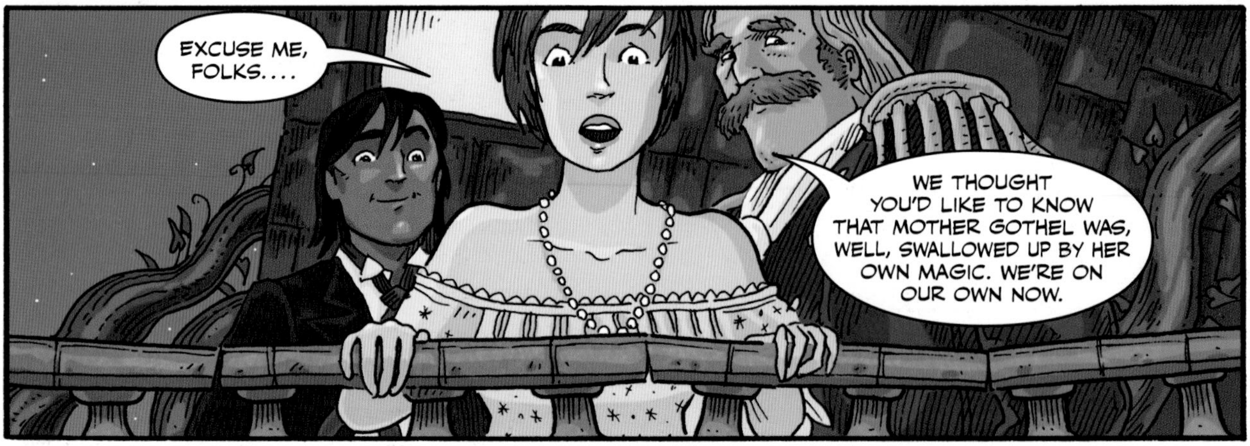
EXCUSE ME, FOLKS. . . .
WE THOUGHT YOU'D LIKE TO KNOW THAT MOTHER GOTHEL WAS, WELL, SWALLOWED UP BY HER OWN MAGIC. WE'RE ON OUR OWN NOW.

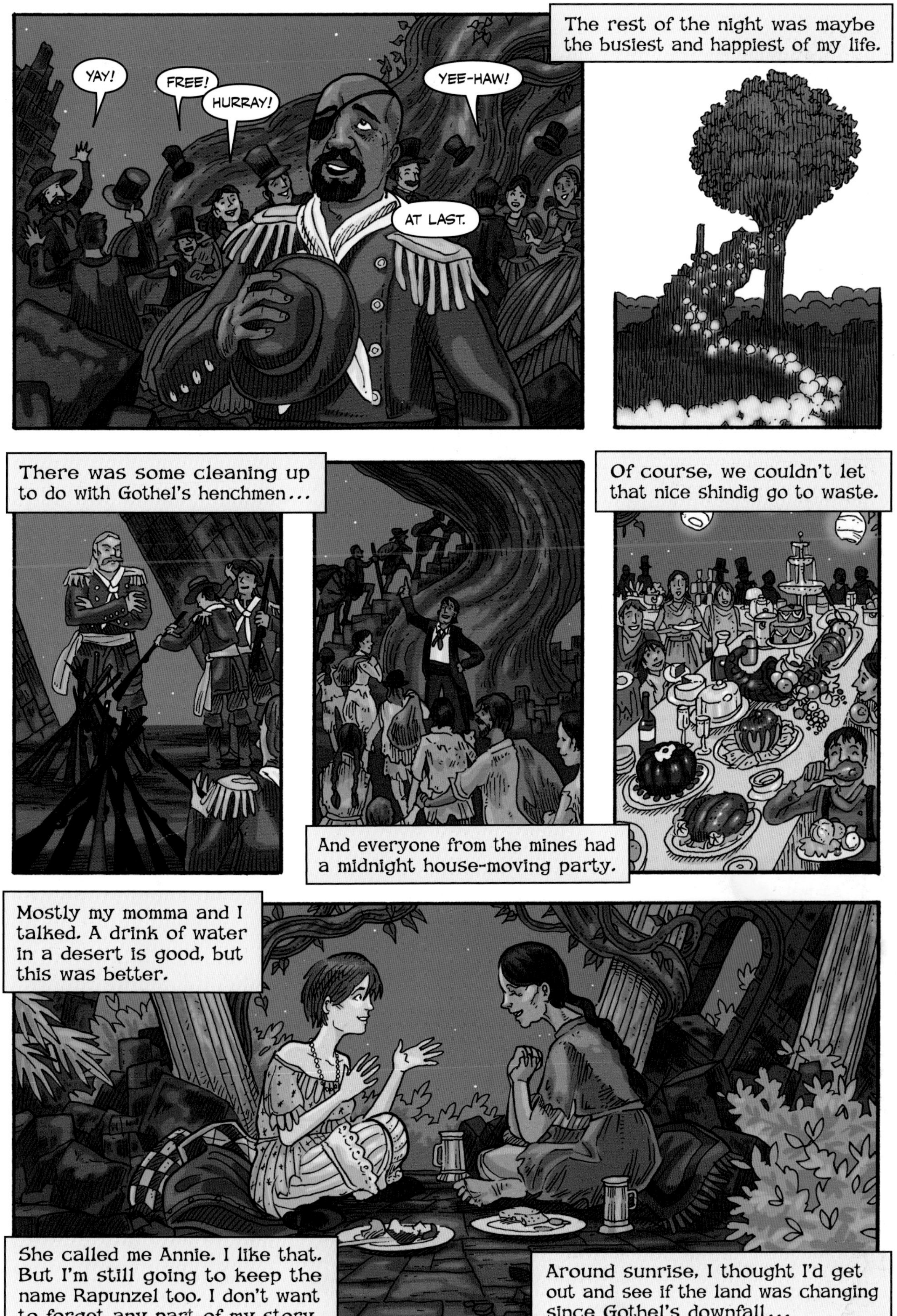
The rest of the night was maybe the busiest and happiest of my life.
YAY!
FREE!
HURRAY!
YEE-HAW!
AT LAST.
There was some cleaning up to do with Gothel's henchmen...
And everyone from the mines had a midnight house-moving party.
Of course, we couldn't let that nice shindig go to waste.
Mostly my momma and I talked. A drink of water in a desert is good, but this was better.
She called me Annie. I like that. But I'm still going to keep the name Rapunzel too. I don't want to forget any part of my story.
Around sunrise, I thought I'd get out and see if the land was changing since Gothel's downfall...

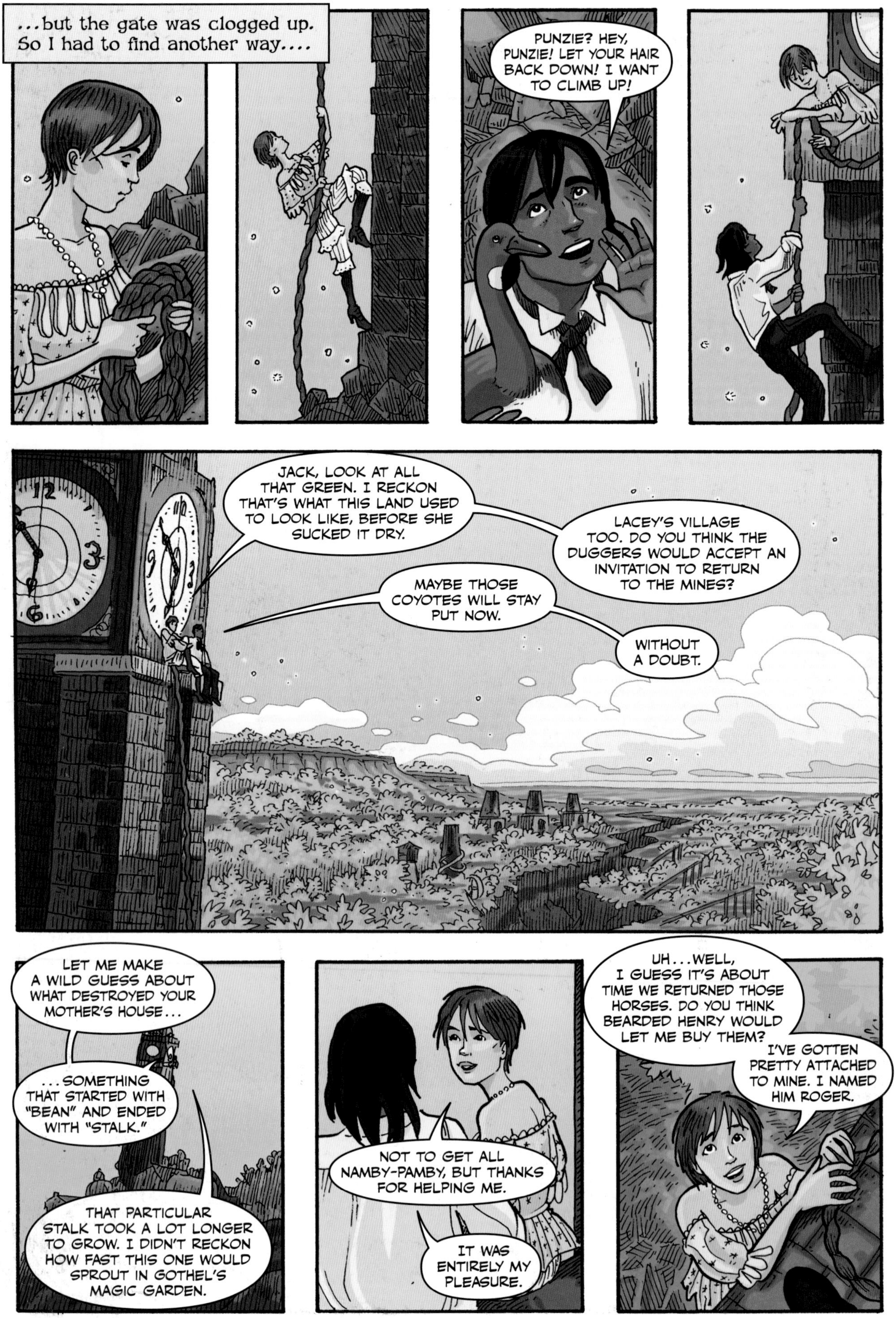

...but the gate was clogged up. So I had to find another way....
PUNZIE? HEY, PUNZIE! LET YOUR HAIR BACK DOWN! I WANT TO CLIMB UP!
JACK, LOOK AT ALL THAT GREEN. I RECKON THAT'S WHAT THIS LAND USED TO LOOK LIKE, BEFORE SHE SUCKED IT DRY.
LACEY'S VILLAGE TOO. DO YOU THINK THE DUGGERS WOULD ACCEPT AN INVITATION TO RETURN TO THE MINES?
MAYBE THOSE COYOTES WILL STAY PUT NOW.
WITHOUT A DOUBT.
LET ME MAKE A WILD GUESS ABOUT WHAT DESTROYED YOUR MOTHER'S HOUSE...
...SOMETHING THAT STARTED WITH "BEAN" AND ENDED WITH "STALK."
THAT PARTICULAR STALK TOOK A LOT LONGER TO GROW. I DIDN'T RECKON HOW FAST THIS ONE WOULD SPROUT IN GOTHEL'S MAGIC GARDEN.
NOT TO GET ALL NAMBY-PAMBY, BUT THANKS FOR HELPING ME.
IT WAS ENTIRELY MY PLEASURE.
UH...WELL, I GUESS IT'S ABOUT TIME WE RETURNED THOSE HORSES. DO YOU THINK BEARDED HENRY WOULD LET ME BUY THEM?
I'VE GOTTEN PRETTY ATTACHED TO MINE. I NAMED HIM ROGER.

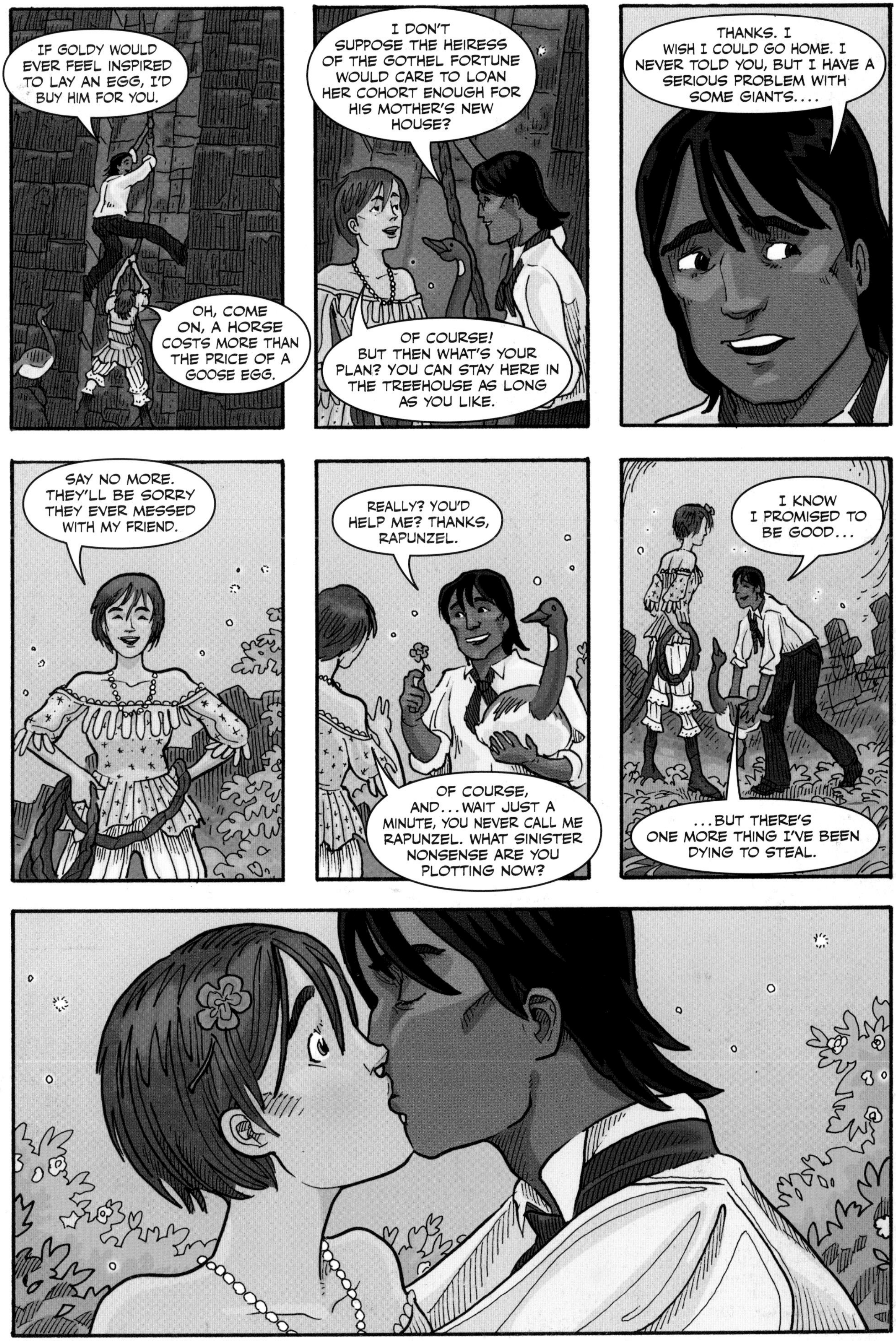
IF GOLDY WOULD EVER FEEL INSPIRED TO LAY AN EGG, I'D BUY HIM FOR YOU.
OH, COME ON, A HORSE COSTS MORE THAN THE PRICE OF A GOOSE EGG.
I DON'T SUPPOSE THE HEIRESS OF THE GOTHEL FORTUNE WOULD CARE TO LOAN HER COHORT ENOUGH FOR HIS MOTHER'S NEW HOUSE?
OF COURSE! BUT THEN WHAT'S YOUR PLAN? YOU CAN STAY HERE IN THE TREEHOUSE AS LONG AS YOU LIKE.
THANKS. I WISH I COULD GO HOME. I NEVER TOLD YOU, BUT I HAVE A SERIOUS PROBLEM WITH SOME GIANTS....
SAY NO MORE. THEY'LL BE SORRY THEY EVER MESSED WITH MY FRIEND.
REALLY? YOU'D HELP ME? THANKS, RAPUNZEL.
OF COURSE, AND...WAIT JUST A MINUTE, YOU NEVER CALL ME RAPUNZEL. WHAT SINISTER NONSENSE ARE YOU PLOTTING NOW?
I KNOW I PROMISED TO BE GOOD...
...BUT THERE'S ONE MORE THING I'VE BEEN DYING TO STEAL.

I'd read about stuff like this, romance and falling in love and such.

I'd even imagined it happening to me.

But I never guessed how it could feel like...well, I may as well just say it... like a good kind of *magic*.

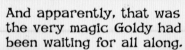

And apparently, that was the very magic Goldy had been waiting for all along.

KLONK!

SQUAWK!